THE TERROR OF TYRANTS

PETER S. FISCHER

THE GROVE POINT PRESS
Pacific Grove, California

Also by Peter S. Fischer

THE BLOOD OF TYRANTS

ISBN 978-0-615-36838-2

DEDICATED to Sinclair Lewis who was first and to George Orwell whose only failing was getting the exact year wrong.

O! what a fall was there, my countrymen Then I, and you, and all of us fell down Whilst bloody treason flourished over us.

WILLIAM SHAKESPEARE

PROLOGUE

The last rays of daylight began to disappear as the sun took its leave on the West Coast. As the grey gloom turned to blackness a great silence fell over the nation. The three nationalized radio and television networks continued to broadcast but one by one, the signals of the 212 so-called independent radio stations flickered off by government decree. They would not resume until 6:00 a.m. local time under pain of losing their license granted on a conditional basis by the FCC. In the interim, anything the government felt its people ought to know would be broadcast by either the American or National or Progressive federal broadcasting systems. The American Network was devoted to breaking news and nationwide sports coverage. The National was the conduit for light entertainment, episodic dramas and sitcoms, game shows, reality programs and federally sanctioned motion pictures produced by the nation's film community. The Progressive Network was dedicated to 24 hour a day hard news and political opinion as well as documentaries on a variety of subjects all reflecting the administration's socialist point of view. Ratings for these networks, if in fact there had continued to be a system of ratings, would have been commercially abysmal, but since they were funded by tax dollars and carried no advertising, other than political propaganda, the administration felt the outdated ratings system no longer had relevance.

One of the administration's higherups had been caught on camera many months before saying, in effect, an informed public is a dangerous public. He and his cohorts were doing their best to see that the populace stayed uninformed, not always successfully. Cell phones and the internet managed to keep communications alive between the dissidents, but the primary reason why the silence was not totally effective was the voice of reason that emanated from Canada.

At precisely 12:00 midnight EDT, the first sounds of wailing bagpipes cut through the darkness hovering over the United States. Starting softly and then increasing in volume, the dirge like melody became recognizable as a deep throated baritone began to narrate the lyrics.

My country 'tis of thee, sweet land of liberty
Of thee I sing.
Land where my fathers died, land of the Pilgrim's pride
From every mountainside
Let freedom ring.

"And good evening, ladies and gentlemen, to all of you, to my gracious hosts here in Canada, to my fellow Americans, to freedom loving people throughout the world, this is Hugo Wheeler speaking to you on the six hundred and forty second day of Exile bringing hope to those who have no hope and the truth to those who will open their eyes and ears and their hearts to receive it. To all of you, I say 'courage'. The outrage that is strangling your country will not stand. You have my promise."

Across Canada, from Vancouver to Prince Edward Island, nine mammoth radio towers picked up Wheeler's words and hurled them to every corner of the fifty states using a primitive technology nearly a century old. Once the sun was down Wheeler's broadcast could be picked up thousands of miles away as it skipped off the ionosphere. And best of all, it was impossible to jam. Each tower was protected by armed volunteers around the clock from possible sabotage. Twice operatives of the three year old Federal Security Force had crossed the border on search and destroy missions and twice they had been discovered, apprehended and incarcerated. Not surprisingly the United States government disavowed any knowledge of their activities, calling them "common criminals pursuing their own agenda." The Canadian Prime Minister responded by informing the American President that "other common criminals of like ilk would meet the same fate and join their predecessors in a maximum security Canadian prison." There was no third attempt to shut down Wheeler's broadcasts.

"Regular listeners to this program," Wheeler went on, "know that I left my native country almost two years ago, hounded from the airwaves by a Socialist government that could not abide criticism and most of all could not tolerate the truth. I would much rather be back at my home on an island off the coast of South Carolina. I would much rather be playing golf several times a week and enjoying the camaraderie of my fellow citizens, sharing a few laughs and many memories and enjoying adult beverages and fine food in five star restaurants. I take no great pleasure in having to secretly move every few days to yet another undisclosed location, eating on the run with my security people as my only companions --and God bless them, I love them, everyone of them. This is not a fit existence for any man or woman, but it must be done. This is my calling. So be it. In a few months, perhaps longer, when the people of America rise up, our nation with its freedoms and liberties will be restored. Until then, I persevere."

A dairy farmer in Wisconsin sits in his kitchen, drinking hot chocolate, determined to take in an least the first hour of the broadcast even though he will have to awaken at five in the morning to start another workday. A trucker carrying oranges from Florida to Charlottesville listens intently, his eyes focused on the road, his mind centered on Wheeler's message. From coast to coast tens of millions of others are tuned in, absorbing the message, wanting to act but not quite knowing how. Their numbers increase with every broadcast.

"And speaking of persevering, how about that Senator from Mississippi? You know who I'm talking about. The Honorable W. Booth Wellington, that courtly good old boy who never met a pocket he couldn't pick. For the third time in three years---count 'em, folks, because this guy does not give up easily-- W. Booth has introduced a bill which would allow the Feds to seize one hundred and eighty acres of beach front property on the Gulf and turn it into a five star resort complete with golf course for the private use of a half dozen national unions who have collectively managed to buy his seat for him the past two elections. Never mind that there are hundreds of private houses on this land as well as two small towns, several schools, a furniture factory, six churches and three cemeteries. Preposterous, you say. Not so, I say, because this time around, W. Booth just might pull it off. How you say? Because this year, the old flim flam artist has included federal office workers in the membership list. Federal office workers. Imagine that. With thirteen percent unemployment and a once robust economy in tatters, these bureaucratic grunts are the only ones who can afford to take a vacation. Ah, folks, isn't it grand? American democracy at its best......"

CHAPTER ONE

He almost missed it. A shadowy movement inside the car parked halfway down the block. The car had not moved for over two hours. It was a strange car for the neighborhood, a dark drab sedan that seemed to shriek 'Feds!' from grille to tailpipe. Truth be told, Edward Vitale had been seeing strange cars everywhere for the past forty-eight hours, ever since that evening when the President's Chief of Staff, Zebulon Marcuse, had barged into his den unannounced to discuss a political stratagem involving the upcoming election. As a Special Assistant to the President for Domestic Affairs, Ed Vitale was often asked for his perspective and advice although the latter was seldom followed. But as a thirty year veteran of party politics and the holder of an impressive governmental resume, Vitale was a good sounding board and, worst case if necessary, a suitable fall guy for a strategy gone wrong.

Vitale let the curtain slide back into place and moved to his desk. If only he hadn't been dictating a passage for his memoirs. If only the voice activated taping system hadn't been operational, none of what Marcuse had told him would have been recorded. But it was and now Vitale had in his possession a tape cassette which, if released, could bring down the administration. He could destroy it. That would be simple. But would they believe he had done so? Probably not. Paranoia was mother's milk to the President and his henchmen. They made Nixon and his thugs look like happy-go-lucky optimists. How had they learned of the tape? He'd told no one. The only call he had made was to a trusted friend, Associate Justice Jacob Blaustein. Yes, he'd mentioned the existence of the tape but not the contents. They had set a tentative date to meet in Blaustein's chambers last night but almost immediately, Vitale began noticing unfamiliar faces following him, dark sedans creeping furtively behind him wherever he drove. Yesterday morning the Justice had called and begged off the meeting, citing a busy work schedule. Apparently Blaustein was not the trusted friend Vitale thought he was.

He considered walking into Marcuse's office and just handing him the tape. Very sorry. Hadn't realized the tape system was activated. No harm, no foul. What's that? The phone call to Justice Blaustein? He had no glib answer for that one. And beyond that, there was a much larger consideration that went beyond party, beyond politics, beyond personal loyalty to a President who had become increasingly self-serving over the past several months. No, Vitale thought, there is a greater loyalty to be considered, a loyalty to the nation and not to the traitorous machinations of Zebulon Marcuse and the President he served.And now there were men outside his house, watching and waiting. Waiting for what? Orders? Almost certainly they were operatives of the Federal Security Force, the President's hand picked mini-battalion of enforcers who kept dissenters in line and who answered to no one but the President himself. Vitale knew they wouldn't hesitate for one moment to eliminate him but they probably would not act precipitously.Their overriding concern would most certainly be to retrieve the tape.

Vitale moved back to the window, reacted as he saw a second car pull up behind the one already parked. The headlights flicked off. A few seconds passed, then two men emerged and moved to the original car. The driver side window was lowered. A moment's conversation as one of the men looked toward Vitale's house. Then two more men got out of the first car and the four of them started to walk slowly but deliberately toward his front door.

He knew instinctively he had to run. He scooped up the cassette and put it into his pocket. He almost doused the room light. No, bad idea. That would only alert them. The light still burning might buy him extra time. He hurried from the room, down the corridor into the kitchen. Grabbing his car keys from the peg on the wall, he quietly opened the door which led into his attached garage. At that moment his door chimes sounded. He ignored them and quickly moved to his car. He slipped behind the wheel . The chimes sounded more frequently. They knew he was home. It wasn't likely they would walk away. His worst fears were confirmed when be heard the sound of splintering wood as they smashed through the front door. He counted to six, giving them plenty of time to get into the house. Pray God there wasn't a fifth agent still sitting in one of the parked cars across the street. He pressed the button on the garage door opener and the door started to rise. He turned the key, fired up the engine of his Mercedes coupe and when he had barely enough clearance, he shot out of the garage , sped down the driveway, and turning onto the street , roared away into the night.

A moment later one of the intruders rushed out onto the front porch, shouted back into the house to the others. Within moments they were dashing toward their cars. Quickly U-turning, they sped after the fast disappearing Mercedes.

Racing down Wisconsin Avenue, Vitale felt the sweat pouring down his chest. His heart was pounding violently. This was insane. Car chases were something you paid twenty bucks to see at the local cineplex. He wasn't a good driver, he was a terrible driver and he knew it. If they were following, it would only be a matter of minutes before they caught up to him. He needed to find people. M Street was coming up. A left turn would bring him to the Four Seasons Hotel in a matter of minutes. Half looking, he swerved into the left hand lane, cutting off a VW Beetle who blared his horn, then slammed on the brakes to avoid hitting the car in front of him as the left turn lane was stalled ten deep. Vitale looked into the rear view mirror. All he could see were headlights and nondescript shapes. For all he knew, they could be right behind him. He stifled an urge to blare his horn. No, bad idea. Don't attract attention. The line started to inch forward, slowly, then more quickly. Vitale's eyes were riveted on the left turn arrow. Move, move. Don't hang me out here. He was fifth, fourth, third. They were still moving. The arrow turned yellow. The car in front of him hesitated, then jumped forward to make the turn. Vitale followed even though the arrow had already turned red. He felt momentary relief. The car behind him was caught at the light. He'd bought himself precious time.

Up ahead he saw the familiar outline of the Four Seasons and across the street, LaChaumiere restaurant. The intersection was jammed. It was the height of the dinner hour on a balmy Friday evening in May. Traffic slowed to a crawl but kept moving. He slid cautiously into the right hand lane. This was no time for an accident. Finally he was able to turn into the underground parking for the hotel and make a beeline for the valet. A plan of sorts was forming in his mind. Create the illusion that he was losing himself in the hotel while, hopefully unobserved, he crossed the street to La Chaumiere. He would hurry through to the kitchen, out the rear door into the alley where deliveries were made. From there it was less than a block to the Georgetown Connector Bus which would take him to the Red Line where he could ride to the end of the line up past New York Avenue. From there God knows what but at least he would be out of immediate danger.

He took the ticket from the valet and hurried up the staircase into the main lobby of the hotel. As expected it was crowded. He sidled over to one of the windows overlooking M street and peered out. What did he expect to see? The two cars had been in shadows, dark colored sedans of indeterminate manufacture. He had no clue what the four men looked like, only that they wore dark colored business suits. If they traveled in a pack he'd spot them, but if they split up he had no chance. Protectively he pressed his hand against his breast pocket, felt the cassette. His plan, which seemed promising on the drive to the hotel, now seemed flimsy at best. He couldn't be found with the tape, that was certain. It had to be safeguarded.

He started toward the hotel entrance, mulling his options which were few. A hiding place somewhere in the hotel? Mailing it to himself or to a trusted friend? Perhaps, although his experience with Blaustein made him question just how many trusted friends he really had. And then, at that moment, a man and woman came through the front entrance. The man's face was immediately familiar. Dr. Kenneth Bannister, a highly respected professor of law at Georgetown University. Vitale had consulted him many times on points of law for the Administration. And on Bannister's arm was his wife Heather who had been Vitale's dinner partner at a soiree two weeks earlier. Without hesitation, Vitale reached into his pocket and palmed the cassette, then moved quickly forward. He would take the chance. He had to.

"Doctor Bannister!" he smiled in greeting. "And the charming Mrs. Bannister. Good evening to you both."

Heather Bannister smiled warmly. "Mr. Vitale, so nice to see you again."

"And you, my dear," he said. He turned to Bannister and put out his hand.

"Good to see you, Ed," Bannister said, taking Vitale's hand. He reacted only slightly, feeling the cassette, as Vitale covered both their hands protectively with his left and moved very close, speaking in a whisper.

"I can't explain. You must trust me. Guard this with your life, Doctor. With your life. I will call you tomorrow." He looked around furtively, then faked an expansive grin and declared loudly, "So nice to see you again. We must get together soon. Ciao!" And with that, Vitale moved quickly to the front entrance of the hotel and exited onto the street.

Heather looked up at her husband who was watching Vitale hurry away, a puzzled look on his face.

"Ken? What is it? Something wrong?"

"I don't know," he said and then without looking, he slipped his hand with the cassette into his pocket. "Come on, let's get the car and go home." He took her by the arm and led her toward valet parking.

Meanwhile, Ed Vitale had made it across the street to the entrance to La Chaumiere. No one had grabbed him or thrown him to the ground. He was beginning to feel almost secure. At the doorway he took one last look around and as he did, his eyes locked on a tall man with a pockmarked face wearing a dark gray suit standing across the street by the hotel entrance. The man zeroed in on him and immediately started for the street, talking into a small microphone clipped to his jacket lapel.

Vitale hurried into the restaurant. He'd eaten there often enough to know the layout and he moved rapidly toward the kitchen situated at the rear of the building. He threaded his way clumsily past the ovens and countertops, apologizing as he jostled several of the cooks who berated him in a variety of languages. He reached the rear door, bolted out into the darkened alley and then headed east toward the connector line. Suddenly headlights pierced the darkness as a black sedan turned into the alley, framing Vitale in its high

14

beams. He turned, started back toward the restaurant just as two men emerged through the kitchen door. They spotted him immediately and ran toward him. In a panic, Vitale looked around and spied a ladder stretching up to the roof of an adjoining building. He grabbed at a lower rung, hoisted himself up and started to climb. He was near exhaustion. Whatever adrenaline he'd had was now spent. He reached up for another rung, then felt rough hands tugging at his legs, pulling him down. He felt himself falling, then a sharp pain as his head struck the jagged corner of a concrete building block laying loose on the ground at the base of the ladder. A sheet of white filled his brain, then there was only a numbed blackness and he lay inert at the feet of the four men who had been dogging him.

The man with the pock marked face turned him over, pressed his fingers against Vitale's carotid, looking for signs of life. He frowned, shaking his head at the others, and then he began searching through the dead man's pockets.

Saturday was Ken Bannister's day to sleep in. It was his one vice and he'd been doing it for years. To say he actually slept would be inaccurate. He usually stirred around nine-thirty and by ten, his wife Heather, a willing accomplice in his morning of sloth, showed up with breakfast on a tray. Bacon, eggs, hot coffee, toast and a huge glass of V8 which was Bannister's one concession to eating his vegetables. Years earlier he would have been curled up with the morning newspaper, but he'd given that up when the pages of the Washington Post began to be filled with predigested pap, courtesy of the Department of Information. Now it was a good book to go with a hot breakfast for at least two hours, sometimes longer.

So it was with no little surprise when he looked up at nine-fifteen as Heather entered the room without his breakfast and a grim expression on her face. "Ken," she said. "Turn on the television. It's Ed Vitale."

He frowned. "What?"

"He's dead."

Bannister picked up the remote and clicked on WDEM, a local station dedicated to local news and sports under the authority of the DOI. A solemn faced reporter was standing at the edge of a rural road. A section of wooden guard rail had been smashed in. Close by were a police car and an ambulance as was a wrecker which apparently was in the process of hauling a vehicle up from below.

"Mr. Vitale was a key member of the President's advisory staff and a long time fixture in Democratic politics. It's unclear at this time why he was driving along this lightly traveled Arlington county road or what factors may have caused him to lose control of his car and crash through the guard rail and down the steep embankment behind me."

Bannister listened as the man's voice droned on but his eyes had already fallen on the cassette which he had placed the night before on his bureau next to his wallet and wristwatch.

"What?"

He was suddenly aware that Heather had been talking to him.

"I said, would you like breakfast now?"

"No, thanks. Just coffee. And honey, would you bring it into the library?"

He went to the closet and slipped into his bathrobe, then took the cassette from the bureau and headed for the library, the room where he did most of his work.

He rummaged around in the bottom drawer of his desk and finally found what he was looking for, a cassette player. He inserted the cartridge and clicked on PLAY. There was a strange timber to the voices, echo-y, as if they were talking in a barrel. He recognized Vitale's voice as well as the unmistakeable voice of the President's Chief of Staff, Zebulon Marcuse. It was obvious Marcuse had no idea

16

he was being taped. He spoke bluntly and rashly and the words that came out of his mouth were terrifying. Bannister knew immediately that Vitale's death had been no accident. Guard this with your life, he had said. Now Vitale was dead and the responsbility had passed to him and Bannister, afraid for one of the few times in his life, had no idea what to do about it.

CHAPTER TWO

He tried to be careful. He was always careful around the rose bushes but even so, now and then he'd catch a finger on a thorn and this was one of those times. He'd tried wearing work gloves but they were cumbersome and more trouble than help so here he was with blood coming out of his index finger. Damn. Between the statens for his cholesterol and the Plavix for his arterial stents, his clotting ability was somewhere near nonexistent. With effort, he managed to raise his 59 year old body off the kneeling pad and straighten up, feeling every one of the slight aches and pains in his knees and back. An iffy heart, joints riddled with arthritis, frequent insomnia. Brian Everett, one time media darling and heir apparent to the mantle of Walter Kronkite, Chet Huntley and David Brinkley, was becoming a physical wreck and there wasn't much he could do about it. He decided to do what he always did in situations like this. He went into the house to get a cold beer.

There were two six packs on the bottom shelf of the subzero refrigerator. If there were no vegetables, no chicken or beef, no mayonnaise or ketchup and no milk, there would always be an ample supply of beer. His one vice and Marnie was no longer around to nag him about it. He wished she were. For one thing she'd be able to tell him where the Band-Aids were although he was pretty sure they were in the top drawer next to the range. He looked. Not there. He tried the second drawer. Aha. Well, close enough. He tore one open, wrapped it tightly around his finger, then popped open the beer and took a long refreshing swig.

The kitchen was not exactly a mess but certainly not the way she would have kept it: chrome shining everywhere, granite counter tops sleek and smooth, windows clear and spotless, dishes stacked in orderly fashion in the glass paned cupboards. She'd have put the pots and pans away; he kept them on the stove. He only used two or three anyway, always the same ones. And dishes. A dinner plate, a coffee mug, a juice glass all of which he rinsed with hot water and dried with a paper towel and left on the counter for later use. One of these days he might contract food poisoning, but until he did he wasn't going to worry about it.

He was a tall man, over six-two, lean with plenty of muscle tone for a man his age. His face was long and leathery, tanned and lined. His grey-green eyes were always alert, often piercing. They missed little. His once deeply auburn hair was now streaked with gray but the roots were holding firm and baldness was probably not in his future. It was his one real vanity. He had no desire to look like either Mahatma Ghandi or Bruce Willis. A man's hair symbolized his virility. He was determined to hang on to every last strand if humanly possible although at times he wondered why. He hadn't exercised his virility since the day his wife of thirty-five years had left him alone.

He walked out the rear door and into the backyard. He stopped for a moment to admire his garden which was in full bloom. Roses of every variety encircling the carefully manicured green lawn, low lying petunias and pansies, multicolored hydrangeas, white lilies, daffodils, jonquils. A panoply of color. He'd started it two years when he'd been left to carry on by himself and it had kept him sane. He felt a pang of sorrow. Marnie had never seen it, had never known the care and love he'd put into it. It was for her. In remembrance of her. Even now he knew that without it, his life would be totally bleak, as bleak as it had been that chilly December morning when he had found her in her bed, a half-smile on her lips, no sign of fear or trauma. An embolism, the coroner said. Instant death. It happened in her sleep. She never knew.

Brian crossed the yard and walked the few steps along the brick pathway to the hip-high wall that backed his property, He looked down at the little town below, the ocean front village of Santa Veronica, still pristinely clean, despite everything that had happened over the past year and a half. Once sublimely ignorant in its leisurely pace of the real world surrounding it, the little town had painfully come of age. The near destruction of the American dollar had had a lot to do with it. The galloping inflation hit hard as did the continuing unemployment. More and more families were out of work, houses and yards fell into disrepair as a general malaise gripped the town's dwindling population.

Still, Santa Veronica managed to maintain a certain dignity. Many businesses struggled but most managed to eke out an existence. People continued to gather at the town park on weekends, cooking up barbecue and trading horror stories about the state of the nation. The local high school still managed to field a baseball team in the spring and a football squad in the fall. They still crowned a homecoming queen and on the Fourth of July, the oldtimers who continued to care were still able to turn out a decent sized parade.

Just off Ocean Boulevard was the church for whom the town was named, gleaming white, it's steeple dwarfing the nearby buildings. Next to the church, the tiny cemetery where Marnie Everett, beloved wife of Brian Everett ,was laid to rest with nearly the entire citizenry of Santa Veronica in attendance. Much beloved was Marnie Everett. Though never much of a churchgoer, Brian vowed from that day forth that he would attend mass every Sunday and he had kept that promise. He was a permanent fixture at the six a.m. Sunday morning service overseen by Father Goodbury who had a standing tee time at 8:30 at the local golf course. Those who did not wish to get up that early were welcome to attend mass at 11:00 at St. Anselm's several miles south.

His gaze shifted to the marina, to Ben Howard's "Yakety Yak", a sleek 32 foot cabin cruiser, equipped for fishing, eating, drinking and with two cabins and eight bunks, other forms of carousing. Ben and Tammy had invited him out for a Sunday afternoon at sea and he'd accepted, even though it meant spending another few hours with the widow Magruder. His matchmaking friends were determined to stir something up between he and Penny Magruder and not even a "No,No,Never!!!" would dissuade them. He chuckled. Their intentions were laudable and Penny was a great gal. Maybe a few years ago if he hadn't been married, maybe a couple of years into the future. Who could say? But right now he wasn't able to return the kind of commitment Penny was looking for. He'd been honest with her and she'd accepted it.

Out of the corner of his eye, Brian spotted the black sedan approaching from below. Even before it turned into his driveway, he knew that the occupants were here to pay a call, probably not social in nature. He'd been half-expecting them, but then that's what you get for opening your big fat mouth in an environment where keeping it closed gets you into a lot less trouble.

With a sigh of resignation, he finished off the beer and started back toward the house.

The two men at the door were wearing very dark grey suits, almost black. Not a good sign. Neither were the bulges showing from inside their jackets. They weren' t carrying wads of money-saving coupons and they weren't from Welcome Wagon. The younger of the two, a shortish bull of a man, perhaps in his mid-thirties, held out his identification, a humorless half smile on his lips which he no doubt thought would put his prey at ease. He was wrong.

"Mr. Everett. Colonel Erwin Conrad, Federal Security Force. This is my associate, Captain Willis Johnson."

Brian looked toward the other man. Black, greyhaired, maybe sixty, gentle brown eyes. He smiled in greeting. It seemed genuine.

"Colonel? Captain? I wasn't aware the FSF was into military ranks," Brian said.

"A newly instituted policy, sir. Helps keep the chain of authority clearer. May we come in?"

"Sure," Brian said, standing aside as the two men entered. Brian led them toward the den.

"I may be a little out of the loop, gentlemen, but I always thought the FSF was centered in Washington and generally wore those dark green uniforms with the gold braiding and carried those three-foot long billyclubs."

"That would be the President's personal security force. Field officers are permitted civilian dress," Conrad said, ignoring Brian's reference to weaponry.

"But aren't you fellas a little far afield? There's no threat to the President around here."

Conrad's eyes narrowed. "There are always threats to the President, Mr. Everett. The FSF has actually spread to all fifty states, not in great numbers as yet but we do have jurisdictional control over local Homeland Security field offices."

Brian was surprised by this revelation but tried not to show it. "Oh? And when did this all come about?"

"Early last week by executive order of the President."

"Funny," Brian said. "First I've heard of it."

"The announcement will be forthcoming in a few days on all three Federal television networks," Conrad said. He looked about the room taking in the many plaques, awards and photos, most of the latter showing Brian hobnobbing with men of power over the past two decades. "A very impressive representation of the old days, Mr. Everett. You were obviously much respected and well connected."

"I was fortunate," Brian said.

"I wouldn't describe your career as the chief newsman at a major television network a consequence of luck," Conrad said. "Your opinions carried a great deal of weight with your viewers but happily, I think, the cult of personality is no longer with us. Our federally operated networks get along very well these days without the encumberance of star power." As if remembering his manners, Conrad continued, sitting in an easy chair and pointing to the leather sofa by the fireplace. "Please. Sit down."

If Brian was annoyed by the man's arrogance, he gave no sign. He sat. With most visitors he would have offered refreshment but he was damned if these two jerks were getting any of his brewskis.

"Well, Colonel," Brian said, "I assume there is some point to this visit and as I have a very busy schedule today, I'd appreciate it if you would get right to the point."

Conrad smiled. "I would wager, Mr. Everett, that your day today is no busier than any other of your days. A call to your daughter in New York City, perhaps a trip to the local market for groceries, maybe a haircut, certainly your usual nap on the backporch between two and three-thirty, answering a few e-mails until five, then after supper, maybe an old movie on a DVD or PPV. Does that about sum it up?"

Brian felt the bile rising in his throat but he remained silent. Get to the point, you son of a bitch, he thought. Oddly, as he was thinking it, Conrad did.

"Two days ago you contributed an opinion piece to the San Francisco Chronicle questioning the President's decision to quell an uprising in western Tennessee."

Brian nodded. "I did. And I would hardly call it an uprising. A half dozen tobacco farmers protesting onerous growing regulations that threatened to shut down their farms. I call that peaceful protest."

Conrad glared at him. "A federal agent was shot."

Brian glared right back. "A federal agent was winged in the arm by a local sharpshooter who could have killed him at a thousand paces while blindfolded and your thug was shot only after he tried to set fire to the man's tobacco field."

"There is no justification for attacking a federal officer. None. The man is in custody and will stand trial for his crime," Conrad said.

"Stand trial? He hasn't even been indicted," Brian said.

"A formality," Conrad said. "The larger issue is, you brought out several facts that were not public knowledge. Where did you get your information , Mr. Everett?"

"That's none of your business."

"And that's where you are wrong, sir. You are aware that it is against the law to publish any opinion piece which mentions government policy and specifically the actions of the President without getting written clearance from the Department of Information."

"Yes, I am, and are you aware that in its three and a half year history, the Department has never yet granted such permission to anyone for any reason whatsoever?" Brian replied.

"I'm not here to quibble procedures, Mr. Everett. I want the name of your source."

Brian shook his head. "Well, you're not going to get it."

Conrad's voice took on a nastier edge. "You probably haven't heard that the editor of the Chronicle was taken into custody yesterday and held for twenty-four hours. He is going to be allowed to pay a fine of $10,000 for his violation and he is lucky to have received that kind of leniency. Now I ask you again."

"And I tell you again, go to hell." Brian looked over at the black man who met his gaze for only a moment and then averted his eyes. Brian looked back at Conrad unflinchingly. "Look, Colonel, if you want to arrest me, then go ahead. I'd welcome it. I still have a pretty formidable cache in this country. It wouldn't bother me a bit to be a martyr for the cause of personal liberty. You remember what that is? Probably not but I do and so do a lot of other people so, fella, do your damndest. Slap the cuffs on me and toss me in the hoosegow." He held up two fists, wrists touching.

Conrad stared at him icily, then smiled. "Not necessary. I can always get a warrant for your computer."

Brian laughed . "Warrant? You guys still bother with those things? My other sources tell me that your idea of a warrant is a 9 mm. Glock."

Conrad leaned back in his chair,staring at Brian with an expression that bordered on amusement. "You fascinate me, Mr. Everett. No, really you do. This opinion piece, this unwarranted attack on the policies of the President. I think most people see it for what it is. A desperate attempt by a man who once commanded the attention of millions, now totally irrelevant, reduced to puttering in a garden in some meaningless little town at the west end of nowhere. You probably feel that in some way we fear you. As for me, I actually feel a little sorry for you."

Brian grinned. "Oh, forgive me, Colonel. I completely misunderstood. Here I thought you had come to reprimand me when you were merely paying a sympathy call."

Conrad's expression turned cold again. He rose abruptly. "I'm sorry. I had hoped we could deal with this amicably." He head nodded toward Captain Johnson and started for the door. "You will be hearing from us again," he said.

"Looking forward to it, Colonel. Next time bring a fourth and we'll play pinochle," Brian said at the front door. "Drive safe."

Conrad strode quickly toward the black sedan. Johnson lingered momentarily in the doorway.

"I'm sorry about this, Mr. Everett. It's the way things are. I wish it weren't so," he said sadly. Then he turned and followed Conrad to the car. It pulled out a little faster than it should have, spinning rubber.

Brian watched the car disappear down the driveway. They'd be back. He'd known this would happen when he wrote the piece for the Chronicle but there were too many people saying nothing, refusing to believe what was happening around them. People like Ben Howard, the town's most successful realtor. A trust fund baby who hadn't had to work ever, but he did because a work ethic was part of his makeup. Work. Civic service. Trying to make things better for those less fortunate. Ben was one of the good guys. He just refused to accept what had been going on around him for the past six years. And then last Tuesday he'd walked into the health club while Brian was doing a couple of miles on the treadmill and his face was an ashen grey. The government had just seized a major oil company which was a substantial part of Ben's portfolio. His net worth had dropped by 24% in less than an hour. At the juice bar he looked at Brian, confused , uncomprehending. What had happened? How could things have changed so fast in so short a time? Brian commiserated. He could have told him about Nazi Germany, how a meaningless party with a scant 8% of the vote in 1925 was able to come to power in eight short years. The Gestapo. The SS. The populace dismissed them as a radical fringe, even when Propoganda Minister Goebbels seized the newspapers and radio stations . Unaware of what was happening until it was too late, the German people suddenly discovered there existed no weapons to ward off the inevitable.

And now, America was being strangled by a Socialist agenda far more attuned to Das Kapital than the Bill of Rights. Total takeover by incremental bites and no one seemed to notice. No, Brian hadn't really wanted to fight these people, he'd really wanted to be left alone but he knew now it wouldn't be possible.

It was six minutes to seven, nearly ten o'clock on the East Coast. He'd just polished off a chicken pot pie and a salad. Years ago that would have been an appetizer but his appetite had shriveled in recent years. Chewing the last remnant of a tomato, Brian called his daughter at her New York apartment. He would find her in. He always found her in. He was secretly hoping for the day when he wouldn't.

"Lissa, it's Dad."

"Hi, Daddy."

"Did I catch you at a bad time?"

"No, just catching up on some reading," she said. It was what she always did. Melissa, the hermit, quiet, shy, satisfied with her own company, loathe to mix it up in a give and take world. She was 25 and attractive in a low key, unflamboyant way and her mind was as agile as a circus aerialist. Her assets were many but she kept them hidden.

"Haven't heard from you in a couple of days. Everything okay?"

"Great," she said.

"What's new at the magazine?"

"Same old, same old. Fixing the coffee, proofreading, getting story approval from the government, talking to writers no one wants to bother with. The life of an editorial assistant is pretty much a treadmill to nowhere."

"Well, you hang in there, Lissa. Sometimes it takes a while to get noticed."

"Dad," she said reprovingly. "It's been fourteen months. I'm on the verge of tripping my boss in the lunchroom just to get him to look at me."

Brian laughed. "Well, that would do it. Dare I ask if there's anything new on the personal front?"

"Don't ask," she growled.

"Subject closed," he said. Then, reopening it: "Have you thought about joining a theater group or maybe a book reading society."

"Dad!"

"Sorry. So have you heard anything from your brother?"

"You're kidding, right? The lieutenant is so busy flitting and soaring over Nellis Air Force Base in Nevada, he doesn't know my area code let alone my phone number. How about you? Dead silence?"

"Dead as it gets."

She hesitated. "That piece you wrote for the San Francisco paper probably didn't help much."

"Probably not," Brian admitted. "Mark's either a true believer or it's the old rebel syndrome. Whatever my Daddy is, I'm not." He sighed. "I can't believe he doesn't see what's going on and where we're headed."

"Daddy, please. You promised. No politics. I just can't deal with it any more."

"Okay, honey. You're right." He hesitated for a second. "Lissa, I think you need to know. I had a couple of government boys here at the house today. Probably doesn't mean a thing , just a little scare-the-old-man stuff---"

"Daddy----". She was alarmed.

"Honey, I'm sure it's nothing, but just in case things get fouled up, you know Henry Blaustein, my lawyer in Los Angeles. Well, whatever you need to know, he knows it."

"Please, you're scaring me," she said, her voice trembling.

"Lissa, I'm sure there's nothing to worry about. This is a just-in-case thing, okay?"

"No, not okay. Do you want me to fly out? I want to be with you."

"No, no. This may be nothing. Please. I mean it . Just if you don't hear from me within the next two or three days, call Henry. Will you do that, honey? Please."

Melissa was unconvinced but she promised and after a few more minutes, Brian hung up. He didn't like to frighten her that way but dammit, there was a real world out there and sooner or later she would have to come to grips with it. And as for him, Conrad's threats could be empty, at least this time around. No way to really tell.

He crossed over to the library shelf where he kept his humidor and took out a Monte Cristo. His last remaining vice if you didn't count suicidal tendencies in opposing the federal government. He clipped one end, then struck a wooden match, and held the flame an inch below the cigar end, rotating it slowly to facilitate an even burn. He strolled out onto the back veranda carrying his cell phone. He was ready to make yet another try to reach his son Mark. It'd be just past supper hour. If he was going to catch him at the base, now was the time.

He stared up at the star speckled sky, so imposing in its vastness. Try as he might he'd been unable to get Conrad's words out of his mind. The man was right. For the longest time, the world had ceased to have any real meaning for him. He rose in the morning, went through the motions, put in the hours and in the early evening, slipped into bed to start the cycle all over again. Certainly the absence of Marnie had much to do with it but more than that, he was constantly being forced to deal with a world he did not recognize. Oppression, regulations, autocratic mandates, the choking off of freedoms once taken for granted, all of these weighed on him constantly but only seldom could he summon the energy to rebel. Bitterly, he thought, the only thing George Orwell got wrong was the exact year.

Suddenly the phone rang, rousing him from his thoughts. He checked caller ID. It showed nothing. He hesitated for a moment, then pushed TALK.

"Yes?" he said warily.

"Brian. It's Ken Bannister." The man's voice was flat, carefully modulated. almost secretive.

"Hey, old buddy," Brian grinned. "My God, it's good to hear your voice."

"Same here, Bri. Too long. Much too long."

There was an awkward silence. "Did I catch you at a bad time?" Ken asked.

"No, no. I'm sitting out here on the back porch enjoying the breeze and hoping to spot a lucky comet."

"Are you alone?" There was an odd quality in his voice. Brian was immediately alert to some sort of problem.

"I'm alone," he said. "What's the matter?"

"I've been thinking, it's been far too long since we got together. If you could rearrange your schedule, we might be able to work something in," Ken said.

"Great," Brian said. "You want to come here or should I hop a plane and fly to Washington?"

"No!" Ken said sharply. "I mean, neither. You know who might join us if he's able. Quentin. You remember Quentin Polsby." He said the name very emphatically, enunciating each syllable.

Again Brian stiffened. Ken was trying to tell him something. Their mutual friend Quentin Polsby had been shot down in the streets of Philadelphia three years ago in a confrontation with one of the administration's unofficial goon squads who were trying to rearrange the results of a Senatorial election with strong arm tactics.

"Yes, I remember Quentin," Brian said evenly. "Always getting himself into scrapes of one kind or another."

"Well, that sort of thing happens to all of us."

Brian had the picture. Ken was in big trouble. This was a call for help. The absence of caller ID. He was calling on a throwaway phone which meant he was being closely monitored. But why? About what? As far as Brian knew Ken was a trusted friend to a few key people in the President's administration. And yet there was no mistaking the fear in his voice.

Brian cautiously played along. "Well, old buddy, if not your place and if not here, where do you suggest?"

Bannister tried to keep his voice light. "I know just the spot. I was dead drunk and you were only slightly sober when you decided to get me home in one piece. You carried me out to the street and I pointed out my car and after you fished out my keys, you tried to open the car door and only succeeded in activating the car alarm."

"Which I could not shut off."

" How I could have mistaken that Mercedes for my Chevy Malibu, I'll never know."

"You weren't functioning all that well that evening."

"But you do remember the place," Bannister said.

"Absolutely."

"Do you think you could make it there by six o'clock Tuesday evening?", Ken asked.

"Not a problem. I'll leave right after morning mass. Will Heather be joining us?"

"No, she's got lots of wifely chores to attend to but she sends her best."

"Tell her I'll miss her. You I'll see on Tuesday."

He shut down his phone and stared pensively up at the inky night sky, peppered with millions of little glints of light. Of all the people in the world who should have nothing to fear in this world, Ken Bannister would be at the top of the list. A highly respected professor of Law at George Washington University, he knew and was known throughout the political power structure. Twice the former President had appointed him to important advisory panels. Nine years ago he'd been awarded the Presidential Medal of Freedom. And yet, there was terror in Ken's voice. After Marnie, he was one of the two or three people Brian had been closest to throughout his life. If Ken needed him, he'd be there though part of him was feeling very skittish about what he might be letting himself in for.

CHAPTER THREE

Sunday morning. It was still dark along the California coastline. Cars in both directions were using their headlights but if you looked carefully toward the east, you could just make out the hazy start of the sun's glow rising into view above the Santa Lucia mountain range. The time was five-thirty five. Traffic was very light on the Pacific Coast Highway heading north. The white van had passed through Morro Bay six minutes earlier and still had about thirty minutes to go before reaching its final destination.

The lettering on the side panels identified the van's owner as Premier Plumbing and Heating, located in a coastal town some hundred and twenty miles south. What it was doing this far north at this time on a Sunday morning was anyone's guess but if they had guessed, chances are they would have guessed wrong.

The driver, a swarthy man with a black beard and mustache, was pounding his hands on the steering wheel keeping time to the music emanating from a Spanish language AM station broadcasting from Tijuana. His other choice was a church service sponsored by a fringe Christian denomination broadcasting from off shore. Hardly his idea of entertainment. He checked his watch. Good. He'd be right on time. No need to speed. Keep the needle under the limit. He knew the California Highway Patrol liked to pounce on the unsuspecting, especially near the end of the month, which this was. Not that his papers were out of order. They weren't. And if some trooper decided to check the back of the van, all he would find were boxes and boxes of pipes and fittings of every description. And, oh, yes, a motorcycle leaning against the right hand wall. He was delivering it to his nephew in Santa Cruz. A belated birthday present.

The only thing that might raise the tiniest of suspicions would be the large stainless steel tool chest shoved up against he back wall of the van. It was highly unlikely that anyone would bother to order it opened, but then again, when the name on your driver's license was unmistakably Arabic, you could never be sure.

Up ahead, on the right, the service station loomed into view. The 24 hour a day convenience store was lit up and open for business. Excellent. Another piece of the plan falling into place. He pulled up to a far pump, inserted his credit card and pumped seven gallons into the tank. He didn't need the seven gallons to get where he was going but that was part of the plan as well.

He entered the small store which was empty except for the bleary eyed teenager behind the counter scanning the latest issue of Penthouse magazine. The van driver moved directly to the cold drink case, rummaging about. After a moment, he turned to the young clerk. "Hey!" he shouted. "Where's the Snapple?"

The young clerk looked up. "The what?"

"The Snapple. Strawberry Snapple. Where is it?"

The kid shook his head. "We don't carry it," he said and turned back to his magazine. The van driver glowered at him.

"Hey, look at me. Every time I stop by here, you always got the Snapple so don't tell me no."

The kid looked up at him, then his gaze fell on the Arabic writing tatooed on the man's arm. He looked up at him again, contemptuously. "I told you we don't carry it. Pick out something else." He turned his attention back to the magazine.

Angrily, the van driver grabbed the magazine from the kid's hands and tossed it against a far wall.

"Hey!", the kid yelled, suddenly fearful.

"I don't want something else, I want what I want, you snot -nosed little pervert."

"Okay,okay," the kid said defensively. "I'm sorry. We just don't have it, okay?"

The driver looked at him long and hard, raised a hand as if to strike him, and then suddenly cursed at him in fluent Arabic and strode out the door. The kid watched him go and then when he was sure the van was totally out of sight, he crossed the room to retrieve his magazine.

Father Goodbury was in the middle of reciting the Gospel according to St. Matthew, a passage he had been citing for many, many years and which he knew by heart. Nonetheless, the Good Book lay open to the words as a precaution since the good Father's memory in recent years had occasionally failed him. Off to one side was the priest's pet acolyte, thirteen year old Danny Olmeda who had been instructed earlier that morning to fill the chalice with an overabundance of wine. Not that the turnout was any bigger than usual, for the most part it seemed to be the same old faces in modest numbers, but that morning, Father Goodbury had a golf match with the Mayor who had a knack for getting under his skin and the only way to combat that sort of gamesmanship was with a healthy intake of the grape. In vino veritas and in addition to the truth, perhaps a calming effect which would permit the good padre to break 100.

Outside the church the little town of Santa Veronica was peacefully deserted. Not entirely, of course. Aside from the early morning parishioners, there was Henny Dilford and her Irish setter romping along toward the beach where no dogs were allowed except on early Sunday mornings when no one was around and nobody cared. Mario Hernandez and his son Lorenzo were in their bakery shop, filling the cases in anticipation of their seven a.m. opening to cater to the churchgoers. 84 year old Waldo Haskell, one of the town's few avowed atheists, was out for his morning constitutional which on every other day of the week passed the church but which, on Sundays, steered a clear path away from the emanations which might be arising from the so-called House of God. Leon Chan drove his pickup slowly down the several side streets while his son, Peter, standing in the truck bed, tossed the tightly wrapped copies of the Sunday L.A. Times toward the porches of their customers. Here and there a bedroom light would go on as the insomniacs would finally give up their futile tossing and turning and rise to face another day. It was still very quiet as Santa Veronica began to rouse itself.

A half mile south, the white van turned off Route One and turned onto Ocean Boulevard heading toward the heart of the little town. The driver was no longer pounding the steering wheel. His radio was silent. His eyes were steely cold, taking in everything. His journey was about to end. His task was at hand.

Slowly he entered the south end of town, keeping well below the speed limit of 30 miles per hour. He passed by the bank on his right, the post office on his left. Down a side street he could see the high school athletic field. Ahead of him on the left hand side of the street he spotted the church steeple jutting skyward toward the heavens. He continued on, reached a side street across from the church and pulled to the curb, shutting off the engine. He looked around. The faint sound of organ music was coming from the church. The mass was still in progress. This side street, more an alley than anything else, was deserted. He climbed down from the cab and shut the door, locking it. He moved to the back of the van and opened the doors wide, then hopped up to the van bed. He untethered the motorcycle from the sidewall and moved it to the rear by the open doors. Then he jumped down and wrestled the lightweight Yamaha YSR50 to the ground. It wasn't the newest or the speediest of bikes but it would do the job.

Glancing around one more time, he closed the rear doors and locked them, then mounted the motorcycle and roared down the alley and turned south, retracing the route he had just taken.

Thirteen minutes and eleven miles later, a weather beaten sign advertising almonds loomed up on the right adjacent to a narrow unpaved road. The Yamaha turned onto the dirt, proceeded for about two hundred yards and then turned left into a small clearing partially obscured by trees and underbrush. Parked under some branches was a ten year old Honda Civic, mud spattered and in need of a paint job. The engine under the hood, however, was tuned like a grand piano and had been checked and double checked three times in the past week.

The swarthy man laid down the bike and popped the trunk of the Honda, revealing a small overnight case. He opened it and took out a change of clothes which he set aside . He removed a compact makeup kit and opened the latches, then started applying cold cream to his beard and mustache. The disguise came off easily. A dab of the cold cream smeared on the arabic "tattoo" and that, too, disappeared. Toweling off, he slipped out of his plumbing garb and donned the change of clothes; well worn levis, a UCLA sweatshirt, and a blue LA Dodgers baseball cap. Quickly he got behind the wheel of the Honda and pulled out of the clearing, leaving behind all remnants of his previous identity.

As he neared the highway, he slowed and looked north along the coast line. He reached into the glove compartment and took out a cell phone. Stopping momentarily at the intersection, he punched in a number. Without hesitation, he hit TALK. A fraction of a second later, eleven miles to the north, a blinding light obliterated the dim morning haze. A second after that the leaves on an oak tree a few yards away started to flutter violently. The Honda rocked gently back and forth several times, then came to rest. The man in the Dodger cap smiled, then pushed the OFF button, slipped the phone back into the glove compartment and took off on the highway heading south toward Los Angeles.

As the last of the parishioners exited the church, souls cleansed of sin for at least another week, the sky over Santa Veronica suddenly turned into an eye-searing sheet of white. The air heated to a hellish temperature as a shock wave of incalculable strength slammed outwardly in every direction, leveling every standing structure, instantly incinerating everything and everyone within its radius of destruction. No chance to cry out a warning, no place to hide, just instant death for almost everyone in Santa Veronica that ill-fated morning. A small town on the edge of nowhere, peaceful, minding its own business, was suddenly no more.

In the large house on the bluff overlooking the tiny village, Brian Everett was in his wine cellar. He had just removed a drain grate from the cellar floor which in fact was not a drain at all but a well disguised floor safe. He reached in and took out several bundles of $100 bills which he stuffed into the various pockets of his cargo pants. Not his usual Sunday go-to-mass apparel but he'd decided the night before to skip this one Sunday in order to get on the road as quickly as possible. He was sure God would understand. He reached in again and extracted the 10 mm G20 Glock automatic he'd bought just before the government had ordered the confiscation of all handguns. The sale had been private. No one knew he had it, not even Marnie who despised weapons of every sort. Even Brian had had second thoughts, putting it away and never touching it again until now. For a moment he hesitated, then stuffed the gun into a zippered pocket in his windbreaker. He looked about, making one last check. His suitcase, containing not only his clothes and toiletries but also his laptop, was in the trunk of the car. He had cash, credit cards, weaponry. Was he forgetting anything?

Suddenly, without his even realizing, it had happened, he was slammed ten feet backwards into the concrete wall of the cellar, his head absorbing a vicious blow. He crumpled to the floor as wine bottles of every shape and vintage flew from their moorings and crashed and splintered into every part of the room. He lay there unconscious for several minutes before starting to rouse. First he smelled the wine, then opened his eyes to view the devastation. The floor was flowing red with merlots and cabernets. Broken bottles were everywhere. Water was dripping from broken pipes above. Part of the ceiling had collapsed around him. He tried to move.The bruises he suffered were painful but as he checked himself out, he was pretty sure the red on the floor didn't include his own blood. He struggled to his feet and gingerly made his way through the debris to the staircase and the open doorway above.

What had happened? Earthquake? They'd been talking about the "big one" for decades . Why had he been so sure it wouldn't hit here in Santa Veronica? Foolish optimism was probably the best answer. Carefully he started to climb the shattered staircase. Half the steps were missing or broken. He had to reach up, grab hold of a piece of stair or railing and hoist himself slowly, foot by foot. Finally he reached the top.

He stepped out into the first floor hallway. He could see into the kitchen. Hanging pots and pans had been dislodged and dozens of pieces of crockery had come tumbling out of the glass paned cases. In the dining room the breakfront had overturned and Marnie's prized mahogany table had skidded across the room to the far wall, breaking into pieces. The living room was no better. Paintings had been tossed to the floor, the picture window had been blown in and glass and splintered wood littered the floor. Broken pieces of plaster and yellowish dust were everywhere. More water was dripping from the ceiling and Brian was sure he could smell the sweet odor of escaping gas. Miraculously, the house was still standing.

He picked his way across the floor into the den. The conditions were the same, everything askew. The french doors leading to the patio hung at warped angles, only half attached to the door frame. And then he saw the smoke rising up from below. The air was foul and the sky oppressively dark as he limped across the lawn to the rear wall, already covered with a thin layer of dust, and looked down on the town.

He staggered as he took in the devastation below and he almost fell to his knees. He leaned forward and clutched at the wall for support. In any real sense the town no longer existed. There were fires everywhere and almost every building had been leveled . He quickly looked for signs of life. There were none. Tears began to stream down his cheeks. Ben and Tammy. Penny Magruder. The good padre with the hitch in his swing. His friends. People he cared about. All gone.

The bile started to bubble up inside his throat and suddenly he began to retch uncontrollably, dropping to his knees and holding onto the wall for support. Earthquake? This was no earthquake. The bastards had finally done it. They'd imported their dirty bombs from Iran and Afghanistan and begun their goddamned jihad against the American homeland.

He struggled to his feet, joints still aching, muscles bruised from the battering in the basement. He moved as quickly as he could around toward the front of the house where he found his car, a vintage Lexus SUV. He had parked it on the graveled driveway the night before and it had skittered sideways onto the neatly manicured lawn. Also covered with a fine layer of dust, it had not, however, overturned. Slipping behind the wheel he was relieved when it immediately started up. He drove forward onto the driveway and accelerated out toward the county road which led to the town below. He glanced into the rear view mirror, watching as his beloved house and all of its precious memories, receded into the distance. He was taken by a very strong feeling that he would never see it again.

Turning right he drove cautiously down the road which was partially blocked here and there by debris, mostly fallen trees and utility poles. Power lines were down everywhere but seemed harmless. Brian doubted there was any power available for miles around. At Hatcher Avenue, he turned right to take the back road into the town, Now the devastation was even more pronounced. The little service station at the corner of Browns Road had been leveled as had the three small Craftsman houses across the street. Brian didn't know the occupants but he knew they had children; he'd often watched them playing in their yard from his overlook vantage point. Now there was nothing left but black charred wood and the stump of a chimney visible where the middle house used to stand. Here, too, the power lines were all down as were the utility poles and as he looked ahead at the carnage, he doubted he would be able to drive through to the main part of town.

He stopped, pondering his next move, when a flash of movement off to his left caught his eye. Fast approaching from the south were three red and white emergency vehicles, each showing the Department of Homeland Security designation. Their lights were turned off, their sirens were silent as if they knew there would be no one to see or hear their approach. Quickly Brian got out of the car and half-ran, half-stumbled past the burned out remnants of the service station so that he could get a better view of what was happening.

The breeze off the bay had stiffened and light debris was skittering toward him across the blackened ground.

The vehicles pulled into what had been the center of town, a block from the now incinerated church, and stopped. The doors of all three of the emergency vehicles opened and white garbed men in Hazmat gear piled out and started to look around. One of the men began gesticulating orders and the others started to scatter in various directions carrying what appeared to be geiger counters.

Brian glanced at his watch. An uneasy feeling began to grip him. Very little time had passed since the blast. Certainly no more than twenty minutes and yet here were DHS technicians already on the scene, in full gear, dispatched from where and how long ago? He recalled the Hurricane Katrina fiasco. It had taken Homeland Security more than twenty minutes just to find New Orleans on a map let alone start dispatching help. This response, if indeed that was what it was, wasn't possible. There was only one other possible explanation for their instant arrival and to seriously consider it was monstrous. No, he dismissed the idea as unthinkable.

Just then he heard the whirr of an approaching helicopter coming up from the south. As it swooped in over the town Brian recognized the dark green and gold colors of the Federal Security Force. What the hell were they doing here? The chopper hovered momentarily over the block where the church had once stood, then abruptly darted skyward and headed toward the bluff overlooking the burned out town. It made a beeline toward Brian's house, hovered and then slowly descended toward his rear yard. The unease which he had been feeling suddenly turned to fear. Any other Sunday he would have been attending mass, a fact well known to the FSF which seemed to know everything about him including the time and duration of his bowel movements. It was not coincidence that had brought them to this place.

Quickly Brian turned and hobbled as quickly as he could back to his car. Now the unthinkable was starting to take the shape of reality. If his assumption was correct, they would not miss either him or his car, assuming both had been incinerated in the blast at the church. They would spent at least an hour going through his papers, opening files, looking for his computer which thankfully he'd had the foresight to pack away in his luggage the night before. By the time they figured out that his car was not among the burned out hulks in the middle of town, he should be well out of harm's way. He could only hope.

He started the engine, backed up and turned around, then drove cautiously back to the county road. A few hundred yards to the south, he turned onto a little used dirt road that led to a dried up lake and then to another road that connected to the highway, two miles south of town. There were downed trees and other debris everywhere and twice he had to get out the car to pull heavy branches from the road, but twenty minutes later, his hands raw and bleeding, he was turning onto Route 1 and speeding south.

Thirty-five miles farther down the highway, another man was heading south, his final destination Los Angeles. Wearing his Dodger cap and his UCLA sweat shirt, he was once again listening to spirited Hispanic music emanating from the powerful station just across the border in Tijuana. His hands were again pounding out the lively rhythms of a bossa nova. He was feeling good about himself. Very good. He reached into the glove compartment and took out the cell phone, punching in a number. When he was connected, he reported in to the operative on the other end of the line.

"This is Sanchez. Mission accomplished. No problems. I should be at headquarters no later than ten o'clock."

He broke the connection and replaced the cell phone, then smiled as the spirited strains of a mariachi band filled the air.

• • •

Three thousand miles away a stocky well-muscled man was showering in the locker room of the Riverview Country Club after a strenuous but losing tennis match with the club pro. General Dwight David MacAndrews was not a man used to losing but he was philosophical when it came to Buddy Finn. Buddy was half his age, once ranked as high as 155th on the pro circuit and he had a killer attitude when it came to tennis. He eased up for no man, not even the Chairman of the Joint Chiefs of Staff. That was one of the things MacAndrews most admired about Finn; he asked no quarter and gave none. These Sunday morning beatings, however, had done wonders for MacAndrews' game and among the 40 and older membership, he was one of the three or four most feared competitors.

He toweled off and dressed and made his way into the lounge where smoking, anathema to the socialist goody-goodies, was still permitted. He went to the breakfront and selected a mild panatela from one of the humidors, then sat down in a leather easy chair where one of the other members had conveniently left a copy of the Sunday Washington Post. He scrupulously avoided the front section containing news of the week which he knew was a government generated pack of lies designed to exalt the President and those around him. MacAndrews was sure if it were ever revealed that a pedophile was among the President's advisors, the man would be instantly labeled a selfless instructor of sexual techniques to a young and inexperienced generation.

He turned to the sports section which, for the most part, had not been tainted by political correctness and self-serving manipulation. You play nine innings. If you score more runs, you win; less runs, you lose. Pretty basic, easy to understand and hard to fuck with. He glowered as he checked the box scores. It had been a bad day for the Nats. A 7-0 defeat at the hands of the Reds. Today's outlook didn't

44

seem much better. The hometowners were going up against Cincinnati's ace, already 8-2 and they hadn't even reached Father's Day.

"General?"

He looked up . Marcus, the lounge porter was standing over him, holding a phone.

"For you, sir. I believe it's the White House."

"Thank you, Marcus," the General said, taking the phone. "This is MacAndrews." He listened and as he did his visage became more intense, turning eventually into a cold anger as he received a thumbnail version of what had transpired at Santa Veronica. "Yes, I understand. I'm leaving now. I should be there in about forty minutes."

He clicked off the phone and sat quietly for a moment, letting it sink in. Those lousy Arab bastards. They've finally done it. And on my watch, too. Well, it had to happen. Everyone knew it was coming, everyone except the President and the dolts surrounding him. We can talk to to them, they said. They'll listen to reason. We'll draw up treaties to ensure perpetual peace. They don't want war, they want to co-exist. We have the answer. We know best.

No doubt the President will be on television later today, he thought, blathering another of his self-serving speeches. In Santa Veronica a couple of thousand souls will be spared the necessity of having to listen to it. They'll be too dead to care.

As angry as he had ever been, MacAndrews rose from his chair and headed for the front door of the club. Like it or not this President was going to get an earful from him and if he didn't like it, he could damn well fire him.

CHAPTER FOUR

Brian was two miles north of Lompoc when he pulled his car into a rest area which had been carved out of the side of the road. A young family of four was standing at the edge of the overlook enjoying the view of the ocean far to the west. They seemed carefree and untroubled which meant they hadn't been listening to the radio or at least not to Liberty National Radio, one of the three government run news stations that blanketed the country. Had they been tuned in, they would have received a great deal of information about the terrorist attack on Santa Veronica and the loss of life which was now nearing eleven hundred. The blame had already been assigned to Al Queida. One of its chief operatives, a man named Hakim Al-Aquba had been identified by a clerk working at a convenience store a few miles south of the town. Al-Aquba had caused a disturbance, threatening the young clerk's life before leaving in anger and heading north. A credit card used to buy gasoline had been issued in the name of Mahmoud Azziri, one of Al-Aquba's known aliases. The clerk was also able to identify the blackbearded swarthy Arab from a grainy photo shown him by agents of Homeland Security. The tattoo in Arabic on the man's right forearm which the clerk remembered vividly was additional confirmation of his identity.

Brian would have laughed at the clumsiness of the scam if it hadn't been so serious. DHS on the scene in Hazmat suits minutes after the explosion, an eyewitness uncovered almost immediately, a credit card bearing the name of a known terrorist used to buy gasoline. Forgetting the fact that no company would issue such a card, how stupid did this so-called terrorist have to be to actually use it? But was it stupid and was clumsiness really a crime? With each passing day the administration became more and more emboldened. With few, if any, survivors outside of himself, the government had nothing to fear and that was particularly true because there was no press to investigate what had really occurred. No, Brian told himself, Al Queida was a bystander in this one. The bombing of Santa Veronica had been perpetrated by some person or persons in the Federal government and the two burning questions were why and just how high up did it go.

The second reason it was no laughing matter was far more serious, at least to Brian. The news broadcast had identified the blast as nuclear with a kill radius of one to one and a half miles. The latter was about the distance from Brian's house to the center of town. He had been protected by the cliff on which his house had been built and to a considerable degree by the wine cellar. But once he had emerged from the house, he had subjected himself to radiation. He calculated that he had been exposed for a period of perhaps twenty-five minutes before he drove away from town. Aware of his danger, he had pulled into the first available service station and used the men's room to wash all his exposed skin areas. He stripped down and put on fresh clothes from his suitcase. Farther down the road he'd turned off into a deserted area and set fire to the clothing. Still, he knew he was at risk, particularly since he was driving a car that had been sitting outdoors when the blast occurred and possibly had absorbed some amount of radiation. He really didn't know. One thing he was pretty sure of. Every minute he spent behind the wheel of the

Lexus could only worsen his condition.

But what to do? In a matter of hours the FSF would discover he had not died in the blast, if in fact they had not already done so. He would certainly become the object of an intense manhunt which meant public transportation was out of the question. His credit cards would be useless as would his cell phone. It might be possible to buy a car for cash, no questions asked, but there was no guarantee the seller could be trusted. The government was more than willing to put up huge rewards when it was in their best interest. In any event whatever he decided he would have to do it quickly.

And then it came to him. The solution. And if God had any mercy in His heart, it just might work. He put the car in gear and sped down the highway toward Lompoc where he stopped at a service station/convenience store. The first thing he did was purchase a throwaway phone and the second thing was to punch up a phone number in Santa Barbara.

"It's Sunday morning," the voice on the line said, "I'm frying up some grits and bacon and you better not be trying to sell me something."

"You and your grits and bacon. I can't believe you're still alive," Brian chided.

There was a long, long silence on the other end of the line and then: "I'll be fucked. Brian Everett, you son of a bitch, where have you been hiding these past three years?"

"Where you couldn't find me, old friend. I still owed you fifty bucks from Super Bowl Forty Four and damned if I was going to pay you."

Buford "Buzz" Shipley laughed. "I always knew you were a deadbeat. That's right. I'm writing a book about it. Brian Everett, America's Most Trusted Newsman and Professional Welcher. Got kind of a ring to it."

Brian growled. "You always were as big as an elephant but I didn't know you had a memory like one. Never should have made this call," he groused.

"Well, you made it so live with it. Is this some kind of obligation? You into a twelve step program, calling to make amends or something? Oh, hell, Brian, it's just great to hear your voice".

"You may not feel that great, Buzz, when I tell you why I called. Have you been watching the tube?"

"Glued to the set. Those sons of bitches."

"Santa Veronica's where I've been hibernating the past three years, Buzz."

A hesitation as it sunk in. "Oh, God, no," his friend said. "Are you okay?"

"Okay enough, at least for now."

"And Marnie?"

"She's dead, Buzz."

"Oh, man, I am so sorry---"

"Not today. Two years ago. I've been living pretty much alone, trying to mind my own business, at least until now."

Buzz' tone immediately became more serious. "You're in trouble."

"The worst kind," Brian said.

"When do you want me and where?" Buzz asked without hesitation.

"Better hear me out first, Buzz. This could be dangerous."

"You haven't answered my previous question."

"I mean it. Don't know why but the FSF is out to kill me."

"The FSF," Buzz sneered. "Jackbooted gestapo bastards. What'd you do, forget to salute?"

"Honest, Buzz, I don't know but they are dead serious."

"Look, could we cut the chatter? What do you want me to do?"

"You're sure?"

"I'm sure."

"Okay," Brian said. "There's a Little League park a couple of miles north of Lompoc on the east side. I'll be in the parking lot."

"Figure ninety minutes, maybe sooner."

"Thanks, Buzz."

"Have the fifty ready. I don't take checks." He hung up.

Brian smiled and shoved the throwaway into his pocket. His gaze fell on a rack of tourist brochures against a far wall. He moved to it, selected a hotel guide for Los Angeles and then stepped outside the store where he dialed the Bonaventure and made a one-night reservation in his own name, giving them his credit card number. As he was finishing up the call, a powder-blue Mitsubishi heading south pulled off the highway and stopped next to one of the pumps. The driver inserted his credit card and the pump started dispensing gas automatically. The driver left the aisle at a jog as he headed for the men's room. Looking around, Brian ambled over to the car and unobserved, tossed his cell phone (clicked to the ON position) into the backseat.

Finally he pumped eleven gallons into the Lexus using his credit card after which he drove out of the station and headed north toward the Little League field.

High over the southern Nevada desert, Air Force Captain Mark Everett started his descent toward Nellis Air Base. On a training exercise in an F-15, he had suddenly received an urgent radio transmission. The country had been put on high alert. He was to return to base immediately. Wheels down he maneuvered the fighter in a perfect landing and taxied toward a nearby hangar. Big John Shepherd, his best friend and constant drinking buddy was there to meet him as he alighted from the plane. Mark knew immediately from his friend's expression that there was news and it wasn't good.

"What's up, Shep? Why the alert?" Mark asked him.

Shepherd just shook his head grimly. "Damned Arabs. They finally went and did it. They set one off, Mark. Nuclear. Not a big one but big enough."

"Shit", Mark grumbled. "I guess we knew it was coming sooner or later. Bastards."

He started off but Shepherd grabbed his arm to stop him. "Mark, they hit Santa Veronica."

Mark stared at him in disbelief. "No. I mean, why? What for? A sleepy little place like that." He hesitated. "Casualties?"

"Over a thousand at least. Just about everyone."

Mark's stomach started to churn. "My father?"

"No one knows. DHS is there. FEMA. They're just getting started."

He felt himself losing it but tried to hide his feelings. No, not his father. Brian Everett was indestructible. A man for the ages. A man he deeply respected even if he had found it hard to love him. What had that been all about? A father wanting so much for a son. A son wanting to go his own way without interference. Oil and water. Flint and flash paper. They'd been at loggerheads since Mark was first able to put "teen" at the end of his age. Marnie had refereed all through high school and college, but when she died, they drifted completely apart. And now he was gone, murdered by a bunch of Islamic bastards with no respect for human life. An emptiness began to consume him as well as a rage and he felt his eyes turning moist.

He shrugged off Shep's arm. "I have to call my sister," he said, hurrying away.

The coffee was bitter and had turned cold but Colonel Erwin Conrad seemed not to notice as he pored over the damage reports coming in from Santa Veronica. The satellite photos were grim. The devastation was horrific and apparently had spread nearly two miles in every direction. There were a handful of survivors but all were burned so badly that their chances of survival were nil. Dying in the blast would have been far more merciful.

So far the cover story was holding and Conrad had no reason to believe anything to the contrary would be revealed. He had no clear idea why the Director, acting on behalf of the President, had ordered the destruction of one sleepy little California coastal town but he was certain there was a logic to it. Not one that he would understand, perhaps, because politics and strategy were none of his concern. He received orders, he carried them out without question or equivication. The one thing he did know for sure was that the Director wanted Brian Everett dead and surely that had been accomplished earlier this morning. Everett, the creature of habit, most certainly had been in the church when the bomb was detonated. Too bad, too. In an odd way Conrad admired the former newsman. He'd always told it straight even when it wasn't popular. And that report in the Chronicle the previous Sunday, that took balls. Everett must have known what he was letting himself in for. But killing him for it? Even to Erwin Conrad, that seemed a little extreme.

The phone at his side rang. He responded. Willis Johnson was on the other end of the line.

"No sign of him, sir. He's gone," Johnson said.

"What are you talking about?"

"Everett. He's in the wind."

"He can't be."

"We got to the house about ten minutes after DHS reached town. The place was pretty beat up but still standing. His car was missing."

"Because he was at the church," Conrad snapped in annoyance.

"Negative, sir. I had the DHS people photograph all of the cars, most blackened and burned out but still identifiable including plate numbers. I went through the photos myself, three times. His car wasn't there."

Conrad pondered that for a moment. "Did you find his computer?"

"Negative again, sir. The den was wired for internet reception. Found the printer and next to it a pad where the computer used to be. From the size I'd say a laptop."

"Damn it," Conrad muttered angrily.

"There's more," Johnson continued. "He's got a wine cellar in the basement. Also a safe built into the floor. It was open and it was empty."

Conrad shook his head. "This makes no sense. Did we say anything or do anything that would have tipped him off?"

"Don't think so." Johnson hesitated. "Do we issue a nationwide BOLO?"

"No," Conrad replied sharply.This was a major fuckup and Washington would immediately blame him for the failure. Better to keep them in the dark while he tried to salvage the situation. "We'll handle it here before we have to drag Washington into it."

"They're not going to be happy."

"Nicely understated, Johnson," Conrad said. " You finished there?"

"Yes, sir."

"Report back. I'm going to need your help."

"On my way."

Conrad hung up, then reached across his desk and picked up the file on Brian Everett. Everything you'd want to know about America's most trusted newsman in 57 concise pages. He started to read.

Sitting on the top row of the bleachers, intently watching the traffic coming up from the south, Brian spotted the jet black Jeep Cherokee immediately. As the car turned into the parking lot, Brian got up and gingerly climbed down the stairs to greet his old friend. Buzz pulled to a stop, got out and waved in Brian's direction. He was a big man, six feet two with dark chocolate skin and black hair just starting to show signs of grey. He probably weighed about 275 although his playing weight with the Atlanta Falcons was probably closer to 220. Fast and fearless he'd been one of the premier wide receivers in the league for over six seasons before a freak hit on a routine catch had put an end to his career. He had believed his life was over but that was before he met Brian Everett. Then he discovered that, with Brian's help, his life—his real life—was just beginning.

The two men embraced warmly in the middle of the parking lot, slapping each other on the back as men are wont to do. Brian hung onto his old friend a moment or two longer than he should have, realizing how much he missed the companionship he had deliberately been avoiding these past two years.

Buzz grinned. "You're still a good looking stud, my man. Maybe a little older."

"And you, my friend, are as fat as a pig. Either that or you swallowed the Goodyear blimp."

"Wrong, grandpa. Without cornerbacks and safeties to worry about, I have gravitated to my natural body weight."

Brian grinned. "Well, gravity seems to be the operative word. Are you wearing a belt under all that gut? It's hard to tell."

Buzz smiled, raising his hands in surrender."Okay. Enough. I know better than to spar with a man who made his living dicing up people with the English language. What's the plan?"

"I need your car for a cross-country trip."

Buzz looked over at the Lexus. "What's the matter with yours?"

"Hot."

"Stolen?" he asked disbelievingly.

"It was parked outside when the blast went off," Brian said.

Buzz frowned. "Oh, shit."

"Precisely."

"And you drove the thing all the way down here from Santa Veronica? "

Brian nodded.

"How do you feel?"

"So far, so good," Brian replied. "I thought to be on the safe side,we'd drive it to some deserted spot in the woods a few miles north of here, burn it so nobody else can get hurt by it, then drive to San Luis Obispo where I drop you off and you hop a Greyhound back to Santa Barbara."

Buzz grinned. "Excellent plan, my man, all except for that last part. I gave up bus travel many, many years ago."

"Thanks, Buzz, but I go this alone," Brian said.

Buzz made the well known buzzer sound which had earned him his nickname on national television. "Nnnnahhh! Wrong answer, compadre. For one thing, in a few hours you might become too sick to drive and for another, this black beauty here belongs to me and where it goes, I goes. The latter being non-negotiable."

Brian stared into his old friend's eyes. "Buzz, I'm serious.This could easily get you killed."

Buzz nodded. "I figured as much. That'd be a problem if I gave a shit."

"What about Valerie?" Brian asked.

Buzz shook his head. "There is no Valerie." Off Brian's sharp and puzzled reaction: "Walked out last year. Went back to Detroit. Took the kids."

"Damn. I'm sorry---'

"My fault. Look, we're wasting time around here."

"You have a right to know what's going on," Brian said.

"I do, and you're going to tell me all about it soon as we get on the road. Now let's move it. We got us a car to incinerate." With that Buzz moved quickly to his car as Brian started to hobble toward the Lexus.

• • •

The White House would normally be very quiet on a Sunday afternoon, but this was no ordinary Sunday. MacAndrews strode down the thickly carpeted corridor that led to the Oval Office, accompanied by the Deputy Chief of Staff. The Deputy, a pleasantly pudgy one-time lobbyist for the paper industry, had met him at the entrance and quickly apologized for disrupting his Sunday. He inquired about the General's health, his family and his tennis game because it was his business to be well versed on everyone who had the slightest thing to do with the White House operation. MacAndrews smiled pleasantly, half-listening, as he noted the increasing number of staffers showing up for duty. And why not? This was a black day for America, the blackest since 9/11 for this White House, which had been shilly-shallying for years on the terrorist situation (which they chose to describe in various politically correct phrases having nothing to do with reality). Week by week, month by month they had been eviscerating the Armed Forces and castrating the CIA, the FBI and other intelligence agencies to the loud applause of their left wing base and to the total dismay of the balance of the country. And now their idiotic folly had brought on this mindless unwarranted attack on innocent civilians. MacAndrews had no illusions that this was an isolated incident. He was dead certain that this was just the beginning of a Holy War to be fought on American soil.

At the door to the Oval office, the marine guard on duty stiffened to attention and threw MacAndrews a snappy salute which the General returned. The Deputy opened the door and the two of them entered. MacAndrews gaze fell immediately on the President's Chief of Staff who was seated on one of the sofas, reviewing some papers. The President was nowhere to be seen.

Zebulon Marcuse, the President's closest advisor, long time friend and administration hatchet man rose, a broad but meaningless smile on his lips. He put out his hand and grasped MacAndrews' effusively, then head-nodded to his Deputy to make himself scarce.

"Thank you for coming on such short notice, General," Marcuse said.

"Nonsense," MacAndrews replied as they sat facing each other across a coffee table. "This is a bitter day for all of us." He looked around curiously. The President's desk was cleared of paperwork. There was no sign he had been in the office that day. "Will the President be joining us?" MacAndrews asked.

Marcuse shook his head. "I'm afraid not. He's in conference with his speechwriters. We're going nationwide on all three networks at five o'clock. Obviously this is a very critical speech. We have to be sure we get it right."

MacAndrews nodded. No surprise there. Speech making was the President's forte; actual governing was an annoying necessity.

Marcuse indicated the silver coffee service on the table. "Coffee, General? It's still hot."

"Sure. If brandy's not available, I'll settle for coffee."

Again, Marcuse trundled out his half-hearted smile as he poured. MacAndrews studied him closely. Marcuse was a young man by Washington standards, not yet forty. A shade under six feet, he was lean, almost gaunt. He wore his hair short cropped, black turning grey. His skin was pale, most noticeably in his face which made the dark circles under his eyes seem almost black. His eyes were grey and cold like those of a timber wolf.

"I asked you here alone, General, so you and I could have an off the record informal chat about today's events and what we should do about them."

"Certainly," MacAndrews said, accepting the cup of coffee, "but are you sure I'm the one you should be talking to? This attack most certainly comes under the jurisdiction of Homeland Security. FBI could get involved, possibly ATF in a peripheral way, but this is not in the purview of the U.S. military."

"You're absolutely right and if this is an isolated incident, the organizations you cited are more than capable of handling it. However, I'm worried—that is to say, the President is worried—that this might be a precursor to similar events all over the country."

MacAndrews frowned. "Have you any intel to back that up?"

"Nothing concrete," Marcuse said. "Bits and pieces here and there, maybe they add up to something, maybe not. But I think we'd be wise to consider the worst possible scenario."

"Which would be?" MacAndrews asked.

"Coordinated attacks on civilian targets through the country, soft targets like Santa Veronica that pose very little risk to the enemy but which could foment widespread panic across the nation. I know that sounds farfetched but then so did Santa Veronica until this morning."

"And just what does the President propose?" MacAndrews asked.

"You are aware of Operation Bunker Hill." It was half statement, half question.

"Been a while since I've read it," the General replied warily. He knew exactly what Bunker Hill was and he didn't like the direction this conversation was taking.

"Stripped of the legalese, it calls for a period of martial law throughout the nation for a duration to be determined by the President. If, in fact, we are faced with insurgency from a host of Al-Queida terrorist cells, implementation of Bunker Hill might become a necessity."

MacAndrews sipped the last of his coffee and slowly returned the cup to its saucer, mulling his response. Marcuse was looking for a 'Yes, Boss, Whatever You Want, Boss' answer and MacAndrews was damned if he was going to give it to him. At least not now.

"I think, Mr. Marcuse, that this is really a discussion I should have with the President."

That smile reappeared. "Actually, General, you are speaking with the President. He and I are on the same page on this, word for word."

"I understand, but that is something I would like to hear directly from him..." adding."...when he's not so busy with his speechwriters".

The eyes of the Chief of Staff narrowed as he stared icily at the four star general across from him. MacAndrews met his look and never flinched. After a moment, Marcuse allowed himself a faint grin.

"Well, as I said when we sat down, General, this is an informal chat, completely off the record. If the situation escalates, and let us fervently hope it doesn't, I promise our next meeting will be with the President. Thank you for coming."

Marcuse stood and MacAndrews followed suit. As they walked to the door, Marcuse again apologized for disrupting the General's day and the two men shook hands in the doorway. The Deputy, who had been waiting outside the door, escorted MacAndrews back toward the main entrance of the West Wing. Unobserved, MacAndrews took out a handkerchief and wiped off his right hand. He hadn't been sweating. He just wanted to wipe it off.

High above the San Diego Freeway, strapped into an FSF helicopter, Erwin Conrad was in a foul mood. For nearly two hours he had been waiting patiently at the Bonaventure Hotel for the arrival of Brian Everett. His operatives, tracking the open line on Everett's cell phone, assured him that their quarry was proceeding within the speed limit south on Rt 1. And then just when he should have exited that highway and turned east toward downtown Los Angeles, he had kept going, continuing south, merging into Rt 5, headed for San Diego or perhaps somewhere beyond. Like Mexico. Yes, Mexico. Of course. Everett was making a run for it , Conrad reasoned and that meant he had pieced everything together. He knew he was being hunted and he was desperately trying to escape. Not that his plan would work. It wouldn't. Immediately Conrad had ordered a roadblock set up on Rt 5 a half mile north of the Mexican border. He would be easily trapped. By the time the fleeing newsman caught sight of the roadblock he would be well past any place he could exit the freeway.

Yes, he would be caught, Conrad assured himself, but he would not be eliminated and for that, he was quite sure he would be reprimanded by his superiors. But better that than having him escape. He looked down. The cars in the southbound lane were already starting to slow. In the distance ahead he could see the roadblock. Cars and trucks were stacked up for miles and he was certain tempers on the ground were short. Well, that was just too bad. An enemy of the state was on the loose and his capture took precedence over all else.

Just then the chopper radio squawked and the pilot responded. A moment later the pilot handed the earphones and microphone to Conrad. Yes? The Colonel frowned. What do you mean he turned off? Where? Into the belly of Chula Vista? Wonderful. He must have been tipped off and was now scambling for an alternate route across the border, although Conrad knew there wasn't one, at least not one close by. What? He stopped? He's parked? Where? Why? The voice had the other end gave him the street coordinates and Conrad relayed them to the pilot. They were already flying over the city of Chula Vista; it was just a matter of getting to the specific address where Everett was trying to hole up.

Four minutes later, the chopper was settling gently onto a residential street in a quiet neighborhood on the east side of the city. Two CHP cruisers and a Chula Vista squad car were parked, blocking the driveway of a small one story frame home with a powder blue Mitsubishi parked in the driveway. Conrad alit from the chopper and hurried toward the front of the house where a copper-skinned

Hispanic was on his knees being held in custody by two beefy highway patrolman. Conrad glanced around, aware that the commotion had already attracted the attention of a couple of dozen gawking neighbors.

"Where's Everett?" Conrad demanded.

One of the CHP officers shrugged. "Don't know anything about any Everett. This is the guy who was driving the car."

Conrad looked down at the man who should have been furious at this shoddy treatment but wasn't. He refused to look up, refused to struggle. Illegal, Conrad thought. Has to be. He wants no trouble.

"Where's the phone? There should be a phone." Conrad said.

The Chula Vista cop stepped forward, holding out a cell phone. "We found this in the backseat of the car."

Conrad took it, then looked down at the man.

"Where did you get this?" he asked.

"No se," the man said.

"Did someone give you this?"

"No se."

"How did this get in your car?"

"No se."

Conrad hesitated for a moment, then turned and hurried back to the chopper where he grabbed the radio-phone.

"This is Conrad. Brian Everett is on the loose. I'm pretty sure he's heading either north or east. I want an immediate BOLO for the eleven western states. You have his car description though it's probable he's gotten rid of it by now. He may also be getting help. I want an immediate check on all friends and relatives, particularly those living in Southern California. There's a file on my desk. Start there. I'm on my way back. By the time I arrive I want to know where this guy is and who he's with".

CHAPTER FIVE

It was close to six p.m. as the black Cherokee approached Jean, Nevada, the tiny dot of a town about twenty miles south of Las Vegas. Aside from boasting one solitary casino and a pit stop for fuel, it's only other function was to provide a home for the Jean Correctional Facility, a major warehouse for most of Nevada's worst miscreants. The traffic was medium light. Across the divider the southbound lanes were already choked with Los Angeles based gamblers, crawling their way home after what had been for most of them, an expensive weekend.

Brian had related to Buzz the reason for their cross country trek, divulging what he knew which was precious little . He had no clue as to why Ken Bannister needed him, only that his good friend was in desperate need of help. Buzz had nodded knowingly. The friend of my friend is my friend. He was in all the way, regardless of what lay ahead.

They had been glued for the past several hours to the Liberty National Radio Network. The news centered exclusively on the horrific events of that morning in Santa Veronica. With each passing hour, the reports became even grimmer. The body count was up to twelve hundred and twenty. Hospitals within fifty miles in any direction were being swamped with burn victims and those displaying the first signs of radiation poisoning. Each time those words were mentioned Buzz glanced over at Brian, looking for some outward sign of exposure. As for Brian, he was trying to convince himself he had escaped the worst of it. True, he'd vomited twice and he was feeling very tired but maybe that was to be expected. And there was a small canker sore on the inside of his cheek, irritating, but probably nothing to worry about.

In fact, Brian had other more important things to worry about. Surely by now Conrad was aware that Brian had not died in the explosion and more to the point, that he was on the run, heading for parts unknown. Conrad would have issued an alert to law enforcement for hundreds of miles in every direction. That meant Brian would have to keep to the car, getting out only when necessary. His face, while older now, was still recognizable to millions of people. On the plus side, Conrad had no idea exactly where he was headed or what kind of transportation he was using. The trip should take thirty hours, thirty-six at the outside. Utilizing service station rest rooms, ordering meals from fast food take out windows, driving in shifts, they could reach their destination sometime after noon on Tuesday. That presumed no unforseen foul ups. They could afford no accidents, no attention from highway patrolmen. It was a high-wire act without a net and Brian was uneasy. What could go wrong? What was he missing? There was something he was overlooking but he couldn't put his finger on it.

"We need a pit stop, boss."

Brian became aware that Buzz was talking to him.

"What?"

Buzz pointed to the gas gauge. "It's pushing empty. I'll fill up at that casino up ahead before we hit Vegas."

Brian nodded as Buzz exited the freeway and headed for the nearest gas aisle.

"They've got a snack shop. You want anything? Probably should eat."

"You're right. Some kind of sandwich. You pick it. Maybe an apple and a Coke. Caffeine'll be good."

"How's your bladder?"

"No problem."

Buzz got out and fired up the pump after paying from Brian's stash of cash. Credit cards were to stay in wallets for the duration. He headed back to the convenience store and went inside. Brian leaned his head against the neck rest, closing his eyes picturing the map. North on 15 into Utah, then east on I70, through Colorado and into Kansas. Interstates all the way. At that moment, for whatever reason he did not know, he opened his eyes and looked toward the nearby casino parking lot where a Nevada Highway Patrol cruiser with its roof lights flashing was creeping through the aisles of parked cars obviously looking for something or someone. He shriveled down a little lower in his seat, never taking his eyes off the patrol car. Common sense told him the officers had possibly been summoned by the casino. Or maybe they had been chasing a speeder and assumed he had exited at the casino in an attempt to evade a ticket. There were dozens of good reasons why they might be checking out those parked vehicles, none of them having anything to do with him. And yet a small paranoid piece of him argued otherwise.

Just then Buzz got back in the car and handed him his sack of eats.

"Let's get out of here, Buzz," Brian said quietly. "Slow and steady. Don't make a fuss." He nodded his head toward the casino parking.

Buzz frowned, observing the police action. "They can't be looking for us."

"Of course they can't ," Brian said wryly. "So like I said, slow and steady."

"Right," Buzz said, throwing one last look at the cops.

A few moments later, they were back on the freeway heading north toward Vegas.

"That lady you called about watching your dog," Brian said.

"Mrs. Segura."

"Call her back," Brian said. "See if you've had any visitors."

"You really think?"

"One never knows," Brian responded.

Buzz took out his cell phone and started to punch in a number.

"No!" Brian said sharply. "Use mine." He handed him the throwaway he'd bought outside of Lompoc.

Buzz nodded in understanding and punched in the number.

"Mrs. Segura, it's me. Senor Shipley." A pause. "Yes,yes, I'm fine. Muy bueno. Si." Another pause. "Mrs. Segura, after I called you this morning, did I have any visitors? People come to my house? Hombres a mi casa?" He listened. "When was that? Cuando?" He frowned. "Yes, yes. No, no problem. Thank you. Gracias. I will call you tomorrow. Manana. Si. Hasta luego."

He clicked off and looked at Brian. "Three men with badges. About two hours ago."

"Jesus," Brian growled helplessly. "They sure as hell weren't Curly, Moe and Shemp." He looked at Buzz apologetically. "Sorry, Buzz. Now they've got you, they've got your car. What the hell do we do?"

Buzz thought for a moment, then smiled.

"Improvise."

Thirty one minutes later Buzz was wandering around the upper level of the long term parking garage at McCarran Airport, small change in his hand. To be specific, one thin dime. As unobtrusively as possible, he was checking out the dashboards of each of the parked cars. Brian sat nervously behind the wheel of the Cherokee, ready to blare the horn at the first sight of a security patrol. He glanced back toward Buzz, but his friend was suddenly nowhere to be seen. He was about to go look for him when Buzz popped up from behind a parked car and jogged toward him, a set of license plates in his right hand. He gestured to Brian to move back to the passenger seat, then opened the door and slid behind the wheel.

"Two Colorado plates. The guy left his ticket on the dash, time stamped an hour ago. Wherever he went he won't be back soon." He handed Brian his dime back. "And thanks for the use of your screwdriver."

Brian smiled. "I'm tempted to say that you are a product of a misspent ghetto youth but in this instance, I guess I'd be wrong about that."

"You betchum, my privileged white suburban friend," Buzz said. "Let's get the hell out of here".

A few minutes later they were back on I15 heading for the Utah state line after a momentary stop in a deserted schoolyard parking lot to switch plates. The dashboard clock read 7:17.

Erwin Conrad took a bite of his now-cold hamburger and chased it down with a couple of swallows of even colder coffee. He hardly noticed. He continued to pore over Brian Everett's file, positive he was overlooking something that would lead him to Everett's destination. They'd been lucky with Buford Shipley. Everett had a half dozen known associates in the Southern California area but according to the file, Shipley and Everett had been extremely close for many years. And when the investigating agents learned that Shipley had abruptly left home in mid-morning and had asked a neighbor to watch his dog for a few days, Conrad was pretty sure he was hooking up with Everett. A BOLO for both men and Shipley's black Cherokee had been issued throughout the western states, but so far no sighting. The Be-On-The-Lookout stressed that the men were not be apprehended or even stopped for any reason whatsoever. Conrad wasn't sure why this was the case, but his orders directly from the top had been explicit. Surveillance only.

The phone rang. Across the desk, Willis Johnson answered the call. He nodded, then pointed to Conrad's computer. "For you, Colonel. The Deputy Director".

Conrad sighed, dreading what was come, and fired up his lap top. The face of Nicholas Lapp, the humorless ex-Navy Seal who now served as the number two man in the Federal Security Force appeared on screen. Conrad didn't let the word 'Deputy' fool him. Everyone in Washington knew that the sallow-skinned, beady-eyed hatchet man with the bad rug was the driving force behind the FSF. The nominal director, a tweedy ex-professor of Asian history, had once served a term as his state's governor. He had been well-liked and totally ineffectual which made him a perfect front man for Zebulon Marcuse's new Presidential goon squad. The 'Professor' had now spent three years regaling Washington society with his wit and charm while Lapp, who boasted neither of those attributes, dealt harshly with the President's political foes, real or imagined.

"Good evening, sir," Conrad said.

"Good evening, Conrad. Where are we? What's going on?" Lapp was not one for small talk.

Conrad filled him in. Shipley. The Cherokee. The lack of sightings.

"So you have no idea where they are," Lapp said bluntly.

" No, sir but I expect to----"

"I'm sure you do," Lapp cut him off coldly. "Everett received a phone call at his house last night around nine o'clock. It was, of course, monitored and recorded. We considered it irrelevant, at least as far as Everett was concerned because we believed that the Sunday morning event would take him out. Or so you led us to believe."

"Sir, I-----"

Lapp ignored him. "The call was initiated by a man named Kenneth Bannister. He is a law professor here in Washington. He and Everett are old friends. Bannister is the object of a search being conducted by the Washington field office. At the conclusion of this call I will be e-mailing you a transcript of that conversation. You will see that the two men plan to meet somewhere on Tuesday evening. Bannister spoke cryptically so we have no clue as to the location of this destination. We will be working the problem from our end. I expect you to do the same. Is that clear, Colonel?"

"Yes, sir, it is."

"Good.To make your task a little easier I am initiating a nationwide alert for Mr. Everett via all three networks and offering a $50,000 reward for information on his whereabouts. We've also alerted all law enforcement entities throughout the country."

Conrad was confused. "Yes, that will be a help, sir, but--uh--the man isn't guilty of a crime. I mean, what's our pretext?"

"Humanitarian. The beloved Mr. Everett was a victim in the Santa Veronica attack. We believe he is dazed and disoriented. We are concerned for his well-being. He may need medical treatment. We want to make sure he gets it."

"An excellent approach, sir. That will be a big help, I'm sure," Conrad said.

"I am also sending you a precis on Bannister's activities over the past several days. Your eyes only, Colonel. Notify me the instant you have an update on Mr. Everett's whereabouts."

Before Conrad could say 'Yes,sir' again, the screen went blank. Moments later the e-mail with the transcript of the Bannister-to-Everett phone call was transmitted. Conrad printed out a hard copy and then sat back in his chair and began to study it very carefully.

In her small, almost tiny, apartment in Greenwich Village, Melissa Everett looked up from the book she was reading and glanced at the clock. It was a couple of minutes to eleven. She put down the book and , as was her habit, flipped on the Progressive Network to get the latest news at eleven. It wasn't really news, she knew that, but the TV provided another voice in the lonely studio apartment. She disrobed and then slipped into a sensible flannel nightgown, one of three she owned, nearly identical but in different colors. She stepped into the bathroom to brush her teeth, leaving the door open as she heard the opening theme for "National News Update". A few moments later she heard her father's name and puzzled, she stepped back into the room to stare at photos of her father and one of his closest friends, Buzz Shipley.

The words being spoken failed to register."...great concern for his well-being.....missing and unaccounted for....may be suffering from radiation poisoning due to the underhanded attack on Santa Veronica.....notify your local law enforcement authorities immediately..."

Melissa could not compute the message, but she knew one thing. Apparently her father was still alive and a shiver of gratitude ran through her body. She wondered if Mark was watching the broadcast in Nevada. Maybe she should call him.What time was it there? Much earlier. She started to rummage through her purse for her cell phone. Maybe Mark, being military, knew more than the broadcast was giving out.

Just then there was a rap on her door. She looked up, puzzled. No one ever came to see her, certainly not at eleven o'clock at night. Another rap and then a man's voice. "Melissa, are you there?" The voice sounded familiar. "Melissa, it's Howard. Please. Open the door."

Howard? Howard who, she thought. Then it came to her. Howard Kaplan, the new guy in page layout at the magazine. The one who'd been furtively looking at her since the day he was hired, thinking of course that she hadn't noticed.

She went to the door and opened it a crack, peering out. Howard peered back at her, then checked out her nightgown and reddened. "Oh, sorry. Did I get you out of bed?"

"No, I was just going."

He looked past her at the television set. "I came to see if you had caught the news. I see you're watching."

"I just turned it on." She opened the door wider. "Would you like to come in?"

"Huh? No. I mean, thanks but no, I have to run," he said. "I just wanted you to know, I mean, they asked me to tell you, they think your Dad may be sick but for now he's okay."

Melissa frowned in puzzlement. "They? Who's they?"

"It doesn't matter," Howard said. "Just trust me. He's alive and we're going to do our best to keep him that way?"

"Howard, you're not making any sense."

"Look, I gotta run. I just wanted to make sure you didn't worry. See you in the morning."

With that Howard turned and hurried down the hallway, then descended the stairs, two steps at a time. Melissa called after him but it was too late. He was gone.

Confused, she went back into the small studio apartment to dig her cell phone out of her purse.

The sun had dipped below the horizon behind them and an inky blackness had settled on the interstate as it wended its its way through the desert of southern Utah. Traffic was sparser now and it became easier to unwittingly exceed the speed limit . The Cherokee's inoperative cruise control, long ago a victim of age and neglect, forced Buzz to constantly power down to keep from attracting the attention of the Utah State Police. They'd driven in silence for the better part of an hour, each man consumed by thoughts of what might lie ahead.

Brian was exhausted but worry was prevented him from dozing off. The one canker sore had been joined by two others, He was suffering intermittent bouts of mild nausea and had been unable to eat more than a couple of bites of the sandwich Buzz had bought him. Now in the past ten minutes he had begun to perspire. He was pretty sure he was running a mild fever. He'd polished off the Coke, now craved a bottle of water. If they ran across a convenience store, they would have to chance a stop.

"Are you all right?"

Buzz was looking at him intently while trying to keep his eyes focused on the road.

"Why? Am I starting to glow in the dark?" Brian asked.

"No, you're beginning to look like my first wife's mother and that's no compliment."

"Buzz, I'm okay. Thirsty. Maybe we could grab a few bottles of water at a pit stop."

"First chance I get," Buzz said.

They were quiet for a few minutes and then Buzz said, "What happened, Brian?"

"About what?"

"Everything. The networks, our jobs, our careers. Everything was going so great and then one day it was gone. How'd it happen?"

Brian shrugged. "We forgot to pay attention."

"You forget, I'm a high school dropout, old friend. Elucidate."

Brian had to laugh. "You're a high school dropout like I'm a scratch golfer. Can't believe you're still pulling that dumb black guy crap."

Buzz shrugged. "Keeps the unwary misinformed and off balance. Also works good with chicks who are suspicious of black guys who use words of more than two syllables." He grinned,then became more serious. "So, without again avoiding the question, how did we forget to pay attention?"

Brian paused, gathering his thoughts, before he answered. "You remember how it was back then, Buzz. The man's first election. The so-called free press, me included, fawning over this supposedly Messianic creature, unwilling or unable to criticize, even when confronted with glaring red flags like his spiritual mentor, his earliest associates of dubious character and blatant political radicalism. No, no. They weren't HIM. They were acquaintances, nothing more. The soaring rhetoric, the persuasive personality, all combined to create the illusion that a savior had arrived to protect and defend the American way of life." Brian snorted. "Kind of funny when you look back on it. But of course it wasn't funny at all. We journalists, those of us who actually were journalists, sold out en masse. No probing, no digging, just blind acceptance of whatever we were told. The naysayers like Fox News---remember them?---- they were dismissed as fascist malcontents and we helped solidify that image. Oh, how we helped, especially the young kids, the 30 and unders who were a product of corrupted journalism schools. Support what you believe in, condemn what you despise and try your best to make it look objective. Neatly coiffed, teeth brilliant, smiles effervescent, brains pretty much empty, they made for good visuals and lousy reporting."

Buzz looked over at him. "That sounds pretty bitter."

"Maybe so," Brian said. "But then I had a ten year headstart on them. I remembered Cronkite and Brinkley and a lot of others who knew who they were and what they were there for. Murrow was before my time but I've seen the archival footage. He was special. But all that disappeared a decade ago. With a few exceptions, reporters became cheerleaders. Access to the power circle was unlimited. Invitations to the best parties within the beltway were automatic.

Discouraging words were discouraged. Too many discouraging words meant ostracism. I caught on sooner than most but by then it was too late." He shook his head sadly. "Those poor silly sycophants, beating the drum for a man who secretly held them in contempt, never realizing that when the time was right for a government takeover, they would be the first to be tossed overboard." He looked over at Buzz. "And that's what I meant when I said, we forgot to pay attention."

Buzz shook his head. "You didn't forget. I heard your final broadcast."

"As I said, Buzz, too little, too late. Three months later the Department of Information was established by executive order, three months after that, the administration assumed control of the major networks under a little known provision of the most recent National Security Law."

"That I remember," Buzz growled. "I was happy as a pig in slop doing color for the Sunday games and a couple of sports talk shows and suddenly, I'm out on my ass. What's football got to do with politics?"

"Nothing, but you were a 'prior', tied to old management. The White House brought in their own people, loyal, beholden and totally clueless. But so what? They were fortifying the stranglehold on the networks and you got caught up in it. Not fair, Buzz, but that's how they operate."

Buzz nodded, then pointed ahead. "Relief in sight," he said as a service station with a snack shop appeared about a mile up the road.

"And not a moment too soon," Brian said as a discomforting urgency shot through his bowels and he sensed the sudden oncoming of diarreha.

• • •

It was quarter past twelve. Conrad badly needed sleep but that was an indulgence he would have to forego, at least until he had unraveled the puzzle that had him in its grip. The FBI offices in Westwood were still abuzz with activity. Johnson was down the corridor meeting with members of the press, that is to say, parroting the information being doled out by the DOI. Local stations had not been invited. Only news of immediate local interest was permitted on L.A.'s two sanctioned non-governmental outlets and none of that could be political in nature. Sports, human interest, music, fashion, the arts, all of that was permissable but the dissemination of political information was strictly limited to the country's three national networks. Exceptions were made for the two weeks leading up to general and special elections but in all cases, copy was carefully screened and often censored by the DOI.

He took a long drag on his Dr. Pepper. He'd long since been sickened by too much coffee but he needed the caffeine. He slipped the DVD into his computer. It was a copy of Brian Everett's final broadcast on what was then NBC. He vaguely remembered watching it and even now, three years later, he remembered that he'd been annoyed by it. He fast forwarded through the news of the day until he got to the tag. Everett was three years younger then but judging by what he had seen of the man yesterday, those three years had not been kind. Maybe the younger man in front of him was a product of lighting and makeup though Conrad doubted it. The current Brian Everett looked tired and disengaged, reflecting every one of his fifty-nine years.

Conrad turned up the volume.

"And so, my friends, we come to the end of this broadcast and I must now tell you that it is also the end of my affiliation with this network". (There was an audible gasp from off-camera, probably a crew member. Everett had told no one of his intentions, not even the President of the network's News Division.)

"For thirteen years I have appeared before you from this chair and I have tried in every way possible to tell you the truth as I knew it. You have been most kind in your support of me and I have considered each and every one of you a member of my family. Well, one does not lie to family and over the past several months it has been increasingly difficult for me to subvert your trust, not in outright lies, but more in the news which I did not cover, the guests I should have had on but didn't, the guests that I did have whom I handled with kid gloves because if I had once asked a difficult question, the genie would have popped from the bottle. Your government has an agenda, often having nothing to do with the truth or your well being as citizens. Every night I am pressured to follow certain guidelines because if I do not, my contract will be terminated. For myself I have never cared about that. But the management of this network, under pressure from the White House, has made it clear that not only will I be fired but so will my team. My producers, my writers, my personal assistants and researchers. Fourteen people in all and I have been unable to bring myself to take that step. Until tonight. Because, my friends, I can no longer face myself. I can no longer participate in this charade. To my co-workers, I am deeply sorry. I wish it were otherwise. As for tomorrow someone else will be sitting in this chair. If you are looking for happy reassurances about the well-being of this country, tune him in. You won't be disappointed. If you seek the truth, go elsewhere. And whatever you choose to do, for the sake of your families and your own sake and for the future of this nation, be wary, be skeptical, and never be afraid to ask the hard questions. I'm Brian Everett, and that's how it went in our world today." He paused for just a moment. "Bless you all and good bye."

Conrad leaned back in his seat. The arrogant bastard, he thought. For the first time in decades, a strong hand had control of the federal government, bringing together disparate factions under one collective roof. No more carping from malcontents about the decreased value of the dollar or whining about the tax base or crying out for more jobs. In the New Economy, of course there were fewer jobs as the country relied on its overseas partners for many of life's necessities at reasonable prices. But generous government programs provided income for all, often at higher than subsistence levels. And Everett, a man earning millions, had dared to turn, traitorously perhaps, on the duly elected government in the nation's capitol. If I'd been in charge, Conrad thought, I'd have arrested him on the spot. Instead he was allowed to disappear into a quiet oblivion, eschewing all interviews, writing no opinion pieces, keeping well out of the public eye. It was almost as if he had ceased to exist. Until, of course, that piece in last Sunday's San Francisco Chronicle.

He picked up the transcript of the telephone call. The words spoken by Bannister were cautious and secretive, revealing nothing about the location of the upcoming rendezvous. He put it aside and turned his attention back to the thick dossier on Brian Everett. He re-read the sections that involved Kenneth Bannister. They were fraternity brothers at the University of Kansas in Lawrence, roommates in their senior year. After graduation they dropped out for nearly a year, touring Europe by bicycle, picking up odd jobs where they could find them to finance their travels. Twice they were arrested for drunken carousing, once in Brussels, a second time in Cologne. Around this time they met a young Austrian would-be poet named Margaretha Steiner who, for reasons not clear, decided to join the two young men as they gamboled across the continent. Most often they stayed at youth hostels, occasionally at cheap hotels or pensiones, depending on their financial status at the time. After eleven months abroad Everett and Bannister made plans to return to the United States. By this time Everett and the Steiner woman, nicknamed Marnie, had fallen in love and they were married in a civil ceremony in Lisbon. A condition of the marriage involved Everett's binge drinking of which his wife heartily disapproved and in fact when the three of them arrived in New York to enroll in postgraduate courses, Everett joined a local meeting of Alcoholics Anonymous at his wife's insistence. The three of them moved into a two bedroom brownstone in Greenwich Village. Margaretha found work as a junior reporter on a German-language newspaper while Everett enrolled in postgraduate classes at the Columbia School of Journalism. Bannister was accepted into the law program at Brandeis University. After earning his Masters degree Everett applied for a job with television station KING in Seattle, Washington. He flew out for an interview, was hired on the spot and within a month he and his wife had settled into a small two bedroom ranch house in a down scale section of Belleview, across Lake Washington from downtown Seattle. Bannister continued to maintain the New York residence until graduation from Law school. According to the file, except for occasional holiday visits and two or three joint vacations, that was the end of any face to face relationship between the two men.

So basically these were his choices; the University, Europe or New York City. Conrad dismissed Europe immediately. There was no way Bannister could possibly leave the country by air. He had barely escaped his house a mere thirty five minutes ahead of the FSF task force. A search of his premises turned up passports for both he and his wife. It was remotely possible he could slip into Canada, that irritating uncooperative frozen tundra to the North, and fly overseas from Toronto or Montreal with a Canadian passport. Unlikely and even if true, where in God's name would he begin looking in Europe. No, he scratched off Europe. He had to.

That left UK and New York. The latter was unappealing as Europe for the same reason. Seven million people. Five boroughs. The proverbial haystack. And then his eyes fell once again on the transcript of the phone call and almost immediately he cursed himself for his stupidity.

Bannister: "I know just the place. I was dead drunk and you were only slightly sober when you decided to get me home in one piece"

Only slightly sober which means, Conrad reasoned, that Everett's new-found temperance following his wedding eliminated New York City leaving just one viable possibility: The University of Kansas at Lawrence.

CHAPTER SIX

It was a Tuesday morning unlike any other the country had known. In major urban areas throughout the nation Imams were being rousted from their beds by squads of investigators from the Department of Homeland Security and forced to open up their mosques and lay open their membership rolls and their financial records. For the past thirteen months every known Muslim in the country had been forced to register with the DHS, photos taken, fingerprints put on file. Although not perfect, the program was closely monitored and tightly enforced, one of the few government programs that was actually run with some semblance of efficiency. Each strike force was accompanied by a reporter and cameraman from one of the national networks to make sure the public appreciated the diligence with which their elected officials were dealing with this latest national crisis.

In Atlanta a quartet of young Muslims, infuriated at the manner in which their imam and their mosque were being disrespected tried to disrupt the investigation. Shouting anti-American slogans they attacked DHS workers only to be subdued by a security force from the FSF which had accompanied the investigators on the raid. The four men were beaten with billyclubs and taken off to FSF headquarters for interrogation. Similar scenes broke out all over the country from Dearborn to St. Louis to Albany and Trenton. All of it was recorded by the three national networks and aired immediately. Commentators expressed contempt for the traitorous actions of the rebellious groups and lauded the bravery of the FSF in quelling the anti-American disturbances. The country, they opined, could rest easy knowing that America was being defended by the highly trained Presidential security force.

What was not known, except to the enforcement squads of the FSF, was the fact that the shiny black truncheons used to restore order were made of lacquered balsa wood and the angry Muslim anarchists were in reality FSF personnel from out of state. Having been taken into the bowels of various FSF headquarters, they were subjected, not to harsh interrogation, but to hot coffee, doughnuts and a lot of hand pumping and backslapping for a job well done.

This pattern would continue over the next two days with well publicized on-camera arrests of several dozen influential imams and mullahs. Furious over the tragedy at Santa Veronica, terrified that the town or city they lived in might be the next target, Americans of every political stripe rallied to the government's side. Root them out, stop them now, regardless of any legal niceties that might be involved. Few stopped to think and consider what was really going on.

One of those who did was Leonard Jaffee, Director of the Central Intelligence Agency. He had been on the phone back and forth with his counterpart in the Mossad, the Israeli intelligence arm, for the better part of the past six hours. Alarmed by what he had been told, he was now sitting outside the office of the President's Chief of Staff, Zebulon Marcuse. He had been waiting for the past thirty-five minutes and if he was annoyed by Marcuse's rudeness, he gave no sign, cheerfully smiling at all passersby and pretending to be engrossed in an article in last month's Cosmopolitan. When at long last Marcuse emerged from his office it was not to invite Jaffee in.

"I've got an unbreakable breakfast date with Howard Jorgenson". Jorgenson was Chairman of the Federal Reserve. "Walk with me. What's the problem?"

Annoyed but keeping calm, Jaffee rose and walked by Marcuse's side toward the main entrance to the West Wing where the Chief of Staff's armored limousine would be waiting. "I've been taking to Malachi," Jaffee said.

"Yeah? How is the old Zionist?" Marcuse asked, not really caring.

"I don't know. We were too busy discussing other things."

" Such as?"

"Hakim Al-Aquba."

"What about him?"

"Your boys in the FSF have it all wrong. He had nothing to do with Santa Veronica."

Marcuse glared at him as the reached the doorway. A uniformed Marine sergeant opened the door for them. "First of all, they are not 'my' boys and second, we have a positive identification. An eye witness, a credit card, even fingerprints."

Jaffee chuckled. "Fingerprints? How'd you manage to rig those, Zeb?"

"Look, just because the guys at FSF are making your spooks look like a bunch of amateurs-----"

Jaffee cut him off. "Al-Aquba's in a cell at an Israeli airbase just outside of Tel Aviv."

Marcuse shook his head emphatically. "No, that can't----"

"They've had him for a week," Jaffee said.

"They would have told us."

"Why? For security reasons, they haven't told you anything for over a year. Why would they start now?"

Marcuse's driver had the rear door of the limo open but the Chief of Staff made no move to get in.

"What are you guys up to, Zeb?" Jaffee said. "You're not stupid. You don't make mistakes like this. What's going on?"

"Malachi's feeding you a line. I'm surprised you're falling for it."

"Nice try, but no sale."

Marcuse glared at him. "Look, Leonard, this is a domestic situation, out of your jurisdiction. But as a courtesy I'll double check with FSF and get back to you."

Jaffee nodded. "You do that, Zeb. I'll be waiting by the phone."

"I'm not sure I like your tone, Leonard," Marcuse said.

"And I am positive I don't like being shined on, Zeb. You and the FSF have been crowding us and the FBI and some of the other agencies a little too hard the past year. If we get in the position of having to crowd back, it could get uncomfortable for everyone."

Marcuse smiled coldly. "I needn't remind you, Leonard, that you serve at the pleasure of the President."

"And I also don't like being threatened," Jaffee said.

"No threat. Just pointing out the obvious. If your enthusiasm for your job has waned, the President and I will understand completely if you wish to step aside"

"I'm not going anywhere, Zeb, certainly not willingly. And if you try to muscle me, well, I've been around a hell of a lot longer than you have. I have at least thirty senators who will come for your scalp if you so much as hint at replacing me."

Marcuse hesitated, then reprised his icy smile. "As I said, Leonard, I'll get back to you." He slipped into the rear of the limo. A few moments later Jaffee watched as the limo went out the gate onto Pennsylvania Avenue.

Just then Jaffee's stomach growled. He checked his watch. Quarter of nine. This was absolutely the last time he was getting up at six-thirty to meet with anyone in the White House, urgent or otherwise.

• • •

He looked at the kitchen table. The places were all set but where was breakfast? He looked up at the clock on the wall The time read 9:23. No, no, this is too late. The kids have to leave for school by eight o'clock . Outside the window he saw Mark playing with his model airplane. But why was he wearing a bathing suit? It was winter. There was snow on the ground. He shouted to him but Mark didn't hear. He just kept running around with that damned model plane. Brian shouted again to no avail. Mark grinned at him through the window and ran off. He looked back at the table. Melissa had suddenly appeared, sitting quietly, looking down at her lap. Brian wished her a good morning and tousled her head. Melissa didn't look up. Then Marnie appeared at the bottom of the stairs and smiled at him. He reached out for her but she backed away, still smiling, and took a box of cereal from the pantry. He glowered at her. Muesli. I hate Muesli. I want Grape Nuts. She wagged her finger. No Grape Nuts. And where's my coffee? No coffee either. From now on, tea. I don't want tea. I don't like tea. She shook her head and took some tea bags from the pantry, then slammed the pantry door. It was a loud slam. It rocked him. It sounded just like the slamming of a car door.

Abruptly Brian opened his eyes. All he could see was green. Leaves and branches pressed up against the Cherokee's windshield. He looked over at Buzz who had apparently just gotten back in the car. He was opening a paper bag.

"What's happening?" Brian asked. "Why did we stop?"

"I couldn't keep my eyes open and you're in no condition to drive. It's okay. I pulled into some underbrush near the highway to get some sleep. Nobody can spot us here," Buzz said. He held out a coffee container. "Fresh brewed and hot. Can you handle it?"

Brian took it tentatively. "I can try."

"Also got hard boiled eggs and cheese and crackers. There's a 7-11 about a hundred yards up the road just off the highway. You hungry?"

Brian shook his head.

"You gotta eat."

"I'm on a diet."

Buzz looked at his friend with concern. "You look like hell, Bri. You need a doctor."

"Right, and as soon as I produced my GovMedCard, the FSF would be down on me like a hawk on a field mouse. Anyway, we've got to be in Lawrence by six o'clock."

"If you live that long."

Brian forced a grin. "It looks worse than it is."

Buzz glared at him. "You die on me, I'm gonna get pretty pissed."

"As well you should," Brian agreed. "Think of all the paperwork you'll have to fill out."

Buzz just shook his head and started the engine. They pulled out of the clearing and drove to the nearest eastbound onramp. It was 10:33 and Lawrence, Kansas, was three-hundred and forty two miles away.

The modified Gulfstream G550 twin engine jet bearing the green and gold colors of the Federal Security Force touched down at precisely 3:42 Central Daylight Time at the Lawrence Municipal Airport. A welcoming committee of three watched as it taxied toward them. Chief among them was Jonas Thibald, head of the Kansas City ,Missouri, office of Homeland Security. He was accompanied by Major Victor Askew of the FSF, also Kansas City based, and Beau Crimmins, Lawrence's Chief of Police. As the plane slowed to a halt the trio moved forward to greet Conrad and Johnson as they deplaned. Following the obligatory introductions, all five men piled into a waiting limousine and headed toward downtown where a war room of sorts had been set up at City Hall.

Following instructions forwarded from Washington, Thibald

had dispersed three dozen operatives to various parts of the city to attempt, if possible, to intercept either Brian Everett or Kenneth Bannister. Covering the bus stations and the airport and the closest Amtrak station was no problem but an arrival by automobile would make their task extremely difficult. Teams of two to a car were parked in advantageous positions adjoining off ramps from I70 where quick scans of occupants would be possible. Routes 40 and 10 were also being covered but with difficulty. Still, spotting either Bannister or Everett on the road was a longshot as Conrad well knew. He was sure their best shot at capture would come on campus, possibly at the dormitory where they both had lived as freshmen or at the Sigma Alpha Epsilon fraternity house where they roomed together in their senior year.

"We're going to have to get very lucky, Colonel," Thibald was saying. He gestured toward the wall. "Look at that map. Damned school takes up maybe thirty percent of the city all by itself."

"If you've got a better idea, Jonas, let's hear it."

Thibald shook his head. "Wish I did." He checked his watch. "Little over an hour to go, assuming they're both here."

Crimmins was studying the map. "I've got eight cruisers in there roamin' around, helping out the campus police force. Guess I could maybe spare two more. No problem long as somebody doesn't decide to rob a bank." He grinned, trying to loosen the tension. It didn't work.

Conrad fixed Crimmins with an icy stare. "Actually, Chief, it might be more effective if you had fewer cruisers on patrol. Unless, of course, you assume Everett and his friend are complete idiots and won't notice the entire Lawrence police force blanketing the area."

"Is that an order, Colonel, or just a suggestion?" Crimmins asked coldly.

"However you want to read it, Chief," Conrad said. They locked eyes for several seconds. Then, with a shrug, Crimmins ambled over to the soda machine to buy himself a Mountain Dew. When he was sure Conrad wasn't watching he took out his cell phone and called headquarters to call off some of his dogs.

Conrad found himself staring at the map. Thibald was right. They needed a break. Anything to narrow it down. Out of the corner of his eye he was aware that Victor Askew was approaching.

"We need to talk," the Kansas City FSF chief said.

Conrad gestured to the folding chair next to him. "Pull up a seat."

"Not here," Askew said. "Let's take a look at the city from the roof." He headed toward a nearby door marked STAIRS. Slightly annoyed at Askew's cloak and dagger behavior, Conrad nevertheless got to his feet and followed. As he stepped though the door at the top of the stairs onto the tar paper roof, Askew was trying to light a cigarette in the fifteen mile an hour breeze, typical for Kansas at this time of day.

"Expensive habit you've got there," Conrad said. Cigarettes were over two hundred dollars a carton, most of that in federal taxes.

"My one remaining vice," Askew smiled, "since I gave up hookers."

Conrad forced a smile. He'd been warned about Askew. The man didn't quite fit the mold. Professionally, an agent without peer but his social conduct sometimes bordered on the bizarre.

"I want clarification on the rules of engagement," Askew said.

"I thought they were clear enough," Conrad replied.

"They're not. Reiterate."

Conrad sighed, wondering who had told him this guy was sharp. "The overriding objective is to retrieve a tape cassette of some sort presumably being carried by Bannister. When he meets with Everett we assume he will play it for him, discuss it with him or hand it off to him. We would prefer that none of these takes place."

"I got that", Askew said. "My question involves Everett. My understanding is that we are to terminate him."

"Yes."

"No arrest, no capture, just a bullet in the back of the head, is that right?"

"It would be preferable to make it appear as if he had resisted arrest, but yes, you have it right."

"May I ask why?" Askew said.

"I don't know why," Conrad replied.

"Just following orders?"

"That's right," Conrad said.

"And it doesn't bother you."

"No, why should it?"

Askew took a long drag on his cigarette. "Now I see why they call you the Icepick."

Conrad smiled humorlessly. "I've heard that." He didn't like the look of disgust on the other agent's face. "Look, I don't have to apologize for following orders, but just so you know, Everett was supposed to die in the Santa Veronica blast. That was my responsibility. Now it's my responsibility to complete that assignment."

Askew nodded. "You're the Colonel. I'm just a lowly major but don't give me the order to put a gun to the man's head. I won't do it and I won't let any of my men do it. Do we understand each other?"

"We do," Conrad said. "It will give me no great pleasure but I'll carry it out myself."

Askew nodded and crushed out his cigarette with his foot just as the roof door opened and Chief Beau Crimmins appeared. He had a wide grin on his face.

"Colonel, the DHS boys just spotted Everett coming off I70 in that black Cherokee. Got a tail on him as we speak."

Unaware that they had been spotted, Brian and Buzz were proceedng south on North Kasold Drive, heading for the University.

Three cars behind them was a dark blue Ford Taurus manned by two operatives of Homeland Security. Three cars farther back was a silver Mitsubishi. One street to the east was a nondescript beige Buick paralleling them. In a few moments the Taurus would peel off and the Mitsubishi would move up. After a minute or two the Buick would turn onto North Kasold and then let the Cherokee pass it. This pattern would continue until the Cherokee reached its destination. The three trailing cars were in constant contact with one another.

Behind the wheel, Buzz's attention was split between the road ahead and his rear view and side view mirrors. The DHS surveillance was well executed. He hadn't yet spotted them.

"I think we're good," Buzz said.

"Keep watching. Conrad's a bulldog and he's not stupid but I doubt he'll make a move on us until we've hooked up with Ken Bannister," Brian said.

"You might be giving this guy too much credit," Buzz said.

"Maybe, but he wants me dead so let's assume worst case."

Buzz nodded. "Sounds like a plan. So just where is this Gaslight Tavern?"

"Tennessee Street, but that's not where we're going."

Buzz looked at him curiously.

Brian smiled. "New location, Buzz. The Tavern reopened there in 2009. Original burned down in the late 70's, nobody knows why, but that's where Ken and I misspent a lot of our evenings, pretending to study and swilling down pale beer. You'd be surprised how hammered you can get on pale beer if you drink enough of it fast enough. We're looking for Oread Street, number 1241, though there's no building there now. It's a parking lot for the Student Union."

"Student Union, eh? Don't suppose I could duck in there for a quick shower. I'm feeling a little gamy. Matter of fact , you're getting to be a little ripe yourself."

Brian smiled. "Be a little risky. And what makes you think you could pass for a student?"

"Professional scholar, working on my tenth advanced degree, hiding behind academic walls to avoid having to go to work. What, you never heard of those people?"

"Sure I have, but you don't fit the profile."

Buzz snorted. "There you go, getting racist on me again. You know when I put my specs on, I look just like a damned intellectual."

Brian laughed. "No, actually you look like a walrus wearing glasses." He pointed. "Turn left up ahead onto Billings and we'll scout the campus."

"You need a pit stop?"

"Not yet," Brian replied.

The Cherokee turned left onto Billings Parkway. A few seconds later, it was followed by a silver Mitsubishi. The agent riding shotgun radioed Conrad. The Cherokee was heading for the campus.

Inside the Student Union dozens of students were gathered in front of the huge Hi Def big screen television that dominated the student lounge. They watched with mixed feelings as the Presidential helicopter hovered over what was left of Santa Veronica. A camera mounted on the chopper caught the gruesome images of the havoc wreaked on the tiny town. It was a sea of black as DHS investigators in Hazmat gear searched through the wreckage looking not for survivors but for identifiable bodies of which there were few. Revulsion was the predominant reaction followed closely by unbridled anger. Two Muslim students had started to enter the lounge but reconsidered when they saw the horrific coverage. They backed out of the room and quickly left the building. This was no time to be found wandering around campus when your names were Hassan and Achmed.

Onscreen the Santa Veronica footage, which had been shot earlier in the day, was replaced by the somber face of the President who was addressing the nation in this hour of national tragedy. As usual he was self-assured and eloquent and also, as usual, his words lacked passion or any obvious heartfelt trace of empathy for the victims. Instead his focus was on the perpetrators.

"This was a deed of consummate evil, perpetrated by one man whose hatred of everything good and noble about this country drove him to this inexcusable act of insanity. But he did not act alone. He was supported by others who shared his apocalyptic view of the world, others who also will stop at nothing to destroy our cherished way of life. Some of these people come from foreign lands, but many others, perhaps a great many others, live and work among us, keeping silent, waiting for the day when they will be ordered to act in the name of Allah. These fanatics must, and will, be identified and punished in the harshest manner possible. Murder, espionage, terrorism, and treason are all capital crimes and will be dealt with as such. This I pledge to you. But, my fellow Americans, we must not forget that the overwhelming majority of Muslims, here and abroad, are quiet, peace loving non-violent adherents to the benevolent and gentle teachings of the Koran. We must not unjustly blame these fellow citizens for the actions of a tiny minority. Now more than ever we need tolerance and understanding. Leave the fanatics to your government. I promise you, I will deal with them with every weapon at my command."

The same picture was simultaneously being beamed to a modest sized TV set in the den of General Dwight D. MacAndrews at his house in McLean, Virginia. MacAndrews eyed the President, as he always did, with a great deal of uneasiness and skepticism. The man had been President for seven years and MacAndrews knew no more about him than he did the day he had been first elected. What he did know was disquieting. If he had been political in nature he might have picked up some vibrations, some warning signs, but his military training prohibited him from doing so. Although he personally disliked the man, his job as Chief of Staff was to serve his country and that meant serving the current occupant of the White House. Any questions or misgivings had to be kept to himself. The military code demanded allegiance to the Commander in Chief. His duty was to follow orders, not question them. And yet as he watched the President glibly pontificate about a tragedy that didn't really seem to affect him, MacAndrews again thought about the benefits of early retirement. The notion had been consuming his thoughts a great deal lately.

There was a light knock at the door. It opened and Grace MacAndrews peered into the room. "Sorry to disturb, dear, but Lee is here."

MacAndrews frowned. Seven o'clock. Dinner hour. His aide Lee Fitzpatrick knew better. It must be important. "Show him in, Grace."

"Shall I invite him for dinner? We have plenty."

MacAndrews shook his head. "No, I'll make this short."

She nodded and went out. MacAndrews pushed the mute button on the television and the President blessedly fell silent. A moment later, Colonel Lee Fitzpatrick sheepishly entered the room. He was a tall man in his early fifties with a ruddy complexion and red hair close cropped in the military fashion. Unlike MacAndrews, a West Pointer, Fitzpatrick had received a battlefield promotion during Desert Storm, had risen quickly through the ranks thanks to Enduring Freedom and been snatched off the battlefield by an observant Major General MacAndrews who was in desperate need of an adjutant he could rely on. Fitzpatrick had filled the bill admirably for the past nine years and they had both prospered within the system.

"Sir, I apologize for barging in like this---" Fitzpatrick started to say but MacAndrews waved away the apology.

"Nonsense, Lee. Sit down," He gestured to the chair across from his desk. "Can I get you something? How about a drink?"

"No, sir, thank you. I won't stay long. It's just that----" He hesitated, fumbling for words.

Again MacAndrews indicated the chair. "Sit, Lee. Sit. Now what's the problem?"

Fitzpatrick sat. "It's Bunker Hill, sir. I just finished reading it and, uh, I found it disquieting."

"How so?"

"Sir, when was the last time you read it?"

MacAndrews shrugged. "I don't know. Maybe five or six years ago. Seems to me I skimmed through it pretty quickly but I know what it's about. As I recall it was a special project of one of my predecessors".

Fitzpatrick nodded. "Put together at the special request of the President when he was first elected. You might recall all those demonstrations. Town Halls, tea parties. The administration was worried they might get out of hand. General Weinberger was only too happy to cobble something together, just as a precaution."

MacAndrews smiled."Right. Against widespread armed revolution. Seemed like overkill at the time. Still does."

"Yes, sir", Fitzpatrick agreed, "and certainly it's a good idea to have a contingency plan in place in the event the unthinkable should happen."

"But?"

"But there are certain provisions, sir. I mean, the damn thing is five hundred and eleven pages. There are things buried in there----"

"Such as? Come on, out with it, Lee," MacAndrews said with a hint of annoyance. Fitzpatrick had shilly-shallied and if there was one thing the old man couldn't abide was indecision.

"I'm sorry, sir. I don't want to give you an abridged second hand version. I left a hard copy on your desk. I highlighted about a dozen sections. I think you should read them for yourself."

MacAndrews eyed his adjutant thoughtfully. Fitzpatrick was not given to either hysteria or paranoia. Whatever he had discovered it had shaken him enough to violate the "no meetings at home" rule which MacAndrews enforced with an iron hand.

"All right, Lee. I'll go over it first thing in the morning and then we'll talk".

Fitzpatrick stood quickly. "Thank you, sir. And again, I apologize for intruding like this. I just thought---"

"No need to explain. We'll chat tomorrow." It was a dismissal. Very formal. Almost curt.

"Yes, sir. Good night, sir," With that Fitzpatrick left, closing the door behind him. Slightly troubled, the General's gaze fell on the muted TV screen. The President was still blathering. He picked up the remote and pushed the power button. The screen went dark. Somehow MacAndrews felt more at peace.

CHAPTER SEVEN

"Quarter past five," Buzz said. "We've got forty-five minutes. How about a pit stop?" They were traveling east on Bob Billings Parkway. Traffic was starting to slow as rush hour took hold. Both men were still unaware that three cars manned by FSF operatives were close behind, ready to move in when contact was made with Ken Bannister.

"I'm okay for now," Brian said, although he wasn't. The aspirin he'd been taking was losing its effectiveness. He knew he was still running a low grade fever and now he was starting to experience stomach cramps. But there was nothing to do for it. He'd have to gut it out until they hooked up with Ken Bannister and after that-----, after that was anyone's guess.Twice he'd coughed up blood. Buzz, intent at the wheel, hadn't noticed and now he could taste it in his mouth. Sour and metallic . Not a great deal but enough to let him know that he wasn't getting any better. He was no doctor but he was damn sure there was no curative treatment for radiation poisoning. Maybe steps could be taken to relieve the symptoms but that was the best he could hope for. The big question was, how severely had he been exposed? If mild he might survive. If not, the next two or three days were not going to be a lot of fun.

Suddenly he was shaken from his thoughts by a loud crash and a lurch forward, restrained only by his safety belt.

"Son of a bitch!" Buzz growled, looking into his rear view mirror at the hulking pickup truck which had just slammed into them as they were immobile waiting for the light to change up ahead. He glanced at Brian. "You okay?"

"Define okay," Brian said trying to ignore what was sure to be a huge bruise on his chest.

Buzz opened his car door and started to get out. "Damned idiot must have been blind," he muttered.

At the same time, the driver of the pickup was alighting from the cab. A big jovial man with greying hair wearing a green checked shirt and levis, he was all apologies as he approached. Buzz noticed a passenger in the cab, a woman who looked to be in her late forties and probably his wife.

"Hey, mister, I sure am sorry," the pickup guy said. "I never saw the light up there turn red and I was just fiddlin' with the radio dial and, well, hell, it's my fault and I'll make damned sure my insurance company knows about it. How bad is it?"

"Let's take a look," Buzz said sourly.

The two of them moved to the impact site and evaluated the damage as agent Lou Abrams of Homeland Security watched from the blue Taurus three cars back. He looked at his partner who merely shrugged. Abrams reported in on the radio and talked directly to Thibald, describing the situation.

"The other driver, is it Bannister?"

"No, best as I can see, it's some rolypoly farm boy. What do you want us to do?"

Thibald hesitated for a moment, then said, "Pull over to the side of the road and monitor. When they start moving again, resume surveillance."

"Copy that," Abrams said, clicking off and pulling to the shoulder of the road, watching as Buzz and the pickup guy assessed the damage which didn't look all that severe.

The heavy set farmer knelt down to get a better look, tugging on Buzz's shirt to pull him in close. He spoke quietly.

"They've had you spotted ever since you left the interstate. Don't react and don't look. The Ford Taurus back there, that's one of them. There's a tan Chevy and a silver colored Mitsubishi. They've been tag teaming you since you left the off ramp." Pickup guy struggled to his feet with a huge grin on his face. He spoke loudly. "Well, hell, man. That ain't nothin'. Little scratch on the bumper is all." Then more quietly as he moved toward the front of the Cherokee: "Play along," he whispered.

He checked out the rest of the car, then peered in the window at Brian who was sitting quietly. "Sorry about the accident, mister. No harm done", he said, again loudly. Then he paused, furrowing his brow. "Say, ain't you that guy?" He looked at Buzz. "I'll be damned. I know this guy. He's uh--what's his name? You know, the news guy. Oh, hell I can't remember his name." He rapped hard on the window, signalling Brian to lower it. Brian looked past him toward Buzz who subtly nodded. The window lowered.

"What's your name?" the pickup guy demanded to know.

Brian hesitated but again Buzz nodded. "Brian Everett," he smiled. "What's yours, cowboy?"

The pickup guy let out a whoop of delight. "I knew it! Soon as I saw you, I said, Bobby Lee you know that man. Brian Everett! I'll be a son of a bitch!" He turned and waved wildly toward the woman in the front seat of the pickup. "Momma! You get over here! Come on. And bring a piece of paper. Yeah, and a pencil, too." He turned back to Brian and put out his hand. "It sure is a honor to meet you, sir. Yes sir, I remember me and Momma watching you every night. We'd just pull up those TV trays and dig into that meat loaf. You were like a --a ritual. Yes, sir, a ritual."

"Well, thanks very much--uh--Bobby Lee?"

"Bobby Lee Huggins and this here is my wife--- Get over here, woman---- my wife Daphne. Honey, you say hello to Mr. Everett. You remember Mr. Everett from the news show."

Daphne smiled and leaned forward. "Very pleased to meet you, sir," she said. "Here's your paper and pencil, Bobby Lee."

Bobby Lee took them and handed them to Brian who looked at the paper. On it was written: NORTH/TAILBACK/THE MEAT CUTTER.

Quietly, Bobby Lee said, "Dr. Bannister said you'd know what this means. You can't go to the campus, they're all over the place. Pretend you're signing an autograph."

Brian nodded and feigned the signature.

"Get yourself onto E 15th Street, approaching the Oak Hills Cemetery on your left. There will be a slow moving funeral cortege that'll turn left onto Oak Hill Avenue, heading for the main gate." Surreptitiously, he handed Brian a small white stick-on triangle which he had palmed. "Place this on the inside windshield by the driver. Then at the last moment, filter into the line of cars. They'll make room for you. Just after you get in the gate watch for a worker in an orange vest and follow his directions without hesitation. Any questions?"

"Only one. Why are you doing this?"

Bobby Lee Huggins smiled. "Oh, hell, man. There are more of us around than you could possibly dream of, Mr. Everett. Now get going." Bobby Lee backed away from the car holding the paper and pencil and spoke loudly. "Thanks very much, sir. You have a good trip now. And God bless you!"

He and Daphne stood back and waved goodbye as Buzz got behind the wheel and they started up again. A moment later, the Taurus pulled into the traffic and followed a respectful distance behind.

"What now, old friend?" Buzz asked. He'd been too far away to hear the conversation. Brian handed him the stick-on triangle and filled him in on the rest. "And just how do I get to this 15th Street?"

"Well. to skip the campus, take a left up there at Rt 59 and then a right on West Ninth Street. I'm pretty sure I can find it from there."

And he did. Twenty-seven minutes later they were heading east on 15th Street with the Taurus lumbering along behind them. The funeral procession, some twenty cars in all was moving slowly, crowding the road. Buzz watched as the hearse turned left just at the edge of the cemetery and the other cars trailed behind. On Oak Hill Avenue they kept well to the right and Buzz made the turn, pulling up alongside the cortege. Up ahead he could see the entrance to the cemetery. He flipped on his right turn blinker. Immediately, the car next to him dropped back giving him room to slide into the procession.

Lou Abrams, at the wheel of the Taurus, was perplexed and immediately radioed in for instructions. He was told to hang back, not join the funeral and a minute or so after the procession entered the cemetery, follow a respectful distance away, then watch and wait. This was almost certainly the meeting place, Thibald thought, and Conrad concurred. A simple matter to abandon the Cherokee and get into one of the other cars which would be carrying Kenneth Bannister.

A huge map of the city dominated one of the walls in the war room and Conrad scanned it, quickly finding the Oak Hills Cemetery. The main gate on Oak Hill was the only way in or out of the cemetery, according to the map. He turned to Crimmins. "Chief, I want a roadblock set up at the main entrance to the Oak Hill Cemetery. When that funeral parade or whatever the hell it's supposed to be tries to come out, we stop and search every car."

"And if Bannister's not there?"

"He'll be there," Conrad said. He looked back at the map. "He's got to be there". Under his breath he muttered to himself. "Got you, you son of a bitch."

Back at the cemetery, Buzz was creeping slowly behind a spiffy Mercedes sedan as the procession started to wend its way forward. Up ahead on the left was a short access road that apparently led to some maintenance buildings. A very large florist's van was parked at the junction and a worker in coveralls wearing an orange vest was leaning lazily against the back of the van. As the Cherokee pulled alongside, the man suddenly stepped in front of them vigorously pointed to the left. Buzz yanked at the wheel and turned down the short road, perhaps fifty feet in all that led to the open entrance of a one story steel frame building that appeared to house lawn care equipment. The van masked the turn sufficiently so that anyone watching from far back probably wouldn't have seen the turn.

As soon as the Cherokee drove into the building another orange- vested man jumped in front of the car holding up his hands . Two others approached from the sides and opened the side doors. A fourth went directly to the rear and swung open the tailgate door to get at the luggage. A few feet away was a parked Honda sedan, doors open, trunk lid up.

"Into the other car, Mr. Everett. Quickly!" said the man on Brian's side of the Cherokee. "We've got about thirty seconds."

The man at the rear of the Cherokee already had the luggage out and was stowing it in the Honda. The man assisting Buzz, who seemed to be the leader of the group, handed him the keys. "Get behind the wheel but don't do anything yet. Not until I tell you." He turned and called off to the side. "Joe! Tommy!"

Two men emerged from the shadows and hurried to the Cherokee. The one named Joe, a beefy black man, slid behind the wheel as his partner got into the passenger seat, slamming the door. The man in the vest backed away. "Stand clear! Go! Go!"

99

Joe expertly backed and filled, drove quickly back down the access road as the stragglers in the procession were approaching. The nearest one stopped to allow the Cherokee back into line and slowly the cortege proceeded ahead.

The head guy walked over to the Honda, lighting a cigarette as he did so. "Mr. Shipley. Mr. Everett. I'd introduce myself if I could but our group operates on a no-name basis wherever possible."

"Better tell that to Bobby Lee Huggins and Daphne", Buzz said.

The man smiled. "I wouldn't go lookin 'em up in the phone book."

Buzz smiled. "Gotcha."

"Probably safer that way," Brian said. "Well, names or no names, thanks."

The man shrugged. "It's a privilege to help out, Mr. Everett. We had a dozen cars forty miles out on the interstate looking for you. Don't know why they're after you, but whatever it is, they'll have to come through us to get to you".

"I appreciate it," Brian said.

"Hell,man, you're one of us. Wouldn't have it any other way." He looked sideways at Buzz. "You I'm not so sure about. You cost me a few bucks every time the Falcons played the Chiefs."

"Friend, you've got some memory." Buzz smiled.

The man nodded. "When it comes to money, I'm like an elephant. Like to shake your hand anyway, if you don't mind."

The man extended his hand. Buzz shook it warmly. "Wish we'd had more time, we could have come up with something better."

"Seems to me," Brian said, "you fellas did just fine."

"They showed you the note from Dr. Bannister?"

"They did."

"Hope you can figure it out. None of us has the faintest idea what it means."

"I'm working on it," Brian said.

The man checked his watch. "We figure DHS'll have a roadblock set up by the entrance pretty soon now." He signaled to one of the other men. "Harry, open the rear door." The man called Harry hurried to the rear of the shed and with the help of others, moved some equipment out of the way, then opened up a rear access door. "Drive out to the asphalt road, turn left and follow it until you get to the fountain, then take the road to the left. That'll get you close to the perimeter road. Someone's out there to show you a dirt road that leads to an emergency gate at the far end of the premises. It isn't used much any more and it doesn't show up on maps. Exit there, turn right and you'll be heading for the north side of the city."

Brian nodded. "I went to school here. I pretty much know my way around."

"All right, then. Good luck." He stepped away from the car. He signaled to Harry again as Buzz fired up the Honda and drove out onto the cemetery road.

Meanwhile on a slight knoll that overlooked a neatly manicured expanse of green dotted everywhere by crosses and tombstones and other loving markers that remembered and honored the dead, Lou Abams and his partner looked down at the parked hearse which was trailed by twenty-one cars of various makes and colors. One of them was the black Cherokee with the Colorado plates. Fifty yards away a gaggle of supposed mourners were doing their best to look shattered and bereaved as a black suited clergyman read a passage from the bible over a coffin which, if anyone had bothered to look, was empty.

It hadn't been easy for the agents to reach this vantage point. Trailing the cortege by several hundred yards, they had been stopped at the suddenly closed gate by a white-maned, florid faced old geezer wearing the uniform of a security guard.

"Can't let you in, boys. Cemetery's closed," he said.

"What do you mean, closed?", Abrams demanded.

The guard pointed. "You see the sign. Cemetery closes at five o'clock."

Abrams shook his head in annoyance. "You just let in a funeral procession."

"Oh, the Peterson party. Wonderful man, young Peterson. Much beloved and a credit to the city. You boys weren't with the procession though."

"Actually we are," Abrams lied. "We got held up in traffic a ways back."

The guard looked at them dubiously. "Where's your sticker?"

"My what?"

"Sticker. White sticker. Can't let you in without your sticker."

Abrams had had just about enough of this old geezer. He dug into his pocket for his identification and flashed it. "Listen, old timer, my partner and I are with DHS and we're on the job so just open the gate."

The guard looked puzzled. "DH who? What? Let me see that again."

Totally irritated, Abrams opened the ID wallet and held it out. "Can you read this, old fella?"

The guard peered intently. "Oh, I can read all right. Just have a little trouble seeing." He put his face close up to the picture ID and read out loud. "Department of Homeland Security." He scanned the photo, then compared it with the scowling Abrams. "Yep, that's you, all right. So what do want to go in for? Mr. Peterson do something wrong. Didn't seem the type to me. Anyways, he's dead now. Can't be that much of a problem for you boys."

Abrams lost it. "Open the goddamned gate, old man , or I'll put you under arrest for obstruction! Do you understand? Now do it!"

The old man put on his finest wounded expression." Well, you don't have to get all het up about it. All you had to do was ask." He figured by now the switch had been made at the shed, but just to be sure, he ambled slowly toward the gate house and entered. Seconds passed. Then more seconds. Abrams blared his horn loudly and then slowly the gate started to swing open.

Now, twenty minutes later, as Abrams and his partner watched, the mourners began to leave. Car after car pulled away slowly and respectfully from the gravesite, ultimately leaving one car still parked and unattended. The Cherokee. Abrams radioed in to Thibald. "The FSF had it right. They made the switch."

A short time later a parade of cars was backed up at the cemetery gate as Erwin Conrad, becoming increasingly irritated, was going through them, interrogating mourners, tossing people and vehicles aside like the kid at Christmas who finds a huge pile of horseshit under the tree and keeps digging in, sure that somewhere in all that mess he would find a pony. He finally realized there was no pony. What there was was thirty-nine people, among whom at least one had driven the Cherokee to the gravesite and then bummed a ride back with one of the other mourners. Conrad knew the whole thing was an elaborate charade, designed to thwart the FSF. He'd been victimized by this sort of thing before but these incidents were becoming more and more frequent, breaking out in all parts of the country. He could open the casket, show it was empty, arrest the lot of them but to what point? One of the "mourners" was the Mayor, three others were city councilman, three more were clergymen, another was the Assistant Dean of Students at the University, and finally, insult of insults, three were highly placed members of the Lawrence Democratic Party. No, discretion called for him to fall back on Plan B. The problem was, he had no Plan B.

The grey-green Honda sedan was heading north on Rt. 59, motoring along at a sedate 55 miles per hour, keeping pace with those around them and being very careful to maintain total anonymity. Brian had just unfolded the map of Kansas they'd obtained on the way to Lawrence and was now starting to examine it in earnest.

"So, have you unscrambled the puzzle?" Buzz asked.

"Actually, Buzz, it's not much of a puzzle at all, and except for the third part, I think you could figure it out."

"I'm not much for games."

"But you'd get this one," Brian said. "North. That's pretty obvious. We're headed somewhere north of Lawrence."

"Yeah. That I figured."

"Halfback. That's a little tougher but think about it. Ken and I attended KU in the late 70's. We had a pretty good football team back then and a really good tailback."

Buzz shook his head, his mind a blank.

"Think Heisman candidate, old buddy," Brian said.

Buzz frowned, then his face lit up. "Chuck Horton."

Brian smiled, nodding. "Chuck Horton. And lookie here, a few miles north of here, the town of Horton, Kansas."

"Amazing," Buzz grinned. "But what about this meat cutter guy?"

"Ah, that's the best part. When we were seniors at the SAE house, one of our fraternity brothers, a premed named Max Devilbiss had his heart set on becoming a neurosurgeon. Well, one day in early September, Ken found this ad in some schlock magazine for the McDermott School of Meat Cutting. Learn to be a butcher! Make big money! So Ken send in Max's name and every week for the rest of the school year, Max would get a promotional letter from McDermott urging him to enroll. Reduced tuition! Last chance! Sign up now!"

Buzz was laughing. "Your friend is pure evil."

"Oh, indeed he is. That's how come he became a lawyer."

"So you think?"

"I think in the small town of Horton, Kansas, we are going to find the home of Max Devilbiss, MD." Thrusting his arm forward Brian shouted. "Drive on, James!"

"Yassah, boss. I'm a-going, boss" , Buzz said obediently, paying satirical homage to the late Manfred Moreland.

The time was 8:40 EDT and the White House, or the People's House as some preferred to call it, was ablaze with activity. Outside the wrought iron fences that surrounded the stately edifice, security had been tripled. Had the Pope attempted to enter without the proper credentials he would have been swatted away like a pesky housefly on a hot Louisiana day. That is, if he wasn't first detained for intensive interrogation. The place was sealed up tighter than a 12 year old jar of stale peanut butter. Inside the fence FSF agents armed with M4A1 carbines and accompanied by attack dogs circled the grounds, poking behind every rose bush and potted plant and finding nothing more dangerous than a previously undiscovered Easter egg.

The real activity was inside the faux Oval Office, a modest sized room rigged as a television set and decorated to resemble the President's workplace, i.e. a small section of it as the camera would not move beyond the scope of the Presidential desk and the flags displayed behind it. At the moment a light-skinned black junior assistant to an assistant was sitting on the Presidential throne as the cameraman and the director fine tuned the lighting for the Chief Executive's address which would begin in less than twenty minutes.

Off to one side Zebulon Marcuse, the President's Chief of Staff and longtime political ally was again scanning the carefully worded speech that the President would be delivering to the nation. In the past seven and a half years, the President had delivered many addresses from this venue (too many, his critics would insist) but of them all, this was the most critical. The attack on Santa Veronica had greatly irritated him. His policy of "to get along, go along" had suffered a humiliating slap in the face. How could this have happened? The leaders of the Muslim nations had given him every indication that detente was imminent, but instead of peace and the world wide plaudits his efforts would have earned he was suddenly viewed as a weak, ineffectual and perhaps even a laughable character. He had no idea, of course, that the attack had been staged by members of his own administration. Marcuse disliked keeping things like this from his old friend, but the President, more often than not, was unable to see the big canvas. If he had played chess, which he didn't, he would have been mated within six moves.

"Zeb?"

Marcuse turned at the sound of his name to face Wendell Comeford, the nation's Vice President and heir apparent to the Presidency. That 'honor' would be bestowed next month at the Democratic National Convention in Boston.

"Mr. Vice President," Marcuse acknowledged.

Comeford checked his watch. "Not here yet? Cutting it close, isn't he?"

Marcuse shrugged. "The President may have a few shortcomings but delivering a speech isn't one of them. He'll be fine."

"I thought that we had decided to find some way for me to participate this evening. After all, come November I'll be carrying the ball."

"We discussed it, sir. Nothing was finalized. In the end the President thought it would be too cumbersome."

"That's funny, because when I spoke to the President this afternoon, he thought it would be an excellent idea."

Marcuse nodded with a chilly smile. "In principle, sir, but the logistics didn't work out and once I explained it to the President, he concurred."

Comeford's smile was even chillier. "You explain a lot to the President, don't you, Zeb?"

"Whenever I can, sir. That's my job."

There was a sudden stirring in the room and both men turned to see the President enter the room, trailed by two Secret Service agents and two uniformed officers of the Federal Security Force. The President's eyes flicked around the room, then settled in annoyance on Marcuse. He started toward him, ignoring everyone else.

"Zeb, we need to talk," he said brusquely without the nicety of a preamble. He turned to the Vice President. "This is private, Wendell. Do you mind?"

Comeford managed a smile. "Of course not, sir." And having been dismissed slinked away to another part of the room.

"You seem upset," Marcuse said.

"You're damned right I am. I had a golf date scheduled for early morning at Congressional, come to find out you cancelled it."

"Yes, sir, I did."

The President's eyes flashed with anger. "That match was arranged weeks ago. Mickelson and Stricker are both in town and they are not going to be happy about this."

"Mr. President, I'm sure they understand, as do you, that a great tragedy befell this country Sunday morning."

"Hell, I know that, Zeb. That's why I'm making this speech but what's that got to do with my playing golf tomorrow?"

"It's a question of perception, sir. The country has to see you as a man of compassion, putting aside trivial things to see to the safety of the nation."

"Sure, sure. But there's nothing I can do personally. Our people take care of all that stuff."

"Perception, sir. You don't want to give your critics more ammunition."

The President glowered. "Right. The damned internet. I thought we were going to do something about that."

"In the works, sir," Marcuse said.

The President nodded, unmollified. "All right, but you make the call to Mickelson and Stricker. Make sure they understand it's not my fault."

"Already taken care of, sir."

"Well, all right then."

The assistant director appeared at the President's elbow. "Excuse me, Mr. President. Two minutes to air."

The President nodded, started off, then turned back. "Zeb, about Wendell. Have you talked to him? Does he know?"

"Not yet, sir. We're going to get together tomorrow."

"Make sure he knows this wasn't my idea."

"I'll do that, sir," Marcuse replied.

The President made his way to the desk and sat down. The make-up lady gave his face a light dusting with powder while wardrobe straightened the knot in his tie. He tossed them his patented charming smile. "How do I look? Denzel or Danny Glover?"

Wardrobe waved a limp wrist at him, grinning. "Oh, Denzel, sir. Absoluteamente!"

"Ten seconds," the director announced.

The assistant positioned himself in front of the desk, held out five fingers, then for, three, two and....

The President, wearing his 'I feel your pain' face looked directly into the camera.

"My fellow Americans," he said. "This evening I want to talk to you straight from my heart," he continued, his eyes flicking to the left to the teleprompter.

The Honda was headed north on Rt 59, keeping pace with the

traffic which was chugging along about 7 miles an hour over the speed limit. Buzz made sure he was always sandwiched between two other cars. Strays who got out ahead of the pack or who lagged behind were fair game for state troopers in need of meeting a quota. Buzz was concentrating on the road. Brian was leaning back, eyes shut. Both were listening to the Presidential address.

"......dastardly and cowardly act by a lone member of an overseas terror group, dedicated to the murder of thousands if not millions of American citizens. I am proud to say your government has done an outstanding job protecting you from attacks on American soil. Special thanks are due to Homeland Security and the Federal Security Force who day after day and week after week have been working diligently, without fanfare, rooting out terrorist cells, thwarting imminent attacks. The dictates of national security prohibit me from relaying to you the details of these operations, but you have my assurance that every day your government is working diligently to keep you, your loved ones and your neighbors safe from devastating attack. And yet Sunday morning, the peaceful little town of Santa Veronica, California, was leveled by just such a tragedy. How could it have happened? Why were we unable to prevent it? Well, my fellow Americans, I will tell you why. It is because we live in a free and open society..."

"Gnnnnnnnn," Buzz buzzed.

Brian forced a smile. "Right on, brother."

The President droned on. No, it was not the fault of his Administration, it was the lawyers who constantly advised their clients i.e. arrested terror suspects, to clam up immediately, thereby denying security forces potentially valuable intelligence. For those who argued that these people should have been arrested and held under military jurisdiction, the President pointed out the 74% conviction rate in civilian courts, an impressive statistic by any standard.

"Let me know when you've had enough of this gas bag", Buzz said.

Brian nodded. "I'll see if I can locate Wheeler. It's almost dark. He could be broadcasting by now."

Brian started to scan through the bands, picking up only the three national radio networks and a handful of local stations, all of which were also carrying the Presidential address under pain of losing their FCC license.

"Too early, Buzz. It's not quite dark."

"Shut it off. I'm getting a headache." Buzz said.

Brian obliged.

CHAPTER EIGHT

Colonel Lee Fitzpatrick exited the Pentagon Grounds onto the Georgetown Pike and then quickly swung onto Chain Bridge Road, heading for his home on the outskirts of McLean, Virginia. Following his meeting with General MacAndrews, he had returned to his office to once again re-read the provisions of Bunker Hill. There had been something of a chill in the general's attitude. Most probably it was triggered by Lee's intrusion into the sanctity of MacAndrews home life but it could have been something else. The President wanted an immediate review of Bunker Hill, indicating it was something he might consider initiating in the future. Otherwise, why review it? To a man like MacAndrews, such a request did not call for questioning, second guessing or disapproval. Having obeyed and given orders for the better part of thirty-three years following his graduation from West Point, his being was totally dedicated and beholden to three precepts. Duty. Honor. Country. And, yes, one more. Obedience. Obviously Lee's misgivings about Bunker Hill had not set well with his boss. The President proposes, the military disposes. It was as simple as that.

As his high beams cut through the blackness enveloping the road ahead, Fitzpatrick became aware of headlights bearing down on him from the rear. A moment later, red and blue lights started to flash urgently from its roof. The car moved up close, threateningly, to Fitzpatrick's rear bumper. Slowly he decelerated and pulled to the side of the road. The police car followed suit. A uniformed officer exited the car and started toward him, lit flashlight in hand.

Fitzpatrick lowered his window as the officer shined the flashlight in his face, then into the backseat to determine if the Army officer was alone.

"Colonel Fitzpatrick?," the policeman asked.

"That's right. What seems to be the problem, Officer?"

The Officer looked up and nodded across the roof of the car. Fitzpatrick turned as a man in civilian clothes opened the passenger side door and let himself into the car. Leonard Jaffee leaned toward the driver side.

"'Thank you, Sergeant," he said. "Please follow us."

"Yes, sir."

The officer turned on his heel and started back toward his cruiser. Jaffee looked into Fitzpatrick's eyes. "You know who I am?" he said.

"I do," Fitzpatrick replied.

"Then drive."

Fitzpatrick started up the car and pulled out onto the road. The cruiser pulled out behind him, lingering a respectful distance behind. Fitzpatrick glanced over at the man who was the director of the one-time most powerful intelligence agency in the world. Fitzpatrick wasn't nervous, merely curious. Leonard Jaffee was one of the President's men, named to the Directorship of the CIA in the second week of the President's first term. Considered a staunch loyalist both to the man and to his political party, you did business with Jaffee at your own risk. Fitzpatrick knew he had to proceed cautiously.

"I knew you fellas had odd ways of doing business," he said. "This is a first for me."

Jaffee smiled. "It's a little out of the box even for me, Colonel, but

I needed to talk with you privately. Absolutely private. No one must know of this meeting."

Fitzpatrick chuckled. "Tell that to the Statie who's on our tail."

"Buchanan? He's one of ours."

"Interesting. And the cruiser?"

"We picked it up at an auction and had it refurbished. At times it comes in very handy," Jaffee smiled. "Yes, yes, I know. Way out of our jurisdiction, but these days who's counting?" Looking ahead, he pointed to the right. "Up ahead there's a roadside picnic area. Pull in there."

Fitzpatrick did as he was told and the police cruiser slipped in right behind him. Jaffee opened his door and got out. "Let's talk at one of the tables. It's a nice night and I need a cigarette."

"Why not?" Fitzpatrick said, joining him at a wooden plank picnic table. Jaffee lit up and took a long drag, then held out the pack. "No, thanks. Never acquired the habit," Fitzpatrick said.

"Lucky you. Tried to quit three times, no luck. And at twenty two dollars a pack, I'd be better off smoking weed." He chuckled. "Of course, that would be illegal. Unseemly for a man in my position." He took another long drag and exhaled through his nose.

Fitzpatrick leaned forward, folding his arms on the table, an amused half-smile on his face. "Well, here we are, alone at last. A full moon, a starlit night, a gentle breeze. So what do you want, Mr Jaffee"?

"Bunker Hill," he said.

Fitzpatrick feigned ignorance. "Excuse me," he said blankly.

"Don't play games with me, Colonel. I have neither the time nor the patience. Bunker Hill. How far along are you?"

Fitzpatrick shook his head. "I have no idea what you are talking about."

"Bunker Hill. A secret blueprint for the imposition of martial law throughout the country, triggered by Executive Order of the President at such time that he, or she, perceives an immediate threat to the safety of the nation. THAT Bunker Hill."

Fitzpatrick stared at him, stonewallng. "I still don't know what you are referring to, sir, but even if I did, even if there were such a contingency plan, I would be derelict in my duty to discuss it with anyone outside of the military chain of command."

They locked eyes. "I see," Jaffee said. "Obviously I'm going to have to approach this from another angle." He hesitated, then lit up another cigarette. "You don't trust me, Colonel. I don't blame you. If I were you, I wouldn't trust me either. I know my reputation. Party hack with just the right connections. Seven years of doing my master's bidding. Not true but it's the perception. Does that about nail it?"

Fitzpatrick stared at him, not sure how to respond. People who criticized the President or his minions often had strange things occur in their lives. Unexplained demotions, dismissal from work, vigorous audits by the IRS, even mysterious disappearances.

"Never mind. You can't trust me, but I am going to have to trust you. Very frankly the future of this country may hinge on it. Will you hear me out with an open mind?"

Fitzpatrick held his hands up in a helpless gesture. "Look, Mr. Jaffee-----"

"I'm sure you know the name Hakim Al-Aquba," Jaffee overrode him.

"The bastard who bombed Santa Veronica."

"Or so the administration would have you believe." Fitzpatrick cocked his head in puzzlement. "That's right, Colonel. Al-Aquba had nothing to do with that attack. Oh, some people went to a great deal of trouble to make it seem as if he were the perpetrator but the truth is, Al-Aquba is in Israeli hands and has been for the past week."

"You're sure about that? It could be a mistake."

"No mistake. I have it straight from Malachi Rabin and it's no mistake on this end. The frame was perfect starting with a credible double right down to the well-known tattoo on his arm. Chew on this, Colonel. Not every one in Santa Veronica died immediately. Quite a few survived the initial blast. Were you aware that within twenty minutes of the blast, DHS technicians in full Hazmat gear were on the scene?"

Fitzpatrick shook his head. "Not possible."

"It is if you know in advance where and when a disaster is going to happen."

Fitzpatrick looked at him in disbelief, shaking his head. "Do you know what you are insinuating?"

Jaffee responded sharply, "I'm insinuating nothing, Colonel Fitzpatrick. I'm telling you. The nuclear blast at Santa Veronica was the work of members of the administration, exactly who I'm not sure of, but you don't pull off something like this unless it reaches far up into the hierarchy."

"But why?" Fitzpatrick was stunned, unable to grasp the enormity of it.

"I'm not sure, but my guess is, it's part of a larger plan. And that's why I ask you once again, where are you on Bunker Hill?"

Fitzpatrick considered his answer carefully. Jaffee's story could be a complete fabrication, but his instincts told him otherwise. The man looked tired, more haggard than Fitzpatrick had remembered from a meeting they'd both attended several weeks back.

"We're nowhere yet. I read it over today. General MacAndrews is going to review it first thing in the morning."

Jaffee nodded. "Then it's not too late."

"For what?"

"To stop it, of course."

"You've read it," Fitzpatrick said flatly.

"Of course I've read it it," Jaffee said in annoyance. "It's my job to read things like Bunker Hill. Are you under the impression, Colonel, that we sit around Langley all day pulling our puds?"

"Sorry. My stupidity." He hesitated. "May I ask, Mr. Jaffee, why are you telling me all this? I should think your loyalties would rest with your President."

Jaffee smiled wryly. "Would you like the long version, complete with The Stars and Stripes Forever, or the short version?"

Fitzpatrick smiled. "Fifty words or less will do just fine."

"I'm a loyal Democrat. Always have been. That's how I got this job. After a year or so, I caught onto what these people were up to. They weren't Democrats, they were so-called Progressives. You know what that means in plain English. Socialists. Neo-Commies. I could have quit but I had two kids in college and two more on the way and I'd already discovered the hard truth about these bastards. Cross them and they took it out of your hide so I went along. Well, my last two boys, the twins, are graduating this year and I don't give a rat's ass any more, not about the Party. But I do care about my country. I care a lot. These people have done a pretty good job destroying every institution that made this nation great, they've wreaked havoc on our financial markets and turned the American dollar into a joke. They've managed to unionize three quarters of American industry, those that are still around, they've nationalized the media and the insurance companies. Congress is comprised of 535 self-serving idiots who go along with anything the White House wants, provided they get a cut of the action. The only bright hope? We still have the Supreme Court but for God knows how long. And meanwhile the people are getting angrier and angrier, weapons are being secretly stashed and unless we can turn things around, surely one day soon there will be blood in the streets".

Jaffee hesitated, then looked into Fitzpatrick's eyes. "That's the short version. Feel free to turn me in if that's your pleasure, Colonel."

Fitzpatrick smiled. "No danger of that, Mr. Jaffee."

Jaffee nodded. "You understand, there is no way the President can be permitted to invoke Bunker Hill."

"I agree, but General MacAndrews is first and foremost a patriotic military officer and he is not political. If the President gives him a direct order he will obey it."

"You'll have to dissuade him."

"I haven't that power," Fitzpatrick replied.

"You'll have to try."

"Or you'll have to find some way to dissuade the President."

Jaffee nodded. "Then we'll both have to try. And God help us, if we fail."

They were huddled in an alley next to the opera house, supposedly one of Prague's finest, though Brian insisted he had seen better looking movie theaters in East St. Louis. Marnie giggled as Brian held her close, nestling his face into the folds of her fur coat. Not mink. Not even rabbit. Just some nondescript animal who had given up the ghost to keep some Czech matron warm but ten dollars American in a seedy thrift shop was a bargain not to be ignored. Gently he slipped his hand under the coat and began to caress her breast. She giggled even more, muttering "No, no" when they both knew she meant "Yes, yes." I'm looking for a little compassion, he told her. That opera was your idea, not mine. You didn't enjoy it? she pouted, knowing he'd hated every minute. He snorted. I didn't even know what it was about. I mean, some guy in prison, then out of prison while the fat lady kept wailing away, keeping the locals awake for ten blocks in any direction. But they had translation above the stage, she said defensively. Great, he said, you speak German, I speak American and the translation is in Czech. Wunderbar! She giggled again, nibbling on his ear as he managed to unhook her bra. No,no, liebschen. Not here, back at the hotel. He growled. Back at the hotel is my friend Ken. She shook her head. Your friend is getting himself drunk at a brauhaus. How do you know that? Because this afternoon I showed him where it was. Good beer, good sausage and even better girls. We won't see him until the morning. That I will promise you, Brian.

"Brian." A pause. Then Buzz' voice, more insistent. "Brian."

He opened his eyes. It was dark. The countryside was flying by. There were few lights visible. It was Kansas farm country. The cows went to bed early. So did the people. Brian looked over at Buzz.

"Where are we?" he asked.

"Coming up on a town called Nortonville. We're probably still an hour and a half away from Horton. Maybe more. I thought you might need to stop."

Brian felt his stomach turning over. His armpits were wet with perspiration and the headache which had come upon him hours ago had refused to go away. He nodded. "I could use a break."

"I'll try to find a mini-mart station. We need water. How about something to eat? Maybe a couple of candy bars. You have to keep your strength up."

"Sure. Whatever you think." He paused. "I was dreaming again."

"I know," Buzz said.

"Was I talking?"

"You were, but nothing I could understand."

Brian fell silent for a few moments, staring out into the darkness. "I miss her, Buzz. More than ever. I can't get her out of my mind."

Buzz nodded. "Only natural. You're hurting and you're scared. You need her. You close your eyes to rest and she's there for you. It's a good thing, Bri."

"Yeah, I guess it is," Brian said, continuing to stare out the window.

A few minutes later an all night service station loomed up on the right. A sign advertised soda and snacks. Buzz pulled in, stopping at the pump closest to the men's room. There were no other cars, no other customers.

"Looks safe," Buzz said. Brian nodded but said, "Let's make it quick."

"By the way," Buzz said, "not to cause any problems but when we get to Horton, just how are we supposed to locate your doctor friend?"

Brian shrugged. "I thought phone book, but maybe that's too easy."

"Sounds like a plan," Buzz said as he got out of the car.

As Buzz headed for the snack station, Brian ducked into the men's room, flipping on the light and pushing the button on the door handle to lock it. The lavatory was small but clean with one commode, one urinal, and a sink. A mirror hung over the sink. Feeling a sudden pang of urgency, he hurried to the commode. Afterwards, he went to the sink and turned on the cold water. He looked up and stared into his reflection. He shuddered. Half his face was covered with red blotches and a dozen sores had appeared . Anxiously he splashed cold water on his face. It felt good but did nothing to change his appearance. He cupped some cold water into his hands and sipped it, sloshing it about and then spitting it into the sink. It was pink in color. He opened wide, examining his teeth. Blood was slowly seeping from several of his gums.

He turned sharply as he heard a rattling of the door handle, then a voice. "Hey, anybody in there?" A pause and then a loud banging on the door. "Hey, open up in there!"

"In a minute!" Brian called out.

The voice called back. " I ain't got a minute, man. I'm about to shit my pants!" The pounding resumed.

Brian patted his face dry with a paper towel, then moved to the door and opened it. A burly kid in a leather motorcycle jacket barreled past him. "About time, old fella," the kid said, then turned and looked at Brian. "Holy crap, man. What happened to you?"

Quickly, Brian turned away and headed out toward the car where Buzz was just getting in, carrying a brown paper bag of edibles. The motorcycle kid hurried out after him.

"Hey!" he shouted. "I know you. Aren't you that guy, you know—uh, what's his name?"

Without responding Brian climbed into the passenger seat and in seconds, the Honda was peeling out of the station. Puzzled, the kid watched them go.

Erwin Conrad stirred restively on the sofa in the office of the Mayor. He'd been without sleep for over twenty four hours but a comfortable bed in a hotel room was out of the question. At eleven o'clock he'd forced himself to lay down, hoping to grab and hour or two of sleep, knowing that if he didn't his judgement would be impaired and he'd be in no fit condition to pursue his quarry.

His quarry, he thought. If he wasn't careful, that quarry was liable to get Erwin Conrad demoted or drummed out of the service. Or perhaps worse. At ten to eleven, just before he had tried to force himself to sleep, Conrad had gotten yet another phone call from Nicholas Lapp, demanding to know why Brian Everett had not been eliminated.

"Do you not understand the nature of your orders, Colonel? Do you need further clarification?"

"No, sir."

"Perhaps you are hesitant because you do not understand the reason for such an order?"

"Absolutely not, sir," Conrad said.

"Just so, Colonel. We do not have to explain our motives. They are part of a larger picture with which you needn't be concerned. But if it will spur you to greater diligence, this one time I will tell you the reason. In the coming days certain events will transpire. Some you know about, some you do not. There is an enemy out there. You know who they are. The leaderless rabble, the malcontents, the selfish naysayers who do not understand the great design being put in place by our President. We want this mob to remain leaderless. That means quelling any voice that might have the power and the authority to bring them together in common cause. Brian Everett is such a man. We thought he had retired from the fray. We were wrong. The attack on the administration printed in the Chronicle last week was an opening salvo. This is a man who now must be silenced. Do you understand me, Colonel? Need I explain further?"

"No, sir," Conrad had said into a suddenly disconnected phone.

He closed his eyes again, hoping to sleep, knowing he couldn't. Willis Johnson was handling communications in his stead. The nationwide BOLO was out to all agencies of law enforcement. Every twenty minutes, the networks put up photos of Everett and his companion, Buford Shipley. The $50,000 reward was prominently displayed. All that was needed was a lucky break, a nugget of gold among all the worthless stones and pebbles that were coming in from all points of the country, including Alaska where the two men had been spotted boarding a fishing trawler in Anchorage harbor. How they were able to drive from Kansas to Alaska in less than three hours defied explanation.

He felt someone tugging at his sleeve.

"Sir?"

He looked up to see Johnson standing over him. "We think we have something solid," Johnson said.

Conrad swung his feet to the floor and stood up. He glanced at his watch. 12:09 on Wednesday morning. He'd been sleeping for a little over an hour. "It sure as hell better be," Conrad growled, trying to clear his head.

"About fifty miles north of here. A place called Nortonville. A young kid, a biker, spotted Everett. He went straight to the local police. They called us five minutes ago."

"Are they sure?"

"They think so. They showed the kid the BOLO with the photos. He says it was Everett. Even with his face all blotched, the kid said there was no question."

They started toward the makeshift war room. "What did he mean, face all blotched?"

"He said Everett had a couple of big red blotches, like birthmarks maybe, and a lot of open sores. He looked like crap, the kid said."

Conrad nodded. "Radiation. Has to be."

"Sounds like it to me," Johnson agreed.

Conrad moved to the large state map on the wall. "What was the name of that town?"

"Nortonville. It's on Route 4."

Conrad traced the route, found the town. He stood there for a few moments, thoughtfully. "Allright. Have our people get on those phones. Contact all police jurisdictions----"

"Sir, we've already done that---"

"Do it again. And for God's sake, Johnson, make sure they understand. Do not apprehend. Surveillance only. We can't take him until we are positive he's made contact with Bannister."

"Yes, sir."

"Then notiify every hospital or health clinic within sixty miles north, east or west. Also get the names and addresses of any private doctors working outside the system. There aren' t that many of them left. Then order up a chopper. I want you and me in the air for Nortonville by 12:30."

"Yes, sir." Johnson moved quickly to the nearest phone as Conrad continued to study the map. He considered momentarily notifying the others -- Thibald and Askew and maybe even the police chief--- but no, they'd ducked out after the cemetery proved a bust. Anyway, he didn't need them. This was his show. Everett was his prey. He'd show the brass back in D.C. that he knew his job. A man as sick as that. He couldn't run forever. It was just a question of time.

Max Devilbiss sat on his living room sofa, sipping a mediocre chablis and smoking a noxious panatela from Honduras. This was a major part of his evening routine and he wasn't about to have it altered, no matter what the situation. Yes, it was twelve-thirty, later than he was used to (his bedtime was closer to ten p.m.) but that was a small concession to make for two old friends, one on the way to his two-story frame house on the outskirts of Horton, and the other pacing nervously around the living room, a cell phone pressed to his ear. Max, a rotund man who had just turned sixty, wore a gravy stained sweat shirt and a pair of size 48 levis. His long white hair was disheveled and he sported a two day stubble on his chin. Max could clean up very nicely when he had to but when he didn't, he preferred the appearance of a homeless derelict. His wife Louise, used to his eccentricities and pretty much numb to them, had retired at ten thirty leaving Max, who never did become a neurosurgeon but had turned into a damned fine general practitioner, to pretend he was scanning a book on lumbar disorders while listening in on his friend Ken's phone conversations.

"When was the last time you heard from him, Mrs. Romano?" Ken listened. "Have you tried calling his cell phone?" He listened some more. "I see, well, if you hear from him, will you call me? You have this number. No, no, I'm not really worried. It's probably some technical problem, a dead spot with no service. They might actually be across the border by now. I'd just feel better if I knew for sure." Listening. "All right. Take care. If I hear anything I'll call you." He clicked off the phone and jammed it into his shirt pocket, then turned to look at Max.

"Not a peep."

Max shrugged. "I think you've got it right. A dead spot. Something like that. This kid Romano, does he know his way around?"

Bannister laughed. "Brought up on the streets of Philadelphia? What do you think, Max?"

"He's still alive. He can't be a complete jerk."

"Brightest kid in all my classes. He's going to make a helluva lawyer in a few years. If anybody can get Heather across the border, it's Mickey Romano." He took his cell phone out of his pocket, looked at it momentarily, then replaced it. He glanced at his watch. "Brian should have been here by now."

Max shook his head with a sigh. "You need a drink. Here. Have some chablis."

Bannister turned up his nose. "Already had some, thanks. Where do you buy that battery acid, Max? Pep Boys?"

"It all tastes the same to me."

"Considering what you're smoking, I'm surprised you can taste anything at all," Bannister said, waving the second hand fumes away. He went to the front window and looked out onto the front porch, then turned back to Max. "The lady on the porch, you sure she knows what she's doing?"

"Don't you worry about Mattie. She can have my back any day of the week."

On the front porch of the Devilbiss home, Mattie Rice sat on the wooden chaise, tucked back in the shadows, hardly visible from the street. An attractive widow of 40, her grey blue eyes took in everything. Her ears picked up every sound. She was sitting with legs crossed and a pump-action shotgun cradled in her lap. As Chief of Police she was responsible for the safety and well-being of Horton's 1500 citizens and it was a job she took seriously, even more so than her late husband, the former chief, who had been killed in a routine traffic stop at the edge of town. That had been a year ago and the town council had immediately appointed Mattie to replace him. They had been a team, Joshua Rice and his wife. Now it was just Mattie and her ten deputies.

The radio affixed to her uniform shoulder flap squawked and she adjusted her earpiece. "Chief?" A woman's voice.

"Yeah, Grace?"

"Thought you'd like to know. Those boys at Federal Security send another BOLO, this one marked extremely urgent." Grace Zisko was holding down the station house while Mattie and five of her deputies stayed on the lookout for the white Honda carrying Everett and Shipley.

"Fuck the boys at Federal Security," Mattie growled, shifting her weight to get more comfortable. "Any sighting yet?"

"Not yet."

"Hang loose."

"Will do." Grace clicked off.

Federal Security, she snorted silently. Damned fascist bastards. Throwing their weight around like they owned the country. Hell, maybe they do, she thought, the way the country's been going. Mail the wrong e-mail to the wrong person, next thing you know you're getting hauled out of your house at two o'clock in the morning and slammed in the pokey, sometimes for three or four days before they get around to an arraignment. It had happened twice in the last month here in Horton. Both times Mattie had played along. She had to or Horton would have had a new police chief by noon the next day. Both times, first chance she got, she called Sidney Fromm, the former Congressman, even got him out of bed once. Sidney was at the jail like a shot screaming about Constitutional rights. Neither case came to anything, but the message was pretty damned clear. Fuck with the Feds at your own peril.

She knew that lesson all too well. Joshua had opposed the President and his Socialist agenda right from the beginning. The fact that so many otherwise rational Americans had voted for the guy bewildered him. The President had made no secret of who he was and what he stood for. He could only surmise that America no longer respected the work ethic, no longer aspired to anything better than government handouts, oblivious to the fact that sooner or later, the economy would be unable to sustain its massive spending and the structure of government would collapse. As indeed it had. For the past seventeen months, unemployment had edged up close to 13%. The dollar was becoming valueless. Joshua had seen it coming, worked to fight against it. Twice the government had questioned him. Twice they had warned him. And then came the traffic stop and he was dead. At the time she did not believe that he was a random victim. To this day she still does not believe it. In all her born days, Mattie had never smelled so much fear in the air. Fear be damned, she thought. Anything she could do to stop the madness she was going to do, regardless of the risk. But like a lot of people she was afraid it was going to end up with guns in the streets.

Her radio squawked again.

"We got him, Mattie," came a man's voice."

"Where are you, Boyd?"

"Comin' off the 159 onto the Two-Oh. White Honda, heading east."

"We don't want him getting lost, Boyd. Bring him in. And try not to scare the crap out of him."

"Will do."

Out on Route 20, Deputy Boyd Shurling took off in pursuit of the Honda. As his cruiser came up on the Honda's rear bumper, he double clicked his high beams, then pulled up alongside, opening the passenger side window. As Buzz Shipley looked over at him apprehensively, Boyd grinned and threw him a thumbs up, then motioned to Buzz to follow. Buzz hesitated for only a second, then reasoned that if this cop was a hostile, he would have activated his roof lights. He fell in behind the cruiser.

Four minutes later Shurling pulled up in front of the Devilbiss house. Mattie and Ken Bannister hurried down the walkway to curbside as Buzz brought the Honda to a stop and hopped out.

"Bannister?" he queried look straight at Ken. Ken nodded. "He's in a bad way. Better give me a hand."

Together the two men helped Brian from the front seat. As Ken looked into his old friend's face, he could barely hide his dismay at his appearance. Brian caught it, forced a laugh. "Forgot my makeup. You'll get used to it."

They mounted the porch steps as Max opened the door and swung it wide open. As they entered, Max, too, had a chance to see the kind of shape Brian was in. His expression didn't change but when Mattie Rice followed them inside, she locked eyes with Max who subtly, almost imperceptibly, grimly shook his head.

CHAPTER NINE

Shortly after 6:30 on Wednesday morning, Joey Keppler pulled his SUV into a parking spot at the 711 on the outskirts of Horton, Kansas. He had been driving for two hours with hardly any sleep and his eyes were drooping like week old lilies. He should have left the night before but he was having too much fun at the hunting lodge with his buddies. Drinking, carousing, poker. After four days of camaraderie you'd think they'd have been sick of each other but 23 year olds barely out of high school have a lot of tolerance for senseless behavior. So now he was on the road, still a long way from Topeka and his job where, if he didn't punch in by nine o'clock, he'd be in a heap of trouble.

Joints rebelling, he eased himself out from behind the wheel and managed to stretch, breathing deeply of the still chilly morning air. As he headed for the entrance of the convenience store, a black man emerged carrying a well-packed paper bag in his arms. The man was wearing a cap slouched down over his forehead and he wore a pair of dark sunglasses, even though the sun was barely on the horizon and the sky was already overcast, threatening rain. A twitch of suspicion registered in Joey's brain, a habit he'd picked up over the past couple of years. The black man placed the bag in the passenger seat, then slipped behind the wheel and fired up the late model white Honda.

Instinctively Joey glanced at the car's license plate, a personalized plate featuring UK's cartoon jayhawk mascot. So the guy was a UK alumni. Funny, the massive black man looked more like a graduate of Leavenworth. Joey shook his head, annoyed with himself. I gotta stop doing that, he thought. Just because the guy's big and black doesn't really mean anything. Not really.

He went inside to order a giant coffee, looked back to take one more glance at the Honda which was disappearing down the street. Then he looked toward the clerk behind the counter.

"Everything okay in here?" Joey asked.

The clerk shrugged. "Sure. Why wouldn't it be?"

It was a few minutes to eight in the Pioneer Room of the Bridge-water Hotel in Atchison, Kansas. It was really nothing more than an overblown motel but it had a restaurant and several meeting rooms and best of all it wasn't crowded. It was serving adequately as a temporary headquarters in the intensive search for Brian Everett.

Erwin Conrad sat at a table in the corner of the room, a phone at his side, dozens of reports laid out in front of him. He had been up since six o'clock after three hours of restless sleep. He refreshed his coffee mug from the ceramic carafe at his side, drank deeply. The brew was only lukewarm. He thought about ordering more, then decided no. His nerves were frayed, his patience non-existent. Another mug or two and he'd be behaving like an out of control lunatic. He picked up a report of a recent "sighting". No, he doubted Everett and Shipley were as far north as Fargo, North Dakota. In fact he was absolutely convinced that the two men were close. Very close. Thanks to that biker in Norrisville they had something to go on. The fugitives were driving a white Honda sedan, the kid was sure of that. And the plate was personalized. A UK alumni vanity plate. The first two numbers were one and one. He didn't get the last two. That information had been added to the BOLO four hours ago. Conrad's instincts told him it was just a matter of time and in twenty-one years of law enforcement, his instincts were seldom wrong.

He put down the report, leaned back and stared out the window at the slowly growing traffic as Atchison started to awake from its nightly torpor. He was not a man given to introspection. Beginning with his four year stint in the Military Police he had learned right away to follow orders without hesitation. A flicker of doubt, a second thought, these things could be the difference between life and death and so he acted. Immediately. Without misgivings. And at the age of 39, he was alive while most of those he had faced down in recent years were not. Yes, he had led a lonely life but it had never bothered him. Somewhere in his maturation he had subconsciously built a wall around himself. If he had ever had a sense of humor, it had been stifled into nothingness. He possessed no social graces and that, too, had never been an issue. An enemy of his country was his enemy . A man like Brian Everett, for instance, who defied the laws of the land, who practiced sedition without apology and threatened to continue. No, such a man was dangerous and had to be dealt with. Eliminate with extreme prejudice. Those had been his orders. As he had always done, Erwin Conrad, without really knowing why, would carry them out.

"Colonel."

Conrad turned to see Willis Johnson striding toward him carrying a sheet of paper.

"We might have something, sir," Johnson said, handing him the sheet. "An all night drug store on Main Street. The day pharmacist came in at six to relieve the night man. When he checked the supply room he found the door unlocked and inside some of the medicine had been moved around. He did a quick inventory and discovered that a supply of potassium iodide was missing."

"And?" Conrad queried.

"Potassium iodide can be used for treatment of radiation poisoning," Johnson replied.

Conrad perked up. He was right. Everett was close enough to smell. He mulled it over for only a moment.

"How many units have we got here in town?" he asked.

"Just two, sir. We're spread pretty thin."

"Okay. Have our people pick up this druggist, check into a low rent motel on the edge of town, preferably one without any guests. And get a room as far away from the office as possible."

"Yes, sir."

"Then contact St. Joe. Have three units here within the hour. Civilian clothes, unmarked cars. I want to keep a low profile. Everett's getting medical help. That says doctor, maybe a nurse. When I get through with this druggist we'll know for sure."

"Yes, sir," Johnson said, turning and heading for the door.

Conrad stared down at the pile of bogus sightings sitting in front of him and with a cold smile of satisfaction, picked them up and dumped them into the wastebasket.

The four of them sat around the coffee table listening to the tape. Bannister, Buzz, Max, and Mattie Rice. Louise Devilbiss was in the kitchen, clattering pots and pans and in other ways showing her displeasure for her husband's actiivities of the night before. He had driven into Atchison, to the only all night pharmacy in the area, shortly after one o'clock to pick up some potassium iodide to treat Brian. He was reasonably sure it wouldn't do much good. Too much time had elapsed since his friend's exposure to the radiation, but he felt he had to do something. Max was honest with the others. Brian was in bad shape. To have a decent chance of survival he had needed a bone marrow transplant as soon as possible but under the government's iron fisted control of the nation's health care system, that procedure was a rarity for just about anyone. For Brian Everett it was an impossibility. There was no way to reverse the effects of the dosage he had already absorbed. Perhaps the worst was over. There was no way to tell. They could only watch and wait.

In the bedroom adjoining the living room, Brian began to stir. He had again been dreaming of Marnie and as he awakened to reality. he tried to bury himself under the covers, to recapture her in his mind. But it was too late. She was gone. And now he was aware of voices coming from the next room. Two men. A heated discussion. Strange voices. He did not recognize them. He caught a few phrases. Martial law? What were they saying about martial law? And Vice President Comeford. What did he have to do with it?

He struggled to get out of bed, not exactly sure where he was. He realized he was wearing his pajamas but he didn't remember putting them on And his robe was lying across the end of the bed. His slippers rested on the floor beside him. His body ached in every joint and his mouth felt like an ashtray filled with week old butts. On the night stand was a fresh bottle of water. He uncapped it, drank greedily, then got to his feet, putting on the slippers and robe and made his way to the bedroom door.

Bannister looked up just as the bedroom door opened and the two old friends locked eyes. Bannister got to his feet and hurried to Brian as Buzz reached over and shut down the tape player.

"Hey, old friend, no getting up. You need your rest."

"I'm okay, Ken," Brian said. He managed a smile. "We sure took the long way around getting together."

"We sure did," Bannister said.

Brian looked around. "Where's Heather?"

"A friend is trying to get her across the border into Quebec. I couldn't bring her, Bri. Too risky."

Brian nodded in understanding, then his gaze fell on Max Devilbiss. "Hey, Max. What happened to you?" As he said it he was eying Max's ample girth.

"Budweiser," Max said, patting his waistline. "Among other things."

He got up and went to Brian's side, putting his hand on his shoulder and squeezing it affectionately. "Ken's right, Brian. You need to go back to bed."

"No time for that, Max. I heard strange voices. What's going on?" As he said it, he looked over at Mattie. "And who's the beautiful young lady?"

"Mattie Rice," Max told him. "The Chief of Police."

Brian tried to stifle a laugh. "Well, I sure have come a long way just to get busted in your living room, Max."

"No chance of that, Mr. Everett," Mattie said, "and it sure is nice to meet you."

"Mattie's one of us," Max said.

"Us? And just exactly who is 'us', Max?"

"A bunch of people, Brian. More than you could possibly dream of."

The two men locked eyes. Bannister broke the silence.

"You spent too long hiding out in that house of yours, Bri. Me, too. There's more going on in this country than either of us is aware of."

Brian looked from one to the other. "So what are we talking about? Guns in the streets?"

"Not yet. Not if we're lucky," Max said. "Ken may have brought us the key to reversing this insanity."

"When I woke up, I heard strange voices. Two men talking about martial law and something about the Vice President."

Ken nodded. "Among other things. Maybe you'd better sit down and we'll fill you in. Buzz, rewind to the top. Brian has a right to know what he's involved in."

133

The funeral mass for Edward Vitale was celebrated at St. Patrick's Church in downtown Washington. Not as well known, perhaps, as its counterpart in New York City, St. Pat's was the oldest parish church in Washington D.C. , an imposing Gothic cathedral that had been founded in 1794 to provide spiritual sustenance to the stonemasons who had been building the White House. Hundreds of Washingtonians, including Senators and Representatives, prayed there regularly. Even one or two members of the White House staff had been known to make an occasional appearance although a belief in God was not a prerequisite to administration employment.

His Excellency Daniel Cardinal Terhune presided assisted by two archbishops. The mahogany casket had been led into the church by pallbearers who had known and loved and respected Ed Vitale in life and by their presence, honored him in death. Three Senators, one a Mormon from Utah. Two Congressmen. A retired Army colonel who had been Vitale's commanding officer during his tour of duty in Viet Nam. His younger brother, a cardiologist practicing in New Orleans. His grandson, studying oceanography at the University of Maryland.

Every seat in every pew was filled. Edward Vitale was much loved, except by those who killed him.

The eulogy was delivered by the President who went on at length as he was wont to do and if one listened carefully, it was possible to realize that hidden in the verbiage were observations that revealed that, yes, in some ways the President did have real affection for his good and faithful servant.

Following the service the funeral cortege wended its way to Arlington National Cemetery where Vitale was laid to rest with full military honors. Originally the President was not scheduled to attend the internment, but at the last moment he changed his mind and now stood, hands clasped in front of him, staring somberly at the coffin that hovered above the gravesite. Close by but standing somewhat apart from the mourners were Zebulon Marcuse and Nicholas Lapp, the Deputy Director of the Federal Security Force.

Lapp was watching the President closely, feeling slightly apprehensive. "I thought he was going straight back to the White House from the church."

"He changed his mind," Marcuse said.

"I was under the impression he only changed his mind when you changed it for him." Lapp turned his head and looked at Marcuse questioningly.

"You give me too much credit," Marcuse said with a smile.

"No, I don't," Lapp replied flatly.

"Stop worrying. He's under control."

"I hope so. The next couple of days are critical. We can't afford surprises."

"There won't be any. The President knows what has to be done. He's on board, trust me."

"I'm going to have to, Zeb."

Marcuse nodded. "And where are we on Dr. Bannister? I assume you haven't located him or I'd have heard about it."

"We're getting close," Lapp said.

"Close won't cut it, Nick. We need that tape back now."

"You'll have it, "Lapp said. "Maybe by the end of the day. We're closing in on Brian Everett. When we find Everett, we find Bannister."

"He slipped away from you in Lawrence."

"It won't happen again. Conrad's my best man. He says Everett is sick. He can't run much further."

Marcuse eyed him coldly. "Pray you're right, Nick."

At that moment Lapp's cell phone vibrated. He checked his watch. It read 11:26. He took out the phone.

"That'll be Longview," he said to Marcuse, then answered the phone. "Yes?" A pause. "I understand." He flipped the phone shut. "Longview," he said. "You'd better get to the President and get him out of here before a lot of other phones start ringing."

Marcuse nodded and started to weave his way through the mourners as the Cardinal sprinkled holy water on the casket. Lapp watched as Marcuse tugged at the President's sleeve, then leaned in and whispered into his ear. The President looked at him sharply, a grim expression on his face and then the two men separated themselves from the crowd and hurried quickly toward the President' s limousine, followed by the Secret Service detail.

General Dwight David MacAndrews, who was among the mourners and who had spent the early hours of the morning reading and re-reading the Bunker Hill protocol, watched the two men with curiosity. What now, he thought. Some fresh new hell for this country? And then his cell phone began to vibrate.

The scene outside of Longview, Texas, was devastating, the carnage stomach-turning. Earlier that morning, an Amtrak passenger train had been approaching Longview from the west. At precisely 10:47, at a point three miles from the city, the powerful diesel locomotive was suddenly blasted from the tracks by a mammoth explosion that tossed it ten feet into the air. The passenger cars that followed were whiplashed from their rails, their steel frames crinkled like aluminum foil as they slammed into one another, some skidding forward on their sides, others overturning and then sliding down the ten foot embankment to the rocky scragland below. The screams of the dying were obliterated by the screech of metal on metal. It hadn't taken long. Two minutes, perhaps three, before the railroad cars became still. Then and only then could the screams of agony be heard. And only the coyotes were around to hear them.

The plume of smoke from the blast could be seen for miles around and within twenty minutes, rescue units from Longview were on the scene. Within the hour more units arrived from Marshall and Henderson and Tyler. Unlike Santa Veronica, there were survivors. A few walked away with hardly a scratch, others had to be pried from the unforgiving twisted metal. Days later, when the official tally was announced, the dead numbered 46. Injured, 77. Camera crews and reporters from the Progressive Network were on hand forty minutes after news of the blast reached their Dallas office and at 11:40, Pearl Jefferson of the Dallas office of Homeland Security arrived to take charge of the scene. She was accompanied by Major Dominic Fortelli of the Federal Security Force, on hand to maintain order and dole out information to members of the government press. The first pictures and reports started airing nationally shortly after noon.

There was no question it was a deliberate act of terror. A freight train had been preceding the passenger train by fifteen minutes all across Texas. The freight train had crossed over the site of the explosion without incident. Someone, or some group, most likely Muslim extremists, had deliberately waited for the passenger train. The reason why was obvious. Derail a few railroad cars of pork bellies and no one cares. Kill helpless men , women and children and in most people, you incite visceral outrage. In others, many more perhaps, you spark terror.

In the hours that were to follow, the government-run network would chronicle the activities of thousands of people, men and women, the old and the young, Democrats and Republicans alike, who were no longer content to wait for the government to take action against these Islamist killers. In all parts of the country, Muslims would come under attack. Mosques would be stormed and vandalized. Shopkeepers would be dragged from their places of business and beaten. Some would die. Law enforcement would make a show of protecting the helpless, peace-loving Muslims but they would do little to quell the madness. The people were angry and they were terrified. Something had to be done. And it would be; another horrific attack later that day on the tracks outside of Paschgoula, Mississippi. And then, a few minutes afterward, a third attack on Amtrak would be launched near Kirkwood, Missouri.

A lesson was being taught to a gullible public. New York was not the only target in America. Regardless of where you lived, north or south, small town or modest sized city, you were not safe anywhere. You cannot protect yourself. Only your government can wage war against these cowardly purveyors of death. Only your government can save you.

CHAPTER TEN

It was pushing noon when Mattie Rice made it into headquarters. Boyd Shurling had been holding things together since early morning and she knew he needed a break. He hadn't seen his wife or his two girls for almost twenty-four hours.

"Sorry, Boyd. Meant to get in here a couple of hours ago. Just overslept," she said.

"No sweat, Chief. Not much happening except for this updated BOLO. I tried calling your cell, guess you must have shut it off. "

She shook her head. "Had it on vibrate and left it in my jacket pocket. What's up?"

"Nothing good," he said, handing her the FSF bulletin. She scanned it, frowned.

"They've got a partial on the car. White Honda, UK Alumni plate."

"Last time I saw it," Boyd said, "it was parked in the street in front of the Devilbiss house. Kinda asking for trouble."

She nodded. "You go home. I'll take care of this."

"Right."

After he left, she unlocked the bottom drawer of her desk and took out the cell phone. Like everyone else in the "movement" she had an untraceable throwaway. She punched in Max Devilbiss' number. When Louise answered she asked to speak to Buzz Shipley.

• • •

Ken laid the G2o Glock automatic on the table between them. "I found this in your windbreaker pocket when we put you to bed last night."

Brian stared down at the weapon. "Ugly looking thing, isn't it?"

"Do you know how to use it?"

"Point. Shoot," Brian said.

Ken leaned down and peered at the weapon closely. "Remove safety, chamber round, THEN point and shoot."

Brian grinned. "Ah, so that's how it works." He picked up the pistol and stuffed it into his trousers pocket.

"Don't you think that's a little dramatic?"

"You never met Colonel Erwin Conrad of the Federal Security Force."

"Can't say that I did."

"Try it some time. It's right up there with a colonoscopy."

Ken Bannister looked at his old friend sadly. "I'm really sorry, Bri. I never should have dragged you into this."

"Forget it, Ken. I haven't had this much fun since my last interview with Nancy Pelosi."

Ken looked away in pain. Brian squeezed his shoulder affectionately. "Hey, quit kicking yourself. I threw down the gauntlet when I wrote that piece for the Chronicle and I knew what it would lead to. But I had to get back into the fray. My choice. Your phone call, well, call that serendipity."

They were sitting at a table on Max's rear patio. After ninety minutes of non-stop television reporting from Longview with its horrific close-ups of mangled bodies, they'd had enough. Anxious to keep things looking normal, Max had gone off to the hospital a few miles north of town to check on two of his patients. Buzz had taken the Honda, looking for a shopping center where he could ditch the car after making a license plate switch. Ken was sipping on a beer. Brian was drinking water and half-heartedly trying to get down some homemade chicken soup, courtesy of Louise Devilbiss nee Rosenberg. Her husband had his pills and potions but Louise had a few ethnic cure-alls of her own to trot out when necessary.

Ken indicated the bowl. "Try to eat."

"No appetite."

"I know but you have to try." Ken looked past him to the kitchen window. He whispered, "She's watching you."

"I know," Brian whispered back , "but if I finish this bowl, she'll come out and refill it. Just like Marnie. Remember?"

Ken laughed. "Oh, yeah, I remember. Have another sausage, liebschen. Have two. Have three! What's the matter, you don't like my sauerkraut?"

"No, my darling, I do not like your sauerkraut. I hate your sauerkraut." Brian shook his head, smiling.

"Did you ever tell her that?"

"Are you serious? I stoically endured for over thirty years. To be fair, she put up with my chili so I guess it was a standoff." Brian hesitated, then leaned forward. "Is she stlll watching?"

Ken nodded and Brian reluctantly took another spoonful of soup.

"Louise says you heard from Heather."

"Early this morning. She's in Montreal. She got picked up almost as soon as she crossed the border. They took her to RCMP headquarters and listen to this. The guy who comes in to question her, he's a former student of mine."

Brian smiled. "No!"

Ken grinned. "Mais oui, mon ami. Not only that, he recognized her right away. I used to have students to the house for Thanksgiving and Christmas dinners, especially the foreigners."

"She's okay, then."

"More than okay. Keith—that's his name, Keith Sunderson—some kind of high placed superintendent. He's trying to work it out so I can cross over."

Brian nodded appreciatively. "He must have some clout. The border's been shut tight for over a year now."

"Heather says he can pretty much call his own shots."

"So when are you going?" Brian asked.

"When I'm done here."

"Old friend, you're already done here."

"Not yet," Ken said. "In law we call it chain of custody. The tape needs to have authenticity. I got it from Ed Vitale. I have to be around to attest to that or they'll be questioning its legitimacy. When it's over, I'll join her, not before."

He fell silent, a pensive look on his face as he looked out over the backyard, fenced for privacy.

Brian watched him thoughtfully. "So tell me, Ken, just why did you call me?" he said.

Ken hesitated momentarily, sipped his beer. "I'm not sure. As soon as I heard what was on the tape, I was scared stiff. For me and Heather, sure. And for the country. Maybe the country most of all, but I didn't know what to do. A few years ago it was simple. Contact the networks or Fox or the Times and splash it all over the country. No way to do that today. Then I thought, if anyone would know how to handle it, it'd be you. You still have contacts. God knows you still have a reputation for the truth. When you speak people believe you. All of that was running through my head."

"Well, I'm flattered but I don't have the least idea of how to get this out in the open either."

"Max and I have been discussing it, Brian. Radio and TV are out but we still have the internet. There are a handful of websites that we started a couple of years back. Seventeen in all. They're all innoucuous looking, low profile. Amphibians of the World. Best Buys in Real Estate. That sort of things. They have chat capabilities built in. We communicate among ourselves quietly, using code words and euphimisims. The government has no idea how far reaching they are or how many people are involved."

Brian looked him squarely in the eye. "And just how many people ARE involved, Ken?"

"Tens of millions."

Brian stared at him incredulously. "I don't believe it. I would have heard. I would have known."

"Maybe not. We're not organized. Oh, maybe at the local level but there's no central authority. We're just a bunch of people from every part of the country. Republicans, Democrats, Independents, farmers, teachers, blue collar, white collar, everybody who is fed up with this monumental power grab by the President and the people around him."

"Sounds to me like you're talking armed insurrection?"

"No, we don't want that. We can't win that way."

"So what do you propose?"

"We still think Congress can turn it around."

Brian shook his head. "Not a chance. Those people are mostly self-serving egomaniacs who are in it for the money and the power. The administration owns them."

"Really? And how long do you think they'll continue to be owned once they hear the tape?"

Brian nodded thoughtfully. "Good point. So what's the plan?"

"Max thinks we should make a video. You on camera, giving some background and then playing the tape. You've got the credibility. The tape speaks for itself. We release it simultaneously on all seventeen sites and then keep repeating it until the government shuts us down."

"Can they do that?"

"They have the technology but we think the message will be already out before they realize what's going on."

"All right. Count me in."

"It could be dangerous, Bri," Ken said somberly. "That'll be your face out there."

"About that. Make sure you only photograph my good side."

"Oh, and which side is that?" Ken asked.

They both laughed. Then Brian smiled. "Buck up, Ken. They're after me already. How much more dangerous could it get?"

They were interrupted at that moment by Louise Devilbiss who had emerged from the kitchen carrying a pot and a ladle. "Too much talking and too little eating, Brian," she said with a broad smile. "Come, I'll heat up your soup."

Brian and Ken shared a look. They were both thinking the same thing. Sauerkraut.

Emma Wasserman sat on a straight backed chair, trying to appear calmer than she was. Given her size (hefty) and her age (over 50), she was more than a little uncomfortable. Not that she'd give these two government goons the satisfaction of knowing it. When the two uniformed FSF officers appeared at her door, she knew immediately what they wanted but Emma, who won regularly at Jocko Babbit's weekly poker game, betrayed nothing in her expression. She smiled guilelessly. What's the problem? Of course I'll go with you. Happy to cooperate. Yes, she'd been sleeping but not to worry. She could nap later. She didn't react when the two men drove her to the outskirts of town to Larry Pritzker's Happy Trails Motel and ushered her into an end unit on the ground floor. Larry, who had rented out the room to the two bozos earlier that day, stepped out of the office when the green and gold FSF squad car returned. He and Emma had exchanged glances as Emma was hustled into the sparsely furnished room. Larry found it odd. Emma could be a tough old broad but he'd never known her to be in trouble with the law. And what were these FSF guys doing around here, anyway?

Emma regarded her two captors with amusement. "Are we waiting on something special or are you boys just planning to have your way with me?"

The taller agent checked his watch. "Shouldn't be much longer," he said.

Emma smiled. "Of course, if it's the latter, I'm not sayin' I'd object all that much. Been a while since I've had a good hump but whatever you decide'll be just fine with me."

The two men shared an amused look. The tall one said, "Not sure I could handle you, ma'am, but I'd be pleased to buy you a coke."

Emma snorted. "My God, a government boy with a sense of humor." She glanced at her watch. "Comin' up on noon. You boys mind if turn on the TV. Judge Jeremiah's on. Always good for a laugh. Man knows as much about the law as a spitoon."

"Won't be on," the taller agent said. "Everything's preempted. All three channels. Muslim fanatics attacked an Amtrak train in Texas."

Emma looked at him curiously. "Muslim fanatics. You don't say."

"Lotta people killed."

"I'm not surprised," Emma said flatly. "Would that be the same gang of fanatics that blew up Santa Veronica?"

The agent eyed her fishily. "You don't seem very concerned, ma'am."

"Sure I am. Innocent people don't deserve to die no matter who's responsible. Funny thing, though. All my born days, never ran into a Muslim fanatic. Oh, I know they're out there. A few of them are still left anyway. Just never met one, that's all. You boys sure it was Muslim fanatics?"

The tall guy glared at her. "Who else could it be?"

"I don't know," Emma said. "You tell me."

The shorter of the two men finally piped up. "Aw, lady, just shut your piehole."

Emma huffed in indignation. "Well, now, isn't that nice language? I was just trying to make an observation. I mean, Muslim fanatics. I could have believed that maybe four years ago when they were threatening to destroy the Great Satan, but then when we started destroying ourselves, they just sort of faded into the wallpaper. We sure didn't need their help tearing ourselves apart, now did we? Just curious why they were suddenly back."

She looked from to the other hoping for an answer. She didn't get one and truth be told, she didn't really expect one. The people she knew already had a handle on what really happened in Santa Veronica. The Texas train wreck wouldn't be far behind.

Just then there was a sharp rap on the door. The taller man opened it. Erwin Conrad strode in like a landlord looking for last month's rent. He glanced at Emma perfunctorily, then turned to the tall agent. "She say anything yet?"

"Waiting for you, sir."

"What's her name again?"

"Emma Wasserman."

Conrad moved close to her, invading her space, looming over her, trying to intimidate. "Well, Emma, I think you know why you're here."

"Got a pretty good idea," she said, "and it's Miz Wasserman to you, buster."

"Last night you dispensed several dosages of potassium iodide. I want the name of your customer."

"Don't know what you're talking about."

"Look, Miz Wasserman, I don't have a lot of time to waste with you. We need that information and we are going to get it. Now you can be a patriotic citizen and support your government or you can refuse to cooperate and we mark you as a subversive and deal with you accordingly. Your choice."

"What's that 'accordingly' all about, Chief? Waterboarding? Electric shock in my tenders? Chop off a few of my fingers?"

Conrad glared down at her. "If I had a few days, madame, nothing like that would be necessary. But I don't have days. I'm not even sure I have hours, so please, do not push me into taking action that will be very unpleasant for both of us."

"Well, hell, mister, I sure appreciate your concern but the fact is I can't help you. Funny thing, I was alone in the store, oh, around two a.m. I guess and suddenly I get this call from nature. Maybe something I ate so I skedaddle off to the john, seeing as how the place was empty and what do you know, when I get back, somebody's busted into the backroom and grabbed some stuff off the shelves. Pissed me off, I'll tell you. Lady can't even go to the john in peace."

Conrad shook his head incredulously. "You expect me to believe that?"

"Hell, no", Emma said, "but that's my story and I'm sticking with it. Now throw the cuffs on me and let's go."

Conrad looked at her coldly. "You're not going anywhere. Not yet."

"Like that, eh?"

"Like that," he said.

She smiled. "Well, Mr. FSF man, just so you know, you picked the wrong lady to push around. I'm a widow and the reason I'm a widow is because last year my husband needed surgery and your birdbrained government refused to let him have it. So he died. At home. In my arms. And my boy, my son, my only child, you and your fascist goons beat the crap out of him at a demonstration in

Cleveland. He damned near died but he made it to Canada where he's made a pretty good life for himself and where you can't touch him. So I'm alone in the world and there's not a damned thing you can do to me except kill me and the way things are going in this country, that might be a blessing. Oh, and did I mention I have a weak heart so it won't take much effort on your part . How's that, shithead? I'm ready if you are. Bring it on."

She glared into his eyes without flinching, daring him, half hoping he'd come at her. As her last defiant act on earth, she was ready to kick him in the balls and put an end to any procreation plans he might have had.

But no. Conrad backed away, shaking his head.

At that moment, his cell phone rang. He answered it.

"What?" His expression turned from annoyance at the interruption to a tight, self satisfied smile. "Horton? Where the hell is Horton?" he asked. He listened some more. Then: "I'm on my way in. Find out what you can about this place. What's the police presence? How big? Have those units from St. Joe arrived?" Pause. "Allright, have them ready to roll when I arrive."

He flipped the phone shut and turned to the tall agent. "Off duty Highway Patrolman coming back from a week of hunting up north spotted the Honda in a town called Horton, about twenty miles from here. Didn't know about the BOLO until he got back to his headquarters in Topeka."

Conrad started for the door. "Get Lt. Stephens over here to watch her. This woman goes nowhere until I give the word."

"Sir, do you want to establish roadblocks in and out of the town?" the tall agent asked.

Conrad pondered it. "No. That would mean bringing in the locals and I'm not sure I want to do that. Not yet. Too many funny things happening. Anyway, we're still not positive that Everett has hooked up with Bannister. Don't want to spook him. You two report to me in Horton as soon as Stephens arrives."

"Yes, sir."

"And while you're at it, find out who's in charge in Horton. Before we let him know we're here, I want to know who I'm dealing with. I don't want another Lawrence."

With that he turned and strode out the door, slamming it behind him.

Buzz drove the Honda at a leisurely pace down one of the side streets that paralleled the main thoroughfare in town. Not fast, not slow. Don't attract attention. He was carefully following directions Louise Devilbiss had given him after speaking by phone with her husband. Turn left at the mortuary, then four blocks to the abandoned grainery. His eyes flitted from one side of the street to the other. No question this had once been a comfortable well-tended middle class neighborhood. Now it had fallen in various states of disrepair. Nearly half the houses displayed "For Sale" signs, many of them weatherbeaten and some hanging at odd angles from rotting posts. Grass and weeds choked off what were once well manicured lawns. Many of the homes had broken windows, falling down porch steps. Most hadn't seen a paint job in nearly a decade. Tattered notices of foreclosure fluttered in the breeze from boarded up doorways. Louise had told him that the town population had been over 2000 as recently as four years ago. Today it had dwindled to 1500. And why not? The small businesses that had once helped Horton thrive were long gone, suffocated by onerous regulations and stifling taxes. Buzz wondered where they had gone to. Certainly Horton wasn't alone. Were things any better in the villages and hamlets of Iowa or Nebraska? He doubted it.

Up ahead he saw it. The grainery. And next to it, the deserted lot heaped high with the town's abandoned junk, mostly worn out appliances and cars too old and beaten up to maintain. He drove onto the lot, threading his way around the debris and finally pulling to a spot pretty much shielded from the road.

He got out of the car, looked around and selected a fifteen year old wreck of a Toyota which still bore its license plates. They were rusted in place but with his screwdriver and wrench he was able to remove them and affix them to the Honda. He took the UK vanity plates and stuffed them down under the rear seat of the Toyota. Satisfied he started to walk back toward the Devilbiss house, hoping that he could avoid drawing attention to himself. He had only been out of the house twice since arriving in Horton but he had quickly learned one thing. Most of the faces here were white, most of the rest were Kickapoo indians and if there was a brother living here, he had yet to run into him.

As Buzz started to retrace his steps, his mind kept wandering back to the happy days, when he had a life and a woman who loved him and two young daughters who had fulfilled him. He had one man to thank for that. Twelve years ago he was just another out of work football player, bounced out of the game by a freak but career ending hit. He had tried to hook on somewhere, in any capacity including gofer, because sports was all he knew. No one responded. Car salesman. Sure, if he wanted it which he didn't. Casino greeter? It was a paycheck but he knew he would have hated it. And then, because he had a quirky sense of humor and a glib way with words, an old teammate convinced a third-tier cable channel to sign him to a six month probationary job on a sports talk show. It was a fun job. He loved the work. But it hardly paid the bills.

And then one night, an insomnia driven Brian Everett happened to catch the show while channel surfing at two in the morning and the next day, Buzz was invited to lunch. Nothing fancy. Lombardi's on Spring Street. Just the best pizza joint in lower Manhattan. When he arrived, he found Everett waiting for him, sipping a house wine, as unpretentious as the restaurant they were eating in. Equally unpretentious was Brian Everett. At Brian's suggestion they shared a large pizza with sweet sausage and roasted red peppers and a house salad and while they were eating, Brian got down to business. Whatever it took to be a television personality, Buzz Shipley had it. The twinkle, the humor, the knowledge, and most of all an ability to criticize without being mean-spirited. All he needed was some polishing and Brian, because he wanted to give back to others the success he had enjoyed, promised to do just that.

For several weeks, Brian worked with him, showed him tapes, showed him how to relate to the camera, to modulate his voice, and then when Buzz's trial employment was up at the cable show, Brian trotted him into the network sports department and got him a one year contract as a reporter-analyst. He started out as a sideline interviewer at major conference football games, then graduated to color in the booth. People loved him and after six months, he was a panel member on the network's highly rated weekend sports program. It was at the network where he met Valerie, wooed and wed her and out of that union sprang his two little girls. For four years everything was perfect.

And then came the "election".

Being non-political, he didn't pay much attention. He was vaguely aware that the Republicans, who should have known better, screwed up royally allowing Congress to fall to the Democrats. And then two years later, a country fed up with massive spending, a war that maybe should not have been waged and a seething frustration that lay just beneath the surface of the national psyche, that country elected a man who promised hope and change, the moon and the stars, and anything else he could get away with to grab your vote. The fawning press completely abandoned all pretense of impartiality, beating the drum for the newly discovered Messiah and beating the opposing candidate with every cudgel at their disposal. In November, the people elected a man they knew nothing about and within a year, he had delivered very little hope and more change than the country was willing to deal with.

Within a year it became clear that the President and those about him planned to convert the United States into a Socialist nation. Riding herd on a like minded Congress and abusing every regulatory device at his disposal, he attempted to spend the nation into bankruptcy, taking over major banks and automotive companies , blackmailing insurance firms, bludgeoning the AMA and the drug companies. By a whisker he managed to pass a health care bill formulated to effectively doom the country to the Socialist design. Opposition obstruction and the courts fought it at every opportunity, essentially to no avail. In one year the President lost any chance of Republican participation, most of the country's independent voters and many of the moderates in his own party. Only the radicals stayed at his side and when the midterm elections rolled around, the Republicans recovered both houses of Congress with room to spare.

And then a funny thing happened. The Republicans, mistaking their victory for a mandate, reverted to their old ways, continued to spend recklessly, swapping useless pork projects with one another as the dollar sunk lower than a snake's belly button in the muck and mire of Washington politics. Had they legislated sensibly, putting the country and its critical problems first, they had a clear road to the White House against the disgraced incumbent. But no, greed and self interest won out and the massive bloc of independent voters, fed up with both major parties, organized themselves to beat them both. It was not to be.

The Republican candidate, a come-to-Jesus Born Again, campaigned on prayer in schools, anti-abortion, and intolerance for gays, ignoring the nation's disastrous unemployment rate and the increasing worthlessness of the currency. The Independent was a former Lt. Governor of a large Western state who promised to turn things around, to clean house in the Capitol, to get rid of the lobbyists, to beef up the military and defeat those A-rabs once and for all, and to drill for oil anywhere they could find it. This populist Lochinvar was leading in the polls right up until early September when it was revealed that not only had he demanded and received massive kickbacks and bribes while in office, he'd been having a nine year affair with his secretary whose name was Frederick. The Independents, disillusioned and having no place to go, went nowhere. They stayed home. The Republican saw the revelations about his opponent as the hand of God at work but in this instance, God didn't work very hard. Blessed with city political machines and a 90% turnout from the loafers and parasites who paid no taxes but received a lot of handouts, the President was swept in to office for a second term with 44% of the vote. Congress was swept in along with him.

After that things went downhill in a hurry. Any firm that needed a bailout got it, even if it meant printing more money. And the price for this largess? Political hacks with no business experience were put in key positions in banks, insurance companies, big box retailers, publishing companies, major newspapers. As the reality of what was happening began to sink in, people started fleeing north. Within months, the Canadian border was sealed tight. No one was allowed in. No one. If there was a bright side to this mess, the Mexican border ceased to be a vacuum for illegal aliens. Most quickly learned it was just as easy to starve in Guadalajara as it was in East L.A.

Buzz had been trying to keep up, to sort it all out, wondering how it would affect him. Then he was shaken to the core when his friend and mentor quit the network on that final and dramatic broadcast. Three months later there was no network. Cable companies were disbanded first with Fox News leading the parade, then came the major broadcast networks, supplanted by the three government operated outlets. Sycophantic administration cheerleaders like Chris Mathews and Keith Olbermann suddenly found themselves out on their respective butts. One time progressive favorites like Joe Klein and Bill Maher who loved to categorize opposition as stupidity and those who practiced it "morons" were relegated to the do-not-invite list. Even the President and his people realized that if you had no integrity before the realignment, you certainly weren't going to develop it overnight.

Around the country the FCC cancelled almost all local station licenses, then relented on some as long as they were operated by minions of the Party. The Department of Information was initiated and all broadcasting entities were subject to its control. Then one cold winter Friday just before Christmas Buzz was informed his services, which had been temporarily transfered to the American (sports) network, would no longer be needed. Out of a job. Out of a paycheck. Out on his ass.

For weeks he brooded, disbelieving, then packed up his family and moved to Santa Barbara where at least he would no longer have to put up with East Coast snow and ice. For days, weeks, and months he vegetated, living off his investments which were quickly shrinking in value.Finally, Valerie had had enough. She moved back to Detroit to care for her ailing parents. Buzz continued to rattle around in the house, surrounded by memories of what had been, and wondering where his life had gone.

A misstep jarred him. So deep in thought was he that he stepped off a curb without looking, nearly falling. Embarrassed he looked around to see if anyone had noticed. That's when he spotted the police cruiser a couple of blocks away. It had started into the intersection, then stopped. Buzz sensed that the driver was watching him.

Out of the corner of his eye he saw the cruiser turn and start down the street toward him. He kept his back to the car. He didn't quicken his step. There was no place to run to. Maybe the turn had nothing to do with him. Maybe it was a routine stop, a black man in a white man's neighborhood. He knew all about that from his high school days. The car was close now. It passed him and then stopped a few feet ahead. The passenger window slid down.

"Buzz!" came the voice from inside the car.

Buzz moved to the window. Boyd Shurling was behind the wheel. "Miz Devilbiss called me, told me you'd be walking. Didn't like the idea of you being out on the streets. Hop in."

Buzz slipped into the passenger seat and the car started off down the street. "Appreciate it," he said.

"Can't be too careful," Boyd said.

Buzz's eyes wandered to the driver side visor where a couple of photos were held in place by rubber bands. A very attractive woman. Two pretty young girls in tee shirts and jeans.

"Good looking family," Buzz said. "Yours I hope"

Boyd smiled. "All mine. Ginny and I have been married thirteen years. Can't hardly believe it. That's Alice Ann on the left, she's eleven and Deborah, she's nine. Don't know what I'd do without them, Buzz. They're the only things that makes any sense any more."

Buzz nodded, thinking of Valerie and his own girls. He fell silent. Boyd looked over at him.

"Look, I don't want to scare you, but a buddy of mine on the force in Atchison is pretty sure the FSF's there. If so, it's just a matter of time before they start to fan out."

Buzz nodded. He couldn't help remembering Joe Louis's quote about the speedier Billy Conn prior to their title fight. He can run, Joe had said, but he can't hide. Soon they'd be running again but for how long and where to?

CHAPTER ELEVEN

Bert Landau, special assistant to CIA Director Leonard Jaffee stared down at the butchery below and was sickened. A veteran of Desert Storm he'd seen the devastation of war close up but he was unprepared for this. Smoke was still rising from the twisted metal of the nine passenger cars that had been derailed. Bodies littered the landscape, some covered and some not. Two ambulances had managed to thread their way to the scene. Others were parked at the perimeter, waiting for their chance to get close enough to save lives, if any were left to be saved. From his vantage point in the Shreveport (La) police helicopter he observed a giant crane trying to right the rear-most car in the sequence. The terrain made it very difficult. No one would be leaving this scene any time soon.

Landau tapped the chopper pilot on the shoulder, then motioned for him to descend. The pilot nodded. As they came in for a landing, Landau looked off to his left and spotted the five green and gold squad cars from the FSF parked on a grassy area near the tracks. Then for the first time, he noticed the dozen or so uniformed FSF officers posted along the track, ostensibly to maintain order. Or perhaps to secure the site and parry questions from those who might ask too many questions about what had happened here.

The helicopter settled onto a relatively flat area about 500 yards from the crumpled engine which lay crossways across the track. Landau hopped down and started to jog toward the cluster of people working feverishly next to the lead parlor car. A hefty black woman in a charcoal pants suit seemed to be giving orders. She was the one he'd come to see.

"Miz Jefferson," he said loudly over the din of workers' voices and the sounds of the metal cutting machinery. She turned to him quizzically , then looked him up and down. "I'm Bert Landau, special assistant to CIA director Jaffee."

"Pleased to meet you, Mr. Landau, but I haven't got time for you just now. We're pretty busy."

"The Director sent me down to see if I could be of any assistance."

"And what kind of assistance would that be? Homeland Security's in charge here---that's me---and..." She pointed to a leathery man with close cropped grey hair who was talking to a couple of EMTs. "And we've got Major Fortelli from the FSF here handling security. Besides, you're out of your jurisdiction."

"Technically, but I had explosives experience in Desert Storm. I was hoping I might be able to help with the investigation," Landau said.

"Thanks for the offer. Our own people are on the way."

"I understand. I just thought that, well, since I'm kind of an expert on the kind of devices these terrorists use, I thought, until they get here, I might help you get a jump start on---"

"Look, Mr. Landau, I don't want to be rude but you've got no business being here and I'd appreciate it if you'd leave. If CIA wants to know what we uncover here, they can make a request through proper channels."

Landau's expression turned cold. "Look, ma'am I jetted down here on the express orders of Director Jaffee himself---"

Jefferson stepped toward him, crowding him. "And I don't care if you were blessed by the President himself on the way to the airport, you're not needed and you're not wanted. Now do you want me to call the Major over here and have him repeat everything I just said?"

Landau looked over at Fortelli. Not a man you'd want to tangle with if you didn't have to. And Landau didn't have to. He'd already learned what he had come to find out. He turned and hurried back toward the chopper.

Jaffee was returning to Langley after a singularly unproductive meeting with a high-ranking Senator on one of the committees overseeing anti-terrorism. Why the Senate always had to have multiple committees and subcommittees with overlapping jurisdictions Jaffee could never fathom. Maybe it was because Senators by nature thrived on meeting and talking and talking and meeting. Perhaps if that was all they ever did and they could give up the notion of passing legislation the country would be a lot better off. He was positive the country would be in far better shape without the services of the blowhard Democratic senator from Connecticut whose idea of patriotism was obeying without question the marching orders he received from the White House who in turn made sure that he shared in the largess doled out by the multi-billionaire patron of the Party, a shadowy figure who rarely, if ever, came out in the daylight.

Jaffee had carefully queried and probed, hoping to glean some sort of information, however slight, from the twice elected bombastic former automobile dealer turned legislator. Like Sgt. Schultz on Hogan's Heroes, he saw nothing, heard nothing, knew nothing. Intel from DHS or FSF was classified. If they wanted to share with the CIA, that'd be their call, not his. The boys were doing a bang-up job containing the Arab bastards, the President had things well in hand. No reason to worry.

As the limo came off the Memorial Bridge and turned north onto the George Washington, Jaffee's cell phone rang. He checked the ID.

"Yes, Bert."

"No go, sir," Landau said. "I was stonewalled from the moment I hit the ground. It's a mess, I mean God awful, sir, but whatever they find or don't find, we won't know about it."

"What about the Jefferson woman?"

"By the book party hack. Also, sir, Federal Security was out in force. Looks to me like they got a lot of units there a lot faster than they should have. Guy in charge is a Major Fortelli. The way he carries himself I'd say ex-military. Maybe Special Forces."

Jaffee frowned. It was about what he had expected but he had needed confirmation. Now he had it. "Good job, Bert. Don't waste any more time down there. See you back at the farm."

The Director clicked off and settled back into the limo's plush seat, troubled and wondering what his next move should be. For the third time that day he seriously considered contacting FBI Director Peter Toussaint and twice he had rejected the notion. He knew where DHS and FSF stood but the FBI was an enigma and so was its Director. Toussaint was a cautious man who rarely showed his cards, sucking up when need be, gently rebelling at other times. It was becoming increasingly critical that Jaffee know where Toussaint stood but to tip his hand, to relay his fears to a man who could possibly be a staunch Administration ally, no, Leonard Jaffee wasn't yet ready to take that step.

General MacAndrews stood at stiff attention on the reviewing stand at the Ft. George C. Meade's parade grounds, eyes straight ahead, hardly noticing the men on parade with their gleaming chrome helmets and uniforms bedecked with medals and insignia. He saluted the colors by instinct alone unable to get his mind around the attack on the passenger train in Texas. California. Now this. What in hell was happening? Two years ago the Muslim fanatics had scaled way back on their Holy War against America. Maybe it was because the Europeans, finally coming to their senses, realized that their sovereignties and safety were suddenly at risk and started pushing back. Or maybe it was because the United States was so busily destroying itself that it needed no help from the mullahs of the mideast. Whatever the reason, Arab terror had not been a major issue for some time. And now it seemed it was back, more terrifying and destructive than ever.

The Irani staredown, following the Afghan conflict, had been one of MacAndrew's proudest moments. 140,000 men on the Iraqi border, poised to attack. Two carriers straining to be unleashed in the Persian Gulf. Over 300 fighters and bombers gassed and ready to go on 60 seconds notice from a newly constructed airbase in Kuwait. Thousands of missiles pointed at Teheran and a dozen other prime strategic targets. Hours away from zero hour, there was one last ditch attempt to prevent bloodshed. Millions of leaflets of warning were dropped into every Irani population center and then, remarkably, that last desperate attempt to stave off all out war had succeeded. People took to the streets in the capital and the Ayatollahs and the Republican Guard backed down. Quickly a general election was held and a military strong man was voted in. His first official act was to sign a non-aggression treaty with both the United States and Israel and for the first time in a decade the boys came home. He did not, however, sign any such pact with a European nation and MacAndrews felt—hell, he was sure—that if and when the Iranis had subjugated the European powers, those treaties with the U.S. and Israel would be as worthless as a soggy roll of toilet paper.

A short time later the parade grounds had emptied, hands had been shaken, salutes exchanged and MacAndrews, accompanied by Lee Fitzpatrick started to walk back toward the limo with the four star insignia flying from each fender.

"I don't get it, Lee. Arabs? I thought we were done with them."

"So did I , sir."

"It makes no sense. You know that privately I'm no fan of the man in the White House but the one thing he did do right was the Iran operation. He stayed with the plan right to the end. I'll never forget that. But dammit, Lee, that was supposed to be the end of it. They're at it hammer and tong in France and Germany and the Netherlands and suddenly, while they've got their hands full over there, they pop up here. Senseless."

Lee hesitated, unsure whether he should take this moment to reveal his conversation with Leonard Jaffee. It might be premature. Better to let the old man stew about it for a while longer. He might be more openminded when he heard what Lee had to tell him.

As they reached the car, Lee's cell phone rang. He answered it.

"Fitzpatrick." He listened intently. His face darkened. "Say again." He listened some more. "I'll pass it along to the General." He flipped the phone shut and looked at MacAndrews grimly.

"What, Lee?"

"Another train derailment, sir. Just outside of Paschgoula , Mississippi."

"Christ almighty," MacAndrews muttered angrily. "Casualties?"

"No word, but it isn't good."

MacAndrews clenched and unclenched his fists. "Oh, Jesus, Lee. I feel so goddamned helpless. That blast in California, all we got was administration bullshit. Same with Texas. And with this one too, I'm sure."

Lee hesitated. "Sir, I know this isn't by the book but maybe it'd be helpful if we could get Army Intel to start looking at these events."

MacAndrews shook his head. "You're right, Lee. It isn't by the book. God knows I'd give my left nut to know what this is all about but we'll have to find out another way. The book is the book for a reason, Lee. Without it, we'd be pretty much lost."

He hesitated, then took Fitzpatrick by the arm and started back toward the administration building. "Let's go find us the Officer's Club. I need a drink."

The good looking young man in the basketball shirt which read "St. Johns 44" was being hoisted on high by his teammates. Toussaint remembered. The boy had scored the winning basket in the final second of the first round of last year's NCAA tournament. They had not fared as well in the second round but for one fleeting moment, Bradley Marcuse had basked in his personal fifteen minutes of fame. There was no question. The glossy framed photo on the wall of the President's Chief of Staff revealed the same lanky thin frame, deep set eyes, the slim aqualine nose. He was very much his father's son.

It was one of the things, one of the few things, that a childless Peter Toussaint , the son of Haitian immigrants, envied about the second most powerful man in Washington. Second most? Some thought that description didn't climb quite high enough. Zebulon Marcuse was not a man you wanted to displease and even a man as powerful as Toussaint, the current Director of the Federal Bureau of Investigation, tiptoed lightly in his presence. There were times when Toussaint envied the audacity of his predecessor, the legendary J. Edgar Hoover who kept secret files on everyone that mattered in the Capitol. Most didn't know what the bantam transvestite had on them and they didn't want to know. He prospered from one administration to another, unfazed by the treacherous shifting of the political sands. Only death finally did him in.

It was rumored that Toussaint, like Hoover, kept his own secret files. He didn't but then he never quite issued a blanket denial. What they didn't know could only help him and the office he served.

The door burst open and Zebulon Marcuse breezed in, barely acknowledging Toussaint's presence except to head-nod him toward a chair across from Marcuse's massive teak and leather desk.

"You were supposed to be here by three," Marcuse scolded. "It's past four." He sat down in his plush cowhide chair and pushed a few papers around.

"Sorry, I got caught up in the train wreck situations."

"Homeland's got that covered."

"So I've been told. But technically---"

"I'm sorry, Pete, but we haven't got time for the technically bullshit today. The bastards are coming at us from every direction and if you and your guys get involved, you'll be stepping all over each other's toes. The President wants it this way. Lean and mean. Besides----"

He stood up and moved to the french doors looking out onto the Rose Garden. He hesitated for a few moments, then looked back at Toussaint. "Besides the President thinks you dropped the ball on this one."

Toussaint tried hard to suppress a glare, managing to keep his voice calm. "No, Zeb, we did not. In fact we were on top of things months ago."

"Then you had intel. Why didn't you pass it along?"

"No. Not intel. What we had was dead quiet. Too quiet. Like the calm before the storm. It was unnatural. There is always something going on but for some reason the normal chatter, the white noise, it suddenly disappeared. Our field offices all across the country were told to intensify their surveillance and to put extra pressure on their confidential informants. We came up dry. The bomb blast, the derailments, they are as much a shock to me as they are to you."

Marcuse regarded him coldly. "Nonetheless, the President is not pleased. Whatever you've been doing in the field, redouble those efforts. As for the sites of attack, don't get in the way. Leave the investigation to Homeland."

The Chief of Staff had just slapped him with the back of his hand. A more violent man might have responded in rage but Toussaint was a man always in control. Don't act in the moment, he'd always said. Wait for the next moment.

"As you say, Zeb. We'll do our damndest to forestall any future attacks. Count on it."

"I am." Marcuse turned his attention to the papers on his desk. Toussaint hesitated at the door, then exited. Marcuse looked up as the door closed and put down the report he had been pretending to scan. Toussaint . Of all the people he couldn't afford to stir up, the FBI director was at the top of the list. Who had he been talking to? What had he learned? He and Nick Lapp had built an iron curtain to keep Homeland's activities free from the prying eyes of the other intel services but no system was perfect. There was always someone willing to talk but the circle around this agenda was so tight, the players so few, it seemed impossible there had been a leak. Maybe Toussaint knew nothing. Maybe he'd been fishing. But if he started fishing around the President, the whole thing could unravel. The President wasn't the sharpest knife in the drawer and his knack for asking dumb questions was legendary among staff. (Never in public, thank God).

Marcuse got up and opened the french doors behind his desk and stepped out onto the patio, breathing in the delicate aroma of the roses that grew everywhere in colorful profusion. Three doors down to his left was the Oval Office where his best friend of twenty years sat behind a massive desk and held the fate of the country and maybe even the world in his hands and for the first time in years, Zebulon Marcuse was starting to question his own judgement. They had both wanted this for years, ever since the day they had met in Chicago at Dukakis headquarters. The President achieving the office he'd desperately sought all his life, Marcuse right behind him, guiding and shaping his thoughts, steering him through the shoals of dirty Washington politics, masking the real man from an adoring public who continued to worship him, all evidence to the contrary. A glib and convincing orator? No question. A deep thinker? Hardly. But from the start Marcuse knew that the man was his ticket to power and he was determined to drive this amiable mediocrity to the top of the ladder. He persuaded him to enter law school where Marcuse would author all his papers, prep him for all his tests. Armed with his license the President-to-be spent hours in store front law offices representing the poor and unwanted for minimal or nonexistent fees. And when he ran for councilman it was Marcuse who engineered his win with the help of a couple of union goon squads. Two years later he was voted into Congress after a bribery scandal made public two weeks before the election destroyed any chance his opponent might have had. (The charges were later proved false). Two years after that he was elected to the Senate when his opponent was killed in a traffic accident. And ultimately, he won the Presidency with a winning smile, a gift of a gab that rivaled a carnival spieler and a campaign that promised all things to all people and for the masses, this cornucopia of goodies would not cost even one thin dime. Yowzah, yowzah, step right up and cast your ballot. Nirvana is here, yours for the taking.

And now, here they were, secure at the top but for one thing. The coming election. In November another man would be elected President and seemingly there was nothing to be done about it. But Zebulon Marcuse was not a man to surrender power easily. He had mulled it over for months and realized, yes, there was a way. It was radical, dangerous, illegal and morally reprehensible, but he had never let little things like that get in the way before. His only quandry was whether to bring the President into the loop and he quickly decided no. A slip of the tongue to the wrong person and they would be doomed. No, better to keep it confined to Nick Lapp and Homeland Security and one or two others. And what about the others? Had they lost their nerve in the face of the terrible carnage? Had they whined to a wife or worse, a mistress? Had there been a leak? If so, the consequences were too dire to contemplate.

At that moment, his cell phone rang. He answered it and listened carefully to the news. By himself, he was not obligated to feign either surprise or horror. An Amtrak passenger train outside of Kirkwood, Missouri, had just been derailed by a mammoth explosion. Another piece of the plan had fallen into place.

CHAPTER TWELVE

Hiawatha Community Hospital some eight miles north of Horton seemed like as good a place as any to start.

"I want a list of every doctor in the area with hospital privileges, and particularly those located in Horton," Erwin Conrad said to the hospital administrator who had never before been bullied by an agent of the United States government. Or at least it felt like bullying to Lila Marie Fortescue, a gentle well-mannered lady who did not take kindly to imperious dictates in a curt manner that bordered on rudeness. Of course that meant she had never had to deal with the bureaucrats in the Medicare wing. That she had left to her assistants so Erwin was a new experience for her.

She smiled sweetly. "I'm so sorry, Mr..uh....?"

"Conrad. Colonel Erwin Conrad of the Federal Security Force," he growled impatiently.

"Of course, of course. I'm so sorry." Her smile of apology seemed so sincere. "Did I ask to see your credentials? I think I did. No, no I didn't. Would you mind awfully showing them to me? There are so many people around these days, mental cases really, posing as doctors and nurses and plumbers and Lord, knows what else. I'm sure you won't mind."

Conrad glared at her coldly, then reached into his pocket and took out his badge. He handed to her, never taking his steely eyes from hers. She looked over the government issue badge, nodding. "Oh, this is really a fine piece of work. I do like that eagle design in the background." She handed it back. "But you know, I was really hoping for some form of photo ID." She smiled again.

"Madam---" he started to say.

"That's Mrs. Mrs. Fortescue. My late husband practised proctology here for nearly thirty years before his untimely passing last November."

"Yes, yes. My condolences---"

"He would have been 81 this coming August. And we had been so hoping to spend our golden years together in retirement."

She smiled again, expectantly. Sighing Conrad reached in his pocket, took out his wallet, displayed his driver's license, his membership card in the NRA and a VISA which also carried his photo.

"I would have brought my passport, Mrs. Fortescue, but I wasn't aware I'd be needing it." For one of the few times in his life, Conrad had made a joke.

Very pleasantly Lila Marie handed back the documents. "These will do very nicely, thank you, Captain. Now why don't you just sit over there in that nice comfortable easy chair while I talk to my people and get this all together for you. It shouldn't take long. Not long at all."

With that she breezed out of her office. Conrad looked around, then rose from the straight back chair at the desk and moved to the far more comfortable chintz covered easy chair by the reading lamp in the corner. Absentmindedly he reached into the nearby magazine rack and took out a six month old copy of "Your Health and Happiness" published by the Department of Health and Human Services. With mild disdain, he dropped it back in the bin.

In the Medical Records room on the main floor, Lila Marie talked hurriedly and quietly to her chief assistant, Maybell Zink who, like Lila Marie , was of an age, but unlike Lila Marie was as brassy as a Victorian doorknob.

"What do you mean, a list? Who is this guy anyway?" Maybell demanded to know.

"One of those Washington gestapo people. And Henry Lutz was right. They aren't very nice at all."

"Bet your ass on that, Lila. He say what he wanted it for?" Lila shook her head. "Sounds like one of our pill pushers has his ass in a sling," Maybell said.

"What do you think we should do?" Lila asked.

"I guess we do what he wants. We just don't do it very quickly. In the meantime we might be able to figure out who he's after."

They were assembled in the Devilbiss basement which had been converted to a recreation room many years ago when the kids were still in their teens. Max and Louise hadn't used it much lately, but now it was being put to good use. A table which substituted for a desk was set up against a far wall. The flag, which Max proudly flew on holidays was stretched out behind the desk. A chair had been put in position. Lamps and other light fixtures had been brought down from other parts of the house and a digital camera sat on a tripod in front of the desk. On the desk was a tape machine that would play the cassette.

"Maybe we should wait for an hour or so," Ken said. "We'll get maximum exposure if we hold off."

"We haven't got an hour or so," Max said. "You heard what Buzz said. The FSF is in Atchison. Only a matter of time before they start poking around Horton." He looked over at Everett. "Brian, what do you say?"

"I think you're right, Max. We all heard it on the tape. Several well planned incidents designed to terrify the public and force them to turn to the government for protection. Well, I think we've seen those incidents. Maybe there are more, maybe not but I don't think we should wait to find out. Let's get this out into the ether. We're not safe until this becomes public."

"And we'll be safe when it does?" Ken asked uncertainly.

"Safer. Now they can arrest us quietly, toss us into a prison somewhere, never to be heard from again. They can't pull that once we've gone public".

Max peered at the back of the camera, adjusted one of the nearby lamps. "Brian, why don't you take your place and we'll start recording. Once the DVD is burned we can set up the simultaneous transmission to the seventeen websites."

Ken shook his head. "I still think we should go live."

Max said, "This'll look live. Anyway, if we fumble or have a glitch we're protected . We have to make sure we get this right."

Brian got up from the old three cushion sofa that was sitting against a far wall and took his place behind the desk.

Max checked the picture, nodded in satisfaction. "Good. Okay, Brian, you do the blah-blah-blah and then when you're ready just hit the Play button on the machine."

"Right," Brian said.

Max looked around. "Everybody set? Okay, ready to go. Everybody quiet----"

And just then Buzz gallumphed down the staircase. "Everything's quiet outside!" he announced loudly. He stopped short, embarrassed, then raised his hands in apology as he tiptoed over to the sofa.

Max pointed a finger at Brian and nodded.

"Hello," Brian said into the camera. "My name is Brian Everett. Some of you may recognize me from my days as the anchor of a network news program. Those who do will wonder what has happened to me. Yes, I have aged a couple of years but the scars and blisters on my face are the result of radiation poisoning I suffered in the bomb blast at Santa Veronica, California, this past Sunday. No doubt you have seen the government bulletins, seeking to know my whereabouts. For compassionate reasons, they told you. I am here to tell you that their reasons had nothing to do with compassion. My good friend Buzz Shipley and I have been on the run for nearly four days, hounded by operatives of the Federal Security Force, whose sole motive in finding us was to prevent us from broadcasting a tape---a taped conversation held last week between the President's Chief of Staff, Zebulon Marcuse, and the late Edward Vitale who died last Saturday as a result of an auto accident. After you hear this tape I will leave it to you to decide just how much of an accident Ed Vitale's death really was. Their meeting occurred last week when Marcuse burst into Vitale's study unannounced as Vitale was dictating notes for his autobiography into a sophisticated recording system built into the room. Marcuse was in a rush, as he always is, and Ed Vitale was so startled by his appearance that he neglected to shut off the recording apparatus. The tape you are about to hear encompasses the entire conversation and has not been edited or doctored in any way. My friends, what you are about to hear will shock you to your core. Its ramifications cannot be ignored. I beg you now to listen with an open mind."

And with that, Brian reached over and pressed PLAY.

Emma Wasserman's ample rear end was aching like a diseased tooth too long ignored. She had been sitting on the hard wooden straight backed chair for more than five hours. Once and only once had she been allowed to use the motel room bathroom and then only if the door was left open and Lt. Stephens of the FSF was allowed to observe. Humiliating. But it could have been worse. Lt. Stephens could have been a man. In fact the lieutenant was a she, tall and athletically built with broad shoulders and muscled arms and legs. She would never win a Miss America beauty pageant but a Bodybuilder of the Year award was certainly within her grasp.

The television set, which had been set to the Progressive channel for the past three hours, droned on, showing and re-showing the carnage from Longview and Paschgoula, the live footage interrupted from time to time by handwringing commentary from the network's on the spot reporters. The body counts escalated with each break-in and every report cited the vicious work of Muslim terrorists although there was no actual evidence that they had been culpable. The heroic work of the Department of Homeland Security and the Federal Security Force was also frequently mentioned.

Emma smiled at her captor. "I don't suppose you'd like to go down to the office and get us a couple of A&W's. I'm getting mighty thirsty."

The lieutenant gave her a dismissive glance. "No one leaves this room. Not you. Not me."

Emma nodded. "Then how about something a little more cheerful on the TV. I heard Bravo was doing a special on cremations."

Stephens didn't even smile.

Emma stole a glance at her watch. Going on five o'clock. The jackbooted thug who was running the show was probably running around Horton by now. Only a matter of time before he caught up with Dr. Devilbiss. Can't let that happen, she thought. Doc's one of the good people, taking a risk like that for the newsman with the radiation poisoning. Got to do something. But what? This muscle-bound she-ape is armed with a taser and she looked like she'd enjoy using it. Even without the taser, Stephens looked like she could handle Arnold, Chuck and JeanClaude all at the same time without raising a sweat.

Just then there was a loud knock at the door. Stephens looked up sharply but didn't respond. Again, an insistent knock, this time louder.

"Anybody in there? Hello!" The door knob rattled.

Stephens moved to the door. "Go away," she said, "we do not wish to be disturbed."

"Can't do that, ma'am. We're the gas company. There's been a report of a leak. We're evacuating all units."

Stephens peered through the peep hole and saw a fish eye view of a man in a hard hat and a uniform which identified him as an employee of the Atchison Utility Service.

"We smell no gas. Go away!" Stephens barked angrily.

"Ma'am, this is a very dangerous situation."

Emma sniffed the air, frowning. "Hey, Brunhilde, I do smell gas. See for yourself."

Stephens turned, inhaled, then a puzzled look crossed her face. She looked at Emma as she drew her pistol. "Get up! Come here to the door!" Emma creakily stood, every muscle and joint resisting. "We will wait outside if need be. Don't do anything foolish."

Stephens turned the handle and pulled the door open. She shoved Emma out in front of her. The gas guy smiled. "Thanks, lady. Just trying to do my job."

And then as Stephens stepped through the doorway, a smelly burlap potato sack was thrown over head as the burly arms of a very strong man encircled her. At the same time a hypodermic needle was jammed into her arm. Within seconds the FSF officer folded up like a flimsy beach chair in a Miami Beach hurricane.

Emma turned, grinned as she recognized her poker buddies: Jocko Babbitt, all 240 pounds of him lowering Stephens to the asphalt; Danny Finsterwald, dropping a disposable needle into a paper sack ; and lovable Larry Pritzker, the motel owner, a dear and close friend, even if he did stutter slightly whenever he had a dynamite poker hand.

"You okay, Emma?" Larry asked.

"I'm fine," she said, " but I know someone who won't be if I don't get to a phone."

"Use the one in the office," he said.

Emma started off, calling over her shoulder. "What about the gas leak?"

"What gas leak?" Larry laughed. "We just punched a hole into the bathroom from the next door unit and ran some tubing from the heating unit. There's your instant gas leak."

Emma just shook her head in amusement and kept moving toward the office.

The taping over, the DVD was ready to be sent to the seventeen sites where it would be downloaded and then transmitted out. The first take had been recorded without a glitch. To be sure, the graphics were hardly inspiring but that wasn't the point. It was the audio, the contents of the tape that mattered and a quick check showed the DVD was in perfect order.

Max hovered over his computer. "I think we'd better send a warning message to make sure someone's ready to acknowledge the transmission." He clicked onto the internet and clicked in the e-mail addresses for the seventeen sites, then composed a short message which conformed to the code system. "Sorry I didn't get back to you sooner. Plumbing backed up. What a mess! Oops. More trouble. Will write back in five minutes. Transmit my regrets to the others." He tapped SEND and the message went out to all parts of the country.

Mattie Rice, who had quietly joined them during the recording, was peering over his shoulder. "They really teach you this 007 bullshit in med school?" she grinned.

"No, no," Max said. "We came up with all this crap by ourselves. You'd be surprised how inventive you can become when you have to." He took the DVD and slipped it into the computer, checking his watch for the time.

Suddenly the screen blipped and a message appeared. It was a glitch he had seen before, usually during a power failure or weather disturbance and once when his roughhousing grandchildren had accidentally disconnected the modem.

"Great", he muttered. "Nice timing." His fingers flew across the keyboard seeking to reconnect to the internet. His efforts failed. Frowning, he called to Buzz. "Buzz, check over that corner and see if the modem is connected."

Buzz did so. "Looks okay to me."

Max tried again. No luck. At that moment Louise appeared at the top of the stairs. "Max, you better come up here. All of you. The President's on TV."

"Who cares?" Max growled.

"You'll care," she said adamantly.

The President, seated behind the desk in the ersatz Oval Office, was wearing his most sincere, most caring, most troubled expression, the one he trotted out when he was about to deliver bad news which, he would be quick to point out, was not his fault.

"These tragic events have shaken this nation to the core. Over two thousand innocent Americans killed or maimed and with each new report, that number grows ever larger. My administration has been working diligently for years, ever since I took office, to root out homegrown terror cells, to thwart alien terrorists from entering the country and to develop intelligence at every level to keep you safe. I have instructed all appropriate agencies to redouble their efforts in this regard. I have absolute faith that these hard working patriotic Americans will perform to the best of their ability. And yet, we must not overlook one fundamental aspect of our society, one of the pillars that make us the great nation that we are. That is our freedom of communication and as your President, I would not have it any other way. However, exigent circumstances call for drastic actions in the name of public safety. Let there be no mistake about this, the people who despise us have no hesitancy in using our great freedom to destroy us and that is why I am being forced to take certain necessary steps to thwart their ability to communicate with one another. Effective immediately, I have ordered the appropriate agencies to immediately shut down the internet for all but emergency government communications."

Brian stared at the television in disbelief. He shot a look at Ken who could only shake his head in disbelief. "Son of a bitch," Max muttered.

The President continued. "This Presidential decree will remain in effect for the next 72 hours. I realize this order will severely impact commerce across the nation but at this moment, I believe the safety of the populace must be my first consideration. This order will not effect cell phone service. Modern technology allows us to monitor almost any call and the enemy long ago gave up its use as unproductive. As for the internet, I have been advised by White House counsel that this action is well within my executive powers. I have conferred with both the Speaker of the House and the Senate Majority Leader and they concur in my decision."

Max growled. "Just like Kermit the Frog says whatever he's made to say." He picked up the remote and shut down the television. He turned to the others. "Well?"

They looked at one another disbelieving. What now? What now indeed?

Just then, Max's cell phone rang. He answered it. "This is Max." He listened intently, his face darkening. He threw a sharp look in

Brian's direction. "You're sure about this? Uh,huh. How long? Uh-huh. Okay, Emma, thanks a lot." He flipped it closed and looked around the room.

"That was Emma Wasserman. The Federal Security Force is here in Horton and I mean, in force."

Mattie Rice shook her head. "No, they would have contacted me."

"You never got a call?" Brian asked.

"Not a peep."

"They might have checked you out, Mattie. You don't always put a lid on what you have to say."

"True enough, but there's protocol."

"I don't think these people give a flying fiddle about protocol," Max said. "So as we were saying, now what?"

Buzz raised his hand. "How about for starters we get the hell out of here?"

"And go where? To do what?" Ken asked in disgust.

"Well, you sure as hell can't stay here", Mattie said. "Look, I'm going to guess that the roads are open out of here. Doesn't mean they're not being watched. Probably are. But to set up roadblocks without us helping, they'd need the Highway Patrol and they haven't called them in yet."

Max looked at her dubiously. "What makes you think they haven't?"

"Because if they had I'd have heard about it from Lt. Potter."

"Bill Potter? What the hell's he got to do with all this?" Max demanded to know.

Louise just clucked her tongue. "Max Devilbiss, I swear sometimes you can be the densest, most unaware human being in the state of Kansas. And you a college graduate."

He turned on her in annoyance. "And just what do you mean by that------?" He stopped in midsentence, looked over at Mattie and frowned. "Oh," he murmured quietly.

"Yes, oh, my knuckleheaded husband." Louise said.

"Sorry, Mattie. Didn't know. Bill Potter. Good man. I like him a lot."

Mattie smiled with a twinkle. "And he speaks highly of you, Max. Which brings me back to the subject of roadblocks. Chances are there aren't any. Heading north, there are several backroads you could take where you'd never be seen."

"Why north?" Buzz asked.

"Because at this point you've got only one logical destination and that's Canada."

Buzz shook his head. "Even if we could reach it, we'd never get across. The FSF would stop us on this side and Canadians would stop us on theirs."

"Maybe not," Ken said, looking at Brian.

Brian nodded knowingly. "Superintendent Sunderson."

"Who?" Max asked.

"Former student of mine, Max. He's a big deal in the Montreal headquarters of the Mounties. Got Heather across the border early this morning. I'm pretty sure he'll help us."

"Okay, then. Case settled," Mattie said taking charge. "Back of the station, I've got an impounded car somebody left by the side of the road last week. No beauty but it runs okay and it's got Missouri plates. Brian, that means you and Ken and Buzz come with me. And bring that DVD. If you cross the border you're going to need it. Max, you and Louise straighten up everything. Get rid of any trace you've had visitors. Emma didn't give you up so they've got nothing." She took out her cell phone and punched in a number. "Meantime I got an idea for a little diversion. Might buy you fellas quite a bit of time." Then, into the phone: "Ephraim, it's Mattie Rice. I need your help and I don't need a lot of backtalk so here's what I want you to do."

• • •

The unmarked Chevy Greenpeace was on Rt, 73, returning to Horton from Hiawatha. It was an underpowered uncomfortable piece of junk but Conrad never complained, at least not in public. After all it was government built and its use mandatory. Whining was not an option but he dreaded the day he ever got into a car chase with something as prosaic as a 4 cylinder Fiat or an electric Prius. Truth be told, the Greenpeace couldn't catch a cold.

He was on his cell phone to his aide Captain Willis Johnson. "I've got the list from the hospital. It includes everyone from the area but we're going to concentrate on Horton. 27 names in all, about half of them G.P.s or internists. I want you to start on this bunch. Surveillance only, Johnson, at least until we're sure we've got Bannister."

"Yes, sir."

Conrad read off the names and addresses of twelve doctors, starting at the top in alphabetical order. Max Devilbiss was number five. "I'm going to check in with this chief of police---what did you say her name was?"

"Rice. Matilda Rice."

"I'm going to see just how cooperative this Matilda Rice is. A lot more so than her dead husband, I hope. Between her people and the Highway Patrol, I think we can seal up 110th Street in both directions, Rt.75 and 36 for sure , maybe 159 if they try to get smart and try to go back south."

"Sir, what if we catch sight of Bannister with Everett? Do we move in?"

"No. Contact me immediately. You and I will handle those two ourselves."

He flipped his cell phone shut, then looked over at his driver in annoyance. "Can't you get this pig to move any faster?"

• • •

Back at the Devilbiss house, Max had fired up the brick barbecue in the backyard and was meticulously feeding it scraps of paper and other potentially damning pieces of evidence. All dishes were in the dishwasher, bedding was in the washing machine as clean sheets and pillow cases were brought out of the linen closet. Within minutes there would be no trace of Max and Louise's surprise visitors.

Out on the streets, Mattie was behind the wheel of her squad car, heading toward the police station. Brian and Ken were in back ensconsed in the mesh cage, their luggage piled around their feet. Buzz was up front because he insisted it would be unseemly, not to mention racist, if he had to sit in the back.

As they neared headquarters, Mattie suddenly slowed and pulled to the curb. Brian leaned forward. "What's the matter?"

"Couple of dudes in black suits just got out of an unmarked car and walked in the front door," Mattie said.

"And?" Brian asked.

"They sure weren't Butch and Sundance giving themselves up." She paused thoughtfully, then took out her cell phone and punched in a number. She waited. Then: "Boyd, it's me. Don't react. Would that be FSF boys in there with you? Uh-huh. Well, you just smile and shine me on like I was some wacky old biddy hearing ax murderers in the basement. Right. Now here's what I want you to do. You know those keys to that old clunker out back. They're in the middle drawer of the desk. Take 'em out, go to the toilet on a whiz trip. Open the window and drop 'em out. Our visitors are going to make good use of that old heap. Right. Do it now, Boyd." She pulled away from the curb, turned down a side street and then approached the police building via a rear alley.

She pointed out the window to the others as Boyd dropped the keys onto the ground by the red '91 Corolla with the slightly cracked windshield and in bad need of a paint job.

"Okay, fellas", she said. "Here's where we part company. Grab your stuff, keep the noise down and good luck. Buzz, you got that map I gave you?"

Buzz tapped his shirt pocket. "Right here."

"All right then." She reached in her pocket and took out a small slip of paper which she handed to Ken. "This is the name of a woman in Rush City, Minnesota. A few miles north of Minneapolis on the 35. You can trust her. We've gotten people out through Lost River State Forest before. If anyone can get you across she can. I'll try to find an untraceable way to let her know you're coming."

"Thanks, Chief," Ken said.

The three men hustled out of the car, gave her a farewell smile and moved quickly across the deserted alley and piled into the Toyota. Five minutes later, they were gone, headed for a dirt road that skirted four farms before emerging in the little town of Purcell on Rt. 20. From there it would be a straight shot to St. Joseph on the other side of the Missouri River.

Meanwhile Mattie was headed to the Horton Municipal Airport just north of town. It's name made it sound grander than it was. It boasted two runways but no control tower and except for an on-again,off-again sometime watchman named Burley Packard it was mostly unattended. Burley was something of a local character, a crackerjack mechanic who could fix a car engine just by looking at it but who had gotten bored by it all and turned his attention to aircraft. He was set up at the airport in his trailer, loaded with tools and equipment, ready to have at the engines of one of the dozen or so small private planes moored on the tarmac just off the runways. A highlight of Burley's day (or week or month) would come when a plane in distress would fly in for an emergency landing giving Burley a chance to work his magic.

Mattie drove up to the field and pulled to a stop in front of

Burley's trailer. She got out of the car and shouted. "Burley, you old horse thief, where the hell are you?"

After a moment, a bald head peeped out from the slowly opening doorway, followed by a rotund little man in an undershirt and a greasy pair of jeans. "That you, Chief? What I done now?"

"Nothin', Burley," she said. "I just came out to chat. You got a cold one in here you could spare?"

"Sure do," the little man said, ducking back inside. Mattie followed him in.

The interior of the trailer was a cross between a Pep Boys outlet and a Motel Six. One end was devoted to shelves and shelves of nuts and bolts and washers and wiring, the other to a small built in range and a refrigerator, an ancient television set and a bed that had more lumps than a can of cheap clam chowder. Mattie knew that out back were two sheds housing all sorts of tools, big and small.

There were two windows in the trailer, one on each side of the doorway. Mattie moved to the far wall, forcing Burley to put his back to the windows as he handed her a Budweiser. He popped one for himself.

"You sure I ain't in some kind of trouble, Chief?" he asked again, a little squinty eyed, head cocked to one side.

"No trouble at all, Burley," she said.

"Ain't like you comin' out here for no good reason," he said. "If it's about Henry White Owl's carburetor, I charged him what I paid for it. Didn't kick it up even a nickel."

"This isn't about the carburetor," she said. Her eyes looked past Burley, out the window onto the field where Ephraim Jones was climbing into the cockpit of his 1964 Piper Cherokee 180. For several years he'd eked out a living ferrying shoppers back and forth between Kansas City or Omaha either because they didn't like driving or didn't have the time to spare. Most Hortonians figured Ephraim and

182

his rickety old single engine wreck of a plane would someday conk out in tandem but as yet, God was Ephraim's co-pilot.

"My God!" Mattie said wide-eyed as the plane started to taxi for takeoff. "Burley! Did you see that?"

"See what?" he said, turning to look.

"Three men just hopped into Ephraim Jones's airplane. Son of a bitch. I was told to look out for those guys!"

"What guys?" Burley asked, confused, as the Cherokee picked up speed.

"Fugitives! And there they go!"

"Yep," Burley agreed. "There they go!"

"Burley, you have to call my office right away. There's a federal agent there. You tell him what you saw. Quick! Don't waste any time," she prodded.

"Well, uh, yes, ma'am but shouldn't you-----?"

But Mattie was already out the door. "You tell that federal man I'm on my way in!"

Burley nodded, peered out the window again at the ascending airplane as it gently banked toward the north. He reached for his phone.

CHAPTER THIRTEEN

In a modest three-bedroom one story house in Livonia on the outskirts of Detroit, Valerie Shipley was dressing her daughters in pale blue organdy. A much loved cousin who lived a couple of blocks away was throwing a birthday party for her youngest daughter who, like Valerie's oldest, was planning to graduate from pre-school the following Friday. Phone calls had been flying back and forth all morning long and the FSF agents who were monitoring Valerie's phone from a supposedly abandoned house on the corner knew that the party started at one o'clock, that chicken fingers and french fries would dominate the menu and that a clown had been hired to regale the dozen or so youngsters in attendance.

In New York City, another team of FSF operatives was carefully monitoring all calls coming into Melissa Everett's apartment phone, office phone and cell phone. These calls were few in number and non-threatening in nature. It was a boring, albeit necessary, assignment.

And at Nellis Air Force Base in Nevada, an FSF agent posing as an Air Force Safety Control officer was keeping close tabs on Mark Everett. It was not a difficult assignment. Brian Everett's only son was either in the air, drinking in the Officer's Club or playing house with his current girlfriend, his apartment or hers, they seemed to have no particular preference.

And meanwhile, across the nation, a great silence had descended. Tens of millions of computers sat mute, unable to communicate. Millions who relied on e-mail or favorite websites like Facebook to chat with friends and neighbors sat staring at screens that had only one thing to say: Internet Service Temporarily Suspended by Order of the United States Government" Some, in frustration, railed at family members who were conveniently close enough to rail at. Others railed at God. Others who wanted to rail at the administration were unable to do so because the internet was shut down. Joseph Heller, were he still alive, would have loved it. The problem was compounded by the fact that, absent the internet, cell phone service was crashing everywhere due to unprecedented volume.

MacAndrews sat at his desk staring bleakly at the manila folder marked BUNKER HILL, TOP SECRET/ EYES ONLY. No question. The world was going mad. Maybe not going. Maybe it was there already. It seemed the doomsayers were right. You couldn't reason with the Islamic fanatics. They would wait patiently and then strike again in force when it was least expected. And it was Islamic terrorism. Forensics at the sites gathered by Homeland Security proved that. But why? To what end? And with all they were dealing with in Europe, why would the fanatics siphon off assets from a battle they were barely surviving.

"David?"

He looked up. His wife Grace was standing in the open doorway.

"I'm sorry to bother you. I've been trying for a half hour to reach Mother on my phone. I can't get through."

"Did you try the hard line?" he asked.

"I've tried them both. David, I'm very worried. You know how her health is. I talk to her at least once a day and, uh.. is there anything you can do?"

"No. I'm sorry," he said.

"But I'm sure if you called someone----Oh, dear, that was a stupid thing to say. I'm sorry."

"Don't be sorry. Your Mother is in no imminent danger. Maybe by tomorrow we can figure something out."

" Perhaps if you called from the Pentagon. I'm sure those phones are operating----"

He snapped at her, more sharply than he should have. "Grace, please! I'm trying to work here!" He saw the look of pain on her face. "I'm sorry. I shouldn't have raised my voice. First thing in the morning, I will check on her from the office."

"Thank you, David," she said quietly, retreating from the room.

He looked down at the folder and then shoved it aside in frustration. Events were careening in one inevitable direction. Tomorrow or the day after, sometime soon, the President would give him the order to implement this Draconian policy. And he dreaded it. Armies in the streets. Survivalists enraged, positive that they had been right all along. Otherwise peace loving citizens grabbing for their guns. Blood in the streets. The blood of innocents. Teachers, students, farmers, those without jobs, those who felt there was no longer hope, these are the ones who would be cut down, not the highly trained, weaponized and armor protected military. It was an order he did not want to give, that he could not, in any moral sense, execute. And yet he would have no choice. Duty. Honor. Country. Obedience.

He got up and went to the sideboard where he poured himself a stiff belt of scotch, neat, and then moved to the window overlooking his backyard. The sun was just disappearing over the western horizon and as he stared at its slowly dimming rays, his thoughts traveled back to a military courtroom in Saigon. The year was 1973. He was a shavetail lieutenant in the Judge Advocate General's corps, assigned to prosecute a case of treason.

Sgt. Nils Olson had been living off base every few days, secretly habitating with a young Vietnamese woman. A violation of the anti-fraternization regulations. A timeline was established which showed that whenever he had spent time with the woman, raids and forays into the jungle the following day were routinely ambushed and American lives were lost. When it was learned that the woman's brother was highly placed in the Viet Cong, Olson was arrested and made to stand trial. MacAndrews went after him relentlessly. The bumbling inarticulate enlisted man was no match for MacAndrews' courtroom skills. Yes, he and the woman had talked once in a while about maneuvers, about assignments he (thankfully) didn't get. Yes, he would sometimes talk about his buddies but never about specific orders. At the end of the trial, McAndrews had successfully painted the man as a liar and an incompetent but in his heart of hearts MacAndrews wasn't sure he was guilty of treason. Nonetheless his own private qualms were of no consequence. He did his duty. He would have it no other way.

Olson was found guilty and sentenced to twenty years in military prison. MacAndrews was later to learn that the woman had given birth to Olson's child. When Saigon fell and the Cong and the North Vietnamese Army swept into the city, the Vietnamese woman was denounced by her brother for living with the enemy, for giving birth to a bastard baby fathered by a round eyes and worst of all, for refusing to supply information which would have aided the Communist cause. Mother and child were summarily executed in the name of the state and tossed into a mass grave along with the bodies of other traitors. When Sgt.Olson learned what had happened, he hanged himself in his cell.

MacAndrews drained the rest of his scotch. Duty, Honor. Country. Obedience. He had no regrets. He had had no choice.

• • •

Conrad and Johnson were intensely grilling Burley Packard at the airstrip. It was still light out but barely. A brisk wind was tearing across the runways and Johnson turned up the collar on his jacket to get a little extra warmth.

"All right, Mr. Packard, let me get this straight," Conrad was saying. "There were three men and they made off with this plane owned by a Mr.---" He checked his notes. "...uh, Ephraim Jones, is that right?"

"Yes, sir."

"And you definitely saw the plane heading north."

Burley pointed. "Yes, sir. North."

"Well, the highway patrol's got a high speed helicopter in pursuit."

Burley nodded. "Probably won't catch 'em. That little old plane's been around a while but she's faster than a jack rabbit with his tail on fire."

"Oh, we'll catch them, don't you worry about that, sir. Now tell me again about these three men."

"Nothing to tell. Three men is all. Not close enough to see their faces."

"I see. And these men, were they white? Were they black? Both?"

Burley pondered. "Well, I don't know----"

Conrad glared at him. "Surely you could have observed that much?"

"Well, I guess they were white. Why don't you ask the Chief? She got a better look at them than I did."

"All white, eh? Just how good a look did you get, Mr. Packard? No, let me ask you this. Did you actually see them at all?"

Burley hesitated. "Well, now that you mention it, no, actually, it was Chief Rice that saw 'em. But she was darn sure, I'm telling you. There was three of them."

Conrad just shook his head in disbelief. He turned to Johnson.

"They're on the road and they've got about 45 minutes on us. Get on the government emergency police bands and issue another damned BOLO. All points north. They're heading for Canada. They've got no other place else to go."

He turned back to Burley. "Thanks for all your help, sir," He chewed off the word "help" sharply. "Now I think I'll have a little talk with your chief of police."

Burley grinned. "You give her my regards, hear?"

"Oh, I'll do that," Conrad said as he and Johnson moved quickly back to their car.

Twenty minutes later, a well-worn Piper Cherokee landed at Eppley Airfield in Omaha. It was met by officers of the Nebraska State Patrol who had been alerted by their Kansas counterparts. They immediately took into custody the pilot who was flying solo. Had there been three people in the plane, somehow they had managed to disappear under the watchful eye of the Kansas Highway Patrol chopper pilot who had the Cherokee in view all the way to the Nebraska border. The pilot, one Ephraim Jones, had no idea what the fuss was all about. He had flown himself to Omaha with the intention of catching a cab to Rosenblatt Stadium and watching the game between the Omaha Royals and their rivals from Round Rock. And if these fellas didn't let him go pretty quick, he was going to miss the free beer and pretzels promotion, not to mention the young girls in their skimpies.

It was dark. Thursday now. Twenty past midnight. They'd been on the road for over four hours. They'd long ago passed through St. Joseph, Missouri, cut across the 36 to Cameron where they picked up the 35 North, a straight shot to Des Moines, Iowa. Ken was driving, Brian riding shotgun, Buzz in the back his hat slouched over his forehead and arms folded across his chest. He seemed to be asleep.

He wasn't. He listened with interest, often amusement, as two old friends relived the days of their youth, wandering aimlessly across Europe in search of wine and women and only tangentially affected by the events tearing apart Southeast Asia.

"No,no", Brian insisted. "His name was Otto. The big guy with the mustache.The little guy, the dwarf. That was Helmut."

"Okay, okay," Ken said. "And Otto, the big guy, he owned the brauhaus."

"No again. The dwarf owned the place. Otto was the bouncer but he pretended to be the owner because, well, who the hell is going to be intimidated by some Kraut pansy three and a half feet tall?"

Ken glanced at him quickly. "You're kidding. Helmut went for guys?"

"What? Little people aren't allowed to be gay?"

Ken scowled. "Can't get my head around that one. So when Helmut goes cruising, he goes looking for other little gay guys?"

"Or big ones. Maybe size doesn't count."

"That's not what that cute little waitress from Dresden told me," Ken said glumly and then laughed. Brian laughed along with him.

There was a long silence and then Ken shook his head slowly. "You were so damned lucky, Brian."

"What?"

"I wanted her, too."

Brian turned to him puzzled. "Who, Marnie?"

"No, Mother Teresa. Of course Marnie, you damned fool."

"I didn't know. Swear to God."

"You weren't supposed to. I made a couple of really brain dead moves. She just smiled. You know, the old Gee-but-I-pity-you smile or the Are-you-kidding-me smile. I gave up pretty quick after I saw how she looked at you."

Brian shrugged. "Well, maybe you didn't get Marnie but you ended up pretty well."

Ken nodded seriously. "Heather? Yeah. I don't know what I would have done all these years without her. I'm just so damned grateful she's safe in Canada."

Brian stared out his window into the darkness for a few moments before turning back to his friend.

"Speaking of that. This DVD which we might or might not get the CBC to air, you know it won't reach far into the U.S. Maybe portions of the northernmost states, that's all."

Ken nodded. "I've thought of that."

"Then maybe you've thought what I'm thinking," Brian said.

Ken glanced at him. "Hugo Wheeler."

"Nothing else makes much sense."

"But how do we reach him? People I've talked to say there's no way. He's constantly on the run, trusts no one."

"Sunderson?" Brian asked.

"I think he'll try to get us across the border. I doubt he can help with Wheeler." He glanced at a billboard before it whizzed by. "There's a 24 hour diner up ahead about a mile off the highway. Easy off, easy on. You want to take a chance?"

"How's the gas?"

"Okay."

"Maybe we should wait."

A loud voice came from the rear. "I vote we eat. Now."

Brian looked back. "Buzz, I thought you were asleep."

Buzz grinned. "My possum pose. Lappin' up the conversation unobserved."

Ken glanced at his watch. "This hour of the night, off the highway, might be quiet. Maybe worth a chance."

"I'm game," Brian said. He looked back at Buzz. "No chitlins, Buzz. They might figure out you're a black guy."

Buzz raised his hand solemnly. "I'm going to have a mayonaise sandwich on white bread with mayonaise. Will that do for you, bro?" he grinned.

Brian grinned back.

The diner was indeed pretty deserted. A lone trucker sat in a booth at the far end reading a newspaper and eating bacon and eggs. Two kids who looked like they were still in high school were pressed up against each other, cooing and giggling softly into each other's ear while they nursed milk shakes.

The three men slipped into a booth at the other end of the diner where they could talk without being heard and less chance they would be seen and recognized. Brian ordered the chicken soup. Filling. Not too heavy. He wasn't feeling any better but he also wasn't feeling worse. He took that as a good sign. Ken settled for a french dip and fries. With a straight face, Buzz ordered the fried chicken.

"Just like your Mammy used to make," Brian chided.

"Only chicken my Mammy ever made me came in a plastic tray with dried out mashed potatoes and rubbery corn. Hated it so much all through college I couldn't look a chicken in the eye. Wouldn't even eat Chicken of the Sea and that was tuna fish. My second year with the Falcons this dumbass rookie from Louisiana comes to camp. Name was Swanson. Soon as I saw his name on that uniform, I decked him one. Never did tell him why."

Brian put up a hand laughing. "Okay, Buzz. We get the picture." He turned to Ken. "Unless you stop him right away, he'll go on like that for twenty minutes."

"If I was watching 'Roots' and Chicken George came on the screen I'd just----"

"Enough, Buzz! We get it." Brian said.

Buzz grinned. "Just trying to entertain you fine gentlemen."

The food came and they dug in. Ken had figured they hadn't eaten since noon the day before. The two kids finally left. Another trucker showed up and sat by himself, ordering and eating quietly, taking little notice of the trio in the far corner. It was while drinking coffee that Buzz got serious.

"I just want to say, and I mean this, that I envy you fellas," he said

Brian looked at him curiously. "What the hell brought that on, Buzz?"

"Watching you both. You going back forty years, friends always. You've got a special relationship, the kind I never did have with anyone. Not even with you, Brian. Close, maybe, but not like you two."

"Now, come on, Buzz---"

"That's how I know you can take care of each other and why I know it's going to be okay for me to leave."

Ken shook his head. "You're wrong, Buzz. We need you."

"Thanks, but no, you don't. Two can slip across the border easier than three. Ever since you two hooked up I've just been along for the ride and honestly, I've got better things to do."

"Such as?" Brian said.

"Go see my wife," Buzz replied. He looked from one to the other. "We all know what's on the tape. In a few days, life in this country may not be worth living. I'm not going to sneak across the border and leave my wife and my little girls behind to face the avalanche of bullshit alone."

"The FSF'll be waiting for you, Buzz", Ken said. "You know they're watching her."

"Yeah, I know that. It doesn't make any difference. I won't argue with you about it. It's how it is. I'll leave you in Des Moines. Should be a bus straight through to Detroit. I might get spotted. Maybe not. I'll take my chances."

Brian reached out and put his hand on Buzz's. "You know I owe you big time, bro. Without you, I wouldn't be here now."

Buzz just shook his head. "It's me that's been owing you, Brian. For a long time now. Thanks for letting me give a little back."

At six o'clock that morning, the beat-up red Corolla turned into an alley in Des Moines, Iowa, a block away from the bus terminal. As part of a plan to facilitate their flight, Brian took out his cellphone and dialed up his daughter in New York City.

"Lo," she said sleepily.

"Lissa, it's Dad," Brian said.

His daughter was instantly galvanized as she sat up. "Dad! Where are you? How are you? What's going on?"

"I'm fine, promise. I didn't want you to worry."

"Well, I have been worried. I've been terrified---"

"Sweetheart, listen to me. I don't have much time. I'm on my way to see an old friend who's living in Sandusky, Ohio. I think he'll put Buzz Shipley and I up for a couple of days while we figure out what to do next."

"Dad, come to New York, Stay with me."

"Can't do it, Lissa, for a lot of reasons. Ken Bannister's been with us a couple of days but he rented a car and he's on his way to upstate New York. He's going to try to cross into Montreal. His wife's already there."

"Yes, but----"

"Call your brother. Tell him I'm okay. This nationwide search is government harrassment, that's all."

"Dad---"

"I have to go now, sweetheart. I love you."

He flipped off the phone.

"Conrad's not going to buy it," Ken said. shaking his head.

"Maybe not, but it might make him think." He turned to Buzz. "As for you----." He reached into his pocket and took out a large wad of hundred dollar bills and handed it to him.

"Oh, no," Buzz said waving him off.

"Take it. It's hardly worth anything now. In a week it'll be as valuable as toilet paper. Besides I've got a lot more."

Buzz hesitated, then took the money and crammed it into the jacket of his windbreaker. He looked from one to the other. "Good luck, guys," he said as he ducked out of the rear of the car, holding his overnight bag. Brian and Ken waved at him as he hurried down the alley toward the bus depot.

At the same time, back in Horton, Colonel Erwin Conrad, who had managed to squeeze in four hours of sleep before arising, was sitting behind the desk of the Chief of Police, sifting through her files. The Chief of Police, Mattie Rice, was sitting on a straight backed chair against a side wall, arms crossed, impatiently tapping her right foot. Captain Willis Johnson was sitting at a table poring over phone records which had been faxed to the office by the local phone company.

"So, Chief Rice, could you tell me how you were able to see three men supposedly stealing Mr. Jones aircraft when it was Mr. Jones-- by himself-- who got into that plane and took off?"

"I wasn't wearing my glasses," Mattie said.

"Your glasses," Conrad said, almost amused.

She nodded. "My distance glasses. Without them I can't see very clearly past thirty yards."

"Must be hell when you're in hot pursuit," he observed.

"Usually have them with me, actually," she said. "Just forgot 'em, that's all, and when it's getting dark like that, well, you know these Kansas twilights. You see all kinds of crazy shadows and things. Just a human mistake. Bet you've had your share, Colonel."

"Bet I haven't," he replied icily. He looked over at Johnson. "Anything popping out at you?"

"Not so I can see," Johnson said.

Mattie watched Conrad carefully. Cold fish. Not an ounce of

humanity in his whole body. Wonder if they make 'em all like that in Washington, she pondered.

"How long you planning on holding Dr. Devilbiss and Emma Wasserman?" she asked.

"Til I'm ready to let them go."

"You know you didn't have to send them all the way to Topeka. You could have held them here until their hearing?"

"What hearing is that, Chief?" he snorted, turning his attention back to the files.

"You know you haven't got a shred of proof against either one of them."

"I have enough."

"And would that proof have anything to do with the law?"

Conrad turned to her angrily. "I have proof that satisfies me, Chief Rice. Once Dr. Devilbiss's name came up, it didn't take me long to discover that he was a fraternity brother and a fellow University graduate of both Everett and Bannister. They did not come to Horton to visit that grimy greasemonkey at the airport. As for Emma Wasserman, she is neither deaf, dumb or blind although she'd like me to think she is. My fellow officer is grabbed, a bag thrown over her head and a sedative jabbed into her arm. Miz Wasserman says it was done by three masked men of average height, average build and from the color of their hands she was able to determine that they were either dark skinned white men or light skinned Negroes. They jumped into a car and raced away. She doesn't know what kind of car it was or its age or its color and here's a big surprise, she didn't get a license plate number. Do you have any further questions for me, Chief?"

He glared her down and she decided that silence, at least for the moment, might be the wisest approach.

The front door opened and one of the FSF agents entered and moved to Johnson's side, whispering into his ear. After a moment

Johnson nodded and fhe man left. Johnson looked over toward Conrad. "Colonel, Rigby came up with something, might be helpful. Yesterday when they were checking this place there was an old red Toyota with Missouri plates parked out back. It's gone."

Conrad looked at Mattie. "You know anything about that car?" She shook her head. "Nope."

Johnson ran his finger down the phone records. "Two days ago there was a call from here to the Missouri Department of Motor Vehicles."

Conrad looked over at Mattie questioningly. She shrugged. "Now that I recall I believe one of my deputies might have found an old wreck by the side of the road. I don't know anything about it."

"What's the date on that call, Johnson?" Conrad asked.

"The 16th, sir."

Conrad started to reshuffle through the files, then stopped and scanned one of the reports. "Abandoned vehicle on 110th Street 1991 red Toyota Corolla, Missouri plate number 552ACW. Towed to headquarters. Missouri DMV notified." Conrad looked up. "This looks a lot like your handwriting, Chief Rice."

Mattie smiled. "In addition to being nearsighted I also have a lousy memory."

Conrad rose from the desk and moved toward her, staring down coldly. If she was intimidated she gave no sign. "You and your husband, cut from the same cloth, determined to destroy the new order, just so you can hang onto your precious position of power and influence. Frankly, madam, you make me sick. I'm going to enjoy putting you away for a long long time."

The phone rang. Johnson answered it. Listening, he started jotting down notes. He hung up and turned to Conrad

"Colonel, we just got a report from the surveillance team in New York covering Everett's daughter. Everett called her twenty minutes ago from Des Moines, said that he and Shipley are headed for Sandusky, Ohio."

"Bannister?"

"He's going to try to cross into Quebec on his own."

Conrad nodded, then crossed over to a nearby bookshelf where he had seen a AAA road map of the states. He thumbed to Ohio and studied it. "Well, imagine that," he said. "Three little islands, very close to Sandusky, reaching out into Lake Erie, then the border in the middle of the lake and a stone's throw away, there is Pelee Island in Canadian waters."

"Shall I notify Sandusky, sir?" Johnson asked.

"Absolutely," Conrad replied, "but only to cover our asses. If Brian Everett told me that the sky was blue and grass was green, I wouldn't believe him, not for one damned minute. I got a call first thing this morning from Washington and the conversation was anything but pleasant. I am told I am incompetent to do my job, to carry out a simple order. So, Johnson, put out a new BOLO. Shitcan the humanitarian angle. These three men are wanted in connection with treason. Up the reward to $100,000 and include the data on the Toyota. Special emphasis on northbound routes from Des Moines. I am going to catch up with this son of a bitch and when I do, I am not going to arrest him or bring him to trial or put him in prison, I am going to put a bullet in the back of his head and be done with him. And then I am going to get on with my life."

CHAPTER FOURTEEN

Chaos reigned. It seemed almost as if anarchy had suddenly gripped the country but of course, anarchy denoted an absence of government and the people were all too aware that they had more government than they knew what to do with. One of the pitfalls of legislative action or governance by executive order is the Law of Unintended Consequences. Raising taxes by 50% on yacht builders does not mean you are going to increase revenue by 50%, it means you are going to put yacht builders out of business and your revenue will sink to near zero. Presidents and Congresses have been pulling boners like that for decades but when it came to shutting down the internet, that was arguably the biggest boner of all.

Crippling communications between Mom in Baltimore and daughter Mary in Denver was bad enough. Depriving students at every level of internet generated knowledge rendered their computers good for little else than playing solitaire or solving crossword puzzles. Planes were grounded. Air traffic control had no way to function. Factories had no way to contact customers. Customers could not order. Shippers could not ship. Restaurants could not order food. The few remaining newspapers in the country had no ability to gather news or to print it. The country was paralyzed because almost no one could remember how any of this was done prior to the internet age. For oldsters who could remember back that far, it was an era of massive telephone trunk lines, telexes, faxes, and God help us, snail mail. All in all, the administration's ill-conceived plan (the networks did not characterize it as such) ground the country to a halt, but it did accomplish one very important thing. It isolated the dissidents from one another, preventing them from coalescing. Seventy-two hours. That was all that was needed. Despite howls of rage and frustration rising up from Congress and emanating from the various State Houses, the President and his minions were determined to see it through just as they had rammed through health care five years earlier. They had to. Everything depended on it.

In the Oval Office, the President was getting an earful from his Vice President, Wendell Comeford , which was highly unusual because in seven years Comeford had been the embodiment of gentility, subservience and quiet obedience to the man who had asked him to be his running mate.

"Shutting down the internet. Just what in God's name were you thinking of?" Comeford demanded to know.

"Now just a moment, Wendell. You are talking to the President of the United States", said Zebulon Marcuse who was sitting off to one side.

Comeford whirled angrily toward the Chief of Staff. "I know who I'm talking to and you keep out of it. And by the way, it's Mister Vice President to you."

Marcuse, totally taken aback by the intensity of Comeford's rage was about to respond in kind but he held back when the President shook his head in warning.

"Wendell," the President said smoothly, "no one wanted to keep you out of the loop but I knew when I took this action it would create national outrage. I wanted to give you deniability."

"Very thoughtful, but considering the fact that I am going to be named the party's nominee at the convention next month, I should have been a part of this decision. Frankly, I've been doing a lot of looking the other way in regard to many of things you've implemented since re-election and I have tried to ignore the slights, not only from you but from the toadies around you." He looked pointedly at Marcuse, then back to the President. "I don't want to fight you. I am grateful to you for the past seven years but this freeze-out stops now."

"Of course it does, Wendell," the President said. He looked over at Marcuse, glaring for effect. "Zeb, you make sure that the Vice President is brought into the picture on every policy decision. We want his input. Is that clear?"

"Very clear, sir," Marcuse said contritely. For effect.

As soon as Comeford left the White House and climbed into his limousine, heading down Pennsylvania Avenue, he picked up the car phone and called the Senate Majority Leader in his office .

"Fletcher," Comeford said. "Clear your desk and don't go anywhere. I'm on my way over. You and I have got to talk."

Neither Comeford nor his driver noticed the black unmarked sedan several car lengths behind that was trailing the limo and its Secret Service escort .

In a similar vein, the occupants of the black unmarked sedan were oblivious to the silver-gray SUV that was stealthily hounding everyone.

Ken eyed the gas gauge with trepidation. It was down to less than a quarter of a tank. Over the past sixty miles, they had passed station after station with handmade signs that pronounced NO GAS. Another by-product of the internet shutdown. Brian caught the worry on his friend's face.

"Maybe we ought to get off the highway and find some small town station that technology hasn't caught up with."

Ken nodded. "Not a bad idea." Up ahead was an exit and he turned off. At the end of the ramp was a sign pointing to the right. "Sylvan 1 Mile."

"Good as any," Ken said, heading down the road.

Sylvan wasn't much of a town. A tiny market, a barber shop, a hardware store, as well as a beat up gas station with two pumps and, best of all, no sign. Ken pulled up and went to a pump. He got out of the car and uncapped the gas tank.

A slattern of a certain age came charging out of the office. "Hold it there, young fella!", she yelled as she hobbled toward them with a noticeable limp, probably an old war wound. She viewed Ken suspiciously. "You gotta pay first, sonny, then you pump. And we don't take no credit cards."

"Do you have gas, ma'am?" he asked.

She looked at him in disbelief. "Course I got gas. What do you think these pumps are for?" she growled.

Brian reached in his pocket and handed her a $100 bill. She looked at it, shaking her head. "I got no change for this," she said.

"Keep it," Brian said. "And we'll take some soda from your chest over there."

She nodded, stuffing the bill into her nearly non-existent cleavage. "Help yourself," she said with a grin. Her teeth, what was left of them, were of an indeterminate color. She limped back toward her office.

Brian took the hose from Ken. "I'll fill it. You call Heather."

Ken nodded and moved a short distance away, punching in his wife's cell phone number and praying that this time, unlike the past few attempts, he would get through. Brian watched as he smiled and flashed a thumb's up.

"Honey," he said, moving even further away because there are some things you would like to say to your wife that even your best friend ought not to hear.

• • •

"Good morning, Mr. Vice President," said Wallace Pinkney, Yale Class of '91, and currently the Administrative Assistant to Fletcher Chase, the illustrious senior senator from Delaware as well as the Senate Majority Leader. "Senator Chase is waiting for you. May I get you some coffee or a soda, perhaps?"

"No, thanks, Wallace," Comeford said. "Your boss is well stocked with what I need just this moment." And with that he pushed open the door to Chase's inner sanctum and pointedly closed the door behind him, making it clear to Pinkney that his presence was neither needed nor welcome.

Chase got up from behind his desk and gave his old friend a hearty handshake and a clap on the shoulder. He was a tall man with a ruddy complexion and close cropped red hair, still as trim as ever after nineteen years in the Senate. He and Comeford had been elected to the Senate in the same year, the Vice President from Florida. Seven years ago Chase had made his bid for the White House and come up short. The nominee, needing Florida's electoral votes, tapped Comeford. Through it all, the two men had remained fast friends. Each had the other's back.

After Chase broke out the scotch, he and the Vice President settled into the plush sofa and silently toasted each other.

"Okay, Wendell, let's have it. I can hear it in your voice. What's going on?" Chase asked.

Comeford shook his head. "That's just it. I don't know." He briefly described his meeting earlier in the Oval Office. "This internet business, it is totally insane. The President is infuriating the nation, almost as if he has a death wish. But he's smarter than that. There's something else brewing, something they're keeping from me. So I'm asking you, Fletch, what do you know, if anything?"

Chase shook his head. "I don't know any more than you do," he said. "Oh, I've heard some pretty bizarre rumors, like that terrorist who was supposed to have bombed Santa Veronica. Not him, say the Israelis, and they can prove it. And this damn business with the Amtrak attacks. I want to hold hearings, find out just how many people at Homeland Security have their heads up their asses. But I'm getting stonewalled. No information available. They're collecting data. Maybe in a week they'll have something for me." He shook his head. "Arabs. I thought we were done with all that."

"So did I," Comeford said.

Chase sipped at his scotch and looked pensively out his window to the Washington Monument in the distance. "There is one thing." He paused for a moment. "Friedman called me this morning, told me that two of the big Army bases in his state had just cancelled all leaves and passes until further notice. Wanted to know if I knew anything about it. Of course, I don't. You?"

Comeford shook his head. "News to me."

Chase asked, "Any ideas?"

"No. Unless..." He paused, mulling it. "All that rancor and dissension out there. Maybe they're worried about street riots."

"Maybe," Chase agreed. "But you don't use the United States Army to quell street riots. Posse comitatus. Regular army cannot be used in a civilian situation except by direct order of the President."

The Vice President frowned, then downed the rest of his drink and slowly settled back into the sofa, a very troubled man.

Ken glanced at his watch.

"It's almost noon. There's a park up there. I'm going to pull in."

Brian nodded and sat up straighter. He'd been nodding off and now his mouth felt dry. He uncapped his water bottle and took a deep swig. I've stablized, he thought. No better, but also no worse. He'd checked himself in the mirror at the last rest stop where they'd picked up provisions. No further redness, no new blisters. Was it a good sign? He didn't know. Did he care? He wasn't sure. Two days had gone by and he hadn't dreamed of Marnie. Where had she gone? He missed her.

The park was enclosed by a chain link fence. Attached to the gate was an official notice. "Closed by order of the Sheriff's Department blah,blah blah.." Inside the fence were a dozen or so boys who either couldn't read or disliked signs. They were playing baseball on the grungy, mostly dirt field. There was a lot of chatter, a lot of yelling and a lot of fun. The game halted in mid-play as the boys eyed the interlopers but when Ken and Brian got out of the car, waved at them with a smile and lazily stretched their legs, they went back to playing.

Ken had prearranged with Heather for Superintendent Keith Sunderson to be at his desk at precisely 1:00 Eastern time. He punched in the number Heather had given him. After several misfires, he heard the ring on the other end. Leaving Ken to talk to the Mountie, Brian wandered over to the fence to watch the game.

Memories came flooding back. Mark in his first "real" game following T-Ball, standing ferociously at the plate and then ducking back five feet when the first ball was pitched. And Marnie, sitting next to Brian with Melissa in her lap, rooting on her son and screaming invectives in German at the umpire whenever he made a questionable call. Mark struck out that first at bat but the second time around, he gritted his teeth, stood his ground and lined one straight at the pitcher nearly taking his head off. Mark was like that. Proud and stubborn. You couldn't intimidate him for long. Brian smiled wryly to himself. Where had the years gone? How had he lost him? A son. A son of whom he was very proud but who he no longer knew.

Brian felt a tap on his shoulder. "Let's go," Ken said.

On the way back to the car Ken filled him in. "Sunderson says he can help us. Heather told him what was on the tape. He couldn't believe it. He says he'll get us across one way or another."

"What about the crossing at Lost River State Forest?"

"The one Mattie Rice mentioned? He's heard of it, but he's never been there. He's checking it out. He's also trying to find how to contact Hugo Wheeler."

Brian grinned. "Great!"

Ken shrugged. "Maybe not. Nobody's had much luck with that. Wheeler's pretty paranoid and who can blame him? Twice they got close enough to kill him. We'll just have to see."

They got back in the car and drove off, heading north

The intercom at Marcuse's desk buzzed. He flipped the switch. "Yes?"

"Mr. Pinkney for you on the first line, sir."

Marcuse was puzzled. "I don't know any Pinkney."

"He says he's Senator Chase's AA, sir."

"Put him through," Marcuse said. "Wait! Did he give you a first name?"

"Wallace, sir."

Marcuse picked up the receiver and acknowledged his caller expansively. "Wallace, it's good to hear from you in person. My people say you're an excellent man to deal with."

"Why, uh, thank you, sir."

"What's on your mind?"

"Well, sir," Pinkney said, "it's probably not important. Nothing really, but I thought you and the President ought to know. That is, uh---"

"Yes?" Get on with it , you twit, he thought.

"The Vice President was here a short time ago to meet with the Senator. He seemed—he seemed annoyed, sir. Angry, maybe. After about twenty minutes they both came out and I was told that they were going to see General MacAndrews."

Marcuse frowned. "I see."

"Ordinarily that wouldn't mean a great deal but Senator Chase told me to tell no one where he was going and uh--- he specifically said to not tell the White House. I know that you like getting a heads up on things like this. I hope I'm doing the right thing."

"Of course you are, Wallace, and the President and I are very grateful for your diligence. Please keep in touch if you learn more."

Marcuse hung up. Slimy little rat fink, he thought.

When the limo carrying the Vice President and Senator Chase pulled up to the gates of the Pentagon, the black unmarked car peeled off and drove the short distance to the parking lot at the Pentagon City Mall. The man behind the wheel radioed his superiors for further instructions while his partner ducked into a nearby Starbucks to pick up a couple of non-fat cappuccinos. Neither had spotted the silver-gray SUV which had pulled into a parking spot a few yards away.

As the Starbucks man approached his car, hands occupied with beverages, he was approached by a burly six-footer in a grey suit who slid in right behind him and talked quietly into his ear.

"When you reach the car put the coffee on the roof and leave your hands out where I can see them."

The Starbucks guy looked back. "What the hell----?"

"Do as you're told or it could get ugly," the man said. Meanwhile the driver had been braced by a second man from the SUV and told to keep his hands on the steering wheel.

The Starbucks guy put the coffee on the car roof. "Look, buddy---", he started to say.

"Why are you following the Vice President's limousine?"

"I don' t have to answer your----"

He stopped when the man behind him grabbed him around the

neck and jabbed a knuckle into a sensitive part of his back. He grimaced in pain. "Careful, fella. You are assaulting a federal officer," he gasped.

The knuckle was pulled back.

"ID," the other man demanded.

"Inside right jacket pocket."

Gingerly, the SUV guy reached around and extracted the man's identification. He looked at it, puzzled.

"FBI?"

The Starbucks guy turned around angrily. "That's right. FBI. And who the hell are you?"

Abashed, the other man took out his ID and flashed it. The FBI guy reacted in confusion. "CIA? What the fuck are you doing here?"

The CIA guy shook his head. "No, no. What the fuck are YOU doing here?"

At that precise moment, two black sedans with US Government plates roared to a stop a few feet away and four men in suits piled out. A heavy set black man with a shaved head strode toward them with fire in his eye.

"All right, who are you people and what's going on here?" he demanded to know.

The Starbucks FBI agent glared at him. "None of your business."

Bald dome whipped out his ID and waved it around. "Special Agent Marvin Lewis, U.S. Secret Service, and it damn well IS my business. So I repeat, who the hell are you people and why the fuck are you following my Vice President?"

Lee Fitzpatrick strode quickly down the corridor, then turned into the waiting room where the Vice President and Senator Chase were patiently waiting.

"Mr. Vice President. Senator Chase. My apologies, gentlemen. I was just informed that you were here."

"No apology necessary, Colonel---" Checking Lee's name tag. "----Colonel Fitzpatrick."

"If we had been told you were coming, sir----", Lee said.

"The Senator and I preferred to arrive unannounced," Comeford said, then smiled. "You'd be surprised how many times people seem to disappear unexpectedly when they've been given prior warning. At least that was my experience in the Senate. We're here to see General MacAndrews."

Lee shrugged helplessly. "I'm sorry, sir, but the General's out of town, attending a testimonial dinner for the retiring base commander at Ft. Bragg."

Comeford and Chase exchanged a look.

"Perhaps there's something I can help you with." Lee offered.

Comeford nodded. "Let's go to your office, Colonel".

Once they were settled in Lee's office, Comeford got right to the point. "We've been told of some irregular things happening at some of our military bases. Perhaps all of them. Fletch, why don't you fill the Colonel in."

Senator Chase repeated what he had been told by his colleague, Senator Friedman. Lee listened intently. None of this was news to him. In fact, he had instigated the no-pass, no-leave policy with MacAndrews' reluctant blessing. If Bunker Hill was possibly imminent, all units had to be on standby and yet, there was no way to call for a general alert. That would have raised all sorts of unanswerable questions. Stealth was the only reasonable course of action. Lee studied the Vice President, wondering just how much he knew about the President's plan. It was common knowledge that Comeford was not a member of the "team" and that only Florida's electoral votes had brought him into the administration, not his political persuasion. He wondered how much he should reveal to the Vice President and the Senate leader, if anything. He decided on nothing. He'd leave the military two-step to MacAndrews .

When Chase had finished, Lee held his hands up helplessly. "I really don't know what to say, Senator. There's been no directive from this office. However, I will say that many of the senior officers in all branches of the military are concerned about the national unrest and posse comitatus not withstanding, they might feel better with their units intact. Just as a precaution."

Comeford stared him down. "And nothing more than that, Colonel?"

"Not that I know of, sir," Lee lied.

Comeford nodded, not sure he believed him.

Lee met his gaze without flinching. There was more to it. A lot more. MacAndrews knew about no-pass, no-leave. What he didn't know was that his trusted aide had been informally querying base commanders, ranking admirals, top Air Force brass and the Marine Commandant with vaguely couched hypothetical scenarios. To a man they said they would obey any order given to them by General MacAndrews, an officer they both admired and trusted. Lee wondered just how far that trust and admiration would go when he implemented the President's bizarre plan to establish martial law.

CHAPTER FIFTEEN

The traffic had slowed considerably once they got within sight of the Minneapolis city limits. As they passed Richfield on the way to downtown Minneapolis, they slowed to an agonizing crawl, even though it was not yet rush hour. Heading north on 35, the highway had forked into East and West and Ken opted to go with west. Neither option looked inviting and there seemed to be no beltway to circumnavigate the sprawling city. At 2:05 they crossed the Mississippi into St. Paul, eyes ever alert for the 35W signs. The last thing they needed was to get lost on the surface streets of Minnesota's capitol.

A sign indicated a hard left up ahead to continue on 35W but before they could reach the intersection, the traffic stopped dead. Totally. Unmoving. Around them horns started to blare. Ken got out and craned to see what was going on. About a half mile up the highway he could see flashing lights. Accident. As if to confirm it, a whoop-whoop warning came up on their rear and an ambulance flew by on the emergency lane. Ken looked around. There was no way forward or backward. They were jammed in for the duration.

He leaned back into the car. "Looks like a fender bender up ahead. Maybe worse."

Brian got out of the car to check. Ken looked around at the nearby cars. Many of the passengers and drivers had gotten out to observe. Conversations were being initiated.

"Bri, maybe you better stay undercover," he said.

Brian was about to comply when he spotted something ahead. St. Paul Metro Police were slowly wending their way on foot past the stalled cars, checking license plates, querying drivers. At that moment, a helicopter swooshed down over the scene. Ken and Brian looked up to see the familiar green and gold markings of the Federal Security Force as the chopper flew by toward the front of the jam-up. The two men exchanged looks as Brian quickly slipped back into the passenger seat.

Ken watched the helicopter intently. It was hovering over the accident site, then suddenly it pivoted and started back along the parade of motionless cars, quickly approaching. As it neared the red Toyota it slowed. Ken could see the pilot staring down at him. A moment later the man appeared to be transmitting on his radio.

Ken leaned back into the car anxiously. "Bri, we've been spotted." Brian leaned out his window, looked up. "We've got to run for it. Now. Can you handle it?"

Quickly Brian got out of the car. "Hell.yes!"

"What about our bags?"

"Leave 'em," Brian said. "They'll just slow us down."

Ken nodded as they rapidly slithered their way through the mass of immobile cars. He stopped. "Do you have the tape?"

Brian patted the pocket of his windbreaker. "Safe and sound."

They hurried away from the logjam and ducked down a side street, looking for cover as the chopper pilot, having spotted them, slowly maneuvered above them.

"Central," the pilot said into his mic. "I have subjects in view. They have abandoned the car and are on foot."

"Location?"

"35W about a half mile east of St. Anthony Boulevard."

"How many down there, Bobby?"

"Two. Looks like Everett and Bannister. I don't see Shipley."

"Keep subjects in view. Backup is on the way."

"Roger that," the pilot said, moving slowly forward.

Below Brian and Ken were hurrying along the surface streets, still exposed, looking for some kind of cover. Ken looked ahead. "There's a shopping mall up there, Bri. We're target practice here. We've got to get to those stores before this neighborhood is crawling with FSF."

"Don't worry about me," Brian replied, trying not to sound winded. His breathing was already labored and he knew he had little stamina but he couldn't stop. They hadn't come all this way just to have it end at gunpoint in some non-descript back alley in St. Paul, Minnesota.

The pilot started to hover lower, turning when they turned, and so intent was he on his quarry that he failed to notice the news chopper from St. Paul's one remaining television outlet coming up on his right side. At the last moment, he saw the danger out of the corner of his eye and he yanked back on the controls going into a steep climb, all the time cursing out the damned fool who had almost killed them both.

He screamed into his mic. "Central, I've got some brain dead asshole from a TV station up here trying to kill me. Get that son of a bitch outta here!"

"We copy that, Bobby," came the reply.

Bobby levelled off and then circled back toward his prey. He scanned the streets and alleys below. They were gone.

Just inside the west entrance to the Roseville Shopping Center, Brian leaned against the Macy's wall, trying to catch his breath. Ken put his hand on his friend's shoulder. "You okay?"

"I'll make it," Brian gasped, his chest heaving. Nausea threatened to engulf him.

He looked around. Midday. The mall should have been alive with activity but few shoppers were visible. Was it the economy or the internet shutdown or both? In a weird way he felt as if he were part of a science fiction movie called, for want of a better title, 'The Day After Disaster'.

Unsteadily he reached into his pocket for a potassium iodide tablet , then moved to a nearby drinking fountain, downing the pill. As he did he noticed a pinkish tinge to the water in the white ceramic basin. He reached in his pocket and took out a Kleenex. He spit into it. His sputum was red. Clearly worried, he tossed the Kleenex away. He'd been taking the pills often, more often than he knew he should, but the hope they provided was what kept him going. Were they losing their effectiveness? Was he starting to go downhill? Whatever his concerns, he was determined to keep them to himself.

Brian looked at Ken with a wry smile. "Okay, partner," he said. "What's your Plan B because I know sure as hell you don't have a Plan A."

Ken laughed. "Not even a B but I could eke out a C."

"I'm game for any of your pea-brained ideas," Brian said, "since we don't have a car, the FSF is closing in and I need to take a leak really bad."

Ken nodded, looking around. He crossed to a nearby mall directory and put his finger on the YOU ARE HERE star. "Okay, here's the men's room here and here's a TTD phone bank so while you are expelling your morning coffee, I'm going to call Rush City and pray---pray very hard--- that Mattie Rice was able to get through to those people."

Brian nodded thoughtfully."Good plan. Almost an A."

"And then you and I have to do some shopping."

• • •

214

Harriet Wayne was in the kitchen of her Rush City home preparing meat loaf for the evening meal. Meat loaf used to be a favorite of her son and daughter in law and Little Sam but once they started having it three times a week, it had lost much of its luster. But with steak at $28 a pound and even chicken only pennies less, there weren't a lot of healthy, hearty meals she could come up with on her limited budget. Once a raving beauty, age and gravity had taken it's toll but her face was still warm and kindly and her chocolate skin was as smooth and unblemished as ever. Outwardly jolly and apparently unconcerned with what was going on in the world around her, that facade hid a steely resolve and a keen intelligence that few knew she had.

The phone rang. She removed her hands from the mixing bowl and wiped them on a towel. She answered the phone.

"Hello," she said cheerily.

There was a moment's silence and then a man's voice. "Mrs. Wayne?"

"This is Harriet Wayne. Who is this?"

" Harriet, I'm calling on behalf of old friends who were supposed to drop in on you today."

"Is that so?" she asked warily.

"Yes. Unfortunately they ran into traffic problems in St. Paul and they're not going to be able to make it without assistance."

"I see. Well, sir, you know I would like to help you but I am in the middle of fixing dinner for my family and, oh dear, I just can't make up my mind what side dish to have with the meat loaf. Would you have any thoughts about that?"

There was a long pause.

"Rice. I would definitely have rice, Mrs. Wayne."

"Uh-huh. Just what I was thinking. Where are you?"

"Macy's at the Roseville Mall. We were in a traffic tie up and spotted by an FSF helicopter. It won't be long before they're all over the area."

"And you're right in the middle of the first place they'll look. Now listen to me. About three blocks north of the mall is Northwestern College. You'll have to walk it. There's no other way. When you get there go to the Nazareth Chapel and wait inside. Someone will come to get you within the hour."

Ken nodded. "Northwestern College. Nazareth Chapel. We'll be there."

"If you're not, we'll assume you've been caught. We won't wait around."

"Understood."

She hung up pensively. Month after month, they kept coming. Afraid and desperate like yesteryear's immigrants. Yearning to breathe free. Mattie Rice said these people were special. She hoped so. Every day brought her closer to the moment when she would be caught. And she had no illusions. That moment would come.

Peter Toussaint had left FBI headquarters somewhat earlier than usual at the request of Congressman Douglas Chan of Hawaii, not only one of his favorite people, but also the ranking minority member on the powerful House Judiciary Committee. Chan had recommended an out of the way Asian restaurant, seldom if ever patronized by Washington's power elite. That meant this was an important "informal" meeting and not for general consumption.

Toussaint found Chan in a small alcove at the rear of the restaurant, safe from prying eyes. He was digging into a puu-puu platter and sipping a nauseous looking beverage from an elaborate glass with an umbrella jutting from it. Chan smiled and rose momentarily as his friend slipped into the seat opposite him.

"You are very prompt, Peter, but you must forgive me. A

committee meeting ran through my usual lunch hour and I was starving. Have a satay." He pushed the plate out into the middle of the table.

Toussaint shook his head and eyed Chan's drink with deep suspicion. "I was warned by my father never to drink anything blue in color. It might be anti-freeze. What IS that thing?"

Chan smiled. "Diamondhead Delight. Gin, rum, pineapple juice and Navy Blue dye with plenty of chopped ice. I'll order you one."

Chan was about to signal the waiter when Toussaint waved him off. "Nothing," he said. "I'm driving."

"As I requested. Excellent." Chan said.

"Okay, Douglas, now I'm here. What's this cloak and dagger all about?"

At that moment, a figure appeared in the entrance to the alcove. Toussaint looked up in surprise to see Leonard Jaffee, his counterpart at the CIA.

"Leonard," he acknowledged in greeting.

"Peter," Jaffee responded.

Chan beamed. "Excellent. You two know each other. No need for me to hang around." He slid out of the booth and gestured for Jaffee to sit. "The platter is excellent. Don't let it go to waste." He started off, then reached back and rescued his Diamondhead Delight and walked off sipping it.

Toussaint smiled at Jaffee. "Somebody here got set up. I think it was me."

"Indeed it was," Jaffee smiled, grabbing for a spring roll.

A lovely Eurasian waitress approached the table with a warm smile. Would the gentlemen care to order? Toussaint shook his head. In a few minutes. In the meantime, he ordered hot tea and sat back.

"And to what do I owe the honor of this ambush?" Toussaint asked.

"Call it mutual interests."

"Such as?"

"The Vice President, for one."

Toussaint nodded. "Yes, I was curious about that. Why the CIA of all people would be shadowing the second most powerful man in the country."

"I might ask the same thing of the FBI."

The two men stared at each other for several moments. Then Jaffee said, "I think it's time one of us put our cards on the table. I'll start."

Toussaint shrugged. Be my guest, he thought. It's your party.

"What do you know about Hakim Al-Aquba?"

"I know he wasn't in California last week."

Jaffee nodded. "That's a beginning. What kind of intel have you gotten on the Amtrak wrecks?"

"Not much."

"Be more specific," Jaffee demanded.

"All right. Intel on the train bombings? Absolutely nothing which, in and of itself, is a great deal of intel."

"Then can we agree that you and I are both being frozen out in equal measure by DHS and the thugs in the FSF?"

"Your language is impolitic, Leonard," Toussaint said, "but yes, you can. Where are we going with this?"

"I got you here today, somewhat deviously, because I have to know where you stand vis-a-vis this administration." He raised a hand as Toussaint started to speak. "You needn't give me a definitive answer. I think I've figured it out. If I'm wrong about you they'll be marching me to the guillotine by the end of the week. So, my friend, have you ever heard of a military scenario called Bunker Hill?"

Toussaint looked at him blankly. "No."

Jaffee nodded. He'd thought as much.

"Then I'm going to tell you about it and I want you to listen very, very carefully."

Brian and Ken waited just inside the main doors of the Nazareth Chapel. They had covered the three long blocks from the Mall to the campus without incident, even though St.Paul Metro cruisers were flying around the area in every direction. Despite Brian's misgivings, Ken had been sure they would have nothing to worry about. And he'd been right.

It hadn't exactly been fun. Ken's new leather pants were much too tight and form fitting. The aquamarine bolero shirt was definitely not his style nor were the oversized chartreuse framed sunglasses he'd had perched on his nose. All of this had been capped off by a faux Aussie hat with a huge feather sticking from the brim. Brian had fared slightly worse. Checked capri pants, White frills and laces for a shirt. A deep shade of makeup that covered his blemishes and also made him look like a mulatto. Whitish lipstick, A frilly hat bedecked with fake tea roses. And best of all, scarlet shoes with two inch heels. Because Brian could walk only with difficulty, Ken got the honor of walking the 3 month old puppy they had purchased at the pet store. Brian carried the oversized satchel holding their real clothes.

Sashaying up the street, they had made quite a sight. Arm in arm, Ken sometimes walking, sometimes dragging the pooch, and Brian lazily swinging the satchel in a devil-may-care attitude. No one had gone near them.

The doors to the chapel opened and a young couple with a pre-school aged little girl entered and looked around reverently. The little girl's eyes fell immediately on the puppy and she ran over to pet him.

"Look, Mommy. Doggie!" she said.

"Susie, don't bother the nice man," the mother admonished.

"No bother, ma'am," Ken smiled.

The child was happily tousling the dog's fur. "What's his name?" she asked.

"Hasn't got one yet," Ken said. "What do you think it should be?"

"I don't know," she said shyly.

"Well, how about Whitey? He's sure white enough."

" I used to have a hamster named Theodore but he died," the child said.

"Then maybe we should name the puppy Theodore. What do you think about that?"

"Okay."

The door opened again and good looking young black man wearing an Anglican collar and fingering a cross dangling from a chain around his neck stepped inside. He, too, looked around somewhat reverently, his gaze falling on Brian and Ken and lingering there for just a moment. Brian and Ken shared a look with each other and looked back at the man who was approaching.

"Good afternoon, brothers," he said. "Are you here in search of divine guidance?"

Brian smiled. "Guidance, absolutely. Divine, I'm not sure. Are you here to show us the way, Reverend?"

"That I am, my brother," the preacherman said. "My car is right outside, waiting to take you to glory and salvation, emphasis on the latter. Shall we go?"

"We shall," Brian said.

As they started out, Ken walked over to the little girl's parents. "Your little girl has just named this puppy Theodore. Be a shame to split them up so quickly." He held out the leash. The parents looked at it.

"Really, we couldn't----", the mother started to say.

"I've just been called out of the country. If you don't take him, then I'll just have to abandon him."

"Oh, no---", the mother said.

"In that case," the father said, "thank you. We'll take good care of him. Susie, it looks like you've got yourself a puppy."

Susie beamed.

At precisely 5:00 p.m. EDT, the President made a short (for him) speech on all three networks. Yes, these are terrible times. The shutting down of the internet is causing hardship everywhere but it is totally necessary in the cause of national defense. Only 48 hours more and everything will be resolved. Your government is here for you. A new era is dawning. We will have peace and prosperity, that is my pledge to you. And, oh yes, God bless America.

After the camera was turned off and the lights dimmed, the President and his Chief of Staff left the small TV studio and walked down the corridor toward the real Oval Office.

Marcuse studied the President's face nervously.

"You look upset, Mr. President," Marcuse said.

"Do I?" The President gave his Chief of Staff a long hard look. "My office. Now. We need to talk."

Several minutes later, the President was seated at his desk. Marcuse sat opposite him . For Marcuse this was not a good sign. When alone he and the President usually chatted across from each other at the coffee table. Not today.

"All right, Zeb," the President said. "What's going on?"

"In what way, sir?" Marcuse said blankly.

The President's face turned cold. "Don't bullshit me. Save it for Congress. Santa Veronica. The Amtrak explosions. What do you know about them?"

Marcuse shrugged. "Well, as you know, most of the intel is still coming in and----"

The President slammed his hand down on his desk angrily and he leaned forward. He was furious. "Didn't I just tell you not to fuck with me? Do you want me to toss your bony ass out of here. I'll do it, Zeb. Friend or no friend, you're close to the edge."

"Yes, sir," Marcuse said, averting his eyes.

"There is a man in California who works for Homeland Security. Early last Sunday he and his unit were put on alert for a possible drill, unusual because drills don't normally take place on weekends. By huge coincidence the radicals attacked Santa Veronica and this man's Hazmat unit was dispatched immediately. The man couldn't believe it. He was sure the blast had just occurred within the past half hour, maybe less. How could that be, he asked himself? It made no sense. A co-worker asked the same question but he directed it to his supervisor. A day later the man was transfered to Montana."

"Mr. President, I-----"

The President ignored him. "DHS has a code of silence. Keep your mouth shut. Do your job. Despite that, this man went to his parish priest with his misgivings about what had really happened. It was not a confession and not under the seal, or so it was explained to me. The priest, upset and bewildered, went to his Senator. You know who I am talking about, Zeb. Senator Trumbull, who scares the hell out of even me, and Senator Trumbull calls me and wants to know what the hell is going on and I haven't got the fucking faintest idea. So now why don't you enlighten me. And I warn you. None of your crap. I want this straight."

Marcuse hesitated as he stared into the face of his longtime friend. Maybe he'd been wrong to keep him unaware. It gave him deniability, of course, but it was more than that. He wasn't sure the President had the backbone to agree and had he agreed, to see it through. But now, here it was, out in the open, and Marcuse knew he had no choice to lay it all bare.

"Mr. President, do you remember a conversation we had last January?"

"We've had a lot of conversations, Zeb."

"You were depressed because you were entering the last year of your Presidency and you would have to step down. And then you and I got to musing whether there was any way you could continue in office and I said to you, let me think about it."

"Yes, I think I remember---"

"And then I came to you a week later and I said I had come up with something that I thought would work. I told you it would be ugly and dirty but it would work and when you asked me what it was, I said it would be better if you didn't know. Do you remember that?"

"Yes, vaguely."

"Not vaguely, Mr. President. Do you remember?" Marcuse's tone was sharp.

The President hesitated. "Yes, I do remember. There was going to be some sort of state of emergency or something and I would be allowed to remain on because of national security. Something like that."

Marcuse smiled indulgently, as always astounded at the naivete of the man. "Yes, sir. Something like that. And you specifically told me to pursue it. No details, Zeb. Just do what has to be done." Marcuse leaned forward. "Now, Mr. President, I want you to listen very carefully because I am going to explain to you in detail exactly what that something is."

For the next twenty minutes Marcuse laid out for the President everything that had happened and everything that would happen. The President's face paled perceptibly and at times he had to look away, so dreadful were the things he was being forced to hear. Finally Marcuse finished.

The President stared at him. "So all those deaths, those people maimed and killed, you were responsible?"

Marcuse shook his head. "No, sir. WE were responsible."

The President shook his head violently. "No, no. I didn't know about it----"

"You knew, sir. You've always known deep in your heart. You're the one who wanted desperately to stay in office. Well, you are getting your wish, sir."

"But there had to be some other way----"

"There wasn't. By tomorrow, when General MacAndrews has mobilized martial law, you will be in total control. No one will be able to thwart you. One more final incident tonight will have the country begging you for protection."

The President trembled. "What incident?"

"Better that you don't know, sir."

"How many dead?"

"We're not sure. A small number. In the big picture it makes no difference. The overriding issue is to save your Presidency and carry on the good work that you have started. Only you can make that happen, Mr. President. Only you."

The President shook his head,waffling. "I'm not sure---"

Suddenly Marcuse hoisted himself out of his chair and leaned across the Presidential desk, his face only inches away from his boss's nose. He shouted angrily. "Be sure, Mr. President! Be very sure! Because if you're not, I am by God ready to walk out of here, call off everything and this November you can go back to being a nonentity in the real world of politics. Tell me now, sir. Which is it? Are you in or out?"

The President sagged back in his chair, then looked up sadly, a beaten man. "This thing tonight. Is it absolutely necessary?"

"I'm afraid it is, sir."

The President shook his head sadly. "We could act on what's already transpired."

"No, sir. We need a precipitous event of sufficient devastation to enrage the public so completely that they will put themselves in our hands without reservation."

"All right, all right," he said wearily. "Just handle it, Zeb."

Marcuse hesitated, then breathed deeply. "Is there something I can do for you, sir? Would you like me to stay?"

The President shook his head. "I'd like to be alone for a while."

"I'll see to it, Mr. President," Marcuse said as he turned and left the office.

The President sat very still for a few moments. Then he reached over to the side of his desk and picked up a copy of that day's Washington Post. He turned to the sports section, looked at it for a moment, and then tossed the paper in the wastebasket under his desk. He swiveled his chair and stared out onto the Rose Garden, lost in thought.

George Wayne, still dressed as a cleric, entered his mother's kitchen through the rear door. He was followed by his two companions. Harriet turned away from the refrigerator and eyed her new guests and their bizarre attire with equal parts of suspicion and disbelief.

"I was unaware," she said dryly, "that Hallowe'en had come early this year."

Brian approached her with a smile. "As a child, Mrs. Wayne, I was taught by my father that the safest place to hide a Christmas ornament was on the tree, out in plain sight." He put out his hand. "I'm Brian Everett and it is a pleasure to meet you."

Harriet nodded, taking in his dark complexion. "I must say, you've changed some since your television days, Mr. Everett."

"I can rectify that, ma'am , if you would just lead me to a sink and some soap and water. And quickly, please. For the past hour I've been fighting this urge to start singing like Ray Charles."

Harriet burst into laughter and jabbed a finger in the direction of the nearest bathroom. She turned to Ken. "And you, Dr. Bannister, you could use a little cleaning up yourself." She eyed his wardrobe with amusement. "Supper in about a half-hour. Properly dressed."

"Yes, ma'am," Ken said.

She looked over at her son. "And that goes for you ,too, Reverend."

"Yes, Mama," George said, tugging at his collar.

Shortly after 5:30 they sat down to eat. They were joined by George's wife, Olive, and their son, Little Sam, a five year old named for his late grandfather. Ken had been able to contact Heather using the Wayne's land line phone. His cell phone was just about dead and he had no recharger. The news was the same. Sunderson was still checking on the Lost River escape route. He had a lead on a contact who could get to Wheeler but nothing definite had been set up. Ken left the Wayne's number.

The meat loaf was so good that Brian was actually eating and enjoying it.

"Bravo, my friend," Ken said, elbowing him playfully. He looked over at Harriet. "This is the first time in days he's actually eaten anything of substance. You are one fine cook, Mrs. Wayne."

"My Grammy can cook anything," Little Sam piped up, fiddling with his succotash.

"Well, I thank you both," Harriet smiled. And then to Brian: "And just what is your prognosis, Mr. Everett?"

Brian looked up from his plate. "I really don't know, ma'am. My friend Max told me I'm never going to get better but with luck I may not get worse. I guess you could say I'm just going day to day."

"As we all are," Harriet said. "Little Sam, if I'm such a fine cook, then stop playing with those vegetables and eat them or no pie for you."

"Okay," he said glumly, shoving a forkful into his mouth.

Ken looked over at their hostess. "Mrs. Wayne---"

"I certainly would appreciate it if you would call me Harriet, Dr. Bannister," she said.

"Harriet. As in Tubman?" he asked.

She smiled. "You know your history."

"The Underground Railroad for slaves. Escape to freedom with compassionate people helping all along the way. I think I see a parallel here."

She nodded. "It needed to be done then. It needs to be done now."

"Do you ever worry about the danger?" Brian asked.

"She doesn't care about that," George said "None of us do. Not after what they did to this family."

"Hush, George. They don't need to hear about our troubles."

George shook his head. "I think they do, just so none of us here at this table forgets what this is all about."

"I'd like to know, Harriet," Brian said. "But I'll understand if you wish to drop the subject."

Harriet paused, looking off absently, lost in thought. She looked back at Brian.

"Big Sam, that was my husband. Big Sam was a surgeon. Practiced right here in Rush City for nearly twenty five years. He had a fine reputation and he was a good provider. And then a few years back these people in Washington pushed through the health care thing. He tried to stay independent but inside a year his practice dried up to practically nothing. He couldn't get hospital privileges because he wasn't in the system. He paid twice as much for supplies and equipment. He was hit with special fees for non-participation. There was a surcharge in his income tax. Finally he had to give up and join them." She paused. Her eyes started to tear up.

"Mama---", George said.

"Hush, George," she said.

"He hated it but he bit his tongue. For me and the others. Then one day an old friend was admitted. Right away Big Sam knew he needed bypass surgery. His friend wasn't that old. 56, I think. But the government people, they wouldn't authorize it, so Sam went ahead and did it anyway. The next day they fired him and a week later they took away his license to practice medicine. Never saw a man as sick at heart and there was nothing I could do to help him. He started working in an underground clinic in Rock Creek. It was a Friday, late in the day, when the Federal Security Force raided the place. They started beating people. Doctors, nurses, even the patients. Sam fought back. One of those people---" She spit the word out. "One of them slammed his rifle butt into Sam's head. He died right there on the floor."

Brian shook his head in dismay and glanced over at Ken who was equally shocked.

"The next day," Harriet continued, "the television carried the story. Sam was described as a rogue doctor, operating an illegal clinic and preying on sick and hopeless drug addicts. Did people believe it? I don't know but I do know there was no one around to call it a lie. No television, no newspaper, no one." She looked over at Brian. "So, Mr. Everett, when you ask me if I ever worry about the danger, the answer is yes. And when you ask me if that will stop me, the answer is no. May they all rot in hell!"

Little Sam piped up, wide-eyed. "Grammy, you said hell!"

CHAPTER SIXTEEN

Conrad hefted the two overnight bags onto the table and zipped them open. They had been retrieved by St. Paul Metro from the red Toyota and brought here to the Minnesota headquarters of Homeland Security. FSF did not yet have their own facility in the state. He rummaged through the bags, finding nothing extraordinary until he opened a canvas bag containing toiletries. At the bottom of the bag was a square clear plastic case holding a DVD. Fearing the worst, Conrad searched through the DHS offices looking for a TV monitor with DVD capabilities. When he found it, he slipped in the disc and hit PLAY.

What he saw sent a spasm of fear through his body. That fear did not subside when Everett started to play the tape and when it was over, Conrad, for the first time, realized the enormity of the situation he was embroiled in. He moved to a nearby desk, picked up the phone and dialed a number. A moment later he spoke into the receiver. "This is Conrad. Put Drago on the line."

At the FSF offices in St. Joseph, Hans Drago took the phone from the hand of his assistant. "This is Drago," he said.

"How are you doing with the woman and her deputy?" Conrad demanded to know.

"I've had better days," Drago replied.

To Conrad, this was not good news. FSF had no better interrogator than Hans Drago who knew every trick, every wile, and if all else failed, every way to inflict pain, even those methods that left permanent scars.

"Where do we stand?" Conrad asked.

"I spent several hours with the woman. She's a hard case, afraid of nothing, not even death. Her hatred runs very, very deep."

"Hans, we have got to know how and where Everett is planning to go across. Does she know?"

Drago responded unemotionally. "She knows."

"The deputy?"

"He also knows."

"Can you break him?"

"I think so but I'll need time."

"We don't have time. Whatever it takes."

Drago hesitated thoughtfully. "Give me an hour. I'll get back to you."

As he hung up, his assistant approached. "There's a Lieutenant Potter from the Kansas Highway Patrol outside. He wants to see Rice."

"Tell him to go back to Kansas."

"He's pretty insistent, sir."

Drago's eyes narrowed into icy slits. "Tell him to leave now or I will arrest him on federal charges of impeding a criminal investigation. If he doesn't move, cuff him and put him in the holding pen."

"Yes, sir."

"And prepare paper work on Chief Rice. First thing tomorrow morning, I want her shipped out to the facility in Brownsville."

"Yes, sir."

As the assistant hurried off, Drago walked down the corridor and entered a cold, barely furnished windowless room where Boyd

Shurling was sitting buck naked on a mattressless cot, his hands cuffed behind him. Shurling looked up at his captor, his eyes revealing no fear, only hatred. His face and shoulders were badly bruised There were visible marks on his chest where he had been tasered.

Drago stared down at him in shocked disbelief. "What the hell is this? What did they do to you?" He turned and screamed out the door. "Sergeant Nolan! Get in here!"

Almost immediately, a pudgy man in uniform hurried into the room, apprehensively. "Sir?"

Drago pointed toward Shurling. "Is this your doing?"

"Yes, sir. I was given orders to interrogate the prisoner---"

"Interrogate!" Drago roared. "Not mutilate. Uncuff this man, give him back his clothes and bring him to my office. Now!"

"Yes, sir!" Nolan gulped as Drago turned on his heel and stormed angrily from the room.

A few minutes later, Shurling was ushered into Drago's makeshift office and seated. "You are dismissed, Sergeant. Keep yourself available." His voice was harsh but since Shurling's head was bowed down, he chanced a wink at the enlisted man who stood at the door. Nolan smiled and winked back, then went out closing the door behind him.

Drago pushed a freshly opened pack of cigarettes across the table. "Help yourself," he said. Shurling just shook his head. He was quiet, unmoving, wary. "Then coffee perhaps?" Drago offered. Shurling looked up, hesitated.

"Coffee. Sure. Coffee. Thank you." He was hungry. Anything to fill his stomach.

Drago got up and poured a mug from the electric pot on top of a filing cabinet. He put it in front of Shurling. "I'm afraid we have no cream or sugar. Stores are closed. Nothing is available. My apologies." He went around the desk and sat as Shurling picked up the mug in two hands and sipped gingerly.

"My sergeant is a fool. He should have known immediately that physical discomfort would have no effect on you." He fingered a file that was sitting in front of him. "I see from your file you fought in Iraq, Deputy. Special Forces?" Shurling nodded . "And three commendations for heroism including the Bronze Star. Yes, I can understand why Sergeant Nolan and his men failed so miserably. I salute your bravery, sir. Your country owes you a great debt of gratitude." He leaned forward. "And now your country calls upon you once again to display that same sort of courage. There are traitors in our midst, Deputy. Self-serving traitors who would love nothing better than to bring this country to its knees. Men and woman who would topple the constitutionally elected government for their own special purposes. I think you know to whom I refer."

Shurling looked up, defiantly. "Yes,sir", he said. "The President, for one."

Drago stiffened but tried to mask his anger. "I was referring, as you know, to Mr. Everett and Dr. Bannister who are trying to elude capture and are headed toward the Canadian border. You would do us a great service, as well as yourself, if you would tell me where and when."

"Sorry, but I don't know."

Drago smiled. "But of course you do."

He opened the folder and took out two photographs, the ones that Shurling had clipped to the visor of his squad car. Drago pushed them forward. "Your wife Virginia. A striking looking woman. Beautiful, in fact. I'm sure you love her very much." Shurling looked up, a knot forming in his stomach. "And your girls. Alice Ann and Deborah. They take after your wife. Such happy smiles. A warm and loving family. They must give you great comfort. I would hate to see you lose them."

"You son of a bitch," Shurling seethed, ready to come across the desk.

Drago smiled. "So I ask you again, Deputy. Where and when?"

Shurling looked away, mute.

"Very well," Drago said. "Let me be more specific. Tomorrow morning, you will be transfered to a FSF correctional facility outside of Spokane, Washington, where you will be assigned a number and all traces of your actual identity will be expunged. In the highly unlikely event that someone comes looking for you, there will be no record of your existence. Your wife ,Virginia, will be shipped to a women's facility in Brownsville, Texas, under the same conditions. As for your children----" He paused for effect. "As for your children, we are in touch with thousands of childless couples throughout the country who have failed to adopt through regular channels. We are not quite so fussy. The children will be given over with a minimum of paperwork. Did I say minimum? I meant to say none and once gone, even God himself couldn't find them."

Shurling, furious, tensed to attack. Drago was ahead of him.

"And if you are intent on doing something monumentally stupid, Deputy, Sergeant Nolan is just outside the door and he is armed. It makes no difference to me if we ship you or bury you, but in any event, if you do not cooperate, your family will cease to exist."

Ken was on the kitchen phone with Keith Sunderson while Harriet and Olive cleaned up the dishes and cooking utensils. Little Sam was in the living room watching a twenty year old re-run of Scoobeydoo while George was poring over his maps in anticipation of the flight north. Brian was in the bathroom, spitting up bloody mucous. His head felt warm and he downed a couple of aspirin to combat a possible fever. He took another potassium iodide, noting that he only had six left with little chance of obtaining more. Tough it out, Everett, he said to himself. Hang in long enough to get the job done. After that it won't matter.

"I understand, Keith. The timing is critical. And please don't sir me."

Sunderson chuckled. "Sorry, sir---uh, Professor. Oh, crap. I'll just call you Doc and be done with it."

"Excellent," Ken said. "Now tell me about the Warroad International Airport."

"Well, it sounds a lot more impressive than it is, but it's no cow pasture. Four runways, a landing beacon, runway lights, an administration building but no control tower. What about your pilot? Does he know it?"

Ken looked over at George and his maps. "He's been there before," Ken said.

"Good. As soon as you land look for the signs for ground transportation. There will be a black Ford SUV parked nearby. The driver's name is Sullivan. Call him Sully. He's an old hand at this trip. He'll take you into the state forest and drive you to the spot where a narrow dirt trail feeds away from the paved road. From there you walk. It's about a three hundred meters to the border. There you will find a fence. It's about ten feet tall, chain link. You'll have to scale it. I'll be waiting on the other side with your wife and a couple of my men."

"What about an alarm system?" Ken asked.

"The only one is on our side. Pressure plates that set off lights and signal a nearby barracks. I've had them disabled for tonight. On your side, well, Doc. I really don't think your government gives a damn about who leaves."

"Except for Brian and me, of course," Ken said wryly.

"Of course," Sunderson echoed. "Now as to the time, try to make it as close to midnight as possible. It's about forty minutes from the airport to the crossing so figure accordingly. Ten or fifteen minutes early or late won't make much difference but you Yanks, despite what I said, do have patrols in the forest and the longer we remain exposed, even on our side of the fence, the less chance for success."

"I understand," Ken said. "What about Wheeler?"

"We go straight from the rendezvous to meet his man who will check you out. Wheeler knows who Brian is and respects him, but he's still being cautious."

"Okay, then," Ken said. Then he added facetiously, "Oh, one thing. Brian said to tell you that our passports were lost with our luggage. Will that present a problem?"

Sunderson laughed. "Only if we catch you trying to smuggle in American beer. That we frown on. As we say in Quebec, bon chance."

"Thanks, Keith. I'm looking forward to seeing you again."

Ken hung up and turned to George. "How are we coming along?"

"Just about set," George said. "A few more minutes and I'll be ready when you are."

"We need to land at Warroad no later than eleven."

George glanced at his watch. "Not a problem," he said.

The staff car that had picked up General MacAndrews at Andrews Air Force Base deposited him at his front door shortly after 7:30. At his request, the testimonial at Ft. Bragg has been moved up two hours and considerably shortened. There was just too damned much going on in Washington that demanded his attention.

As he stepped into the living room, he found Lee Fitzpatrick in polite conversation with his wife. He had called his aide earlier and ordered his appearance, unnerved and irritated by some of the things that he had learned. He embraced his wife fondly and acknowledged Fitzpatrick.

"My study, Lee."

"Yes, sir," Fitzpatrick said, leaving the room. He had been anticipating this moment. Dreading it. Nothing left to do but put it all out in the open.

"Can I bring you some coffee, David?" Grace asked.

235

"No, thank you, dear," he said.

"I made a chocolate cake this afternoon."

"Thank you, no, Grace. Lee and I have a lot to discuss. If anyone calls, I'm unavailable."

She laughed. "Even for the President?"

He looked at her straight in the eye unsmiling. "Unavailable," he said, softly but firmly. Her smile faded.

"As you wish, David," she said and she left the room.

MacAndrews found Fitzpatrick staring at an old black and white photo on the wall. A 23 year old infantry lieutenant who had graduated the year before from The Point and now, no longer wet behind the ears, was a grizzled veteran of the Viet Nam conflict. He was sitting on the fender of a jeep,holding an M16, surrounded by eight grinning enlisted men in various states of dress and undress. Second Lieutenant MacAndrews was grinning,too. They were all alive. That had to count for something.

"I can tell you all of their names," MacAndrews said, "and where they came from and which two didn't make it, one of them saving my life."

"It must have been hell, sir," Fitzpatrick said.

"It's all hell, Lee. Always has been, always will be."

MacAndrews crossed to the breakfront, extracted two glasses and a bottle of scotch. He sat down at his desk and half-filled both glasses. He slid one across the desk to Fitzpatrick and leaned back in his chair.

"All right, let's hear it."

Lee hesitated, took a sip of his drink and set it down on a convenient coaster. "I've been contacting base commanders throughout the country, informally feeling them out on the ramifications of Bunker Hill, should that order be given."

"And on whose authority have you made these contacts?"

"My own, sir," Lee replied.

"And did it occur to you that I ought to be consulted on these so-called informal queries?"

"Yes, sir, and I decided against it."

"May I ask why?" said MacAndrews.

"Yes, sir. If the President initiates Bunker Hill—and that is still a big if—if he does, we will be taking a step never before taken in this country and it will have a profound effect on how the citizenry views the military and even how we view ourselves. It was my feeling, sir, that the base commanders and other key people from every branch would be more likely to give me a more honest answer than they would you."

"I see," MacAndrews said quietly.

"No disrespect, sir, but I was trying to avoid the politics of the situation, military protocol and all that."

MacAndrews nodded. "Military protocol."

"Yes, sir. Your commanding officer says jump, you jump without reservation. It's instinctive. But this situation goes deeper than that. I believed, and still do, that we need to know the guts of a man to know how he is going to react if this thing ever comes to pass."

Again, MacAndrews nodded thoughtfully. "A moment ago you mentioned politics. Are you a political man, Lee?"

"I never have been, sir," Lee responded.

"That's not an answer."

Lee paused, then picked up his glass and took another swallow. "I believe in the Constitution, General. I took an oath to protect and defend it. When I see those in power ignoring its basis tenets, trashing everything it stands for, slowly but surely taking away the liberties that the Constitution guarantees to every man, woman and child in this country, then yes, I guess you could say I'm political."

"And our electoral process, would you say that that, too, was a part of the Constitution?"

"Of course, sir."

"Then what am I to gather, Lee? That you find yourself qualified to pick and choose among the various articles, defending those you agree with and subverting those you don't?"

"That was not and is not my intention , sir---"

"Isn't it?" MacAndrews said harshly, raising his voice for the first time. "There are those who would characterize your actions as treasonous."

Lee shook his head, fighting back. "Sir, these men you command, you have no idea the respect they hold you in. They would follow you anywhere----"

"That's enough, Colonel!" MacAndrews roared. "There is a reason why the military cannot, not ever, become embroiled in the nation's politics. We hold the sword and a mighty sword it is. It cannot be wielded unilaterally and its control must stay in the hands of the civilians. That's what your Constitution says. Respect it. Abide by it."

"Yes, sir. My apologies, sir. You will have my resignation on your desk first thing tomorrow." He started to rise. MacAndrews waved him back into his seat.

"Oh, sit down. I don't want your resignation, Lee. I depend on you too much. All right, you exceeded your authority. We've all done that. And you did it for what you believed were good and sufficient reasons. They weren't , but it's not a firing offense. Next time you want to go off half-cocked, talk to me first. I might surprise you." He raised his glass in a salute and drank.

"Yes, sir," Lee said.

MacAndrews looked woefully at the half empty bottle of scotch. "If my wife were out of town, I would suggest that the two of us get stinking drunk. But-----. He shrugged.

"Maybe some other time, General," Lee said.

MacAndrews nodded. "To another time."

They finished off their glasses.

• • •

It was a few minutes past seven. Drizzle was falling from the sky. Not rain but just enough moisture to slick down the roads. George turned his Izusu Rodeo into the airport access road and sped quickly toward the tie-down area for the city's private planes. The Rush City regional airport was small like the town in which it was located but it served a purpose. In the absence of decent rail service and a paucity of reliable bus lines, airport to airport was often the quickest and easiest way to get anywhere in this part of the country.

George pulled up a few yards from a 1981 Cessna 182R. "That's her. Let's go."

The men piled out of the car and hurried to the plane. They carried no luggage, just the clothes on their back. If they made it across, plenty of time to shop. If they didn't it wouldn't make any difference.

"What's the weather like ahead?" Ken asked as they hopped into the plane.

"Haven't a clue." George said. "With the internet down, no information is coming through. I've got a stormscope but it has limited range. If it shows bad weather, we'll be in it before we can do much about it."

"Sounds good to me, Brian. How about you?" Ken smiled.

"Couldn't be more thrilled", Brian said as they strapped themselves into the two seats at back of the cockpit.

"Well, if we don't run into anything severe, we should be okay. I figure we have about a half hour leeway if we hit a glitch," George told them.

George checked the sock for wind direction, then fired up the engine and taxied onto Runway 16. He had not filed a flight plan because after 3:30 there was no one around to file it with. Just as well. George disliked lying to friends. At the far end of the runway he pivoted the plane and then giving it full throttle into the wind , sped forward, lifting off within a hundred yards of the far end. The drizzle had not abated but the prop wash was keeping the windshield clear. Because of the dark clouds, visibility was not what it could have been.

George turned to his passengers, speaking loudly enough to be heard over the sound of the engine. "I forgot to ask. Either of you fellas prone to airsickness?" When they shook their heads, he said, "Hope you're right. We're going to be hedgehopping all the way, staying low beneath the radar. Nobody's supposed to be in the air right now."

"No problem," Brian said, looking out the window as the tops of some pine trees passed by some twenty feet below.

He looked over at Ken who, despite his protestations, was starting to look as green as those tree tops.

CHAPTER SEVENTEEN

The President leaned back in his chair and lit up a cigarette, even though he already had one burning in the crystal ashtray on his desk. He glanced impatiently at the clock on the wall. 9:13. This all should have been resolved an hour ago. The delay was unconscionable. He neglected to remind himself that shutting down of the internet was the key reason nothing was happening. Nicholas Lapp, the deputy director of the Federal Security Force, was sitting at the coffee table, phone at his side, tapping his foot nervously while he continued to imbibe massive amounts of black coffee. Marcuse was sitting opposite him, calmly working on the Times crossword puzzle. The room was deathly quiet.

The clock moved to 9:14. The President turned his attention back to Lapp for the fourth time in the past ten minutes. "What's the holdup, Nick?" he said. "Why aren't we hearing anything?"

"It's complicated, sir. Without confirmation on the wire transfer of the funds they won't act," Lapp said.

By now the President had come to terms with reality. What had come before was heinous. What was to come was in many ways worse. But damn it, this was his Presidency at stake and he was damned if they were going to take it from him. Zeb Marcuse was right. Either they saw this through successfully or they were doomed.

There was no way back if the truth came to light.

The President shook his head in annoyance. "We should have given them cash."

"Ten million in old small denomination bills, that's a little un-wieldy , sir", Lapp said. "And I'm not sure how we could gather that much together without arousing suspicion."

The President just glared at him. Before he could say anything, his intercom buzzed. The President flipped a button. "I said I didn't want to be disturbed."

"Yes,sir," came a woman's voice, "but it's the Vice President. He's standing right here at my desk."

Marcuse looked up sharply from his puzzle. Lapp raised his eyes to heaven. The President hesitated only momentarily. "Send him in," he said.

Lapp looked frantic. "We can't have him here----!"

"He won't be," the President said, overriding him. "Leave him to me."

The door opened. Wendell Comeford was ushered in. The Vice President looked around. "I was told there was a party going on here. Looks more like a wake."

The President nodded. "We're waiting for some intel on the Am-trak derailments, Wendell. Just routine stuff. Nothing you really have to be concerned about."

Comeford glared at him. "Don't you think, Mr. President, since I am very likely going to be sitting in that chair come next January that you might extend me the courtesy of deciding for myself what's important and what isn't?"

The President got up and came around the desk. "Wendell, please. My apologies. We've all been on edge and remiss in some of our ac-tions. I know you've been busy all day, keeping up your contacts with Senator Clark and the Joint Chiefs." He paused. Comeford didn't take the bait. The President continued, taking his Vice President by the elbow and leading him toward the door. "Why don't you go back to the residence? We'll let you know if you're needed."

Comeford angrily shrugged off the President's grip. "If I'm needed. Well, thank you but I'm well aware of when I'm needed. Ribbon cuttings. A funeral for some despotic tin soldier in central Africa. A fact finding mission among the volcanoes on Iceland."

Marcuse rose, coming to the defense of his President. "Now look, Wendell----"

Comeford turned on him angrily. "No, you look----". He stopped, looked from one to the other. "I almost called you 'errand boy', Zeb, but lately I've been wondering which of you actually runs the errands."

"That is treasonous!" Marcuse fumed.

"No," Comeford replied, "that's insulting. But probably accurate. Look, I didn't come here this evening to get into a pissing contest. I came to ask a question. Something General MacAndrews' aide asked me this afternoon, just in passing, and I didn't have an answer. Embarrassing, eh? Vice President of the United States and I didn't have an answer. So now I'm going to ask you. All three of you and particularly you, Mr. Lapp. After the train was derailed outside of Longview, Texas, why wasn't the rail system immediately shut down as a precaution?" He looked from one to another.

The President stood mute, looking toward Marcuse for help. Marcuse looked to Lapp. Lapp cleared his throat. "We didn't see the need. Our best information indicated this would be an isolated incident----"

"Oh, so you knew about it in advance," Comeford charged.

"Of course not. I mean, there had been chatter but nothing specific about a time or a place. We hear these things all the time. Seldom do they amount to much."

"Any reason why the FBI wouldn't have heard the same chatter? Because they didn't. I talked to Toussaint personally. These attacks came out of the blue."

Lapp sneered. "Yes, well I would expect the FBI Director to protect his people. It's a skill he's honed very well."

Comeford stepped toward Lapp. "But you had heard the chatter. You had a clue and what did you do about it?"

Lapp responded in kind. "What did you expect me to do, shut down the whole rail system on a rumor? Anyway, that's not my department, that's a call for Homeland Security."

"Oh, yes, FSF and DHS, the devil's disciples, joined at the hip."

Lapp became even angrier. "Don't tell me how to do my job, Mr. Vice President." He spat out the word "Vice" as if it were a diseased housefly that had suddenly flown into his mouth.

"Stop it! The both of you!" Marcuse screamed, startling not only the combatants but the President as well. There was an awful silence and in that silence a phone rang. Lapp looked toward the coffee table, then moved quickly to get his phone.

"Yes?" he said anxiously. He listened, then looked toward the President helplessly, nodding.

The President, understanding that this was the call they had been waiting for, once again took Comeford by the arm and steered him to the door.

"Time for us all to calm down, Wendell. Tomorrow we'll all be able to think more clearly. Now go home and get some sleep."

At the door, the Vice President again shook off the President's grip. "I'm tired of playing good little soldier. Something's going on around here. Something rotten. I don't know what but I'm going to find out. If it costs me the nomination next month, then so be it. Be careful, Mr. President. Be very careful." With that, he walked out the door, closing it behind him.

The President, visibly shaken, looked over at his Chief of Staff and then to Lapp who was in conversation on the phone.

"Yes, yes. I understand. Execute immediately. Tonight must be the night and time is wasting. Yes, I'll be here. Call me when it's done." Lapp turned to the others. "The money went through. Everything's in motion."

Fighting the wind and the ever-strengthening rain, the little Cessna plowed ahead, clawing at the turbulence as it tried to maintain speed and attitude. As the plane bucked and yawed, George's grip on the W shaped yoke became lighter and lighter, guiding it with nothing more than four fingers. A less experienced pilot might have had the controls in a death grip but George knew better than to strangle the yoke. In weather like this he abided by a tried and true maxim: don't just do something, sit there. His eyes peered into the darkness ahead. Despite his outwardly calm demeanor, he was terrified. Suddenly he felt a tree top brush against the bottom of the fuselage, not enough to do damage but enough to cause him to pull back on the controls.

"We're going up!" he shouted.

"What about the radar?" Ken shouted back.

"Screw the radar! This is going to get us killed!"

"Can you get above it?"

George looked at the stormscope. "I don't think so but if we keep low, sooner or later we're going to plow into something."

The little plane reached for the heavens, shuddering and weaving, fighting to keep stabilized.

"How far behind are we?" Ken asked loudly leaning in close.

George checked his watch. "We're still okay but we're losing our cushion!"

"Any idea where we are?"

"I can guess," he said checking the instrument panel. "Maybe coming up on Leech Lake but without a visual, I can't be sure." He glanced back over his shoulder. "How's Mr. Everett doing?"

"Asleep," Ken said. "He's exhausted."

Suddenly they hit an air pocket. The plane dropped ten feet before it righted itself.

"He'd have to be to sleep through this," George said.

Although his friends would argue the point, Brian was not on the little plane struggling to make its way to Warroad. He was relaxing on a leather covered seat in a sailboat on Cape Cod Bay, a drink in one hand, the tiller in the other. Marnie was digging around in the picnic basket looking for the jar of pickles she'd brought along to spice up the sandwiches she'd prepared that morning. Bavarian ham and knockwurst, potato salad ---German style, of course---grapes and a half dozen chocolate chip cookies. To drink: Bock beer. The tastes and smells of Oktoberfest running rampant in the middle of May. Triumphantly she extracted the pickles from the basket, popped the lid and took a loud crunchy bite, grinning as she did so. Then she picked up a cookie and started to eat that as well, alternating bites. Brian shook his head. What are you doing? You're going to get sick eating like that. She smiled. Haven't you noticed? I've been getting sick every morning for the past week or maybe you think that's just because I'm a lousy cook. The smile never left her face. Brian stared at her for a moment and then he, too, began to smile. He tossed his drink overboard, let go of the tiller, and scuttled to her side, taking her in his arms and holding he as close and his tightly as he dared. Salty tears ran down his cheek.

Another air pocket jostled the plane violently. Brian did not notice.

Conrad and Johnson hurried from the elevator, through the street level doors and jumped into the FSF staff car that was waiting at curbside. "Holman Field!" Conrad shouted at the driver. The car sped away, horn blaring at any civilian vehicle that had the temerity to slow its progress.

Conrad could feel his heart pumping wildly. At least 120 a minute, he figured. Drago had come through and a lot faster than Conrad had any right to expect.

"Lost River State Forest," Drago had informed him. "A dirt trail off the paved road, a few miles east of the border crossing at Pinecreek. He doesn't know when but probably tonight, if they haven't already crossed. He says they were in a hell of a hurry."

"I'll bet they were. How hard did you go at him?"

Drago chuckled, somewhat proudly. "I never laid a glove on him."

Conrad frowned. "Then how can you be sure----?"

"I threatened to ship his little girls to a family of perverts in East Jesus, Wyoming. Five minutes later he was crying like a baby. He knows if he lied it's all over for him, his wife and the kids. He gave it to me straight."

The car flew across the bridge that spanned the Mississippi. Several minutes later, it skidded to a halt next to a hangar at the west end of the field. Conrad and Johnson jumped out, hurrying through the soft drizzle that had just started to fall a few minutes before. A grizzled looking pilot with the name "Bob" stenciled on his jacket, was standing next to a 2004 Citation CJ2 painted in the green and gold of the Federal Security Force. Nearby a younger man was carefully giving the plane a last minute inspection.

"I'm Colonel Conrad, this is Lieutenant Johnson. Are we ready to go?" Conrad demanded.

"We're not going anywhere, mister. Not in this weather," the man called Bob said laconically.

"Weather? Its drizzle, for God's sakes," Conrad replied.

Bob pointed north. "Not out there."

"Now, look----"

"No, you look. We've got information. Limited information. Two phone calls I made to buddies up along the line who stuck their faces out the window and told me what the skies were like. We call that low-tech analysis. We'd be using hi-tech but the assholes in Washington who shut down the internet fucked up all kinds of electronics everywhere in the country. Bottom line? Lousy weather. I stay put."

Conrad moved to him threateningly. As he did the young man dropped what he was doing and moved closer to listen. "Mister, I am ordering you to fly this plane."

Bob smirked. "Mister, I don't work for you and I'm ordering you to get your nose out of my face."

"You're not FSF?" Conrad asked, puzzled.

Bob shook his head. "You're nearest pilot is in Duluth and he can't get out."

Conrad hesitated. "How much were they going to pay you?"

"Twenty-five hundred."

"I'll make it five."

"I said no!"

"Ten!"

Bob shook his head. "Mister, you could make it fifty and the answer's the same. I plan on waking up tomorrow in a warm bed."

The younger man butted in. "I'll do it. For ten, I'll do it."

Bob glared at him. "Timmy, no!"

Conrad looked at the kid. "Can you fly that thing?"

The kid nodded. "I'm the co-pilot. I can fly it."

Bob was furious. "Don't be crazy. You'll get yourself killed out there!"

"Okay for you to say, Bob. You got money put away. Me and Mom, we haven't seen that kind of money in a couple of years. Hell, we got no money at all, you know that."

Bob looked at his young friend grimly. "Tim, you have no idea what's out there."

"It's a good plane."

"Sure. And the instruments won't be worth shit. You might not be able to see---."

Tim looked at Conrad. "Ten thousand. In cash. Now."

Conrad started to shake his head. "Cash? I'm sorry, I'm not able to-----."

"Then get yourself another pilot," Tim interrupted , starting to walk away.

"Wait!" Conrad called out. He turned to Johnson. "Back at headquarters, they have emergency funds in the safe. Go get it and hurry!"

Johnson started off.

"Make it twenty," Bob said. "Ten each".

Conrad nodded with a smile. "Ten each."

Bob turned to Timmy and smiled. "Hell, kid, when we're going down, you're going to need somebody to hang onto."

Forty minutes later, the plane lifted off. In the interim, two envelopes containing ten thousand dollars each had been given to the airport administrator to hold until their return. Or given to their nearest loved one in case they didn't.

The ball buzzed in, high and hard. Felipe Machado, ducked his head back a few inches. The umpire growled something that sounded like "grulk" and raised his right fist. Strike two. Machado glared at him and stepped out of the box. He looked down to the third base coach. Hit away. What else with two out and no one on. He looked around the stadium at the sea of empty seats. Machado was used to seeing things like this in Tampa but this was Fenway Park. The Red Sox filled the seats. Always had. Tonight there might be four thousand, no more. Okay, it was a nothing game and yes, the cheapest seats had ballooned to $85 but still, this was America and baseball was America's game. Or was it? Maybe there was no America's game any more. People had to eat. Kids had to be clothed. Maybe the time had come when Joe Six Pack was no longer a part of the picture. Maybe the sports writers were right. It had become a television game with the government owned networks picking up the salaries. Pretty soon the government would probably own the ball clubs as well. Why not? They owned just about everything else.

The next pitch swooped in, darting down and right at the last second. He didn't bother swinging at it. "Grulk" shouted the umpire and Machado headed back to the bench.

Bottom of the seventh. Time for the stretch. The crowd stood as the organist whipped up a gusty "Take Me Out To The Ball Game." Kids ran for the concession stands for their last shot at peanuts and a soda while their Dads headed for the Men's to unload several innings worth of Sam Adams. Out on the field the motorized corps was re-smoothing the infield and re-chalking the lines. In the visitor's bullpen, a kid who'd just been called up from the Durham Bulls was loosening up. With the score 9-0 Sox and the starter beginning to throw very slow big fat balloons, the Rays had nothing to lose by giving the kid a chance to get belted around by the best.

The scoreboard clock read 10:12.

If it was relatively quiet inside the stadium, it was even quieter on the streets that surrounded the little bandbox stadium, capacity 35,000, over a hundred years old and rivaled in tradition only by Wrigley Field. By modern standards it was an antiquated broom closet but no amount of political chicanery or owner venality could persuade Bostonians to upgrade or "improve" their lovable ball field. By any benchmark it was an American treasure along with the Old North Church and other sentimental landmarks.

Landsdowne Street was dark and relatively deserted. A few fans were leaving early with the game well in hand and school threatening the next morning. Now and then a cab cruised by looking for a fare. At the far end of the street a large black sedan turned the corner and headed slowly along the outer perimeter of the stadium. It came to a stop just below the wall, the Green Monster, which dominated left field. A short distance behind, the sedan had been followed by a van which carried no signage.

At this exact moment, a Boston Metro squad car was approaching from the opposite direction. At the wheel was Vinnie Russo, a six year veteran of the force, former altar boy, failed seminarian, and an ex-MP with eight years learning his trade in Iraq. Next to him was his partner DeDe McConnell who, if she had had balls, would have had balls. Nobody messed with DeDe who was as tough as a gator with a toothache and twice as mean.

As they approached the car, Vinnie observed the front visor being flipped down, revealing a crucifix and some sort of designation. A priest stepped from the car, closed the door and locked it, and then looking up, noticed the squad car for the first time as it pulled to a stop alongside him. The priest froze in his tracks, seemingly confused. He looked back toward the van.

Vinnie lowered his window. "Good evening, Father," he said. "Can I help you?" He noted that the priest had a dark complexion but certainly wasn't Italian or even Black Irish. The placard on the visor read: "Cathedral of the Holy Cross". The priest looked at Vinnie uncertainly.

"I..uh... one of my people called me from the baseball game. I think he is sick. He asked me to come."

"Does he need a doctor? Or an ambulance?"

"No,no," the priest said quickly. "He..uh...he is a very important contributor with a morbid imagination and...I'm just here to humor him. I'm sure he's all right." The priest started to move off.

"Father, you can't leave your car here," Vinnie called to him.

The priest kept moving up the street toward the entrance to the park. "I won't be more than a few minutes."

Vinnie opened his door and got out while DeDe exited on her side. Her attention was focused on the van. She could see that there was someone behind the wheel but whoever it was was just sitting, lights out, unmoving. The short hairs on the back of her neck started to bristle.

Vinnie took a few steps in the priest's direction, shouting now. "Father, come back and move this car. No parking here at any time."

The priest turned back toward him, said nothing, and again looked past the black sedan toward the van. DeDe slid back into the squad car and grabbed the mic, ducking out of sight. "This is 313. McConnell . Badge 4545. Request backup immediately. Landsdowne Street at Fenway. I think we got big trouble." A voice came back. "We copy that, 313. We're about four blocks away and moving."

"Come in loud," she said, exiting the car again and unholstering her service revolver. She looked toward the van. The overhead dome light had gone on. The driver side door started to open. In the distance she could hear the wail of an approaching siren.

Vinnie took two more quick steps toward the retreating priest. "Hold it, Father!" he shouted. "Right there!" He opened his holster flap and pulled out his Glock 17 nine millimeter. At that moment, the priest turned back toward him, a pistol in his right hand. Flame belched from the muzzle as the sound of the shot reverberated in the near empty street. Vinnie felt a tug at his left sleeve and slight sting in his arm. He dived forward onto the pavement, rolling to his right and then coming up in a two-handed stance. He fired two quick shots. The priest spun around and crumpled to the ground, then tried to get up and stagger away.

For a split second, DeDe had turned away from the van to check on her partner. When she looked back, a swarthy bearded man was standing next to the open van door holding an AK 47. As he ripped off a dozen shots, DeDe ducked back into the squad car, then popped out immediately and sent four quick shots in the direction of the van. The rear doors suddenly opened. Two more men appeared, both armed. They fired in Vinnie's direction and he shuddered momentarily as one of the bullets hit him in the leg. He dropped to a knee as DeDe resumed firing at the occupants of the van who were jabbering in a language she did not know.

At that moment a Metro squad car, lights flashing, wailed around the corner at the far end of Landsdowne and raced forward toward the scene. The three men, caught in a cross fire, scattered as the squad car skidded to a stop and two uniformed officers bailed out, guns drawn. They fired and two of the men were cut down in a hail of bullets. The third turned to see what had happened and then suddenly, screaming something unintelligible in Arabic, he started to race toward the policemen, his weapon spewing bullets. The policemen ducked behind the squad car for cover. Thirty yards away, DeDe took careful aim and got off a single shot which separated the top of the terrorist's skull from the rest of his head.

Meanwhile, the priest, severely wounded, was still trying to hobble away. Vinnie got to his feet and fighting the pain, limped after him. The priest stumbled, tried to rise and fell back. Then he reached into his jacket and took out a remote control device. As he fumbled to activate it, Vinnie took two giant steps and kicked the remote from the priest's hand. Frantically, the priest who was muttering in Arabic, struggled to pick up his fallen gun. Vinnie kicked that, too, off to one side.

"Not tonight, Mahmoud," he said, his muzzle aimed right between the man's eyes. He felt himself growing dizzy. Then suddenly DeDe was there, holding him up. Gently she lowered him to the pavement, took one look at his leg wound and whipped off her belt.

She tightened it around his leg in a make shift tourniquet.

One of the other policemen hurried to them. "Ambulance is on the way," he said. Then he grinned. "Nice work, Russo. Got a feeling you and McConnell bagged yourselves a big one."

CHAPTER EIGHTEEN

The sturdy Citation knifed its way through the ominous clouds and howling wind, faring far better than the little Cessna carrying Brian and Ken northward. Bob, the pilot, had tried without success to climb above the storm. Nevertheless he found himself in reasonably decent shape at 8000 feet on a beeline for Warroad. His fears about the flight had been allayed. The turbulence was significant but the plane was airworthy. Unless something unexpected happened, they'd be setting down in less than an hour.

Erwin Conrad was shouting into the radio microphone, trying to make himself heard through the static. The connection to Warroad Airport was tenuous at best and the voice of the woman at the other end kept cutting in and out.

"I said, have any planes landed within the last two or three hours?"

Crackle. "....nobody flying in. Got a real bad storm...." Crackle.

"A small plane! Two men on board! Anything like that?"

"Had a twin engine come in from Canada about three hours ago. Wasn't too bad then. Old man and his two grandchildren...." Crackle. ".....no problem with customs..."

"If a plane comes in, I want you to detain the passengers!"

"Say again. I didn't catch that."

"I said detain the passengers!"

"Oh, we have no way of doing that, sir," the woman said. "We have a couple of private security people here but they couldn't detain anybody....." Crackle. ".......Warroad police department if you want....... give you the number..." Crackle.

"I don't want the number. You call them. Get them to the airport now!"

Crackle. ".......who'd you say your name was...."

"Colonel Erwin Conrad of the Federal Security Force and we'll be landing inside an hour."

"....pretty much closed down....."

"Well, you'd better pretty much open up and I want those police there at the airport when I get there. Do you understand me?"

Crackle. Crackle. Crackle.

"Hello! Can you hear me? Airport, can you hear me?"

Crackle. Crackle. Crackle.

The street was closed off at both ends with squad cars posted to keep out gawkers. Two ambulances had been summoned to the scene and Vinnie Russo was being attended to in one of them as it got ready to pull out and speed the few blocks south to the V.A. Medical Center. Two camera units and several on-camera reporters were making pests of themselves but no one dared interfere with them. They were, after all, government employees doing the work of the government. Happily, no fans were stumbling onto the scene. The umpires had wisely called the game giving the win to the Sox and the patrons were herded toward the exits at Yawkey Way.

DeDe McConnell had cuffed the bogus priest and had him up against a squad car as she started to search through his pockets. The swarthy man looked at DeDe with hatred in his eyes and spat out an obvious curse in Arabic at her. She leaned in close to him, smiling as she cupped his genitals in her hand and squeezed hard. "Sorry, I didn't catch that," she said sweetly.

The priest howled in pain. DeDe shrugged. "Sissy boy", she muttered under her breath. She reached into a trouser pocket and pulled out a cell phone. "Well, looky here" she said with a grin of triumph. "Ryan, watch this guy," she said to a nearby uniformed as she went in search of her captain.

At the same time, one of the reporters on scene was checking in with the network's news director in New York. Shortly thereafter the news director would be in touch with the Director of the Office of Information. It was a good story. A big story. But no one ever got ahead at the network by taking initiative. Buckpassing was a favorite sport among the nation's bureaucrats and in the case of the networks and the DOI, the bigger the story, the farther the buck got passed.

Nicholas Lapp glanced at his wrist watch. The time was 11:17. Something was very wrong. He should have received the call by now. He cursed himself. Why in God's name had he recruited those fanatics from a New Jersey cell? His informant, an FSF agent who had wormed his way into the mosque, had assured him that these people were highly trained and totally dedicated to their twisted cause. No, he should have used his own people as he had in Santa Veronica and in the Amtrak derailments. Secretly he had hoped that in the aftermath of a successful detonation that the men might have been killed. Real fanatics in the country illegally would only underscore the national danger and keep the path smooth for the next step.

A phone rang. It wasn't his. Zebulon Marcuse reached into his shirt pocket and took out his cell. The President, who had been leafing through a two week old issue of People Magazine looked up in annoyance. The wrong phone was ringing.

"Yes?" Marcuse said into the phone. He listened intently , then furrowed his brow as he looked angrily in Lapp's direction. "Say again." He listened for a long time. "Yes, yes. Go with the story. We have no choice. How many dead? Uh-uh. The name of the survivor? He's not, eh? Didn't I just say okay? Put it on the air. Give Boston Metro some credit but beef up our side of it. You know the drill. FSF had these people under surveillance for several weeks. Working hand in hand with local authorities. Don't make me write it for you. Okay, okay. Just make us look good."

Marcuse flipped his phone shut and turned to the President. "A couple Boston cops stumbled into the middle of it. Three dead, one taken into custody, the explosive device disabled by the Metro bomb squad. The network wanted permission to run with the story. I gave it." He looked back toward Lapp, furious.

Lapp got to his feet and held his hands out placatingly. "Look, it's not my fault. We got unlucky. One of those damn things that happen in this business. But it's not a complete disaster----"

"The hell it isn't!" Marcuse said sharply.

"No, no, don't you see. We're heroes. We're doing our job, protecting the people----."

Marcuse shook his head violently. "Lapp, you really are a damned fool. We needed this. A precipitating event that would send the American psyche over the edge, that would so scare the shit out of them that they'd sit still for anything. Blowing up Fenway, that would do it. Thwarting a gang of terrorists, that doesn't do jackshit. On the contrary, now there is no way the President can give that order to initiate Bunker Hill. Weeks of careful planning down the drain. We are totally fucked!"

"Maybe tomorrow we could improvise something," Lapp whined, trying to salvage his dignity and perhaps even his job.

Marcuse looked at him angrily. "Improvise? Now there's a hell of an idea. Why should we do that, Nick, when you people are so good at what you do. Even with weeks of preparation, you screw everything up. And now you want to improvise?"

"I just thought---"

"Don't think. Just do all of us a favor and shut up!"

Just then Lapp's phone rang. He looked puzzled as he checked the caller ID. "Wait a minute," he said quickly. "This is my guy. Maybe the TV people have the story wrong." He answered the phone.

"Hello?"

A momentary silence, the the voice on the other end of the call asked, "Mr. Lapp?"

Lapp frowned. "Yes, this is Nicholas Lapp. Who is this?"

In his office at police headquarters in Boston, Chief Darrell Flynn pressed the OFF button and then laid the phone down on his desk, staring at it it thoughtfully. Then he looked up at Ray VanHoog, the FBI's SAC in the Boston office.

"You were right. That Washington number. It belongs to Lapp. Ray, what the hell is going on around here?" the Chief asked.

George cut back on the power and activated the flaps. Visibility was perfect. The rain had abated, the clouds had scutted away, a million stars and a nearly full bright yellow moon helped light up the inky sky.

The Cessna swooped onto the runway in a perfect two-point landing onto runway 13/31 and then slowing, taxied toward the administration building. "Nice ride, George," Ken said. "Six Flags couldn't have done it any better."

"Thank you, sir. I'll take that as a compliment, seeing as how a few miles back, you seemed ready to bail out."

Ken smiled. "A paucity of parachutes changed my mind."

"Wouldn't have changed mine," Brian groaned. He sat up shakily, unbuckling his safety belt. His complexion was ashen. Deep dark circles underscored his eyes.

"You okay?" Ken asked.

"Will be as soon as I hit the men's room," he replied. "I'm going to need a few minutes."

"Take all the time you need," Ken said. "We're not going anywhere without you."

The plane came to a halt and George opened the door. Brian was first out and hurried toward the administration building. Ken stepped down onto the tarmac. The air was clear and crisp and he breathed deeply. George was right behind him.

"He doesn't look good," George said.

"I know."

"Can he make it?"

"He has to," Ken said grimly.

The men's room right off the main lobby was clean and brightly lit. Brian emerged from a stall and moved to a sink, stared at his reflection. Dead man walking, he thought. His joints were stiff and aching, partly due to the confinement of the cockpit, partly because the radiation was giving him no respite. There was blood in his stool, loose as it was. His urine was reddish and his gums were starting to bleed. The moments of fitful sleep on the plane had not energized him. He just wanted to close his eyes but he knew it was impossible. He and Ken had to reach Canada. They had to make contact with Hugo Wheeler. Nothing else mattered. He reached in his pocket and popped open the pill bottle. One iodide potassium left. He put it in his mouth, cupped his hands to catch some cold water and drank. Water. He needed water to keep hydrated. He dried his hands with a paper towel and walked unsteadily out in to the lobby in search of a vending machine.

Outside, Ken and George had found ground transportation which consisted of one lonely cab driver sitting at the wheel of his Honda Civic, poring over a newspaper.But, as promised, there was also a black Ford SUV parked at curbside. The chassis had been slightly raised, it sported heavy duty deep tread tires and atop the roof, a bank of four floodlights. Leaning against the driver side door, smoking a pipe, was a burly man in a red checked wool jacket. His face was soft and starting to get jowly. His hair was greying blonde and cut short military style. Thirty years earlier, he might have been Special Forces or Black Ops, but time had worn away the hard edges. Yet there was something about him. Maybe it was the 10" serrated knife he kept in a scabbard down by his right boot. Or maybe the ice cold look in his hooded blue eyes that warned you not to underestimate this beer-bellied old man.

Ken approached him. "Sully?"

Sully nodded. "You'd be?"

"Ken Bannister. This is George. He flew us in."

"How you be, George? "

"Good as ever, Sully," George said.

"That bad, eh? Wasn't sure you'd be getting through."

"Matter of talent and fortitude, Sully," George said, "which I have plenty of in equal parts."

Sully nodded, looked at Ken. "He overlooks the fact that insanity runs rampant in his family." He looked around. "So where's the other one?"

Ken pointed as Brian came around the corner carrying four bottles of water. Sully studied him. "They said he had the sickness. Don't look good."

"It's not," Ken said.

Brian forced a grin. "All present and accounted for. Let's hit the road."

"Bri, say hi to Sully," Ken said.

Brian fumbled with the water and managed to stick out his right hand. They shook. "Pleasure to meet you, Sully."

"Likewise", Sully smiled and then added, "And that's how it went in our world today." It was Brian's traditional sign-off.

Brian nodded. "You've got a good memory."

"For some things," Sully said. "All right, as Mr. Everett said, let's hit the road."

They were about to climb into the SUV when a woman came hurrying out of the administration building carrying a clipboard. She waved at them. "Hello there! Just wait a minute, please!" Breathing heavily from the exertion of her run, she reached the small cluster of men.

"You fellas just landed in that Cessna?"

"That's right," George said.

"You shoulda radioed in for landing clearance."

"Didn't need clearance," George said testily. "Ten miles out I declared an emergency. Check your regulations."

The woman glared at him. "No need to get huffy, young man. Just doing my job. You come in without clearance, FAA says I have to file a report." Subtly she lifted her eyes to scan the southern skies, then looked back at George. Ken caught the look and glanced over at Brian. He'd seen it too.

"Look, ma'am," George started to say.

"Ida May Polsby. Assistant Manager. And I know my regulations. Now you all come up to my office and we'll fill out these papers."

George shook his head. "You don't need these men. They were just passengers."

"Don't tell me what I don't need, young man."

"Besides I'm about to hop back in that plane and take off like we never even landed here. So don't you worry yourself, Ida May."

Angrily, she muscled in on him. "You want me gettin' security out here, mister?"

Sully laughed as he stepped toward her. "Yeah, that'd be fine, missy. You get Roscoe and his lard ass out here to scare us to death. Hell, he don't even have bullets in that popgun he carries around."

She shook her head. "You won't be laughing if I call police headquarters and talk to Chief Garrity".

Sully laughed again. "Oh, lady, Garrity's not in his office. He's out at Frannie Victor's place playin' bump and tickle and he sure ain't gonna hop out of her bed on your say so."

At that moment, from far off to the south, there was the sound, almost inaudible, of an approaching airplane. Ida May turned her eyes to the sky. Ken saw it, turned and looked.

"Let's get the hell out of here!" he shouted as he hurried to the SUV and yanked open the rear door. Now the others had heard it. Brian moved quickly to the shotgun seat as Sully opened the driver side and slipped behind the wheel.

"Wait!" Ida May yelled, then turned toward George who was racing toward the Cessna. "Don't you go near that plane! You hear me!!'

As the SUV spun wheels and then raced out of the airport onto Rt 313 heading north, the FSF Citation emerged from a cloud bank, its red warning lights blinking, and started to descend. George fired up the engine of the Cessna and started to taxi, then took a sharp turn and moved quickly onto the 4/22 runway. George moved the small plane directly into the landing path of the Citation and waited.

Inside the cockpit, Bob saw what was happening at the last second and pulled back on the stick. "Holy shit!" he screamed as the plane suddenly climbed, missing the Cessna by a matter of feet.

"What's going on?" Conrad shouted.

"Damned if I know," Bob said, starting to circle back to take a closer look and a possible landing. His eyes flicked to the alternate runway and he banked slightly to move into position for a landing. George saw immediately what was happening and quickly taxied to 13/31 and again parked in the landing path.

In the cockpit of the Citation, Bob sized up the situation, eye-balled distances and muttered under his breath, "Fuck you, Charlie." He cut back on power, activated the flaps and took dead aim at the Cessna. Conrad leaned over his shoulder and realized what he was up to. "Are you crazy?" he shouted.

"Sit down and shut up!" Bob ordered, easing forward on the controls. Lower came the plane, a bare 40 feet off the ground with the Cessna dead ahead. Timmy gulped hard, frozen. Conrad sat back and raised his eyes to heaven. Johnson leaned forward for a better look, seeming to enjoy the moment.

"Piss your pants, motherfucker," Bob whispered as the Citation flew over the smaller plane, missing it by less than 10 feet. With not much runway left, Bob powered back and gently tapped the brakes. A stand of trees was dead ahead and rushing up quickly. More pressure on the brakes. Gently, not too hard. The plane continued to slow, almost to taxi speed. Bob turned the wheels carefully and the Citation edged leftwards just before it was going to slash into the trees. Finally, it came to a stop five yards from disaster.

Bob looked out his window. The Cessna was racing down the runway now, flaps up, picking up speed and then lifting off into the night sky.

"I want that son of a bitch arrested!" Conrad said from the back of the cockpit.

"Good luck with that," Bob muttered to himself as he started to taxi back toward the administration building.

Peter Toussaint was seated at his desk in the study of his modest three bedroom home in Georgetown. The clock on the wall read 12:17. The radio nearby was tuned to Canada Free Radio and the FBI Director was listening to the evening's report on the American debacle as seen through the eyes of Hugo Wheeler. Across the room, a 56" hi-def television set was tuned to the Progressive network. The sound was muted temporarily as reporters and cameramen covered the aftermath of the Fenway Park attack.

"The van parked in the shadow of Fenway Park," Wheeler was saying, "contained enough enhanced RDX compound to blow away the green monster and most of the seats all the way to the third base line. The timing device was super-sophisticated, the kind supplied by the Iranians to the Palestinians during the years prior to the detente."

Toussaint couldn't help smiling as he shook his head in wonderment. Where does that man get his information? Accurate and fast. Very fast. Toussaint knew there were tens of millions of dissidents in all parts of the country, all in a seething rage, ready to oust the President and the Congress and anybody else who was trying to turn the United States into a worker's paradise. He snorted. How can you have a worker's paradise when upwards of 13% of the country was out of work?

"Of the four Islamist terrorists involved, three are dead thanks to the quick work of the Boston Metro Police and no thanks at all to the government's Federal Security Force who, as usual, was no place to be found but will certainly be there to accept plaudits when credit is passed around. As for the fourth member of this grimy quartet, the FSF has no idea who he is so I thought I would help them out. Stealing a close up from the government TV broadcast, I compared it with my own private data base of known or suspected fanatic followers of the Great Allah, the Unmerciful, and what do you know, bingo, ladies and gentlemen. In less than one hundred and forty seconds, I had my match. I hold here in my carefully manicured fingers a print-out of none other than Khalil ibn Hakim, the number two man in a mosque in Hoboken, New Jersey, once overseen by the Blind Sheik of Twin Towers fame. Failure edition."

Unbelievable, Toussaint thought. If I'm not careful, this guy could get my job.

Just then, the phone at his elbow rang. He lifted the receiver as he muted the radio. "Toussaint."

"Director, this Ray VanHoog, SAC Boston Office. I'm calling from the office of the Chief of Police."

"Good morning, Ray," the Director said because it was indeed Friday morning. "I don't suppose you've been listening to Wheeler."

"No, sir", the FBI agent said. "Been a little busy for that."

"Well, write down this name. Kahlil ibn Hakim. He's your surviving terrorist. Wheeler just ID'ed him for us."

"Son of a bitch!" VanHoog blurted. Toussaint could hear Van-Hoog's muffled voice away from the phone. "Write this down. Kahlil ibn Hakim."

"Don't take it badly, Ray. We could use a hundred more like Hugo Wheeler. So what's going on?"

"Sir, we got a cell phone off this Khalil guy. I checked out the last call he made. A Washington number. We got the user name from the server without a warrant."

"Go on," Toussaint said carefully.

"I called it, sir."

"And who answered?"

"Nicholas Lapp."

Toussaint stiffened. "You must be mistaken."

"No mistake, sir. He said, hello. I said, Mr. Lapp. He said, this is Nicholas Lapp. I even recognized his voice." There was a long silence. "Sir?"

Toussaint let out a small sigh. "There is no accounting for the stupidity of some people."

"No, sir."

"What's the name of the Chief?"

"Flynn, sir. Darrell Flynn."

"Put him on."

VanHoog handed the phone to Boston's Chief of Police. "Director Toussaint, this is Chief Flynn."

"Good morning, Chief. Sorry our first conversation has to be under these dire circumstances."

"No problem. I understand completely."

"Ray VanHoog will fill you in on everything we know. I don't play turf war games."

"I've heard that, sir. It's much appreciated."

"I'm going to ask you one favor. Grant it or not, your call. I want you to put this Khalil ibn Hakim in solitary confinement. Totally incommunicado. No comment to the press. If a lawyer shows up, run him around from precinct to precinct. You know the drill. As for the FSF, they don't get near him for any reason whatsoever and if they try to get tough, claim jurisdiction. I'll back you all the way. If that doesn't work, arrest the bastards and I'll have a dozen of my agents on the scene in fifteen minutes to help you out. Any questions?"

Chief Flynn grinned. "Only one, sir. If we arrest them, does that mean we get to strip search them?"

Toussaint laughed. "You're the Chief, Chief."

After he hung up, Toussaint called another number. After two rings, a man answered.

"This is Jaffee."

"Peter Toussaint here, Leonard. You and I need to talk. Now."

CHAPTER NINETEEN

Almost immediately after leaving the airport, Rt. 313 deteriorated into a substandard road as it cut into the eastern boundaries of the Lost River State Forest. The night sky, which had been so bright at the airport, dimmed as the towering trees blocked the rays of the moon. As a shroud of darkness enveloped the SUV, Sully flipped a switch beneath the dash and the array of lights on the car roof lit up, throwing beams of illumination a hundred yards ahead.

"Hang on now," Sully warned. "Gotta turn here and it's gonna get a little bumpy up ahead. Slippery, too. That rain didn't help these dirt roads much."

Brian clutched his seat with both hands and braced his feet against the engine compartment. Ken tightened his seat belt and grabbed tight to an arm rest. The car shuddered as it hit a pot hole and couple of ruts but didn't lose speed or traction. Looking out his window, Brian watched the pine trees fly by. He could barely make out a thicket of willows up ahead and then they were out in the open for a few hundred yards. The road snaked through the deciduous forest turning ever so slightly to the west. The Canadian border was very close. All they had to do was find the right trail to reach Sunderson and safety.

"You fellas got any idea who was in that plane comin' in?" Sully asked.

"I'd guess FSF," Ken replied, "but I don't know for sure."

"They know this was where you were planning to cross?"

"Not to that I know of. I don't know. Maybe they spotted the plane. Maybe they caught up with George's mother. Could be anything. Could be that plane had nothing to do with us."

Sully snorted derisively. "The way Ida May was waitin' for it, I don't think so." He glanced in his rear view mirror. "They'll be back there somewhere, how far I don't know."

"Can they catch us?" Ken asked apprehensively.

"Depends. Fella in the cab waiting for a fare, that's Deucy Jacobs. Don't think he knows this road all that well, but he's a pistol. Got a lead foot and no fear. If they followed immediately, they might be ten, maybe fifteen minutes back. Maybe farther if they wasted time."

The car started to slow down. The lights were only reaching out for twenty or thirty yards as the road started to twist and turn. "Road gets real bad from here on in," Sully said. "Gotta take it a lot slower". He looked over at Brian who was staring straight ahead. "You okay, Mr. Everett?"

"Hangin' in, Sully," he said hoarsely. "Hangin' in."

As soon as the Citation rolled to a stop, Conrad shoved open the door and hit the ground running. Johnson was right on his heels. He made a beeline for Ida May Polsby who was standing in a bewildered state wondering just what was going on and who was who. She quickly found out who Erwin Conrad was.

"I told you people to detain the passengers of that plane," he shouted. "Are you deaf and dumb or just plain stupid?"

"Mister, there's no cause to get abusive---"

"Those men are fugitives from justice and you have just put yourself in serious jeopardy, madam. Now where the hell did they go?"

She pointed to the airport exit. "Headed into the forest, seems like. Probably going for the border."

"Yeah. Probably," Conrad echoed sarcastically. He looked around. "Do you have a rescue helicopter here?"

Ida May nodded toward the nearest hangar. "In there."

"Where's the pilot?"

"Most likely in bed," she said.

"Well, get him up and get him over here. Now."

"Oh, no, I couldn't do that---"

Conrad yanked out his ID and shoved it in the woman's face. "You'll do it or I'll toss you in jail for a week, maybe longer," he said. "And meanwhile I'll close down this airport so when you get out, you won't have a job to come back to. Do you understand me?"

"Yes, sir," she whimpered.

"Then tell this pilot I want him to use his floodlight to locate those men who just landed and when he does, follow wherever they go and keep that light on them at all times. He gets it right, it's worth $10,000. He screws up, he'll be in the cell next to you. Is that clear?"

"Yes, sir. I'll get him over here right away," said Ida May, scared out of her mind.

"Johnson, let's go," Conrad said as he started to jog toward the taxi still parked in the transportation area.

Deeper and deeper the SUV plunged into the forest. The road narrowed and at times leaves were brushing up against the side of the car. Now and then the lights would pick up the huge yellow eyes of a Great Gray Owl as it stared down at them from the safety of a tree limb. Suddenly a deer would dart into the road and then freeze, staring into the oncoming headlights, Sully would have to brake sharply and the SUV, despite its all-wheel drive, would slide on the muddy surface dangerously close to the edge of the road which, in places, dropped off several feet. Sully would mutter something unintelligible under his breath and then start off again. Ken kept checking his watch. They were cutting it close.

Suddenly Ken was aware of the whop-whop sound of helicopter blades . He looked out the window and high above them, he spotted the rescue chopper with its floodlight beaming down. Almost immediately, the high powered beam zeroed in on the SUV whose bright lights helped find the road ahead, but also made them an easy target for anyone trying to find them.

Sully also looked up. "Damn," he mumbled. "These people are getting serious."

"What is it?" Brian asked. He'd been half dozing, his eyes closed.

"Chopper overhead. Got us in his sights," Sully replied.

"FSF?" Ken asked.

"Doubt it. Most likely Joe Running Deer's rescue helicopter, if I was to bet."

"Can we lose him?" Ken asked.

"Sure. If we turn off the headlights and the rooflights".

"Dumb question," Ken admitted, chagrined.

Sully nodded. "We all come up with 'em from time to time." He yanked at the wheel as the road jogged slightly left, then straightened.

"How far?" Ken asked. "Could we walk it?"

Sully considered it for moment. "About a half-mile. It'd be hard going, dark as it is." He pointedly looked at Brian, then back at Ken.

"Don't worry about me", Brian said. His eyes had been closed but he was tuned in.

"It's up to you fellas. I can slide the car sideways across the road. That'll put the people behind us on foot as well."

Brian didn't hesitate. "We walk."

Ken shook his head. "Are you sure, Bri?"

"Like this we're target practice, Ken. On foot we have a chance. We can't let them catch us now. Not now."

Ken nodded. "Okay, amigo. Your call."

Sully nodded, moved ahead about fifty yards to where the road narrowed down, then expertly skidded the big SUV into position, blocking any possible passage. He killed the lights, cut the engine and slipped the keys into his pocket. He reached into the glove compartment and took out three flashlights. "A life lesson I live by. Hope for the best but be prepared. Batteries are fresh this afternoon."

The three men exited the SUV and started slowly up the road. "Keep to the sides where the overhanging branches are thickest," Sully continued. "Try to keep your light pointed mostly down, not ahead. And watch your step. The footing is lousy."

Heather Bannister, Superintendent Keith Sunderson and three of his Mounties had left Middlebro on the Canadian side twenty minutes earlier and now, at a couple of minutes before midnight, they were positioned near the fence at the point where Heather's husband and Brian Everett were going to try to make good their escape. The first thing Sunderson had noticed when they'd arrived was the helicopter a half mile or so away, circling with its powerful floodlight searching the forest below.

Sunderson's sergeant moved up alongside him and spoke quietly so that Heather wouldn't hear. "Don't like the looks of that, sir."

"Me, either. The good news is, they've probably made it this far, but with that chopper circling, it's going to be tough getting them over."

"Especially if it's an Apache or another of FSF's lethal toys," the sergeant said.

Sunderson nodded. "Have Laveque go back to the truck, grab three roadside flares and then head west along the fence, maybe a thousand meters." He checked his watch. "At 12:15 have him lay down the flares, light 'em up and then hustle back here. Make sure the chopper doesn't see him."

"Right, sir," the sergeant said, moving off quickly.

Heather moved to Sunderson's side. She pointed. "That helicopter, Keith. What does it mean?"

He smiled. "It means your husband is close by, Mrs. Bannister."

She frowned. "But----"

"No buts. My men and I are dealing with the chopper."

He was so smooth and confident, she almost believed him.

Without roof lights and relying solely on headlights, the taxi nearly slammed into the black SUV parked sideways across the road. As it was, the cab skidded badly on the muddy surface and the front wheels ended up jutting out over the five foot drop off on the left side of the road.

"Jesus!" Conrad screamed, more an oath than a prayer.

"Looks like they're walking," Deucy Jacobs said as he got out of the cab to check for damage.

Willis Johnson looked up, spotted the helicopter a short distance ahead. "Guess they had to," he said. "Chopper must have had them pretty much pinned down."

Conrad got out of the car. "We're going to have to walk it," he said to Deucy.

"Guess that's your only choice," the diminutive cabbie said.

"I said 'we'. That means you, friend."

He shook his head. "Fare didn't include any walking, mister. You want me to take you back? No extra charge."

"I have to catch up with those men," Conrad said angrily. "You're coming with us. If you don't I blow our fucking head off here and now." Conrad drew his Glock and pointed at Deucy's head, right between the eyes.

The little man shrugged. "Since you put it that way----"

"We need flashlights," Conrad said.

"Got one on the trunk. And a battery operated work light."

"Get 'em," Conrad said looking past the SUV, down the narrow darkened road.

Johnson moved up next to him. "Maybe they're over by now."

Conrad looked at his partner. "If they are, I'll be right behind them. One of us is going to die, Johnson. Everett here tonight or me in a week or two. The FSF deals with its own and there are no second chances."

"This is it," Sully said as they reached a spot in the road where a narrow dirt trail shot off to the right.

"How far?" Ken asked.

"Pretty close," Sully said. "Maybe three hundred meters." He turned to Brian. "You holdin' up, Mr. Everett?"

"Hell, yes," Brian said, spitting a glob of blood toward the mud. "Having the time of my life."

"If you need help----"

"I can do it."

Sully nodded. "Okay. I'm going to move up the road, wave my flashlight around. Maybe I can draw Joe Running Deer's attention and lead him off in another direction."

"You don't have to----" Ken started to say.

"I know that," Sully smiled. "See you boys after the war." And then he hurried down the road, disappearing into the darkness. Ken and Brian started up the dirt trail. Three hundred meters. After nearly 2000 miles, just three hundred meters. Overhead the chopper circled aimlessly, hoping to get lucky.

They moved slowly. Ken checked his watch. They were still okay on time. Eleven minutes past midnight. They'd been given leeway. It ought to be enough. Brian groaned and fell to the ground awkwardly. He had tripped over a root growing out onto the trail. Ken helped him to his feet.

"Can you walk?" Ken asked.

"I can limp a little," Brian smiled.

Behind them Deucy had found the turnoff. "I found it! The turnoff!" he shouted, loud enough to be heard in Manitoba. That, of course, was the whole idea. Deucy Jacobs didn't much care for Erwin Conrad. In fact the trail that he had found was thirty yards short of the real one. Conrad peered into the darkness to the right. He saw and heard nothing.

Ken, on the other hand, had heard Deucy very clearly and supporting Brian, he picked up the pace. Unfortunately, when Brian had stumbled he had tried to brace his fall and inadvertently turned his flashlight skyward. It was only for a moment, but in that moment, Joe Running Deer had spotted the beam and now he was flying back to their location. He stopped, hovered directly above them, as Ken and Brian froze in their tracks under some tree branches as the shaft of light danced back and forth dangerously close to their cover.

Conrad, a hundred yards away, watched the chopper hover, then started to run. "This is the wrong trail!" he shouted to Johnson. He ran forward, cautiously, his eyes flicking between the dark road and the whirring helicopter. Within moments, he found the trail that Ken and Brian had taken. "This way!" he shouted and started in. Johnson followed. Deucy Jacobs stayed put. He wanted no part of any of this.

High above the tree tops, Joe Running Deer stared into the darkness below, manipulating his searchlight, inching slowly along the path, looking for the slightest movement. Suddenly out of the corner of his eye he saw a bright flash of red light on the ground about a quarter mile to the west. Then another flash. Some sort of signal. He swooped the chopper to the left and raced westward along the fence line keeping his searchlight trained on the American side of the fence.

As soon as the helicopter flew away, Ken held Brian tight and started to move. "We have to run for it, Bri," he said. "Stay with me."

Hobbling and slipping, they made their way north on the trail, no longer disguising their flashlights, hoping not to fall. Up ahead they saw what looked like a small moonlit clearing and just beyond it a chain link fence. Ken thought he saw shadowy figures in the darkness on the other side.

He and Brian stumbled into the clearing as Keith and Heather dashed to the fence from the Canadian side. Heather put her hand to her mouth and instinctively spoke his name. "Ken!"

He grinned and blew her a kiss.

"Time for that later, Doctor. Up and over, gentlemen. No time to waste," Sunderson said.

Ken helped Brian to the fence. "Come on, Bri. I'll give you a boost," he said. Brian laced his fingers into the mesh of the fence as Ken cupped his hands.

Just then a shot rang out, reverberating through the forest, as Conrad and Johnson charged into the small clearing, guns drawn. Conrad's was pointed directly at Brian.

"Stop right there. By authority of the Federal Security Force I am placing you both under arrest!" Conrad said, moving forward. Johnson grabbed Ken shoving him against the fence. As he did Brian fell to the ground.

Heather clawed at the fence, screaming at Johnson. "Get your hands off of him!" Sunderson tried to pull her away, but she was having none of it. "Leave him alone, you bastard!"

The Mountie sergeant unflapped his holster and started to draw his weapon. Sunderson put his hand out, staying his action. "No, Sergeant," he said quietly.

Conrad kneeled down and rolled Brian over onto his back, then began rifling through his pockets. A moment later he retrieved the tape cassette from Brian's windbreaker. He held it up, examining it. With a smile, he stood up, looked around, spotted a nearby rock. He put the cassette on the rock, then stomped down hard with his boot. The plastic case shattered. He stomped again . The cassette disintegrated into a dozen pieces. He turned back to Brian, who was still lying on the ground. Pistol at his side, Conrad walked over to him. "Get up!"

When Brian didn't move, Conrad jabbed him with his foot. "I said, get up!" Still Brian didn't move. "All right, I'll drag you out of here like the dog that you are." Conrad leaned down and grabbed the back of Brian's windbreaker by the neck and started to drag him through the mud, back toward the trail.

Brian wanted to fight, to struggle, to work himself free but he had no strength. Conrad was a deceivingly strong man and he twisted Brian's jacket around his neck, cutting into his skin and choking off his windpipe. Brian gasped in pain, struggling to breathe as he was tugged along in the muddy slime of the trail.

Suddenly a shot rang out. Conrad loosened his grip and then he fell in a heap right in front of Brian, who raised his head and opened his eyes. He found himself staring into Conrad's face or, rather, what was left of Conrad's face. Most of the right side of his skull was gone, blood and brains seeped from the gaping wound. The one eye that was left was staring at Brian, wide-eyed, in shock. Brian struggled, turned to look back. Willis Johnson was looking at him, a smoking pistol held at his side.

After a moment, Johnson replaced the gun in its shoulder holster and he moved to Brian, reaching down and helping him to his feet. Half carrying him, the beefy FSF officer brought him to the fence and then looked at Ken.

"Give me a hand," he said.

Quickly, Ken made a stirrup of his hands and with Johnson's help, they boosted him to the top of the fence. The Mountie sergeant jumped to the fence from his side and scrabbled up, grabbing hold of Brian and helping him over the top. With a firm grip, he eased him down slowly to free Canadian soil.

In a flash, Ken was up and over, dropping down to the other side. He got to his feet and moved to Heather, enveloping her in his arms, holding her close. "Don't cry," he murmured. "Don't cry."

Brian struggled to this feet and moved to the fence where Johnson was watching.

"Look, I don't know why-----"

"Got my reasons," Johnson said.

Brian's eyes started to moisten. "Thank you," he said.

Johnson nodded and started to turn away.

"Come with us," Brian said. "There's nothing back there for you."

Johnson managed a wan smile as he shook his head. "Too much blood on my hands", he said. He looked to include the others. "Good luck to you," he said and then he turned and started to trudge back down the narrow trail.

CHAPTER TWENTY

It was nearing 2:00 a.m in Washington and no one was sleeping. At least not the movers and shakers who were trying to make sense of what was happening. A terrorist attack on Fenway Park? Unthinkable. And yet four brazen Islamic fanatics had tried just that and if not for the officers of Boston Metro who accidentally stumbled into the middle of their insidious mission, thousands of Bostonians would be dead or maimed and much of one of the country's most beloved ballparks would be reduced to rubble. Radio and television reportage indicated that the Federal Security Force also had a major role in the operation though hardly anyone with an ounce of brains could make that compute.

Lee Fitzpatrick and Leonard Jaffee, at their respective homes, were following the coverage closely as they compared notes by phone. What they were coming up with was not a pretty picture.

"Trust me on this, Colonel," Jaffee was saying. "I just got off the phone with FBI Director Toussaint. For a supposedly smart terrorist, this guy Hakim takes this year's Dumbo Award. He showed Nicholas Lapp's cell phone number as the last call he had made on his own cell before he was arrested."

Lee frowned. "But that means----"

"Of course, that's what it means. Feel free to call Director

Toussaint to verify. I'll give you his number."

"That won't be necessary."

"We've been suspicious of Lapp for some time now. All of these attacks, well, hell, Colonel, we went over this the other day. Now we have proof positive. The administration is engineering all these crises for their own political ends."

"Just a moment, sir. The only one you can legitimately implicate is Lapp. There's no evidence the President knows anything about this."

Jaffee responded in anger. "For God's sakes, man, do you really think a toadie like Nicholas Lapp would do all of this on his own? Use some common sense."

"Even if I agreed with you, Director, it won't be enough for General MacAndrews. If you want him to disobey a direct order from the President, you'd better have a smoking gun. Ifs and maybes and hearsay aren't going to cut it."

"Damn it, man," said Jaffee, "if your General had the love of country that I do----"

"Stop right there. No one, and I repeat, no one has a greater love of this country than Dwight David MacAndrews and if you show him proof that the President is involved in this, he will disobey that order. But it will have to be hard, rock solid proof. Until then, we have nothing to talk about. Good night, sir."

Lee hung up gently, resisting the temptation to slam the receiver down on the cradle.

They were sitting around a circular table in the middle of the restaurant at Pond's Motel on Rt. 12 in Middlebro. Ken and Heather, Keith Sunderson and a man named Stimson. The sergeant was off on an errand of mercy to pick up a fresh supply of potassium iodide after Sunderson had rousted the druggist from his bed and explained the situation. The other enlisted men were sitting at a nearby table eating sandwiches. The owner had kept the restaurant open as a courtesy to the RCMP Superintendent .

Ken looked across the room toward his old friend, watching as Brian sat hunched over, talking on the phone, a couple of bottles of water at his side. Ken's heart was breaking. It was too late for the medicine, too late for a bone marrow transplant, too late for anything. Everyone knew it.

"Lissa, sweetheart. Don't cry. Please. I'm okay with it.", Brian was saying to his daughter.

"Dad, it's just not fair."

"Chin up, kiddo," he chuckled. "A lot of life is like that. You go with the punches. If you can get up, okay. If not, well, that's okay, too. God didn't put us here to live forever. We had good times. Let's keep those close to our hearts, okay?"

"Okay," she finally agreed, unwillingly.

"Now you listen to the broadcast tonight. I'll be on pretty soon. You'll hear everything that's happened, what it's all been about. And call Mark. I tried twice. I couldn't get through. Problems with the base switchboards. Something like that. Tell him I love him. I admire him. Tell him I was always on his side. Remember always that I loved both of you very much." With that he hung up. He could no longer stand to hear his daughter cry.

Just then the sergeant hurried to him with the bottle of pills which he had already uncapped. "Sir," he said as he held out the bottle.

"Thanks," Brian replied as he popped two in his mouth and washed them down.

At the center table, the man named Stimson was shaking his head uncertainly. "I don't know. Look, I was told--- Hugo was told--- there'd be a tape. Now you tell me it was destroyed."

Sunderson nodded. "Smashed to pieces by the FSF officer."

"And there are no copies?" Stimson asked hopefully.

"There was one," Ken said. "A DVD we made that we were going to broadcast on the internet before they shut it down. We had to leave it behind when we abandoned our luggage in St. Paul."

Brian came to the table carrying his water. He was about to sit down.

"You see my problem. Hugo doesn't put just anything out on the air. I mean, it's his reputation. The stuff that floats around, much of it bogus. Without the actual tape---" He threw up his hands helplessly.

Brian stared down at him. "Are you saying he wouldn't accept my word?"

Stimson shook his head in embarrassment. "No, no, it's just that—"

"Just that what, Mr. Stimson? Do you think I came all this way, sick as I am, to subvert the trust of an old friend whom I respect and admire? Is that what you think this is all about?"

Brian stared into the man's eyes, unflinching. After a few moments, Stimson shoved back his chair and got up. "Excuse me for a moment," he said as he took out his cell phone and moved to a far corner of the restaurant.

Those at the table exchanged looks while still keeping an eye on Stimson.

"So, Mr. Everett," Sunderson said. "How long have you and Hugo Wheeler been old friends?"

Brian thought for a moment. "I met him once at a broadcasting convention in Chicago back in 1997, I think it was."

"Ah," Sunderson said, as if that explained it all.

Stimson returned to the table and put a hand on Brian's shoulder. "All right, Mr. Everett", he said. "Let's go."

With a sigh of relief, Ken started to get up.

"No", Stimson said "Just Mr. Everett . Everyone else stays here."

Ken looked at his friend with concern. "Brian----"

"I'll be okay, Ken," he said.

"It's close by," Stimson said. "Give us an hour. Maybe ninety minutes. No more."

Ken and Heather moved around the table to Brian. Both embraced him. "Good luck, buddy. Don't let your old friend give you any crap."

Brian smiled and then he and Stimson went out the door, heading for Stimson's pick-up truck.

Stimson hadn't lied. After driving for a short stretch on Rt. 12, the pickup turned right onto an unpaved road that would lead eventually to Whitemouth Lake. A half-mile in, Stimson turned onto an unmarked driveway and drove toward an unprepossessing ranch house that lay directly ahead. Before they could reach it, Stimson slowed the truck and then came to a halt as a man in fatigues carrying an AK 47 stepped out of the shadows. He flipped on his flashlight, played it on Stimson's face, then moved it for a better look at Brian. Satisfied, he stepped back with a nod and Stimson pulled forward. Only then did Brian realize that there had been an armed man in the shadows on his side of the car as well as a third man directly behind them , also carrying an automatic weapon.

They pulled up in front of the house where Stimson parked. Two more men in fatigues stepped out onto the porch. One carried a machine pistol. The other, the taller of the two, had a .45 automatic holstered to his belt. As Brian stepped up onto the porch, the tall man put out his hand, palm forward, halting him.

"Hands over your head, please, sir," the man said. Brian did as he was told and the tall man patted him down expertly. Satisfied, he stepped back and opened the door.

"Mind the light," he said to Stimson. "He's about three minutes away from a commercial break."

"Right," Stimson said as they went inside.

There was nothing unusual about the foyer or the living room. A sofa, coffee table, stuffed chairs, a couple of lamps, a table top TV in the corner. Off to the right Brian could see part way into the kitchen. Off to the left there seemed to be a corridor leading to at least one bedroom, perhaps two or three. Straight ahead was another corridor leading to the rear of the house. Brian couldn't make out what was down there but he was aware of the blinking red light wired into the hallway ceiling.

Stimson gestured for Brian to follow him, putting a finger to his lips as he moved slowly and gingerly. When they came to the end of the corridor, Brian realized that an entire new addition, perhaps twice the size of the original house had been added on. On his left was a floor to ceiling glass wall which allowed onlookers to observe Hugo Wheeler hard at work behind the microphone in his sound proof studio. On his right was a corridor which led to a half dozen bedrooms where staff and security were presumably housed. Those few individuals allowed to visit might, if they were sharp enough, have wondered where the transmission tower was since it was obviously not on the premises. They would have learned that it was over two miles away, on the shores of the lake, and that it was 580 feet tall, the tallest of the nine towers used to broadcast Wheeler's program to all corners of America. The tower was connected by an underground hard line from the ranch house. Each of the nine towers was interconnected to the others by a combination of hard lines and laser capabilities. Each tower, like this one close to Middlebro, was serviced by an out-of-the-way ordinary looking ranch home that had been modified for broadcasting. If Brian had asked he would have learned that tonight was Wheeler's last broadcast from Manitoba for at least ten weeks. Tomorrow he would be traveling with his staff to an undisclosed site in western Ontario.

The red light overhead went out and Hugo Wheeler looked up at his guest through the glass wall, smiling broadly as he rose and came through the studio door to welcome Brian with a warm handshake.

"Mr. Everett, this is a pleasure as well as a distinct honor," Wheeler said. A man with a steel backbone and a take-no-prisoners combativeness in his public persona, in private he was a kind, sympathetic man with a rascally sense of humor.

Brian smiled. "The honor is mine, Mr. Wheeler. I'm happy to see you again after these many years."

Wheeler scoffed. "Oh, bullshit," he said with a smile. "As my Jewish friends would say, I'm the pischer in this twosome. And by the way, may I say that you look like crap." He waved at Brian's face. "Does this have something to do with what we're going to talk about tonight?"

"Everything," Brian said.

The digital clock on the President's coffee maker read 2:27. Depressed by the events in Boston, angry with those who were letting him down, he had left the Oval Office for his living quarters on the second floor. He wanted to sleep. He knew he needed it. He also knew he was far too agitated to get any sort of rest. He started to brew some coffee, then sat at the little round table in the middle of the kitchen and stared at the Norman Rockwell print that adorned his wall calendar. May. May had always been a good month for him. Not this year. Far from it.

Zebulon Marcuse had gone to his office to review the situation, hoping to find some magical solution to his dilemma. How could Boston have gone so wrong? One thing he knew for sure. Nick Lapp was an idiot. He wouldn't be around long. Marcuse would see to it. Out of habit, he flipped on his radio which was alway tuned to Canada. Sometimes it was useful to hear what the chubby son of a bitch had to say for himself.

As for Lapp, he was in the backseat of his limo, being driven to FSF headquarters where he hoped to salvage something from the evening's debacle. He was talking on his car phone with Darrell Flynn, Boston's Chief of Police. Lapp was not happy.

"What the hell's going on up there, Chief? I dispatched two men to take your prisoner into federal custody."

"Yes,sir. They're here. Got 'em in the third floor lockup for safe keeping until they cool down."

"What are you talking about?" Lapp fumed.

"Well, they came in about twenty minutes ago, kind of highhanded, you know, demanding that I turn over the Arab fella and I had to explain to them that the prisoner fell under my jurisdiction, not theirs, but that if they wanted to take it up with a judge tomorrow, they should go right ahead. Well, they didn't take kindly to that and started making all kinds of threats, screaming like alley cats. Thought for a minute I might have to turn a hose on them, but no, we just threw them in the cage. They stopped yelling about five minutes ago."

Lapp was even more enraged. "Chief, I am ordering you----"

"No sense ordering, Mr. Lapp. They're staying put. Same goes for anybody else you send over. Now, if you'll excuse me, you're wasting my time."

Lapp stared at his phone in disbelief. He'd been cut off.

The wind was whistling with gale force through the streets of Kingfisher, Oklahoma, but the customers at Rosie's Burger and Fries all night diner paid no attention. It was warm and quiet and the food, as always, was top notch. A trucker from Abilene sat at a booth scarfing down bacon and eggs and gallons of coffee while outside, his rig shuddered in the wind. At the counter a Kingfisher policeman on supper break was flirting with Maisie who was Rosie's younger sister and who always worked the ten to eight night shift. Rosie, for her part, always worked the eight to six day shift which worked out well for both of them since they hadn't spoken to each other in over six years. The AM receiver on the shelf behind the counter was tuned, like tens of millions of others throughout the country, to Canada Free Radio. The clock on the wall read 1:49 CDT.

"Folks," Wheeler was saying, "we hardly ever have guests on this program but tonight we make an exception. Sitting across from me is a man I think you all know. A man who devoted a lifetime to the honorable profession of journalism at a time when it really was a profession. He is a man I am proud to call my friend and he is here to relate to you a harrowing story of betrayal, near death, and an agenda totally committed to the destruction of the United States as you and I have always known it. This agenda is not being put forward by outsiders but rather by those in the highest positions of power within the current administration.

"When I was first made aware of this story, I was told there was an incriminating audio tape that would prove every allegation. Unfortunately in his struggle to get to this microphone, my guest was momentarily arrested by officers of the Federal Security Force. The tape was totally destroyed on the spot. You all know that I am suspicious of accusations made without proof so normally I would say, no tape, no story. But because of the reputation of the man who has literally defied death to be here this morning, in this one case, I make an exception.

"My friends, I now turn this microphone over to Brian Everett, for two decades the voice of the news at one of America's major networks. I will try not to interrupt. I will let him tell you his frightening story in his own words. Listen with an open mind. Believe what he has to say. I know that I do." He paused. "Brian."

"Thank you, Hugo. And good evening, my fellow citizens. If my voice sounds strange, a little weak, please bear with me. I am sick. Very sick. Less than a week ago the tiny town of Santa Veronica was destroyed in a low level nuclear bomb blast. I lived in Santa Veronica. I was there when the bomb was detonated. I have severe radiation poisoning. My chances of survival are nil."

The trucker looked up from his breakfast and began to listen. The policeman stopped flirting. Maisie quietly poured herself a mug of coffee, attention totally fixed on Brian's voice.

"What I am about to tell you is the simple unadorned truth. I have nothing to gain by lying to you. I never lied to you before. I won't start now. This story begins, not last Sunday, but the previous Friday. It involves a man named Edward Vitale, a one time Washington insider who, you may recall, died last week. It also involves another man. Zebulon Marcuse, the Chief of Staff to the President of the United States."

In the small ranch home they shared in Palm Beach Gardens, Florida, 55 year old twin sisters, Abigail and Amanda Forbes, both insomniacs, listened attentively to the radio as each plied her hobby; Amanda knitting and Abigail working a jigsaw puzzle.

"Vitale was dictating his memoirs into a recording system built into his den. Uninvited, Marcuse angrily charged into his den and started berating Vitale who, as I said, was a powerful Washington insider. The interruption was so sudden and so bizarre that Vitale never thought to deactivate his recording system. Consequently, every word of their conversation was committed to tape. I have heard that tape. I listened to it a half dozen times. I know precisely what was on it. Marcuse was furious that Vitale had not contacted Vice President Comeford about the upcoming party convention and a change of plans. The Vice President, as most people are aware, is the presumptive nominee since the President cannot by law run for a third term. But Comeford was not going to be allowed to succeed to the Presidency. Why? I'll get to that shortly.

"Vitale told Marcuse he would ask the Senate Majority Leader,

Fletcher Chase, to break the news to him since Comeford and Chase were the closest of friends. Marcuse became angry. He said, 'And bring someone else in on this? Are you insane?' Then he said, 'We have the events carefully planned in a certain order starting with California over the weekend. We cannot widen out the circle without risking exposure and particularly with Senator Chase. I'm not sure he would go along.' I think it's obvious that the California event was the destruction of Santa Veronica on Sunday morning, not by Islamic terrorists, but by some faction within the federal government. Because of Mr. Marcuse's involvement, that faction very well might include the President himself. And why do I say I don't believe it was a terrorist attack?" Brian went on to detail the much too early arrival of the hazmat clad investigators from Homeland Security as well as the appearance of the FSF helicopter that landed on his front lawn within twenty minutes of the detonation.

On the second floor of a brownstone on North Charles Street in Baltimore, a Johns Hopkins graduate student who had been busy editing his master's thesis found himself staring at his radio. Lev Blaustein, a Democratic activist, could not believe what he was hearing. He could feel an eggplant-sized knot growing in his stomach.

"It was obvious to me", Brian was saying, "that the actuality of what Marcuse was saying had stunned Mr. Vitale. He as much as said he thought all these so-called plans were theoretical in nature. Marcuse became more impatient. Was Vitale so dense that he didn't know that revolution was breeding in every corner of the country? The time to take control was now and to do it by any means possible. He said, and Hugo and my fellow Americans, this is a direct quote from Marcuse—'the President and I are determined that this plan go forward now without delay.'" Brian looked at Hugo whose face was ashen and yet his host did not interrupt, giving Brian a subtle wave of his hand to continue.

"That's when Marcuse reiterated the need for the followup acts of terrorism, the derailment of the Amtrak passenger trains. Vitale was shaken. You could hear it in his voice. He asked, 'Isn't there some way to do this without killing people?' Again, Marcuse scoffed. Only with the blood of Americans can we muster the support for Bunker Hill. 'We have to scare the crap out of three hundred and fifty million people and especially General MacAndrews.'"

Hugo finally interrupted. "Excuse me, Brian. Bunker Hill? What is that?"

"It's a highly secret military contingency plan to establish martial law in the event that public safety is seriously compromised," Brian said.

"I see," Hugo said. "So the President creates the panic so he can institute martial law."

"Precisely."

"To what end?"

"I'm getting to that," Brian said.

"Continue," Hugo said.

General MacAndrews and Lee Fitzpatrick sat across from each other at the coffee table which separated the sofa from two easy chairs. Each had a drink in front of them. Neither was drinking. Earlier Superintendent Keith Sunderson had contacted the RCMP Commissioner of National Security Criminal Investigation and repeated to him what he knew of the situation based on Heather Bannister's recollection of what was on the tape. The Commissioner had in turn telephoned Canada's Minister of Public Safety. The Minister called Peter Toussaint, the Director of the FBI who in turn had called Lee Fitzpatrick. His message to the General's aide was short and to the point. Time to fish or cut bait.

MacAndrews sat staring grimly into space, unmoving as if comatose.

Brian continued. "With the populace terrified, the President and his Chief of Staff knew that the people would go along with any edict that would ensure their personal safety. Understandably, because it is a top secret document few people were aware of its provisions. But here are two which Marcuse reiterated to Vitale that evening. With martial law in place, the President would have dictatorial powers unfettered by Congress or anyone else. That would presumably include suspension of habeas corpus, search and seizure, closure of churches and other organizations deemed a threat to the government. Once in force, Bunker Hill provided that it could not be reversed unless and until the President, in his sole judgement, considered the national crisis to be over."

Hugo Wheeler shook his head in disbelief. "My God," he said softly, "an absolute dictatorship."

"Yes. And worst of all, because he had those powers, the President was going to announce the cancellation of the political conventions this summer and a suspension of the November elections."

"Marcuse said that? In so many words?" Hugo asked.

"No, Hugo, in those exact words. That is why it is so devastating that I don't have the tape to play for you. Because it is so evil, so unbelievable. And yet, I swear to you, all of this is true." A pause. "Anyway, the conversation ended the way it had begun, with Marcuse berating Vitale. It is your job to take the Vice President aside and fill him in, not a week from now when it will all be moot. He has to be told now that he is not going to be President, not in the forseeable future, and that if wants to continue being a member of this team, he had better be prepared to go along. And that's about it. The next evening, Vitale, apparently being chased by dangerous people, slipped the tape to Dr. Kenneth Bannister in the lobby of the Four Seasons hotel in Washington. Later that evening Vitale died in a so-called freak accident on the outskirts of the city. Within twenty four hours, Bannister found himself being stalked . He knew what was on the tape and he knew who was after him. He and his wife fled for their lives."

"What have you done to me?" the President screamed, his voice at least an octave higher than normal.

Marcuse, who was standing in the middle of the living room in the President's private quarters, raised his hands defensively. "Mr. President, I swear to God, I thought Everett had been dealt with."

"Well, obviously he wasn't," the President hissed. He had not invited his Chief of Staff to sit and had no intention of doing so.

"It's Lapp, sir," Marcuse whined. "He told me Everett was dead along with that other traitor, Dr. Bannister."

"Yes, well, it's always handy to have someone else you can shove the blame onto. You have a real talent for that, Zeb. How am I supposed to survive this?"

Inwardly, Marcuse rankled. It was the "I" word again. Not "we". It was never "we" with this President . Anything favorable brought out the "I" word. Negatives elicited an instant search for the other guy. The guy to blame. This whole scheme was doomed to failure from the start, he saw that now. Oh, how he now regretted that day not long ago when he mused in passing how the President might be able to stay in power despite the Constitution. The President had seized on it like a mongoose thrashing a cobra, hanging tight, never letting it go. Make it happen, Zeb, the President had exhorted, never asking for details. Make it happen and nothing on earth can stop us. One of the few times when the "us" word supplanted the "I" word in the President's vocabulary.

Yes, they were faced with disaster. And yet---- Marcuse wrinkled his brow thoughtfully. The President saw it. "What?" he demanded.

"Just a thought, sir."

"Think aloud."

"This man Everett. We've been chasing him across the country for almost a week. His picture on television. Police alerted in every state of the union. Wanted for treason. A huge reward offered."

"For all the good it did," the President grumbled.

"He escapes the country, joins forces with another known traitor, Hugo Wheeler. He goes on the air and relates this bizarre story for which he has not one shred of evidence."

The President leaned back in his chair. "Go on."

"Mr. President, it's all a lie. Everything he said. All of it created out of thin air. Where's the proof? This so-called tape? Has anyone actually seen this tape or heard it?" Marcuse was getting excited now, starting to roll with it as the picture in his mind took shape. "There was no tape. This was nothing more than the desperate act of a desperate man, no longer relevant in today's world. What is he up to? I'll tell you what he's up to, Mr. President. Very simply this was a call to armed revolution, to bring the people into the streets, to take this legally elected administration and bring it down by force of arms."

The President shook his head. "I'm not sure-----"

"Be sure, sir. This is it. This is your precipitating event. Everett and his followers must be stopped. What could be more dangerous to our democracy than armed rebellion? It cannot go unchallenged. Take this moment. Phone General MacAndrews now. Activate Bunker Hill effective immediately."

"But---"

"There are no buts, Mr. President. Yes, this is a bold step but you must take it because if you do not face this man down and put the lie to his accusations, we are lost. But if we succeed, then everything is within our grasp."

The President sat quietly for several moments, then reached over and picked up the phone. "Get me General MacAndrews at his home." He replaced the receiver and stared up at Marcuse. He gestured toward a chair. "Why don't you sit down, Zeb" he said.

Marcuse sat. A few moments later the phone rang. The President answered.

"General MacAndrews, this is the President. Have you been listening to the Canadian broadcast?"

In his den, with Lee Fitzpatrick by his side, MacAndrews said, "Yes, sir, I have."

"I am appalled by what I have just heard, General. Appalled and frightened. The rebels have finally come out into the open and frankly, General, I fear for the country. Lies like the ones told tonight have the potential to bring down this government."

"It was certainly chilling, Mr. President," MacAndrews conceded.

"Oh, yes. Frightening, like most fairy tales. How convenient that this so-called incriminating tape was destroyed. Brian Everett is deranged, of that I have no doubt, but governments have been toppled by less. That is why, in the interest of public safety, I am ordering you to implement Operation Bunker Hill immediately." There was a considerable silence. "General, did you hear me?"

"Yes, sir. I did."

"Did you understand that I have given you a direct order to implement Operation Bunker Hill?"

"Yes, sir."

"And are you going to carry out that order?"

"Yes, I am, sir."

The President permitted himself a smile. "Very well, then. Please do so immediately. We need to get a handle in this situation before dawn."

"I understand."

"And please be in my office at eight o'clock tomorrow morning. We will have a great deal to go over."

"Yes, Mr. President."

"Good night, General."

"Good night, Mr. President."

MacAndrews lowered the receiver onto the cradle. He looked over at Lee and then picked up his now warm, watered down scotch and tossed back a sizeable swallow.Slowly he settled back in the sofa and stared off into nothingness, lost in the confusion of a million different thoughts.

CHAPTER TWENTY ONE

As the first rays of sunlight began to illuminate the eastern seaboard, three massive A1A2 Abrams tanks rumbled down Pennsylvania Avenue and took up strategic positions at the several intersections surrounding the White House. They were followed by a quintet of M2 Bradley fighting vehicles. Three of these drove onto the White House grounds along with two armored troop carriers holding several dozen Army infantrymen armed with M4A1 carbines as well as M249 SAW (Squad Automatic Weapons). Two of the Bradleys stationed themselves at the south entrance with orders to bar access to all vehicles that had not been expressly authorized by either General MacAndrews or his aide, Colonel Lee Fitzpatrick.

Throughout the city military units moved with speed and precision to carry out the Presidential order. Copies of the order had been handed to the various departments and armed units had secured their various buildings. Only the most essential personnel were permitted to enter. All others were instructed to take the day off. F550 BATT patrol vehicles equipped with loudspeakers roamed the streets informing the populace of the imposition of martial law by order of the President. They were told to watch their television sets at 6:00 that evening when the President would address the nation. In the meantime, they were strongly urged to stay off the streets for the remainder of the day.

Those who had already turned on their TV sets found nothing to watch except a waving American flag backed by patriotic background music and the notice: Transmission Suspended. Tune to Presidential Address 6:00 pm EDT The one remaining independent television station and the two radio stations were not broadcasting, having been shut down shortly before 6:00 a.m. Likewise, the presses at the Washington Post sat silent. If there existed any opposition or outrage regarding this turn of events, it had no opportunity either to organize or to voice itself. No television, no radio, no newspapers, no internet, just the rumble of tank treads on asphalt and beyond that, silence.

Similar scenarios were playing out in major metropolitan areas throughout the nation: New York, Chicago, Philadelphia, Boston, Dallas and points west. FBI offices were put on alert to support the military and liaised with local police. The smaller towns in America, cut off from information at every turn (except cell phones) remained clueless about the military takeover. They did know that the President would have something important to say that evening. Few planned to miss it.

The President looked out of his second floor window onto the avenue below.The flag was flying proudly over the grounds, tanks were protecting the perimeter of the White House, armed infantrymen were everywhere, guarding the national residence and those in it. As he slipped his red and grey silk power tie under the white collar of his shirt and then tied a perfect Windsor knot, the President felt a great exhilaration run through his body. He had done it. Long months of agonizing, of planning, of keeping dark and terrible secrets, it was finally paying off. Soon he would have a free hand to deal with the nation any way he pleased. No more sucking up to Congressional leaders, no more lies and half truths about his plans for the country. The power was now his and he would exercise it judiciously, with compassion when called for, with a strong hand when needed. A new America was being born this day. His America. The one he had been taught by his mentors would truly be of the people and by the people and for the people.

He felt badly that his wife wasn't here with him to share his moment of glory but she was on a good will tour overseas, a tour that he knew consisted mainly of shopping in London, Paris and Rome. Governments would fall in Europe but no matter what, Gucci and St. Laurent would survive. And while school children in New Mexico went hungry because their parents could find no work, there would always be room in a White House closet for another $15,000 evening gown.

The President crossed to the coffee table and picked up the TV remote, then stared in confusion at the message on the screen. A Presidential address that evening? He'd made no such plans. Undoubtedly Zeb's work. More and more the man was overstepping his authority. He would have to be dealt with firmly. In this case, however, he was probably right. The people needed to be reassured by their President. He would get Ray Screbant and his other speechwriters on it immediately.

The President slipped into his jacket and moved to the phone sitting on a nearby table. He lifted the receiver. There was no sound, no dial tone. It was dead. Odd, he thought.

He opened the door and stepped out into the corridor. Two Marine sergeants in full dress uniforms and carrying M9 9mm pistols in their patent leather holsters were stationed on either side of the door.

"Good morning," the President said.

"Good morning, Mr. President," said the sergeant whose name tag read Stepkowski.

The President looked around, puzzled. "Where are Stutzmann and Durant?"

"The Secret Service has been temporarily relieved of responsibility for the time being, sir. General MacAndrews wlll explain it, I'm sure. He's waiting for you in the Oval Office."

"Excellent," the President said as he strode down the hallway toward the elevators. The two sergeants fell into step beside him, flanking him.

General MacAndrews was, indeed, waiting in the Oval Office, seated on the sofa which faced a large oak coffee table. Seated beside him was his aide, Colonel Lee Fitzpatrick. Seated opposite in one of the plush easy chairs was Zebulon Marcuse, the President's Chief of Staff. Marcuse rose quickly as the President entered.

"Good morning, Mr. President," Marcuse greeted him.

"Good morning, Zeb," the President replied. "And good morning to you, General," he said to MacAndrews who had not gotten to his feet but was shuffling through some papers.

"Good morning, Mr. President," MacAndrews said. Lee followed suit. He, too, remained seated.

"Well, perhaps we ought to get some coffee in here," the President smiled.

"Already taken care of, sir." MacAndrews pointed to the silver service on a table nearby. A large selection of danish and rolls was on display.

"Well done," said the President who walked over and poured himself a mug of coffee and picked off an apple cruller. "That was a very heartwarming sight I woke up to outside my window this morning, General. You seem to have things well in hand."

"I do," MacAndrews said. He gestured to the empty chair. "Please. Sit down, Mr. President, we have several things to discuss."

"Indeed we do." He started for his desk. "Let me hold all my calls."

"I've already taken care of that." MacAndrews said evenly. The President looked at him curiously. Something strange was afoot but he couldn't quite put his finger on it. Again, MacAndrews gestured toward the empty chair. "Please," he said.

The President put his roll and coffee on the table and sat down. He shook his head, almost in amusement. "You know, I still can't get over that broadcast last night. Really unbelievable. Did the man really think he could get away with those wild accusations?" He laughed as he looked over at his Chief of Staff. "Didn't realize you were such an anarchist, Zeb."

"Well, Everett is certainly desperate, Mr. President. And dishonoring Ed Vitale like that. He obviously has no shame." Marcuse said.

MacAndrews eyed the President without smiling. "So in your opinion, Mr. President, there's nothing to it?"

"A fairy tale, General."

"And there's not the slightest doubt in your mind that Mr. Marcuse here could never have plotted such an outrageous power play, with or without your permission?" MacAndrews asked.

"Do you even have to ask?" the President said smiling, shaking his head.

"Yes, Mr. President, I do because I am going to convene a board of inquiry into the charges made last night by Mr. Everett."

The President stared at him in disbelief. "You are what?"

"We are going to investigate Mr. Everett's accusations to see if they have merit."

Marcuse butted in. "You can't do that," he said.

Lee smiled and leaned toward the Chief of Staff. "He can and he will."

The President's face darkened. "General MacAndrews, I have told you that Everett's story is a complete fabrication. You have my word on that."

"Yes, I know," MacAndrews said drily.

"What's that supposed to mean?" the President demanded angrily. "Are you calling me a liar? I can have a dozen people over here inside of an hour who will-----"

"Yes, yes, I'm sure you can. And we will be talking to all those people, under oath. The Secretary of Homeland Security, the Director of the Federal Security Force----"

The President exploded. "Excuse me, General, but you are not in charge here!"

MacAndrews smiled. "As a matter of fact I am. On your command, Mr. President, this country was placed under martial law according to the provisions of Operation Bunker Hill. As you are Commander in Chief of all military forces and I , as the Chairman of the Joint Chiefs , am your immediate subordinate, I am now relieving you of that command under the provisions of the Universal Code of Military Justice, Article 92. I am charging you with derelicition of duty, failure to uphold your oath to the Constitution and aiding and abetting the premeditated murders of several thousand United States citizens."

"This is preposterous!" Marcuse fumed, rising from his chair.

MacAndrews looked coldly in his direction. "And you, Mr. Marcuse, face the same charges so if I were you I'd start flipping through my Rolodex for the name of a good lawyer."

"We'll see about this," Marcuse said, striding to the President's desk and lifting the receiver from the phone. "This is Zebulon Marcuse. Put me through to the Attorney General immediately."

A male voice responded. "I'm sorry, sir, but I am not authorized to relay any phone calls except those initiated by General MacAndrews and Colonel Fitzpatrick."

Furious, Marcuse slammed down the phone. The General looked over at Sergeant Stepkowski. "Sergeant, summon a guard unit to accompany Mr. Marcuse to his office. He is to remain there until further notice."

"Yes, sir," the sergeant said. He stepped out of the room for a moment, then returned with two Army MP officers who moved directly to Marcuse and started to take him by the arm. He shrugged them off as he headed to the door under his own power.

"You'll never get away with this, General", Marcuse said over his shoulder.

"Maybe not", MacAndrews said. "Maybe down the road some court martial board will throw my sorry ass into a stockade for the rest of my life, but until then, I am in charge and I am, by God, going to do what is best for my country." To the MP's: "Now get this sorry piece of garbage out of here before I puke all over this beautiful carpet."

The two MPs muscled Marcuse out the door as MacAndrews turned his attention back to the President. "Why, Mr. President? Why did you do it?"

"I did nothing wrong," the President insisted.

"You're going to tell me that that obnoxious little ferret carried out all of this on his own without your knowledge?" MacAndrews narrowed his eyes in disbelief.

"I'm saying I knew nothing about any nefarious plot to seize the government and suspend elections. And I can't believe Zeb Marcuse would condone such a thing, let alone instigate it. I know he's ambitious and often chooses expediency over good sense but this? No, it's almost too hard to believe."

MacAndrews looked from the President to Lee Fitzpatrick, sharing a knowing look, as if to say---now it starts. Did you hear that word 'almost'? In a matter of hours, the rats , like brides-to-be in Filene's basement will be turning on one another and it won't be a pleasant sight.

"Mr. President, as of now, you are confined to the upstairs living quarters. You will have no visitors until after my address to the nation this evening. Starting tomorrow, you will be allowed no more than six visitors a day and no more than two at a time. Anything you need will be brought to you. In the event we are able to bring criminal charges against you, your attorneys will be exempted from the visitation quotas. Is that clear?

"Perfectly," the President said coldly. "There is only one traitor in this room, General, and it isn't me."

"That remains to be seen." MacAndrews signalled to Stepkowski. He and the other sergeant escorted the President from the Oval Office.

"Now I know how Caesar felt when he crossed the Rubicon," MacAndrews said. "We've got a rough few months ahead of us."

"Yes, sir. Shall I put that call in to the Vice President now?" Lee asked.

MacAndrews nodded. "Yes, I need to see him as soon as possible. And Lee, this afternoon, I want to see Mr. Jaffee and Mr. Toussaint. Set it up."

"Anything else,sir?"

"Yes," MacAndrews smiled. "If I start to act like a politician you have permission to kick me in the ass until I come to my senses."

For the remainder of the day, MacAndrews kept very busy. He spent nearly two hours with Vice President Comeford, discussing which steps he should and should not take to put the country on an even keel. The General made it clear that Comeford's role would be advisory only but he soon learned that he and the Vice President agreed far more than they disagreed. Almost immediately, regular army units and some national guard commands took control of not only the Washington headquarters of the Federal Security Force but all fifty-eight field offices as well. FSF agents were disarmed, their credentials confiscated and then sent home until further notice. Homeland Security was kept active but the Director, a hack political appointee, was relieved of his position and a non-political career administrator was named interim director.

The nominal heads of the three television networks and their radio counterparts were dismissed, their places provisionally taken by proven veterans of the industry without radical political leanings. They geared up for the evening address and were told to be ready to resume programming the following morning. They were also told it would no longer be necessary to get content clearance from the Department of Information, a bureaucratic monstrosity that MacAndrews happily abolished with a single stroke of his pen. MacAndrews and Comeford also agreed that the internet should be reinstated but not until after the address to the nation. MacAndrews wanted to make sure he got his message out before the citizenry started comparing opinions before they knew the facts.

As for the CIA and the FBI, they were given the full backing of the military regime. CIA was charged with contacting its counterparts across the globe and to reassure them that a military dictatorship was not in the offing and that democracy was still alive and well in Washington DC. Watch the broadcast, they were told. All will be revealed. Simultaneously the FBI was charged with collecting any and all evidence relating to Santa Veronica, the Amtrak disasters and the failed attempt at Fenway Park. Both MacAndrews and Comeford were determined to bring charges against the guilty parties as soon as possible. Toussaint was instructed to bring all data directly to Lee Fitzpatrick and not to the Attorney-General. The AG was another political appointee but his positions were closely held and no one was sure exactly where he stood. He would be left in place for the time being for the sake of continuity but he was warned that any statement or act that could be deemed anti-Constitutional would be grounds for his immediate dismissal.

At 4:00 MacAndrews left the Oval Office, leaving instructions that it be locked up until the nation was able to elect a new President. He strolled down the corridor to a smaller office which had been prepared for him. He settled in behind the desk, left word that he was not be disturbed and then started jotting notes on a yellow legal sized pad. He would not need the notes that evening nor would he need a teleprompter. He was a man who knew what had to be said and he had the skills to say it in plain language that anyone could understand.

At exactly 6:00 p.m. EDT , tens of millions of television sets were powered up, their screens still displaying the American flag. And then in an instant that image was replaced by a wide shot of the floor of the House of Representatives, the familiar two aisles which partitioned the arced seating area into thirds, the imposing high ceiling, and the gallery which on any other occasion would have been crowded with onlookers but on this night was empty. On the floor, 433 Representatives had been joined by 99 Senators. All were seated quietly. By order of the Chairman of the Joint Chiefs of Staff, there was to be no mingling, no group chats, no camaraderie (false or otherwise) and during the address, no applause. Each man and woman was to remain in his or her seat. Violators would be ejected immediately. Two Congressmen and a Senator had already been removed. The others apparently had gotten the message. They had been told the identity of the man who would address them that evening but nothing more, not even the reason for the convening of the two houses although most could guess at the purpose. When the General strode down the aisle toward the podium, there would be no standing, no reaching out for a handshake or to touch the man. Protocol must and would be observed.

At 6:02, one of the rear doors opened. A voice rang out. "Ladies and gentlemen, the Chairman of the Joint Chiefs of Staff, General Dwight David MacAndrews. "

MacAndrews entered, resplendent in his dress uniform, a bevy of ribbons displayed on his tunic. Two armed Marines in dress blue entered with him, then remained by the door as it was shut tight. At the same moment, other duos of armed marines entered and took up positions, standing at parade rest, by the other exits.

The General strode with military bearing down the aisle, eyes front, his visage serious but not grim. He passed the area where the members of the Supreme Court would normally be seated. They were absent at his request. He briskly climbed the steps to the podium, went directly to Vice President Comeford who was seated to the right, the American flag hanging proudly behind him. Comeford rose. The two men shook hands. The Speaker of the House also rose and put out her hand. MacAndrews pointedly ignored her as he turned to the lectern. He removed his hat and placed it off to the side and then let his gaze pan the room. There were six cameras in the hall. Two were devoted to MacAndrews, a wide shot and a closeup. The other four would cover the assemblage.

"Good evening, my fellow Americans. For those of you who are not quite sure what you heard a few moments ago, let me introduce myself. My name is Dwight David MacAndrews, a general in the United States Army, as well as the Chairman of the Joint Chiefs of Staff. I am also, de facto, the current head of state of this country. Very early this morning the President lawfully ordered the country to be placed under martial law. Subsequent to that, as the second highest ranking military man in the nation, I used the authority granted to me by the Uniform Code of Miiitary Justice to relieve the President of his command. Those of you who heard the broadcast from Canada last evening will understand why this step was taken. The President has not been convicted of any crime. He has not even been formally accused. Think of this as an arrest until more information and evidence can be gathered. Better men than I will eventually decide on his guilt or innocence but in the interim, the charges are so severe that steps had to be taken to remove him from a position of power. The President will continue to reside at the White House. His needs will be met. But he will not be leading this country in the foreseeable future.

"For those of you who did not hear the broadcast, I will summarize the charges. Dereliction of duty. Violation of the oath of office. Most importantly, and most dreadfully, the use of the office of President to aid and abet the premeditated slaughter of more then two thousand American citizens in an effort to circumvent the Constitution and turn this nation into a Socialist dictatorship. He was assisted in this endeavor by a few executive staffers, and a small group of Cabinet level appointees as well as one or two highly placed party officials. As I said, these are the charges. The courts will adjudicate them. Meanwhile it will be my duty, with the help of your Vice President, Wendell Comeford, who had no knowledge of any of this, to restore to you, the American people, the liberties and privileges that have been taken from you over the past seven years.

"Immediately following this broadcast, the three national television networks will resume broadcasting around the clock. Local television and radio stations that had their licenses revoked will be reinstated. Local and regional newspapers will be permitted to restart publication. None of these entities will be required to report to the Department of Information which I dissolved by executive order early this afternoon. In addition, access to the internet is being unblocked even as I speak."

In the basement of his farmhouse a couple of miles west of Lawrence, "Bobby Lee Huggins" had put down the window frame he was repairing and sat quietly on a keg of nails, listening to MacAndrews on the radio. He sipped slowly on the cold beer "Daphne" had brought him as tears of relief and gratitude started to well up in his eyes.

"It is my hope," MacAndrews continued, "and the hope of Vice President Comeford, that this restoration of free communication within our borders will result in greater awareness of the political world we live in and the God given responsibility each of us bears to make certain that never again will we allow a handful of power seeking radicals to attempt to overthrow our government. We have averted a catastrophe. We have been given a second chance. Let us not squander it by slipping back into lethargy and disinterest."

As Grace Devilbiss drove north from the Topeka jail cell to their home in Horton, Max stared straight ahead, taking in every word of MacAndrews' address to the nation. He still felt the throbbing ache where his shoulder had been dislocated and then reset and the myriad bruises on his chest and abdomen, but for the moment they were unimportant. For the first time in ages he felt real hope. He looked over at Grace and smiled. She smiled back, grasping his hand and squeezing it gently.

MacAndrews took a sip of water from the glass that had been placed there for him. "Those who know me know that I am not a political man. I am a citizen. I vote. As a military man, that should be the extent of it. But I am also not brain dead. Like many of you, I have been appalled by the direction this country has been taking for the past seven years. Someone once said to me that you need not be a pig farmer to know that pigs love to wallow in filth. Similarly, one need not be political to understand the workings of Congress. I say this with deep apologies to the pigs of America."

At this point the four cameras covering the assemblage began to slowly pan across the faces of the Congressmen and Senators sitting quietly in their seats.

"I have charged the administration with malfeasance of office but there is another villain in this story. A collective villain and, ladies and gentlemen, you are looking at them this very moment. At the beginning of this speech I began by addressing you, my fellow Americans. Protocol demanded that I first acknowledge these members of Congress you see before you. That I could not do because these people sitting here are just as guilty as the President and his minions for the sorry state this country finds itself in. These people, with few exceptions---" He took a moment to look back at Comeford. "---with few exceptions are just as much to blame for the destruction of the dollar on the world market, for unemployment figures that hover near 13%, for confiscatory taxes that squeeze the life blood from families just trying to survive from one week to another. These people that you are now looking at with their platinum plated health care insurance, unavailable to you ranchers in Montana or farmers in Wisconsin or apple growers in Washington. They indulge themselves like royalty while you and your children wait for endless hours, trying to see a doctor, fighting to be granted a life saving procedure that you know may never come. These people with their backroom deals, their mutual backscratching, the bribes from lobbyists, the perks from industry. Look at their faces. These, too, are the people who have brought you to this point. Some of them are Democrats, some are Republicans. Can you tell by looking at their faces which is which? Of course you can't because they are, for the most part, all of a piece. Venal, greedy, self-centered and oblivious to the fact that they are not American royalty but servants of the people. Look at these faces carefully. Memorize them. Stifle any compulsion you may have to vote for them again,for surely if you do, they will bring us right back to the abyss into which we are now staring."

On the outskirts of Detroit in a small three bedroom home, Buzz Shipley sat watching the address. His arm was clasped tight around his wife. Their two girls sat cross legged at their feet. It was his youngest that noticed the tiny trickle of tears starting down her father's cheeks. Why are you crying, Daddy? she asked. He just smiled.

Just happy to be home with you, sweetheart, he said. And your sister and your Mom. He tousled her hair. She smiled up at him.

"Tomorrow," MacAndrews continued, "I will announce guidelines for the coming election. Each political party will have until August 31 to nominate candidates for President, Vice President, Congress and where terms will be expiring, U.S. Senator. Election Day will remain the same, the first Tuesday in November. As for those Senators whose terms do not expire this year, I make a special plea to the various states to ease the conditions under which these men and women of either party may be recalled by the voters. I truly believe that a clean sweep is needed, that the existing Congress be voted out by you, the electorate, and that a fresh new crop of legislators, citizen lawmakers whose first duty is to their country, be swept into office. With God's help they may be able to undo the damage of the past seven years."

In the kitchen of her house in Rush City, Harriet Wayne was brushing barbecue sauce on a pan full of chicken thighs, her eyes raising up every few seconds to watch the General on the little TV that sat on her kitchen counter. A good man, she thought. Big Sam would have liked him very much.

MacAndrews paused for a moment, collecting his thoughts. "My friends, despite everything I have said, there are many true patriots in high places who have been trying in their own way to protect this country. Your Vice President, of course. The Director of the FBI, Peter Toussaint. The CIA Director, Leonard Jaffee. Senate Majority Leader Chase. We will uncover many others before we are through and we will need the help of all of them. As for me, when this nightmare has ended, when you have elected new leaders, I will step down and submit myself to a military board of inquiry. They will decide whether or not I have acted rightly or wrongly and whatever their judgment, I will not question it. What I am doing, I am doing for love of country. I will stand by that.

"As for you out there watching, I implore you once more. Pay attention. Educate yourselves, Vote knowing who and what you are voting for. If you do these three simple things, this nation will survive."

He paused again, looking out over the Congress sitting in deathly silence. He looked back at the close-up camera, staring intently into the lens.

"Finally, and regrettably, I must end this address on a sad note. Early this afternoon, America lost one of its great patriots. Brian Everett died in a hospital room in Canada from the effects of radiation poisoning sustained in the nuclear explosion in Santa Veronica last Sunday. At his side were his son, Mark, an Air Force pilot, and his daughter, Melissa, a journalist living in New York City. Despite his illness Mr. Everett struggled for six days, along with his good friend Dr. Kenneth Bannister, to reach Canada and to bring to the American people the terrible truth about their government. Tonight, and for many nights to come, I will pray for this man. I hope that those of you out there who believe in the power of prayer will join me "

With that, MacAndrews donned his hat, squared it sharply and moved briskly down the podium steps, up the aisle and out of the chamber.

The following November, on the first Tuesday of the month, the American people went to the polls and voted.

THE END

ABOUT THE AUTHOR

Peter S. Fischer is a former television writer-producer who currently lives with his wife Lucille in the Monterey Bay area of Central California. He is a co-creator of "Murder, She Wrote" for which he wrote over forty scripts. Among his other credits are a dozen "Columbo" episodes, several made for TV movies and mini-series. In 1985 he was awarded an Edgar by The Mystery Writers of America. His first novel, "The Blood of Tyrants" was published in 2009.

TO ORDER ADDITIONAL COPIES

If your local bookseller is out of stock, you may order additional copies of "THE TERROR OF TYRANTS" through The Grove Point Press, P.O. Box 873, Pacific Grove, CA 93950. Enclose check or money order for $10.95. We pay shipping, handling and any taxes required. All copies personally signed by the author. 10% discount on all orders of 3 or more. Copies of "THE BLOOD OF TYRANTS" are still available at the original cover price of $8.95. If you wish to order both books, they are available as a set for $13.95.